My Thanks

This is my first novel and I would like to give special thanks to three people.

Jennifer Macedo was a very kind, sweet girl who I knew back in High School (Go Whalers!). We were never more than friends, but she was the very first person I ever showed any of my stories to. I used to keep them in notebooks hidden in the back of my closet. I was your typical fat, near sighted nerd and my stories were way too personal to expose to actual criticism.

When I mentioned I liked to write she begged to read some of my stories. She told me she really loved them and that I should always write. Hearing that meant a lot to me, and I promised her that if I ever wrote a book I would dedicate it to her. We lost touch after High School and I have no idea where she is now or if she will ever read this.

But promise kept.

Kelly Kilroy is my best friend. He is the sort of friend who will tell you you're being an idiot when no one else will. He will also listen when you really need to talk. I once quit a dead end job and moved down to Florida with him because he told me, 'I need a roommate and I know you won't steal from me.' He gave me a whole lot of crap at times, but he also gave me a lot of good advice that I wish I had taken. While he didn't specifically help me with writing this book, he has helped me more than any other person outside of my parents. He has always been there when I needed him and is everything a best friend should be.

And Kelly, if you're reading this, 'a sphere had no sides to it!'

(Yes, I know a sphere has infinite sides to it. It's a private joke.)

1

Mistress Winowyll, and no, that's not her real name. We have never physically met, spoken on the phone, or even been in the same state. We met online because she liked some of my fanfiction stories. We got to talking and discovered we shared two things in common. Our love of writing and a pathological need to inflict pain and humiliation on lesser people.

Also, we're both really into leather.

Over the past six years we have constantly IMed one another with story ideas. Our chats have been the inspiration for a lot of my writing. We love to inspire and mock each other and can share harsh truths when called for.

I have spent over two years writing this book. She has been there the whole time, bouncing ideas, giving me her opinion, and acting as both my editor and beta. She even helped me come up with the original story concept.

You have my deepest thanks and appreciation. Hell, I even used both l's on your name. If that's not love I don't know what is.

Credits

The cover art was done by **Jennifer Aucoin** at **Panoramictour.net**. She has my thanks. I know how difficult it is to work with rabbits.

__Prologue__

A woman in black robes quietly approached a wooden door.

"*Pyro*." With a single word a small fire materialized in the palm of her hand.

She entered the nursery as quietly as she could.

It was night time, and the only source of light was the magical flame.

The baby did not stir. He continued to sleep peacefully in his crib.

The woman simply stood there, looking down at him. He was only three days old, pink, perfect, and healthy. He was her seventh child. Like all of his brothers and sisters she would protect him and teach him how to be a powerful mage. Being the seventh and youngest made him lucky, his older siblings would not see him as a threat. That meant the chances of having an, 'accident' were much less. It was a small mercy.

It was not as though he would have a peaceful life. Being born into this family made that impossible, but things would be much easier than if he had been the first or second.

"Things will be hard enough for you my son," Lilith whispered.

It always amazed her how pure and innocent the children were, how free of corruption and sin. Within her heart she felt a twinge at the thought of the things she would teach him. The things he would be made to endure to toughen and strengthen him. Their world was a dark and dangerous place; you could not afford to be gentle.

Reaching down she touched his cheek with a single finger. His skin was warm and so very soft.

"How I wish you could always be safe, but as my son that is not something you are entitled to."

For just a moment, she wondered if he would be better off if he'd been born in a peasant hut in some far off land. He would never see the rivers of fire. Never get to taste Illsyrian wine or wear silk. Never study magic and experience its wonders. Never know what power felt like, or see that marvelous look of terror in a person's eyes just before you ended their life.

He would instead have an ordinary, common existence. His meals would be gruel and turnips and he would labor in muddy fields from dawn to dusk. His life would be one of servitude, at the mercy of petty lords. One day he would marry some homely girl from his village and have a family of his own. He would live an entire lifetime never going more than twenty miles from where he was born.

But at least he would be safe, she thought.

Lilith chuckled and shook her head. Such silly, pointless thoughts. There was no way her child could ever be ordinary, not with the blood that flowed through his veins. She was an archmage and head of a very powerful family, while his father had also been extraordinary. Surely this child would accomplish great things.

In the back of her head she felt a presence approaching, her familiar. Still standing over the crib she turned her face slightly towards the door. It opened without a sound, and an emaciated form enter the nursery. In the fire's light she could see the veins beneath his skin and the outline of his bones. His shadow flickered and danced on the wall behind him. He seemed very much at home in the darkness.

"Feeling maternal today?" He asked in his feather soft voice. His tongue ran over his bloodless lips as he cast his eyes towards the crib.

4

Hungrily.

"What do you want Enver?"

Short, shuffling steps brought him to her side to peer down at her son.

"His scent is rich and tempting, his blood would taste sweeter than summer wine I'll wager." His fingers twitched and he leaned forward ever so slightly.

"You are forbidden to touch or harm any of my children." She brought the fire close to his face and forced him to step back. "Never forget who your master is."

He took a couple additional steps back away from her and held up his hands. "I am not likely to."

"You do it all the time," she grunted. He was her familiar, and bound to her by their contract. That didn't keep him from trying to find all sorts of ways to cause mischief. "Why are you here?"

"I was curious," he said softly. "I wanted to see if it was true. Are the boy's eyes yellow?"

"I prefer to call them honey colored."

Lips twitched and a wheezing laugh filled the chamber. "It's so then? He has the blood of Avalon in him?"

"He has my blood, and that is all that counts."

"People won't see it that way."

"What does that matter?"

"The other families won't like it."

"They have no say in this."

Inhuman eyes stared at her though the fire light. "He will be hated."

"That would be true regardless. Those with power are always hated. He will learn to accept it as I have."

"So cruel," he teased. "You could make him a sacrifice you know. Offer him up to the Dark Powers, a child with the enemy's blood. Surely you would be rewarded."

"We sacrifice the deformed or the sickly. My son is healthy and strong."

He opened his mouth with a fresh retort.

"Be silent." Lilith said with annoyance.

His jaw snapped shut. Defiance marred his face, but he made no sound.

"Go," she commanded. "I do not want to see you again until tomorrow."

Body stiff and movement rigid he left.

When he was gone she again turned back to her son.

"You will have a hard time my son, but there is greatness inside you. Your life will not be an easy one, but I am sure it will be filled with wonders." She placed a soft kiss on his forehead. "Sleep well Waldo."

With that she quietly departed.

Chapter 1

The First Quest

The Shattered Lands held more than a thousand nations. Kingdoms, Duchies, Baronies, Republics, Oligarchies, Magocricies, Theocracies, Tribal Federations, Dictatorships, and lands with no law at all could be found. Each individual nation was independent. So called kings had no more authority beyond their borders than a baron or high priest did. There were alliances and treaties, but no ruler ever swore fealty to another. The human nations shared a common tongue, a number system, a calendar, and a coinage system; but there was no single law or authority. Wars were constant, as were corruption and sickness. Monsters roamed the land, crime was endemic, and many feared their own rulers. Nations were born and swallowed up. Peace was fragile and justice an illusion. It was a world filled with magic and bloodshed.

One of these nations was called Alteroth. It was located near the very heart of the Shattered Lands. It was among the largest and most powerful countries; for it was a land of Dark Mages and dark magics. Undead soldiers patrolled the borders and enforced the laws. The dead served and the living obeyed. Those who could use black magic held absolute power.

Seven families ruled here. Though suspicious of each other, they were bound together by mutual need. The rest of the world hated and feared them, and would gladly destroy them if they could. The neighboring nations were too divided to form a coalition, and would not dare challenge Alteroth's might. So long as the Seven Families stood united they were far too powerful to attack.

For those who practiced the Dark Arts, Alteroth was a sanctuary and a haven. The Seven Great Families sought influence and wealth in the wider world. They reveled in the fear and terror they inspired, and treasured their reputations. The Seven

Families thrived on the dread they inspired and did all they could to appear terrifying, both to their own people and to the world in general.

That was the reason the Council of Seven was meeting.

XXX

Within the vast council chamber, six men in black robes sat about a round table eying one other. There was no leader of the Council, no one was allowed to stand one inch higher than the rest. Each member was the head on one of the Great Families, and a master of the Dark Arts. They were not friends and they did not trust, they worked together because of need. Enslaved elven maidens poured wine, eyes downcast and properly attentive. There was an uncomfortable silence as attention flickered to the single empty seat.

"This is dangerous," Loram Blackwater muttered. "Not announcing a meeting to one of our own."

"I sent a message," a sickly man with rotten teeth said. "I suppose the slave was slow in delivering it. I'll have him killed in apology."

"That's not going to fool anyone Dante." Baldwin Blooddrinker said. He had forest green eyes and ears that were slightly pointed. His features were smooth and delicate, almost feminine.

Dante Poisondagger offered a putrid smile. "I know that, but it's enough to cover us. Mistakes do happen."

"We need to come to a decision before she arrives." Gawreth Wormwood said.

The others all nodded wearily.

"We should just kill him!" Darius Heartless shouted. "He's a disgrace! An embarrassment! He has no place among us!"

8

"He is heir to one of the Great Families, and you cannot deny he has skill with magic." Xilos Soulbreaker said.

"You call what he does talent?" Heartless challenged.

"Well he can use magic," Soulbreaker said defensively. "Some of his spells are quite effective."

"I've seen the things he can do." Heartless said with contempt. "It's *white* magic. He will never make a fitting head of family! Much less a member of this council."

"None of us are arguing about that," Gawreth said. "The question is what do we do about it?"

"Kill him," Darius said flatly.

"How?" Gawreth asked. "The boy never leaves the castle. I swear he is better protected than a virgin sacrifice."

"Is there any way we could convince her to choose another heir?" Xilos suggested.

"Have you ever tried changing her mind about anything?" Dante asked in annoyance.

"Can't Walter be the heir?" Darius demanded.

"Don't be stupid, Walter is dead." Gawreth reminded.

"He's only mostly dead."

"The dead cannot rule the living." Baldwin stated in his usual, well-bred manner. "Heads of families must meet certain criteria. For instance, how exactly would Walter father an heir?"

Darius shrugged. "He could stitch one together I suppose. He would still be more fitting than that miserable disgrace."

9

"Who's a miserable disgrace?" A cold voice said from the doorway.

The six men turned to the new arrival, the seventh member of the council, and the most powerful necromancer in all Alteroth; Lilith Corpselover. Pale, alabaster skin, long straight raven hair, with a full feminine figure that her tight fitting black robes showed off nicely. In her hand she held a wand carved from human bone. Drawing a wand was always a provocative step, the other members all carefully placed hands on their own. No one else actually drew one out though.

"Just who is a disgrace?" Lilith repeated, gripping her wand with both hands.

"I think you know who." Darius told her.

"Lilith, the time has come for us to address the situation." Blooddrinker said. "Let us sit down and talk about this rationally."

"The fact is your youngest cannot be your heir." Soulbreaker said.

"Since when does the council decide who the heir of a Great Family is?" Lilith demanded. "That has always been the choice of the family head."

"Lilith," Baldwin said sounding pleasant. "Even you must admit he is not someone who could replace you, either as the head of the Corpselover family or as a member of this council."

"Why?" She demanded. "Because his blood isn't pure enough to suit you? I can name someone here whose ancestry isn't exactly unmixed." She stared pointedly at his ears.

Baldwin spread his hands before him. "His parentage is not the question here Lilith, we are not uncivilized after all. Whatever it

10

is that runs through my veins, no one has ever questioned my ability as a Dark Mage. It is your son's talent that is the issue."

"He has immense natural talent. He can do things even I can't manage."

The six men looked at each other.

It was Dante Poisondagger who decided to force the matter. "Your son is a White Mage."

Lilith snapped. She grabbed the small man about the neck with her free hand and began to shake him as a dog would a rat. Instantly the other five were on their feet pointing their wands at her. Despite having the advantage none of them dared cast a spell.

"Say that again you rotten mouthed dove!!" Lilith screamed into his face.

"Let's just calm down, shall we?" Baldwin asked serenely. He had his wand pointed at her and a killing spell on his lips. "I'm sure Poisondagger did not mean to insult you. Isn't that right Dante?"

"That's ri… right," Dante managed to get out as he was being rattled. "Pl… please forgive me."

"Fine," she spat out and released her grip, dropping him unceremoniously onto the floor. Though only slightly appeased she knew there were limits to what even she could get away with. "I shouldn't expect anything better from a Poisondagger."

"Shall we all sit down and talk now?" Baldwin suggested.

Nodding, Lilith took her usual seat; the others put away their wands and returned to theirs. Poisondagger looked paler than usual and avoided even glancing in Lilith's direction. As soon as they were all seated Baldwin spoke again.

"Lilith, you know how important it is that we guard our reputation as ruthless and powerful Dark Mages. Fear is our shield. Were the other nations to see any sort of weakness they might try to attack us."

"Especially Avalon and the Alliance." Darius put in.

Baldwin nodded. "I beg you; see this from our point of view."

Lilith shifted in her seat. It had to be Baldwin who brought that up. It would have been so much easier if it had been Darius with his bluster or Dante with his usual double talk. Baldwin was always sensible and as fair as anyone here could be. "I am willing to admit my son is a bit unusual for a Dark Mage, but he has the potential to be extraordinary. He will definitely prove to be a worthy successor."

"Do you truly believe that Lilith?" Baldwin asked, a sudden glimmer in his eyes.

"I do."

"In that case, would you agree to a test of his abilities?"

Lilith frowned. "What sort of test?"

XXX

In one of the highest towers of Castle Corpselover a young man in black robes was down on his knees. At his side were several opened books as well as scrolls with hand drawn sketches. In his hand was a piece of chalk. On the stone floor he had drawn a summoning circle, with a myriad of arcane symbols and runes surrounding it.

"This time it will work," he muttered to himself. "I know it will." He had checked the formula time and again and was certain it was correct. He was going over the chalked symbols he'd written with exquisite care. He was determined that this time there would be no mistakes. Everything had to be perfect.

As he was bent over studying the runes and symbols the door to the room slowly and silently opened. A figure with tattered and filthy black robes slipped inside. From a distance it might have passed for human, up close it never would. The skin was an unnatural shade of grey. The eyes were milky white and without pupils. Its fingertips ended in razor sharp, bony talons. The lips were bloated and an inky blue, when they pulled back in a ravenous grin they revealed sharp pointed teeth. The creature stretched out its arms and readied to tear apart its unsuspecting victim.

Still bent over and studying his handiwork the teenage boy waved a single hand. "*Repulso.*"

It felt magical energies take hold and slam it into the far wall. "Aaarrrrrrrgh!" The creature screamed in frustration, not actual pain.

"Hello brother," the boy said without ever bothering to look up.

The creature struggled against the magical energies that were holding it pinned to the far wall. It knew it was hopeless but still fought to get free.

"I don't mind you wanting to kill me, but could you please wait until I'm done?"

The zombie stopped struggling and bore its teeth in a hateful snarl. "I want to tear out your throat! I want to gnaw on your bones! I want to feast on your still beating heart while you watch!"

"Yes, I know, but could you at least wait until after I am done? Is that too much to ask Walter?"

"How did you know I was here?" Walter Corpselover demanded. "You couldn't have heard me; I was as silent as the grave. You didn't have any wards set up."

Sighing, he slowly got up and faced his brother. His face was boyish and looked young even for sixteen. He had small, delicate hands and a thin, undersized frame. His short cropped hair was the color of gold and his eyes were a bright, clear shade of yellow. "You're a zombie Walter. No matter how well preserved your body is, it still stinks of rot; there's no way I wouldn't smell you from twenty yards away. Besides…" he waved a single hand.

Hidden runes on the cell floor suddenly revealed themselves.

"Even if I had done nothing, you'd have been held in place as soon as you took one more step."

Walter's whitish eyes widened as he saw all the trap spells that had been set for him. "How… how did I not notice?" Ordinary humans could not sense hidden wards and circles, but mages and certain monsters could.

The undead could not sense or feel magic.

Waldo Corpselover looked at his brother with sympathy. In this family death was not the ultimate tragedy; weakness was. Walter had been three years older and, for a time, the designated heir. He had been powerful, arrogant, and ruthless; in other words, a typical Dark Mage. A glorious future had stretched out before him. Everyone assumed that eventually he would replace mother and take over her position as head of the family.

Then one day grandfather ate him.

Not all of him, just his heart.

Mother had done what she could, raising him as a zombie. She had done an incredible job. He retained most of his memories and could still think and feel emotion. Walter could even still use some minor spells, with the exception of liches that was considered impossible for the undead. He was an exceptional zombie, but still only a fraction of what he'd once been.

In life Walter had always treated his younger brother with contempt. In death he openly hated him. Not simply because he was still alive, but because everything Walter had wanted and treasured had been handed over to his Waldo. Walter could no longer smell a flower or feel a warm breeze on his face, but he could still feel hatred.

"Is that pity I see in your piss colored eyes? Hah! What a joke!"

"You know I never wanted to be heir."

"Liar," Walter cursed. "Don't pretend. The joke is that even like this I am a better Dark Mage than you will ever be."

Still pinned to the wall Walter glanced at the summoning circle Waldo had been working on. Walter could no longer perform the deeper magics, but retained his knowledge.

"You're trying to summon a homunculus this time? I summoned one when I was just nine. Don't you feel pathetic that you can't manage that when you're sixteen?"

"Big talk from a zombie who can't even move right now."

"If you really are the next head of the family I weep for Corpselover."

"Can zombies weep?" Waldo's right hand sliced the air in front of him. "*Nunc.*"

The spell ended and Walter was once more free.

"If you'll excuse me, I still have work to do." Waldo went back to his summoning circle.

15

"You're turning your back on me?" Walter growled.

"Why not? We both know you can't touch me."

Waldo did not have to turn around to know that would make his brother furious.

"I really am going to kill you."

"Yes, I know, but wait until after I am done here. Close the door on the way out."

Still not bothering to look Waldo heard the footsteps and the door slamming shut.

XXX

In this castle there were undead servants and living slaves; the only people who were, 'free' were the members of the family. He'd read plenty of books about the people who lived in other countries. Folk who in their whole lives never saw the dead walking, and would be terrified just by a single unarmed skeleton shuffling towards them. For Waldo dark magics and the undead were the stuff of ordinary life.

He had been born into this world and, to his eyes, it was all normal. Waldo loved Alteroth, with its volcanoes and slow flowing rivers of magma. He loved the way they glowed at night, and how they rumbled and sent ash up into the perpetually grey sky. Waldo had witnessed several eruptions and thought them beautiful beyond words. He loved the city of Alter, with its clean and logical design. The squat, identical houses packed in their neat rows, the avenues that all ran in perfect lines, the city was a monument to order and control. He didn't get to actually visit it often, but he could stare at its lovely symmetry for hours from his window. It was a joy to behold.

In this world power was everything.

All his life he'd been taught not to fear death; only weakness. Being weak was the only unforgivable sin. Waldo wanted to be strong. Not really for himself, but for his family and for his mother. He did not want to fail or bring them shame. For the sake of his family, he wanted to be a great Dark Mage.

His mother had, had a total of seven children, of which he was the youngest and only one still currently alive. Four were dead, and two (including Walter) were mostly dead. They had all died violent deaths, none of them living to reach nineteen. All had been born with the gift of summoning mana and an ability to use magic.

Their individual talents had differed. Roland (who Waldo did not remember) had specialized in fire magic. Gwen had taken after mom and been a natural at necromancy. Walter had always had a gift at summoning and controlling monsters. All of them had been talented with great potential. All of them had been a credit to their House.

Waldo thought about his own abilities and let out a frustrated grunt.

Healing and protection magic, that was what he was best at. He had absolutely no talent at necromancy, he couldn't even reanimate a mouse. Whenever he attempted any sort of destructive spell it always went horribly wrong... and not even in the good sort of horribly wrong. When he tried to summon monsters...

He let out another frustrated sigh.

The ability to use magic was, in itself, a rare trait in humans. When it manifested, it differed from person to person, both in depth and in direction. Some would never have the strength to do much more than levitate a book or light a candle. Others could summon giants or tear open the earth. The amount of mana a person could draw was an inborn ability. You could learn spells

17

and train to draw the energy more easily; but the limit was in your blood.

There were written spells and incantations, rules of magic, runes, and wards; things that a magic user could learn and study. Spellbooks, wands, rods, magical rings, scrolls, and other items made casting certain spells easier. Yet magic was much more of an art than a science. In theory every magic user should have been capable of casting any spell, so long as it did not require too much mana. In practice it was nothing like that. The sorts of spells a wizard could work were a reflection of his soul.

Waldo stood. The summoning circle was perfect. He would bring forth a homunculus and bind it to his will. Being sixteen, it was long past time to have his own familiar. He began performing the required hand gestures and spoke the incantation. *"Ithkaros venti setarros abro homoculi tenos arrilo venti sem apparos!"*

The circle and the symbols he had so carefully chalked suddenly blazed with light. He felt the mana flow out of him and into the circle.

It's going to work this time! I know it! Waldo thought.

The interior of the circle vanished, as space and time were momentarily shattered.

"Bring me my servant!" Waldo shouted into the void.

Bending to his will the spell brought forth a living creature.

"Chirp. Chirp. Chirp."

There within the summoning circle was a confused blue bird.

"Oh not again!"

XXX

Six skeletons in rusted chainmail walked along the hall. With each step the scabbards attached to their bony hips clicked. These were just a handful of the guards who protected Castle Corpselover. They would patrol these corridors again and again and again, without fail, until their bodies broke down. The guards of this castle never tired, never complained, and would never betray their mistress. If a stranger appeared before them they would draw their swords and fight to the end. How could anyone ask for more than that?

Waldo passed them without a second thought. They were as much a part of his home as the paintings on the wall or the furniture. They shuffled past unheeding.

Waldo was thinking about his most recent failure. The summoning circle had been perfect and so had the enchantment. He understood that the more difficult the spell the easier it was to make a mistake. Something as basic as say lighting a candle could be done with nothing more than a thought. More difficult tasks might require a word or two or a hand gesture. Complex spells needed a specific incantation and hand signs or the use of an item like a wand or magical ring. Summoning a creature without a contract was a high end spell and demanded an incantation, hand gestures, and a summoning circle with a proper containment for the specific creature.

I did everything right, Waldo thought. *I did! Why didn't it work?*

In a sense the summoning had worked… sort of, but a blue bird was not a homunculus. The only positive he could take from his recent effort was that at least he could summon. He couldn't even use necromancy. For a Corpselover that was worse than embarrassing, it was downright humiliating. His family was known for its ability with raising and using the dead. It was where their damn name came from! His mother was acknowledged the greatest necromancer in all Alteroth. Being unable to use it at all made Waldo feel unworthy. He wanted so much to make mother and the family proud of him. How could

19

he ever do that when he was such a complete failure at the family specialty?

As he neared a corner in the hallway he waved his hand. "*Repulso.*"

Even unseen Walter was thrown from the hiding spot and sent flying down a side corridor. His brother cried out in frustration as Waldo kept going.

Healing spells, wards, spell traps, and protective magics all came to him easily. **That** was his gift. That sort of magic did have its place and its uses, but in Alteroth that place was quite low. No one respected healers. The ability to destroy or to control was what mattered.

Behind him Walter shouted. "Why do you always just let me go? Why don't you destroy me?! Am I so pathetic to you?"

"It would make mother sad."

He heard Walter curse him. Waldo knew his brother really would kill him if he ever got the chance. Mother would be upset, but she wouldn't punish Walter if it happened. Children were protected until they knew enough to put on the robes as apprentice mages. From that point on you were expected to protect yourself. Not just from outside enemies, but from your own family as well. The world was hard and you had to be strong enough to not only face it but to take what you wanted from it. There was no place in the family for the weak.

Waldo wondered if that was what he was.

The truth was he had no wish to kill anyone, not even Walter. He had no desire to control others or acquire power. All he wanted was to make mom proud of him. Waldo wanted to be a powerful Dark Mage and a proper Corpselover because that was what would make her proud.

He had talent with magic and the ability to draw on quite a lot of mana. What he didn't have was the same mindset as everyone else. Why did he have a problem with killing? Why didn't the idea of having power over others excite him? Why had he never hungered to be heir?

"What is wrong with me?"

XXX

Castle Corpselover had nine towers and five dungeons. The main castle itself had five floors, each with dozens of rooms and a different lay out. The hallways twisted and turned with various side corridors that came to abrupt ends or went in a circle. Some of the stairways only went up or down one floor and the walls were riddled with secret passageways and hidden rooms. It was not hard at all to go from one end of the castle to the other without ever stepping into the main hallway, if you knew what you were about.

On the fifth floor he took the second corridor on the left off the main hall. Halfway down it there was another side corridor. This one curved around like a fishhook until it ended in a small alcove. Hanging on the wall was a full length mirror, six feet high, with brass trim that was polished so that it shined like gold.

The mirror itself was made of ordinary glass. Standing before it Waldo could not see himself or the corridor around him. There was no reflection; there was only a perfect grey emptiness there.

"Sister, will you come and talk to me?"

He waited. She usually came when he asked, but not always.

He waited for a long time while nothing happened. He was about to go when he saw some of the mirror's grey melt away. Colors swirled, like mixed paint in a bucket. A figure slowly began to take form.

It took a few minutes, but finally she was standing there on the other side of the mirror; his sister Gwen. She had been sixteen when she died on her First Quest. It had happened outside the borders of Alteroth so there had been no way to recover her body. Mother had instead bound her soul into this mirror.

Waldo had been only twelve when Gwen died, still just a child under mother's protection. Gwen had always been gentle with him. Unlike Walter, and most of his other siblings, she had never mocked his eyes or teased him about his many failures. Gwen had never bullied him, and he had loved her almost as much as he had mother. She had taken after mother both in looks and talent. Gwendolyn had been a promising necromancer and candidate to be heir. The sweetness she had shown him had not affected her ability to be a Dark Mage.

She appeared before him dressed in black robes that highlighted her attractive figure. She had long straight black hair, auburn eyes, and the same delicate features as mother. Her skin though was a bleached white and her throat was slashed from ear to ear, the cut slowly bled all the while she stood there.

"You look sad little brother." The words came in a rasp, her wound quivering with each syllable. "Did Walter try and eat you again?"

"Yes he did, but that was no big deal."

Gwen's pale lips twitched into an amused grin. "I would have destroyed him a long time ago. You are truly merciful."

"Please don't insult me."

"I am only being truthful," Gwen croaked.

In Alteroth, and within the Corpselover family, mercy was not a virtue but a weakness.

"I just don't hate him," Waldo confessed. "I know I should. The Dark Powers know he was never fair to me even when he was alive, but I just feel sorry for him now. He was the heir and a Dark Mage. Now what is he?"

"You have a kind heart."

"If you're going to keep insulting me I'm leaving."

Gwen gave a slow rasping laugh. "I truly love you little brother, even though you are strange."

Waldo sighed. "I love you too."

In this world love was also seen as a weakness, but it was at least an accepted one. It was only natural for human beings to feel love, even if they were necromancers. In Alteroth parents still loved their children, children loved their parents, husbands and wives (sometimes) loved each other, and people could love their friends and companions. Love alone though was never an excuse for being soft or indulgent. Seeking power had to come before all else.

"If Walter is not the cause, what has you so glum?"

"It's the usual I suppose," Waldo admitted. "I tried to summon a homunculus and wound up with a bird instead."

"What did you do with it?" Gwen asked curiously.

"I sent it back."

Gwen rasped out a laugh. "Anyone else would have killed it you know."

"I know," Waldo said miserably. "I just don't like killing. There's something terribly wrong with me isn't there?"

"Yes, but it's all right; I like you as you are. You have your own strengths and your own way. Don't worry so much. In the end you will be the head of the family."

Waldo felt his stomach turn. She had told him that before, and made him promise not to tell anyone. Those who were spirits could look into both the past and future. When Gwen made a prediction it *always* happened.

"There's no way that someone like me could ever be head of the family." Waldo muttered. "Even if it can't be Walter there are other branches to the family line. Mother will find someone else, it would never be me."

Gwen smiled at him. Her eyes sparkled and she spoke in a slow melodic tone as if reciting the words to a poem.

"When mother, sister, and brother are gone, you shall receive that which all others covet, and the cost will be that which you treasure most. They shall kneel down and acknowledge you, and your crown shall be made from ashes and blood."

He felt a cold shiver go down his spine. "Is… is that a prophesy sister?"

"Remember that there is more than one path to get to wherever it is you want to go, and sometimes the long way is best. Find your own road, and don't worry about how others would make the journey."

"Gwen, what you said before, was that a prophesy?"

His sister was grinning at him. "Little brother, did you know that when a girl falls in love with someone she will do anything for him? If she gets a little possessive sometimes try to endure it; it's a sign of love."

"Huh? What are you talking about?" He had no interest at all in girls. His life was difficult enough as it was.

24

Gwen rasped out another laugh as her form began to dissolve. "Don't be late to dinner little brother, mother has important news for you."

"What news? And what did you mean before?"

"You'll see." She winked and said nothing more. Soon she was gone completely and the mirror was once again empty.

"That's just great! I have a zombie brother who just wants to kill me and a ghost sister who just likes to confuse me. I don't know which of you is more annoying!"

No reply came from the mirror.

Sighing in frustration Waldo left the alcove.

XXX

Having had two run ins already, Walter had decided not to show up for dinner. Waldo did not mind. Watching a zombie rip apart a pig carcass had never done anything for his appetite. He wondered if his brother would take out his frustration on one of the slaves.

There was a long ornate dining table with forty seats down in the grand hall. This was where the family always took its meals. On occasion members of the extended family or members of one of the other Great Families would be invited. It didn't happen often. Waldo had grown up in relative isolation. He'd known his mother and siblings, his teachers, and the slaves. Outsiders were not welcome. There were people the family did business with and others they ruled over. There were no friends. For the Corpselover family the people of the world were divided into three categories; those with less power, those with similar power, and those with greater power. Those with less power were treated as slaves or servants. Those with similar power were treated with wary respect and never trusted. Those with greater power were feared and obeyed. (The family did not currently acknowledge anyone to be in this third class.)

To Waldo friendship was an alien concept. He understood liking certain people better than others, he preferred certain slaves and teachers. Within the family there was a strict hierarchy, and how you were treated depended on just where you ranked within it. Some family members could be more gentle (Gwen) some more harsh (Walter) but it was always understood who was more important and who was less.

For almost his entire life Waldo had been at the very bottom. He had been the youngest, and as a child had had no power. When he was thirteen he was allowed to wear the black robes as an apprentice, but was still the weakest. At each meal mother sat at the head of the table and the children sat in order of who was strongest. The stronger you were the closer you sat to mother, with the one sitting to her immediate right being the heir.

The order was not set, and he could remember it changing many times. His older brothers and sisters competed and fought with each other to prove themselves. Mother would reward or punish them by changing their seat at the table. It was not love or favoritism that decided the order; it was just a reflection of who was the strongest.

Waldo was always the one seated furthest away and he was always seated on the left side of the table. He was never really angry about that. He accepted that he was the weakest, and it was enough that there was a place for him. Growing up all that he wanted was to be worthy of his family.

Then one by one they began to die.

Dark Mages were expected to go out into the world and **take**. The strong took from the weak; that was the way things worked. Every member of the ruling family was expected to add to its wealth and fearsome reputation. A Dark Mage's worth was reflected in the amount of gold and slaves they could acquire, and by how many enemies they could kill. These were the true measures of a Dark Mage's power, and each of his brothers and sisters were determined to prove themselves the strongest. That meant facing constant danger, and the usual consequences.

There were never any funerals.

If a body could be recovered it was given a pyre as the family bore witness, but there were no prayers, no ceremony. If the body could not be recovered mother would just make an announcement. 'Karl is dead.' That was all. There were no prolonged mourning periods. Mother would be sad but she would never say much. There would be one less place at the dinner table; one less competitor for the title of heir. No one would ask how they died or want to remember them. Bit by bit they were simply forgotten.

There were the living and the dead and the mostly dead. Going from one to the other was just accepted. If you were strong enough you would survive no matter the dangers. If you were not it didn't matter what became of you.

When Gwen died Waldo had cried for her at the table. His mother had gotten up and slapped him. "If you have to do that then at least do it where no one can see you!"

It was just one of the many hard lessons he had been forced to learn.

As a child Waldo had moved up the table, as one brother or sister after another disappeared. By the time he put on the robes there was only Walter left ahead of him. The two of them were seated next to mother, with him on her left. When Walter died they switched places. Waldo found himself on mother's right; in the seat reserved for the heir.

"The dead cannot rule the living," his mother had said after raising Walter. "The heir must provide children and must be able

27

to make contracts and work the greater magics. You are heir now Waldo."

That was how he had come to his current position, he hadn't done anything to earn it; he was just the last one breathing.

As he approached the head of the table mother silently watched him. She looked tired, she'd had her robes on when she had suddenly left, but wasn't wearing them anymore. She had a comfortable, loose fitting brown shift on and some slippers. Though she was at home, Waldo noted her wand was still tucked into a large pocket.

His mother's long black hair was tangled and messy. The occasional strands of grey were getting more numerous and noticeable, as were the lines radiating from the corner of her eyes. His mother was still a beautiful woman and more powerful than she had ever been, but there was no denying that she was getting older. (Not that Waldo would ever say so out loud. He wasn't suicidal.)

"Did everything go well mother?" Waldo asked as he took his seat.

"No it did not, but we'll discuss that after dinner."

Waldo felt a sudden nervousness. Growing up in this family he'd learned to be wary of any change in routine. His mother had never discussed meetings with the Council with him before.

"Did something special happen?"

Lilith turned to face her son. "I dislike repeating myself. Must I?"

"No, mother. Please, forgive me." He apologized quietly.

She nodded and then glanced to her left at the empty seat. Zombies didn't have very good table manners and preferred to devour their food raw, and still struggling. When Walter joined them he usually just had half of a pig carcass placed on a large silver tray. "Your brother did not want to dine with us today. Did anything happen between you two?"

Waldo shrugged. "Nothing unusual, he just tried to attack me twice."

His mother nodded slightly, that was routine. "Why haven't you destroyed Walter?"

"Do you want me too?"

"No, but that was not my question. It has tried to kill you many times, it is your enemy."

Never spare an enemy. Never show mercy. Those were rules that had been drilled into him since childhood. He hesitated and answered carefully, his mother had regularly tested his other siblings. She had never really tested him before but it was certainly possible. "Walter is no real threat to me, and... and I know you would not be happy if I destroyed my brother."

A slight grin touched her lips, but it only made her appear sadder. "You have always been a thoughtful child."

Just what does that mean?

She gestured to one of the waiting slaves and trays of food were brought out of the kitchen.

"Let's just have a nice meal together."

"Yes mother."

The slaves brought out a small feast for just the two of them. They both picked at their food in near silence. Freshly baked bread, roast pork, beef, chicken and other delicacies went untouched and Waldo guessed the slaves would get to enjoy them.

29

Something very strange was going on.

Everything had been normal this morning before she had set out for the council meeting. It did not take a genius to see that something had happened there. His mother ran the family affairs completely on her own. Whatever occurred must have been of great importance if she felt the need to discuss it with him.

Once the dishes had been cleared away, and the slaves had departed, she told him what was going on.

"It's time Waldo. You will be leaving on your First Quest tomorrow."

Waldo blinked. "Oh."

His mother lifted a single eyebrow and looked slightly amused. "Is that all you have to say? 'Oh?'"

"Well, I am sixteen, and it's not like I didn't know this day was coming. I… I would have liked a little more warning I suppose."

"This is how it has always been done. You have been preparing for this since the day of your birth. You should not need any more time."

"You're right mother, of course I am ready." Inside Waldo was anything but sure of that. "I will come back with servants and piles of treasure. I will definitely make you proud."

"Servants and piles of treasure," his mother echoed quietly. "Will you also bring back the heads of the enemies you have killed?"

"I… I will try to." Waldo answered hesitantly. "I will do my best."

"Is that what you'll say when you're facing a charging knight or a hill giant?" His mother slowly shook her head. "This will be your first time facing real danger. Oh I know Walter has tried to kill you, and that some of the others might have if you had put the robes on sooner. But those were all threats you were familiar with, ones you knew to watch for. When you leave this castle, and then leave Alteroth, you will be alone and surrounded by enemies. This is the rite of passage every Dark Mage of a ruling house must endure. You must prove you are worthy, not just by surviving, but by shedding blood and returning home with treasure. Do you expect to come back empty handed and just say, 'I did my best'?" She gave a rude snort. "That would be fine if you were a Poisondagger."

Waldo's face reddened. "I'm not a coward mother."

"My son, if I'd ever thought you were I would have killed you myself. I **know** your worth. That is not what concerns me."

"Then what is it?"

"You don't remember your brother Roland do you?"

Waldo shook his head.

"Well I'm not surprised; you were only three at the time he died. He was my first born, his father was Martin Wormwood. Martin was very skilled at fire magics. He would definitely have become the head of his family if the Poisondaggers hadn't murdered him."

Lilith Corpselover had never married. Had she, her husband would have become the family head. Instead she had enjoyed a long series of lovers; each of her seven children had had a different father. The men came and went, and none of them were allowed to have any part of her children's lives. Among the Great Families there was no stigma in being born out of wedlock, so long as there was one parent with elite blood and the child had the ability to use magic.

31

"Roland was just like his father; a powerful and ruthless fire user. I taught him everything I knew and he never disappointed me. When he was just fourteen, I took him with me on a trip to the Barren Mounts. I wanted some new goblins, and I thought it would be a good experience for him. Would you believe we ran into a giant? Twenty feet tall at the very least, and a tree for a club in his hands. Roland was closer to him than I was, and I called for him to get clear so I could deal with the brute. Calmly, as if it were just practice, he lifted his wand and poured enough fire on that stupid beast to roast him in less than a minute. I was fifty yards away and I felt as though I were starting to bake." She sighed wistfully. "We ate his flesh for the rest of our trip."

"He killed a great monster at fourteen?" Waldo was impressed. Killing a Great Monster was quite a feat for anyone who was not a master. "Why did I never hear about that before?"

Lilith shrugged. "Because he is dead, so what does it matter now? The point is he was everything I could hope for in an heir. When he set off on his First Quest I was certain he would come home with an army of slaves, piles of gold, and the heads of at least a dozen knights. I really was sure he would be fine."

Her eyes drifted, no doubt recalling his long forgotten brother.

"He died," his mother said simply. "He went to the Kingdom of Lothas and never came back. A knight defeated him and left his head on a pike. As strong as he was he ended up as rotting flesh somewhere far from home."

"I've always known the First Quest is dangerous mother."

"Three of my children have died on their First Quests," his mother said. "All of them were as well prepared as I could make them, and all of them had learned how to kill by the time they set out. Yet they still died. Do you truly understand? No one cares about doing your best, the point is to survive. That means doing what you *need* to, not what you *want* to."

32

"I know that mother. It's not like I fail on purpose." He answered quietly.

"My son, I don't believe you are a failure or weak. You simply have different strengths. I have tried to bring you along, slowly, in the hopes that your special talents would develop on their own. I had been planning to put off your First Quest for a while."

"How long were you planning to wait mother? I'm sixteen; everyone usually goes between fifteen and seventeen."

"I was hoping to put it off until you were thirty."

Waldo stared at her with his mouth hanging open.

"Or until you managed to kill someone," his mother added pointedly. "Whichever came first."

"So the fact you're sending me now is a sign you believe I'm ready?"

"No," his mother said. "The council has forced my hand."

"Wait, my going on the quest now was a decision made by the council?"

His mother nodded unhappily. "Not only are you going on your First Quest but there are set conditions you will have to meet before you can return."

"Conditions?"

XXX

Lilith narrowed her eyes. "What sort of test?"

"Your son is sixteen is he not?" Baldwin asked.

"He is," Lilith answered suspiciously.

"Isn't it time he went on his First Quest?" Baldwin inquired in a reasonable tone.

Around the table heads began to nod.

"If he really is worthy of being your heir then let him prove it." Darius said.

"I will be the one who decides when he should go." Lilith stated. "It is always the family head that decides."

"Not always." Baldwin remained placid. "There have been other occasions when the council insisted someone take their First Quest early. There is precedent for it."

"If your son is strong enough to replace you, then he should be strong enough for this." Gawreth said.

"You cannot keep him hidden inside your castle forever." Xilos added.

"If he can succeed that would certainly convince us and this whole matter would be closed." Darius said.

"You have to admit that it's only reasonable." Loram piled on.

Lilith's eyes went to each of them in turn. Only Poisondagger had not spoken in favor of sending her son out, and from his previous comment it was obvious where he stood. *They have already decided*, Lilith realized with sickening certainty. While she would not hesitate to take on any of the other Houses, even she did not have the strength to fight all six.

"So, you intend to force me into this?" Lilith asked.

"Why do you even need to be forced?" Darius snarled. "You sent your other children out when the time came."

"I sent them when I felt each was ready." Lilith answered coldly. "He is my only living child now. Do you blame me for being cautious?"

"From our perspective it looks more like you are acting out of love." Darius said.

"I do love my son." Lilith admitted. "However I would never try to protect him just because of that. I have good reason to be patient. He is my sole remaining heir."

"He is your only remaining *child*," Baldwin clarified. "If the tree dies you take a healthy branch and plant it. You have cousins and other relatives. Just how many branch families are there in Corpselover?"

"Forty seven," Lilith admitted. In the extended family there were a dozen masters, and probably at least that many with the potential.

"All of them better," Dante muttered.

Lilith sent him a sharp look and he seemed to shrink into his chair.

"Don't blame us if your child is weak." Xilos said.

"My son is unusual I admit, but he is not weak." Lilith said. "Even the strong do not always survive the First Quest."

"Then we must make absolutely certain he is strong." Baldwin said. "If you are to choose him over the branch members of your family it needs to be obvious he really is the best choice."

Lilith had an unpleasant suspicion of where Baldwin was leading.

He continued, confirming her misgivings. "We require he meet certain conditions before he will be permitted to return home."

"That is not how the quest works! Each individual decides when they have done enough. The only absolute requirement is that they leave Alteroth and visit a foreign land."

"Which means he might cower in some cave just over the border for a few days and then run home!" Xilos said.

Darius nodded "It's happened before. It's disgraceful, but it has been done."

"My son would never do something so cowardly!" She sent a cold look in Dante's direction. "He's not a Poisondagger after all."

"What does that mean?" Dante asked even as he squirmed.

"Your son Daryl spent what, three days in Galisia before running back with his tail between his legs? What about your son Pyrus? He killed a couple families out in the Barrens and that was all. I never heard any complaints about his worth."

Dante fumed, but no one spoke up in his family's defense.

"We are not all Poisondaggers." Gawreth said pointedly. "I lost Cersei, my daughter from my third wife just a month ago."

"My son Kiska was burned alive at the stake in Dregal." Baldwin said.

Darius held out his hands and began ticking names off on his fingers. "Aban, Astera, Casper, Daria, Ewa, Faraz, Jasmin, Melchor, Razin, Shayan." All ten fingers were up. "I can still continue. We have all lost children on the First Quest."

"Except for Dante." Xilos pointed out.

"Yes, except for him." Darius agreed.

Poisondagger seethed but could not deny it.

"We have all made sacrifices to the First Quest," Baldwin told her. "You cannot pretend you are the only one. It is a cruel custom, but necessary. It is the only way to ensure that every member of a ruling family is worthy."

"Unless you're a Poisondagger of course." Lilith sneered.

"At least all of mine have killed! Isn't it true yours never has?" Dante said accusingly. "Not even a slave?"

"Killing is easy." Lilith gripped her wand with a single hand. "Shall I demonstrate?"

The others placed hands on their wands as well.

"There is no need for that." Baldwin said. "We are all members of the Council of Seven."

"So what? We'd all kill each other if we could."

"Very true," Poisondagger muttered.

"We don't kill each other openly." Baldwin said.

Gawreth nodded. "That would lead to civil war and our ruin."

"No," Lilith said bitterly. "Instead we send each other out on impossible quests and let someone else do it."

"If your son is strong enough he will survive." Gawreth said. "If not then he is of no use to you."

"Just what are the conditions you intend to place on him?" Lilith asked.

Baldwin told her.

"I see," Lilith said. "Do you even still pretend this is anything but a death sentence? Only someone with the potential to be a Grand Master would have any hope at all!"

"I am sorry Lilith." Baldwin told her. "I know this is drastic, but you have forced us to act."

He wasn't sorry. They wanted her son gone, and this was their way of going about it.

"If the six of you are determined then I suppose I have no choice."

Her son was doomed.

XXX

"Yes," Lilith said. "The council set three conditions you will have to fulfill before you will be allowed to return home."

"I've never heard of that before."

"It's rare, but not unheard of son."

"All right mother. What are the conditions?"

Lilith had to struggle to keep the fury out of her voice. She wanted to at least give her son hope that it was possible. "You must make a contract with at least three monsters and bind them to your service. You must defeat at least one knight in battle." She struggled to get out the last, most impossible, requirement. "You must acquire a dragon's egg or a dragon and return with it."

Waldo stared at her hoping she would suddenly laugh at him and tell him this was all some huge joke. Her somber manner convinced him it was not.

"Bind three monsters, defeat a knight in battle, and bring back a dragon's egg or a dragon? Is that all? Why don't I slay an army or capture a castle while I'm at it?"

"Careful son, they might add those."

Waldo stopped and considered the situation.

Making a contract with just one monster was extremely dangerous and quite a feat. Getting three would be an even greater challenge.

Knights and White Mages were the deadliest threats most Dark Mages could face on a First Quest. Only the strongest candidates, or the most desperate, would deliberately seek out a knight.

Dragons were far and away the rarest and most powerful of the Great Monsters. Even his mother, an experienced grand master, would never try and face one alone. That was work for an entire army and dozens of skilled mages. Unless you had some sure method to keep the mother far away, stealing a dragon's egg was nearly as dangerous.

"Why does the council want me dead?"

"They are afraid you are too weak to replace me as both head of the family and as a member on the council."

"Well I can't say I'm surprised. Do you agree with them mother?"

"No. Never."

"Even though I have never managed to kill anyone?"

"Killing is the easiest thing in the world my son. All it takes is not caring about your victim. You care too much, you feel too much. It's only ever hard when you let yourself care." She knew how true *that* was.

"I'm sorry; I can't seem to help it."

His mother looked at him wistfully. "You remind me of your father."

Waldo had never known who his father was. He had asked his mother a few times, but she had never given him any information. From the color of his eyes it was obvious his father was from Avalon, the home of the White Mages.

"Is that a good thing?"

"To me it is." Lilith sighed. "I had hoped that eventually you would learn to harden your heart. Unfortunately there is no more time." She paused. "If you were to find a place in the greater world no one would come after you."

"You mean go into exile?" Waldo said shocked. "Never come home again?"

"If the only choices are exile or death which do you prefer?"

"If I can't come home there's no point to any of it. All I have ever wanted is to make you proud of me mother. This is the only place where I belong, the only place I have ever wanted to be. I want you to be proud to call me your son."

He really is like his father. Lilith thought fondly. She felt an ache in her chest and forced herself to ignore it. "If that is your choice then so be it."

His mother surprised him then by placing a soft kiss on his cheek.

"Whatever happens, I am already proud of you."

Chapter 2

Setting Out

Waldo was in his room getting ready.

It was tradition that he would have one last meal and then leave. He would not be permitted to take any coins or precious metals. Waldo would have to travel alone on foot, without any slaves or undead. From the moment he stepped outside the castle gate he was expected to rely on his own strength.

Whether he went north or south, east or west, it would take weeks to reach the border. Though he would be without money Waldo did not expect any problems until he left Alteroth. The peasants would give him food and shelter. They would not dare refuse one who wore the black robes. Once he was on foreign soil he truly would be on his own.

Come the morning Waldo would be given a couple waterskins, as well as a week's worth of travel food. He had a backpack where he would carry spare clothes as well as some other items. These were spread out over his bed, and he was going over each of them.

First and foremost was his spellbook. Inside it was every spell and ward he had ever been taught. (Including the ones he had never managed to get right.) The basic ones, that he used constantly had long since been memorized, he could perform them without a second thought. The more powerful and complicated magics he would need to study and memorize first. Along with his spells and wards were the recipes for all sorts of potions and remedies. Waldo was skilled at making potions, and was an expert at using different herbs and ingredients to bring out the most potent effects.

As he walked through Alteroth he planned to spend as much time as possible going over the binding ritual. Getting that right was of particular importance; it was the only way he could force monsters to obey him.

The order in which he would need to attempt things was obvious. He could not even think about acquiring a dragon's egg yet. Fighting a knight with his current abilities was akin to suicide. He would have to start by acquiring monsters. Once they were bound by magical contract he could use them to do his fighting. It would be dangerous, but it was his only choice.

Next to his spellbook was his wand.

Like all Dark Mages, his had been carved from human bone. Etched into it were three words; Corpselover, pride, and power. He tapped it with a couple fingers and frowned. A wand was supposed to magnify the effects of its user's spells. The way a hammer multiplied the force of a blacksmith's blow. It was the most basic tools used by mages. One of the *many* things that had frustrated Waldo over the years was the fact he'd never gotten much out of his.

Oh he could *use* them; the problem was there was never a real difference in the spell's effect. When his mother used her wand the spell was usually two or three times more powerful. When he used his the results remained frustratingly the same. This wand was his fifth. He'd asked for new ones in the hope it would help; but the results never changed.

There were small cloth sacks, each bound up tight and with a description written in ink. Ginger, mandrake, basalt, sulfur, wolfsbane, ground obsidian, and a dozen other spell components. He had were two pens and a bottle of ink. Beside them were six knives, to a magic user daggers were both a useful tool and a weapon of last resort.

Next were the maps.

Alteroth was a large nation and nine countries touched its borders. To the north were three kingdoms. From west to east they were Wylef, Lothas, and Dregal. To the east was Abura and to the southeast Dacia. To the south, running from east to west were Rutenia, Galisia, and the Barony of Lemur. On the western border, between Wylef and Lemur, was Viscaya.

Within Alteroth, the nations of Wylef, Lothas, and Dregal were collectively known as the northern kingdoms. The ruling families of all three were related to each other and had firm control over their lands. All three kingdoms held a feudal tradition, going back almost to the time of the Shattering. Knights and armed men swore fealty to local lords, who in turn were sworn to serve their King or Queen. There was no slavery to the north, but only nobles could own land. The peasants who worked the fields were allowed to keep a share of what they produced and did enjoy certain rights, but were forced to rely on their liege lords for protection and enforcement of the law.

The northern kingdoms were blessed with fertile soil and plenty of water. There were thick forests, marshes, abundant farmlands, and thriving towns and cities. Lothas also had vast iron deposits and forged large quantities or iron and much smaller amounts of steel. They were rich lands and Alteroth had a profitable trading relationship with Lothas and Wylef. The growing influence of the whites was stirring up trouble, especially in Dregal where the king was weak and easily influenced. Because of the White Mages trade with Dregal was almost nonexistent.

Abura and Darcia were also feudal kingdoms, but there the ruling families were not as well established. They often struggled to enforce their rule over their nobles. Some of the local lords barely acknowledged any sort of fealty to the crown. They tried to rule over their lands autonomously and often did not bother to send any taxes to the capitol. Dacia had only just recently come out of a long civil war. The old ruling family had been exterminated, and a new one installed. The new king had to be very cautious as to how much he demanded of some of his retainers. Many still considered him a usurper.

The lands to the south were arid and mountainous, the border region was a desert called the Barrens that was especially unforgiving. The Barony of Lemur was ruled by Baron Artimus Fabri. The Fabri were the only nobles in Lemur, they'd annihilated all the others generations ago. The baron saw the country as being his own personal property and used his extended family to rule over it and drain every last bit of money. Every tax collector was a Fabri and every Fabri was a tax collector.

Galisia was the poorest of all the lands that bordered Alteroth. Its territory was mountainous and dry with the people living in scattered villages scratching out an existence with sheep and goat herding and a little subsistence farming. The country had no one ruler, each individual village or settlement was cut off from the others by the rugged terrain; all authority was local. The land was overrun by goblin and orc tribes who raided each other and the humans. It was perhaps the poorest and most wretched spot in the world.

It was however a wonderful source of slaves.

Rutenia also had many goblins, orcs, and other monsters. The land south of the Barrens was a bit more hospitable with hills and lowlands in place of mountains. Here various clans held power over stretches of territory. Loyalty was to the family or clan and battles were **always** personal. In Rutenia feuds and vendettas could last for generations and even the most minor slight could be cause for bloodshed.

Viscaya was an anomaly, the people who lived there had very bizarre notions about power and government. There the commoners held political power. They practiced a strange form of organized anarchy that was referred to as, 'democracy'. The people there had no respect for blood, and did not permit any noble titles or special privileges. They loudly insisted that all men were equal and ought to be treated that way.

The idea was so patently ridiculous Waldo couldn't imagine how anyone could be blind enough to actually believe it. To say nothing of actually having a nation based around it. Waldo could only imagine it as mobs roaming the streets and claiming to be a government.

Oddly enough, Viscaya was actually quite prosperous. They were a center for artisans and trade. It made no sense, but it was so.

Where to go was the first decision Waldo had to make.

It was funny, even though he'd been preparing for this his entire life he had never thought about the specifics. There were advantages and disadvantages to whatever choice he made. The northern kingdoms were rich with many towns and cities. There were wild goblins that he could try to capture. The problem with going north was the fact there were knights and the occasional White Mage infesting the countryside. Despite trading with each other Dark Mages were feared and hated. Anyone with black robes might suddenly be attacked, as his brother Roland had apparently discovered.

Abura and Darcia had the same issues, while being poorer.

By contrast in Lemur, the knights were little more than armed tax collectors. All the southern lands were poor, with monsters running free. Lemur made a lot of coin by selling slaves to Alteroth, and the local authorities would likely look the other way at anything he wanted to do there. In Rutenia and Galisia people only worried about themselves and were not about to try and fight a Dark Mage unless they had to. In any of the lands to the south he would be at liberty to try and capture as many monsters as he could. Capturing an orc or goblin was perilous, but not as dangerous as facing a knight. With luck he could capture and make a contract with three or more of them and that would be one task completed.

In Viscaya there were few monsters roaming the wild, and the people there actually expected Dark Mages to tamely submit to their laws. They really were filled with strange ideas.

He had individual maps for all nine nations. He picked up the one for Galisia. It was commonly accepted that candidates who felt confident in their power or really wanted to impress went north. Those who were less certain or less ambitious usually went south. All of his brothers and sisters had travelled north.

I think my best option, Waldo thought. *Is to go south and try and contract some monsters. I need three, but I can always get more than that. If I have ten or twenty goblins and orcs in my service that will be a fine start.*

There was no limit to how many monsters you could have under contract. The advantages with using familiars were that they were permanently bound to your will. They could be summoned instantly without a circle. They were bound to obey their master's every command. They could not lie or inflict harm on their master, even when they hated him.

Making the contract could be done against the monster's will. All that was required was physical contact between master and servant as the binding spell was cast. The servants kept their free will and often openly hated their masters; but they were bound regardless. This *could* lead to trouble if a master was careless. Familiars could tell lies of omission and could find subtle ways to cause trouble.

Contracts could not be made between members of the same race, so it was impossible to make a human a familiar. You could also not make a contract with the undead. Contracts could only be made with living beings of other races. Once a monster was contracted to you, you were also responsible for feeding and providing for it just as you were with slaves.

Waldo knew he would have to overpower and capture the first orc or goblin and then force a contract on it. After that he would have a servant to do his fighting for him and things would be much simpler. Waldo was nervous at the prospect of that first run in. Maybe he could set up a trap where it would be caught by some hidden wards. That was likely his best option.

Galisia would be the place to start his quest, once he had enough monsters under his control he would have to travel east to seek out a knight. After that... well he no idea where to go after that.

One step at a time, he thought. *Just this will be more than hard enough.*

Waldo was carefully studying the maps; he would need to have plenty of water with him while he crossed the Barrens. It would not be out of the realm of possibility to be attacked there. He was going over the different scenarios in his mind when he heard a soft rap at his door.

Waldo knew immediately who it had to be.

His brother was not stupid enough to announce himself. His mother never came to his room. A slave would knock once and announce himself. The undead never knocked; they weren't very big on courtesy.

"Come in Enver."

The door to his room opened and slowly swung wide. There in the doorway was a rail thin man barely five feet tall who might have weighed ninety pounds. You could make out the lines of his skull beneath the slightly yellow skin. His fingers were long and bony thin and his wrists looked like they would break off if shaken hard. He had short black hair and was dressed in a tailored made suit with a vest and long coat draped around his thin shoulders.

His eyes were blood red and slitted. Two long canine fangs dominated his mouth and made him appear just a bit more

47

menacing. Despite eyes and fangs he did not really look all that dangerous. He actually looked rather frail.

Waldo knew better. Except for his mother, this was the most dangerous person who lived here.

Enver cast his eyes down on the bare stone floor. There were no markings there to see.

"It always amazes me how many protective wards and trap spells you have in your room." Enver said in that slightly superior, mocking tone he always used. Being what he was he could sense the magic, though all the runes and inscriptions were inverted and hidden from view.

"Do you think I'd be able to sleep at night without them? I swear zombies have short term memory loss. Walter keeps trying to sneak in here."

"You should have destroyed it long ago." The condescension was just a little more blatant. "It's hard to believe you are her son. Why she let such a weak, defective creature as you live past childhood is a mystery to me."

"Did you come here for something or did you just want to get in a few more insults before I leave?"

Enver's head shook in mock disappointment. "No need to be hostile, have I ever harmed you?"

"You threatened to kill me all the time when I was growing up."

"Well I am a vampire. You looked like such a tasty treat when you were little." His inky lips peeled back in a ghoulish grin. "Truth to tell, I would still like to have some of your blood."

"If you ever tried that I would kill you." Waldo said and meant it. He felt sympathy for the slaves and even for Walter. Enver was different. The vampire had tormented him constantly until he took on the robes, and he had done it just for his own amusement.

"I have never actually harmed you." Enver reminded him.

"Only because my mother gave you a direct order to never touch any of her children."

"More is the pity. It's boring only being able to torture the slaves."

"What do you want? If you're just here to annoy me then get out. I have a lot of things to do."

"You will be leaving in the morning, so I will not see you off. I do hate how I am in the day time."

"I can't tell you how sad that makes me."

Enver looked at him with those inhuman eyes. Waldo could see the amusement there. He only took pleasure in the pain of others.

"You know Waldo, I want to help you survive your First Quest." Reaching into a pocket he drew out a folded piece of paper. Knowing better than to step any further into the room he gave a flick of his bony wrist and tossed it across the floor to land near Waldo's feet.

Waldo looked at the paper suspiciously and made no move to touch it. "What is it?"

"A gift." Enver said with a bloodless smile.

Waldo did not reach for it.

"You don't trust me?"

"Why would I?"

Enver spread his hands. "I have no reason to deceive you, and I would gain nothing from your death."

"Except a good laugh."

Enver gave a slight shrug and did not deny it. "It would please me more to see you return. You have always been my favorite victim, and I do miss your tears and screams."

Waldo's eyes flickered to the wand lying on his bed. He'd never killed anyone, but he thought he could destroy Enver without any regret. When he was a child the vampire had often cornered him and threatened to rip out his throat and drink him dry. Waldo had been forced to watch favorite slaves be tortured and slowly killed. Enver would never try to quiet them. He enjoyed their cries and pleas for mercy as he tore into their flesh and greedily drank their blood. He always made it last as long as he could.

As they were being killed, the slaves would always turn to *him* for mercy. Those pleas had always bothered Waldo more than the actual killings. Slaves were common and easy to replace.

The way they would look at him though, the way they would beg him for help... it had given Waldo nightmares. He had gone to his mother and asked her to make Enver stop. His mother had been unhappy with him. She told him to accept it or find the means to deal with it. A Dark Mage could not be affected by his victims' cries. Mother forbade Enver from harming or even touching him, but she didn't care about nightmares. In her eyes it would only make him stronger.

Waldo eventually learned not to show any favor on the slaves. He learned not to care when they died in front of him, and Enver finally grew bored with that game. The vampire would then threaten to kill him and would make a point of bending iron bars or crushing stones in his bony little hands.

"I'll kill you and drink every last drop of your sweet blood," Enver would growl and approach him menacingly. The vampire wanted to hear screams and see Waldo shaking in terror.

Waldo had learned how to deal with him by the time he was apprenticed. "Who are you trying to scare? You can't touch me and we both know it." Waldo would then walk past him, daring Enver to prove him wrong.

The vampire never did and it made the monster furious.

Waldo knew that if Enver were not bound by his mother's command the vampire would tear his throat out in an instant. The day his mother died the contract she had made would be broken and Enver would be free. On that day (if they were both still alive) one of them would die. Waldo knew and accepted that. If Enver turned out to be the first person he ever killed he would be very happy.

"So you want me to live so you can kill me yourself one day?"

"Exactly," Enver smiled. "I've dreamed of tearing out your throat for so long, I would simply hate to be denied that pleasure."

Waldo knew that was true and, oddly enough, it did give Enver a reason to want to help. Reaching down he slowly and carefully unfolded the paper. He saw it was a map of Lothas with a path marked on it and three distinctive X's.

"What is this? A treasure map?"

"Of a sort, if you follow that it will lead you to three Great Monsters."

"Great Monsters?" Waldo said disbelieving.

There were ten races that were classified as Great Monsters due to their superior power. They were; Dragons, Vampires, Giants,

Ogres, Werewolves, Trolls, Succubi, Griffons, Medusas, and Elementals. Capturing a Great Monster and making a contract with one was a challenge even for an experienced Dark Mage. For a novice to capture one, let alone three…

Waldo tossed the paper aside.

"You must think me a complete idiot. Either the map is a fake or you really are trying to get me killed."

"Not at all," Enver said. "You cannot return until you have made a contract with at least three monsters correct? These three will be of far greater use to you than some lazy goblins would be."

"My mother told you about that?"

"Why are you surprised? She always shares everything with me. I am her trusted confidante."

"You're her familiar."

Enver gave a careless shrug. "Six of one, half a dozen of the other. The point is that once I learned of that I drew up this map for your benefit. If you can capture these three creatures they will be a major help to you on your quest. Who knows? You might actually survive, though it is unlikely."

"Just overpowering some goblins or orcs is going to be hard enough. You expect me to take on giants and vampires?"

Enver's lips quirked and twisted in a silent laugh. "Oh, I think you might manage with *these* monsters."

Waldo knew that tone much too well. It was the one Enver always preferred before performing some particularly cruel jest. "Just what are you up to?"

"I am simply trying to help you survive in the hopes of eventually making a meal of you." He turned back to the door. "I

52

have given you my help. You may accept it or not as you wish. I will not be seeing you off in the morning, so this will be goodbye. I wish you success and will hope for your return." He flashed a cruel and mocking smile. "Though I won't expect it, even if you do follow my advice."

Enver left closing the door behind him.

The vampire's visit had completely ruined his mood. He didn't need a reminder that this quest was nearly impossible. Picking up the maps of the southern lands he went through the motions of trying to select which one he should visit first.

All the while he kept glancing at the paper lying there on the floor.

Waldo did finally pick it up and look at it again. More out of curiosity than anything else. Lothas was the richest of the northern kingdoms, and also the one most infested with knights.

"Maybe he really does want to get me killed."

Contemptuously he crumpled up the treasure map and tossed it in the trash. He went back to the southern maps and studied them more seriously as he packed for his journey.

XXX

Waldo got no sleep that night.

His backpack was ready except for the waterskins and travel rations. His spellbook was in there, while his wand would be in one of the many pockets sewn into his robes. It would be hidden but always in reach.

He had finally decided to go south to Galisia. He would stay there just long enough to make contracts with ten weak monsters. It would not be much, but it would be the most he could hope for. With that done he would move on to trying to defeat a

53

knight. If he managed that much he would then try to figure out what would come next.

When Waldo really stopped to think about it, the requirements of his First Quest did seem impossible. Rationally, no one would ever expect a young, inexperienced, mage to have any hope of acquiring a dragon's egg. Capturing any three monsters would be a great accomplishment. Defeating a knight an even greater one. For someone lacking combat magic those feats were already nearing unbelievable. Dragons were the fiercest and most terrible of all monsters. Their lairs were always well hidden and far from human civilization. Just discovering one would be an immense challenge. Sneaking into one unnoticed? Stealing an egg? Escaping with one alive? When Waldo tried to imagine the odds against it the number he came up with was depressingly large.

Since he couldn't sleep, he spent a lot of the early morning hours just staring out his window. Like every night the world was complete blackness; from the skies above to the city below no flicker of light marred the perfect dark. The only light was from the ever churning volcanoes and the slow moving rivers of lava of the Forge. They were many miles away but were clear through the pitch black.

Waldo just stood there for hours gazing at the rivers of fire shining through the dark. It was just so beautiful.

XXX

When the skies began to shift from utter darkness to the tiniest hint of grey, Waldo knew the time had come. He would have a last meal with his family, gather his food and water, and then set out on foot. The idea of leaving not just the castle but everything he knew scared him. Down deep he was afraid that he was as weak and useless as most had always thought. For all his brave words he knew he would probably never return. Death was not something to be feared. Waldo knew it was a failing that he could not think of his own death without a cold knot in his stomach.

Had the others been afraid to die?

The slaves always begged and screamed; but they were only slaves. Waldo was thinking of his siblings; those brothers and sisters who had sat at the table with him. The ones he had always been compared to, and to whom he'd always been found wanting. Had any of them ever been scared like this?

They'd all been so strong and sure of themselves. Each one had fought to be heir and had been a true Dark Mage. He didn't think any of them could have ever been afraid.

Along with the fear there was something else. In his life he had stepped outside the castle walls on only a handful of occasions. What he knew of the Shattered Lands he'd mainly read in books or heard about from his mother. Now he was going to go and see it for himself. The idea of exploring and facing dangers was exciting. For the first time in his life he was going to be on his own. It was a thrilling thought. Excitement and terror warred inside his heart.

Before heading down to breakfast there was one more thing he needed to do first.

XXX

"Sister, will you come and talk to me?"

He waited as the colors swirled and Gwen took form.

His sister appeared before him; throat slashed and skin stark white. She was looking at him with just a hint of amusement. "Hello little brother," she said in her gasping voice. "Have you come to say farewell?"

Waldo nodded. "I'm leaving on my First Quest today. I didn't want to go without saying goodbye to you."

Gwen gave a slight nod. "I will miss you until your return."

"You sound very sure I'll come back."

"I have told you, one day you will lead the family. Trust your big sister."

Waldo looked at her longingly; he wanted any kind of hope. "Will I do well in Galisia?"

Gwen slowly shook her head. "You are not going to Galisia."

"Yes I am." Waldo said. "I'm surprised you wouldn't know that." Maybe she couldn't see everything that was going to happen. That was not a comforting thought.

She shook her head again and spoke with rigid certainty. "You will not travel to Galisia or Lemur or Rutenia. If you go south you will die. If you go to Viscaya or Abura or Dacia you will die. If you go to Wylef you will die. If you go to Dregal you will die."

Waldo felt the ice in his stomach start to crawl up his throat. She had named off eight of the nine places he could travel to and announced they were death sentences.

"Are you saying I have to go to Lothas? Isn't it the most dangerous of the northern kingdoms?"

She made no reply. She simply stared back at him.

Thinking of going to Lothas something immediately occurred to him. "Wait! Are you saying Enver was being serious last night? Are you telling me I should actually follow his treasure map?"

"Listen to me very carefully now brother," Gwen said in a somber voice.

Waldo gave a nod and paid her his full attention. When Gwen asked for him to take note it was always something important.

Gwen spoke in a rhythmic voice.

"Moon rises and sun sets, day turns to night and summer to winter. Five winters shall pass before you shall return. Long will your journey be and difficult your challenges. Three shall follow you; claws, horns, and fangs devoted to your service. They will journey with you to the forgotten keep, where you shall find your treasure. Your return shall be glorious, but turn to ash in a moon's turn. When brother, sister, and mother are gone you shall stand above all others. What is broken you will make whole."

When his sister finished Waldo just stood there staring back at her. Obviously this was another one of her prophesies, but he really wasn't sure what to make of it. A lot of it made no sense to him. Her words did seem to suggest that he would return in five years' time. He also took special note of, 'three shall follow you.'

"Are you telling me I should follow Enver's advice then? You're saying he was actually serious last night?"

Gwendolyn tilted her head to the side and blood spurted from her wound. "I have given you my help. You may accept it or not as you wish."

Waldo stiffened.

"If you want me to follow Enver's map why don't you just say so?" Waldo asked. "Why does all your advice have to come in riddles? Why can't you just tell me what is going to happen?"

"I am dead little brother. You have to grant me a bit of fun."

"I'm glad I amuse you."

"You always have," Gwen responded with a rasping laugh.

Waldo shook his head. "Thank you for helping me sister. You have always been very kind to me."

"If you are going to insult me I am leaving." Gwen scolded.

As her form began to dissolve she looked at her brother with real affection. "I will not say goodbye to you little brother. We will meet again. Whatever happens, no matter how hard, do not give into despair. Remember that you are destined to return home again. In glory and in blood."

His sister was gone and the mirror once more was empty.

"Thank you sister."

Waldo hurried back to his room to recover the treasure map he had thrown away.

XXX

Enver's map was taken out of the trash, neatly folded, and slipped into a pocket. Waldo would study it later. His plans from last night were now tossed aside, but all that really meant was that he would take the north road out of Alter rather than the south.

Hurrying along a hallway Waldo came to a halt and glanced towards a partially opened door to his right.

"Really? Do you still want to play this stupid game, even today?"

The door flung open and Walter rushed out.

"*Repulso!*" Waldo waved a hand.

Walter had not made it more than two steps before magical forces slammed him into the wall and pinned him there.

"Damn you! Why can't I kill you?"

Because I can always sense you.

He'd always had the ability to sense the undead. It was a rare talent that sometimes ran in his family. Waldo had told his mother but no one else about it.

"I've told you before," Waldo said. "No matter how well you hide there's no way to disguise that stink."

"It's your fault, all of this is your fault! When you're dead I'll be heir again, and I'll have everything that should be mine!"

Waldo wanted to laugh at the sheer stupidity of it. "Yes, I've heard that before."

"You stole my place!"

Waldo was sick of being the target of his brother's hate. Sick of the idiocy and the mindlessness. Since this was the last time he would be seeing Walter until his (hoped for) return he decided to go ahead and say a few things.

"The reason I took your place is because you're dead. The dead cannot rule the living. You know that!"

"If you were gone she would have to make me heir! There is no one else!"

"Wrong! There are the other branches of the family. Mother would choose one of them."

"No she wouldn't!" Walter denied. "She would choose me! I'm her son! She would never pick some cousin or uncle or nephew she hardly knows!"

Waldo shook his head. "Whoever leads the family must be able to make contracts, perform the greater magics, and provide an heir. A zombie can't do any of those things. Even if mother did choose you, the council would never allow the choice to stand. Your chance to be heir ended the day grandfather killed you! I never had anything to do with it! Mother only put me on her right because she had to. I didn't do anything to replace you, and even if you killed me it wouldn't change anything."

"Liar!" Walter hissed and thrashed about trying to somehow free himself. "You were always just like the rest! Always plotting to destroy me and take what should be mine! I know it was you! I know it! I know it! I know it!"

Watching the pointless display of fury only made Waldo shake his head.

"You're pathetic," Waldo left with him there. "Goodbye brother."

Walter screamed after him but Waldo didn't bother to listen.

XXX

As was tradition Waldo had a big breakfast before setting out. His mother said very little and did not ask him what his plans were. Waldo could remember her acting the same whenever the others went out.

The kitchen slaves brought him two full waterskins and a pack filled with jerky, nuts, dried bread, and other travel food. The slaves spoke well wishes and hoped for his safe return while keeping their eyes lowered.

When the meal was finally finished he put on his backpack and waterskins and proceeded out of the castle proper, through the courtyard, and towards the main gate. His back was bending forward just a bit under the weight. Having to travel so many miles on foot toting everything on his back was going to be wearying.

The morning sky was a barely visible ash grey. His mother was the only one to accompany him. When his brothers and sisters were still alive they would come and see whoever was leaving. Since Gwen and Walter could not join them it was just mother. He wondered what it was like for her to be sending the last of her children off on a First Quest. It had to be hard, especially given the circumstances.

Whatever she was feeling his mother gave no sign; her face was rigidly set and her demeanor utterly calm. She was certainly not behaving like this might be the last time she ever saw him.

"I will definitely come back," Waldo said as they came to the open gate.

The wooden drawbridge was down over the dry moat with its rusting iron spikes. Beyond was a rutted dirt road that led down to the city of Alter. From there he would follow the north road and begin his journey.

Now that the moment had really come Waldo felt scared. He looked back at the dreary castle and the undead shuffling along the battlements. He looked out at the volcanoes in the distance spewing ash into the sky and bleeding lava into the rivers of fire. The morning breeze was heavy with the stench of sulfur. How he would miss this place!

His mother looked at him and there was a miniature smile beneath solemn eyes. "I am sure you will," she agreed.

Reaching into her cloak she produced a leather sack that jingled in her hands.

"Take this; it is a hundred gold coins. I made sure they are all foreign mint, you will only find ducats and denari; no gold skulls. It's all I can do for you."

"Isn't this against the rules for a First Quest?"

"Oh it's completely against the rules, but then so is setting impossible conditions. Now go ahead and take it."

"The whole point of the First Quest is to prove yourself as a Dark Mage. You're not supposed to take anything with you beyond the necessities."

"That's how it normally goes," Lilith agreed. "But if the council is going to bend the rules I am too."

"Did you ever give any of the others money when they went out?"

"No," Lilith admitted. "But they all went on normal quests."

Waldo looked closely at the purse his mother was holding. Not having to worry about acquiring gold would make things easier.

He shook his head. "I can't take this."

"Why not?"

"Because it's against the rules and I want to face this the way I am supposed to, the way the others did."

"The others went on normal First Quests," Lilith reminded him. "For them it was a fair test of their abilities and their courage, so I didn't give them any extra help. Your situation is completely different."

Waldo again shook his head. "I want to do this the right way so that when I return you can know I succeeded on my own and be proud of me."

His mother blinked. "You really mean that? You honestly don't want this gold?"

"I mean it."

His mother stood there a moment, still holding the leather sack. "You are very brave my son."

"Thank you mother."

"You are an idiot, but a brave idiot."

She grabbed him by a shoulder and roughly turned him around. He could feel her tugging and opening up his back pack.

"Mother what are you doing?"

"What else? I'm putting the gold in your pack."

"But I said I didn't want it!"

"I heard you, why do you think I called you an idiot?"

He opened his mouth to try and argue but his mother cut him off.

"What did I always teach you about following rules?"

Waldo sighed. "That rules only matter when you know you'll get caught."

"Exactly, results are all that count my son. Just succeed and come home, that is all I care about. We are Corpselovers; we are bound by no laws."

That was the family motto. "Not even the ones made by the council?"

Finished Lilith tied shut his backpack. "We have to follow their dictates of course, at least as far as they can see. You don't ever need to worry about what I think of you. I am only sorry I cannot do more."

"It's okay mother. It makes me happy just to know you would defy the council for me."

"Well of course I would," his mother said and placed an affectionate hand on his cheek. "After all you are my son, and more important to me than anything else."

Waldo blushed and a simple happiness filled his heart and pushed away all the fear that had been there just moments before. His mother had never really shown him a lot of warmth growing up. "Thank you mother."

She gave a single nod and withdrew her hand. "I will pray the Dark Powers to watch over you and see you safely home. I will offer a hundred sacrifices."

"Ah, I would be grateful for the prayers, but please don't make any sacrifices for my sake. I have never liked having people die because of me, even if they are only slaves."

Lilith gave an amused shake of her head. "You have always been a bit strange my son, but if that is your wish I will honor it."

"Thank you. Goodbye mother. I will see you again."

"Goodbye my son. I will wait for your return no matter how long it may be."

Taking a deep breath Waldo took a step out onto the drawbridge and began his journey.

Chapter 3

Melissa

Peabody was a small village in northern Lothas. It was located near the marshlands that were infested by goblins. Thousands of the vile creatures festered there, living in their filth and squalor. They kept mostly to themselves, but small packs would often go out to do a little hunting.

It was said that human flesh was a goblin's favorite food.

There were forts and strongholds all along the frontier, manned by local militia and the King's troops. They did what they could. The soldiers patrolled constantly and killed or captured any goblins they came across. The men couldn't actually go into the bogs, those who did never came out again.

Every few years the goblins would come out in force and go on a rampage. Whole families would be slaughtered and eaten, villages and forts would be burned to the ground. When that happened the king would raise the levies and lead the army into battle. The goblins would always be crushed and sent fleeing back into the marshes. The army would follow after, in hopes of being rid of them once and for all.

It never happened, in their bogs they knew how to disappear when they wanted to. The army would burn down the thatch huts they found and kill a few stragglers, but most of the goblins would simply vanish and be impossible to find. After a couple of weeks the men would start to complain and want to go home. The army would disband and the cycle would continue again.

"They lack commitment," she said to herself. "You can never accomplish anything lasting without commitment."

This world belonged to man. Monsters, all monsters, were an abomination, a disease that needed curing. And the only real cure was to purge them from this earth, with fire and steel. It was a plain and obvious truth, and if you asked most people they would agree with you. Yes, get rid of all the monsters and the world would be a much better place. If words alone were enough the world would have been purified long ago.

The problem was that most were unwilling to pay the price.

Creating a new age of peace and justice would not come easily. Ridding the world of monsters demanded tremendous sacrifice, of both blood and treasure. Most of the nations were unwilling. They fought when they had to, when the danger was obvious, but then sought accommodation rather than continue fighting to achieve a lasting victory. There were monsters all across the Shattered Lands, in almost every country. Most rulers chose to compromise with them and tolerate their existence within limits. Much as they would accept a certain amount of corruption and crime.

"Compromise." She spat as if to get the taste of that foul word out of her mouth. *There can be no negotiation or agreement with evil. What is just is just, what is wicked is wicked, there can be no compromise.*

"Those who do not understand that must be taught the error of their ways."

XXX

Like every village near the marshes, Peabody was surrounded by a wooden stockade. There was a single watch tower that was manned day and night. The people here and in the other villages lived in fear because their king was not strong enough to do what was truly necessary.

As she approached the people inside the village proper all quickly noticed. It was not surprising, people in white robes were a rare sight, especially in a place like this. A small crowd of twenty to thirty gathered near the gate, openly gawking at her.

She was used to this reaction and did not hold it against them. A White Mage always drew stares and made people nervous.

Her hood was down so that they could get a clear look at her face. She was attractive and exotic for this part of the world, with the blonde hair and yellow eyes.

She came to a halt before the villagers and offered them a slight bow. "Hello, I am Mistress Melissa Cornwall, an archmage of the Order of Mist."

The locals looked nervously at one another and turned their focus to a burly man with a salt and pepper beard.

The local chieftain, she thought.

Stroking his bead he took a hesitant step forward and gave her a much lower bow than she had offered. "Greetings to you Mistress Cornwall. Welcome to Peabody, my name is Lorimer, it has been a long time since a White Mage has visited us. To be honest I am not sure one ever has."

"Well, there are only so many of us outside of Avalon."

Still stroking his beard Lorimer looked around, as if asking for help. Everyone remained silent.

"Well then Mistress Cornwall, is there some special reason you have come to visit us?"

"I was told there was an attack by a very strong monster in this area. I have come here to rid you of it."

Her words produced an excited murmur.

Lorimer took on a stern air. He motioned for silence and everyone soon quieted. "You heard right, there was an awful attack two weeks ago at the Hampton place. The whole family, father, mother, and four children were all done in. We have all been very nervous about it."

There were unhappy nods and folk drawing circles over their hearts to ward off evil.

"I would be happy to deal with this monster for you."

"For how much?" Lorimer asked. "I do not mean to be rude Mistress, but we are a poor village and do not have much in the way of coin. We might be able to pay you with a fat sow or some chickens, but if you were hoping for silver or gold we have none."

Smiling she spread her hands. "I require no payment, I am more than happy to do this without charge."

That caused fresh whispers and had Lorimer once more stroking his beard. "When do mages ever do anything for free? We've had to hire one from time to time to make it rain or to help us drive off some wolves. We always get charged at least four healthy pigs or a cow in her prime."

"But you have never dealt with a White Mage before have you?"

"No, like I said, you are the first any of us have ever seen."

"The members of my order do not work for money. We serve a higher cause. I will destroy this monster for you because it is the right thing to do. All I ask for in return is that you remember."

She could see Lorimer had his doubts, but the villagers were clearly willing to accept her help. Eventually it was decided that they would agree and Lorimer would personally act as her guide to the Hampton place.

XXX

Before setting out the chieftain insisted on putting on a worn leather jerkin and got a spear with sharpened stone tip.

Melissa had tried to explain it was unnecessary, that she would keep the both of them from harm.

"When Lord Durmoor heard about the attack he sent a squad of guards to go look for what did it. Ten strong and healthy men, all with iron or bows. It ambushed them, a huge beast they said, skin green as moss and big as a bear. Their arrows wouldn't pierce it, their swords and axes wouldn't cut it. It tore them limb from limb, the way a man can tear apart a rabbit." He shuddered.

"I see."

He gaped at her. "How can you be calm? I am a man and I will tell you I am afraid."

"There is no reason to fear, I have fought many monsters. I am sure I can deal with this one when we find it."

He began to stroke his beard. "You really expect no payment for this?"

Melissa shook her head.

"Then why? Why are you doing this for people you don't even know?"

"Because it is the right thing to do and will make this world a little better place." Her demeanor was calm and at ease. "I know the sorts of stories they tell about my order, and why people fear us. But I assure you, innocent folk like you have nothing to be afraid of. We exist to protect and serve people like you."

He hesitated. "Lord Durmoor doesn't think that."

"Those in power usually fear change, no matter how beneficial or necessary that change may be."

"Why do things need to change? They're all right."

"Tell that to the Hamptons or to the soldiers who didn't return."

"Well I'm not saying the world's perfect or anything, but what can you do about it?"

"Unite the Shattered Lands to bring Unity. Grant all people everywhere the protection of the law to bring Justice. Kill every last monster and servant of evil to bring Peace. That is what you can do, that is what my order believes in."

"That's a bit much don't you think? No one could ever do all that."

"No one person could, but I am only one member of the Order, and every one of us is dedicated to working towards this ideal. It is what I believe in, and what I gladly give my life for; Unity, Justice, Peace."

"Forgive me for saying this Mistress, but it will never happen. The world's too big a place, no matter how many of you there are. Things have always been the way they are."

"It will not happen in my lifetime, but even if it takes a thousand years it will happen."

Lorimer stared, obviously not comprehending. "Why would you spend your life working for something you know you will never get to see?"

"Because I know that all my sacrifices will not be in vain. That is enough for me."

XXX

It was early summer, and the lands they passed through were all green and vibrant. The fields held wheat, rye, and other crops.

On gently rolling hills cows and other animals grazed. Melissa noticed that everyone she saw was armed. The people clearly noticed her as she and Lorimer passed them. Most of them stopped working just to stand there and gape.

A few drew circles over their hearts.

They don't understand, she thought sadly. Why did so many fear the Order? She understood their reputation was not pristine. The Order was not above committing violence when it was for the greater good. Many of the rulers in the Shattered Lands were corrupt and had to be dealt with harshly. Kings and noblemen who stood in the way of progress had good reason to be afraid.

Our ends are truly honorable and worthy, they justify even the bloodiest means.

The common people had nothing to fear. It was for their sake that the Order had been founded. They wanted to protect the ordinary folk and help them lead good, decent lives.

The people didn't understand that because their rulers deliberately lied to them. They spread false rumors and tried to paint every action in the worst possible light. Wherever White Mages went those in power always tried to interfere with their good work. That was true here in Lothas as well. Melissa was here to recruit someone and then travel to the local court. She would try to bring some of the officials there over to the right side.

XXX

"We're here." Lorimer told her. He was clutching his spear against his chest.

They had gone about four or five miles from the village and were at a small farm like all the ones they had passed. The home was set back from the road behind a field of wheat.

71

"I am sure the monster is long since gone," Lorimer muttered.

"You have done enough, you can wait here while I take a look."

"A man can't leave a woman unprotected."

Backwards notions, but these people haven't been taught better yet. "As you like."

She entered the wheat field with him close by her heel.

What she found was a simple cottage with a thatch roof. The door had been smashed to kindling. A sudden breeze brought the smell of rotting meat.

Lorimer rubbed at his nose and shifted from one foot to another.

Melissa calmly drew her hands together and cast a spell. *"Taranos evel monstri desu noratal est aki est avaratos."*

To her eyes a reddish glow began to emanate from inside the cottage.

Reaching into one of the many pockets of her robe she took out her wand. "It's here."

"What?" He tightened his grip on his spear and spread his feet to get a solid stance. "Are you sure?"

"Yes."

It only took a moment before a massive creature with skin the color of moss and two yellow tusks jutting out of its jaw crouched through the doorway. When it stood to its full height it could have reached up and tapped the top of the roof. Its entire body was muscle and it was looking them over hungrily.

"Fresh meat for Toola! Toola happy!" It began to stride towards them.

"So it was an ogre." Melissa calmly pointed her wand. *"Evaros ventus est corti."*

Lorimer gasped as he saw the air above Melissa's head warp and solidify. He could make out four separate semi-circles hanging above her, each about four feet across.

"Now pay for your crimes you disgusting abomination!" She flicked her wand.

The four wind blades flew, covering the distance between them in the flicker of an eye.

The hide that could defeat arrows and sharpened iron was no match at all for an archmage's spell. They cut clean through, slicing not just the skin but the flesh and bone beneath. One blade took off the monsters head along with most of his right shoulder. A second cut through his chest about two thirds of the way up. Another chopped the legs off just above the knees. The last one severed the left arm from the rest.

It was so quick and clean there was not even any time for cries of pain. Lorimer actually saw a look of surprise on the monster's face as his head was in the air. Blood gushed from the neck and the other cuts. Then all the pieces just fell to the ground in one massive bloody heap. It was just that quick. One moment he was getting ready to die, the next the beast was nothing but bloody chunks.

He bent over and threw up.

As he emptied his stomach he felt Melissa's hand gently patting his back.

"Are you all right? I know it can be a bit much if you're not used to it."

He straightened, feeling ashamed. "I am sorry."

"Nothing to be sorry about. As I said, it can be hard to take the first time."

"How many times have you done this?"

"Killed a monster? More times than I can count. It's one of the things I am best at."

He shook his head.

"Well now that my work here is done please go back to your village and tell everyone that they are safe."

"Aren't you coming with me? Let us throw you a feast in your honor. That is the least we can do."

She shook her head. "No. I didn't come here for feasts any more than I did for coin. I have to go and meet someone I hope to recruit into the Order. Please go back and tell them what you saw, and ask them to remember that it was a White Mage who came and helped when they were in need."

"I will," he promised. "Is that really all you want?"

"Yes, it is enough for me." She gave him a polite nod of her head. "Goodbye Lorimer, I wish you and your people the blessings of Unity, Justice, and Peace."

With that she started towards the road and her next task.

Chapter 4

Blue Skies And Sunshine

The city of Alter was the heart of Alteroth.

Located near the volcanoes of the Forge and the Rivers of Fire, the Seven Great Families had founded the city and built their castles here. Originally they had come to establish a sanctuary and escape the persecution and mistreatment of their native lands. They soon discovered that the lands near the Forge were a treasure trove. Gold, silver, iron, and precious gems could all be found in abundance. With slaves and undead to work vast mines the wealth poured in. The riches of the Forge allowed them to build their ideal city and to begin raising armies to conquer neighboring lands.

The skies above Alter were always overcast with ash, and at night the only light would come from the Forge and from the Rivers of Fire. Nothing grew here, not a tree, not a shrub, not a blade of grass. There was always a trace of sulfur in the air, and when it rained the rain was black and filthy. Undead soldiers marched along the wide and perfectly straight streets. The people who lived here obeyed every law without question. The members of the Seven Families were the only ones truly free, anyone who wore the black robes could walk the earth like a god. They had the power of life and death and answered only to the Council and the families.

Waldo had spent all his life in Alter, residing inside Castle Corpselover. Everyone agreed that Alter was the most wonderful place in all the world.

He never doubted it. His travels would only prove just how wonderful and special his home city truly was.

XXX

The very first thing that bothered him was when the sky disappeared.

As he walked along the north road he noticed the daytime sky overhead growing less and less dark. It slowly changed from charcoal to slate grey to ash grey until the sky was the unnatural color of cotton.

On his third day he saw tears in it. Rather than the constant cover that was normal, the sky began to break apart and he saw horrible patches of blue! His immediate inclination had been to turn back and run home. What else would a sane man do when the very sky seemed to be dissolving?

By the fourth day the sky had disintegrated completely; there was nothing but the unnatural blue, with only occasional bits of white. Staring straight up into that vile and terrifying emptiness he expected to have something come crashing down on him at any moment. Without a comforting ceiling above his head he felt completely vulnerable and exposed.

As bad as the lack of cover was, the 'sun' was a hundred times worse.

Waldo had been taught science along with math, history, and other subjects. He was not an ignorant savage, and knew that the Sun circled the Earth. It was, after all, what made the daytime bright enough to see back home. He'd never once seen it of course, but he knew it existed as he knew about the oceans or about dragons. It was the great ball of fire that circled the world and provided heat and light. It sounded curious, but not as interesting as say dragons or snow or the oceans.

The first time he'd seen it he'd stared at it until he was forced to look away. He could feel the heat of the thing. It made walking along with his heavy pack that much more tiring and made him sweat. Waldo also noticed that his black robes seemed much hotter; as though they were slowly being burned up. (It never once occurred to him to remove his robes. They were a symbol of his status and he would sooner travel the whole way on hands and knees as go without them.)

While he knew from his studies that the sun would not fall from the sky, he couldn't help but have that impression. He also wondered if he would suddenly burst into flame or melt from the heat. Those first few days were a misery. He was often under a clear blue sky with a bright sun overhead.

It was just horrible.

The world around him was much too bright and filled with abnormal colors. The land itself began to come to life the further he got from his home. First there were patches of straggly yellow grass poking out of the greyish brown soil. Occasionally there were a few shrubs and other vegetation within sight of the road. Once you left the Forge, Alteroth became a land of rolling hills and wide fields. Mile by mile the grass began to thicken and turn from brown or yellow to green. (He had used grasses and other plants in various potions. He was just not used to so much of the stuff.) It grew on either side of the road as tall as his chest. When the wind blew he could see the grass bend and ripple.

While the sight of all this vegetation did not bother him the way the blue sky and ball of fire did, he learned there were terrors hidden in those fields of green.

One day, as he was just walking along, a horrible creature suddenly came hopping out of the grass right into the middle of the road in front of him. The small monstrosity stopped there, as if in challenge. It had wide eyes, a constantly twitching nose, and long deformed ears. It was the most disgusting thing he'd ever laid eyes on.

Waldo stopped and pulled out his wand. He stood his ground and did his best not to show fear. Waldo glanced towards the tall grass on either side and wondered if a horde of these vile things might be hidden, waiting to pounce on and devour him. He did not attack out of fear of angering the creature and possible others.

At last, after what seemed like an eternity, the foul thing hopped away into the grass and vanished. Waldo took off running and hoped he would not encounter any more such revolting animals.

There were odd sounds. Chirps and squawks and hoots and caws. The air itself was off, as it lacked the familiar scent of sulfur. Instead there were strange and exotic fragrances that made his eyes water.

Even the night, which should have been comforting, was alien.

There were tears in the darkness; the countless 'stars' which were the souls of distant and uncaring gods. His mother had mentioned a few times how beautiful the clear night sky was. Waldo found no beauty in the pinpricks of light. To him they ruined the comforting blackness. Along with the stars was a crescent moon shining down with a coppery sheen. After enduring the ball of fire it wasn't so bad. He tried to sleep out in the open as best he could, but didn't get much rest.

He heard the various sounds coming from the tall grass and imagined a horde of those monstrous long eared creatures just waiting for him to fall asleep.

The next day he came across a company of undead skeletons marching lifelessly. Such patrols were common all along the borders and roads of Alteroth. Empty eye sockets turned to him, and skulls dipped in a sign of respect. They recognized him as a Dark Mage. Waldo was sorely tempted to take two or three of them with him. They were instructed to obey the orders of any Dark Mage they came across. The idea of a few undead corpses standing over him in the dark would have let him sleep much more peacefully.

He didn't, that would be against the rules for a First Quest, but he wanted to. Waldo walked along with them for as long as he could, before tiring and watching them shuffle too far ahead and out of sight.

Mercifully, he began coming to the small villages that were scatters along the way. The heads of the Seven Great Families resided in Alter, where political and financial power was concentrated. Few of them bothered to spend much time in the countryside, where most of the population lived and where most of the food was grown. The landscape changed from wild grass to neat fields of wheat and barley and other crops. Across open hillsides he could spot flocks of what he assumed were sheep peacefully grazing. Most of the villages were no more than a dozen or a few dozen simple thatch huts clustered about a central Inn or Hall.

In some of the larger villages and towns, there would be a mansion or master house, where one of the branch families would reside and act as local overseers. Waldo would have been able to call on them for hospitality, but the places he stopped at were too small.

The villagers always looked at him with honest fear, and fell over themselves to bow and show respect.

"I am a Corpselover." He would say proudly and people would break into a fresh bows and proclaim how honored they were to have him staying in their village for the night. Waldo would take a meal at the Inn, spend the night in a decent bed and leave after a hearty breakfast with fresh bread, smoked mutton, and full water skins. All the while the people near him looked terrified.

It made him feel right at home.

In Alteroth only the seven families were allowed to own land. Everything belonged to them; and that included the people who lived in the countryside. The first village he stayed at happened to belong to the Poisondagger family. If Waldo had felt like murdering the villagers or taking them as slaves the cost to him would have been one silver rib per person. (Gold coins minted in

79

Alteroth were skulls, silver coins were ribs, and copper coins were knuckles. The different nations gave their currencies various names, but all coins were minted to the same standards.)

That was how much a peasant's life was worth.

The standard rate of exchange was twenty silver coins to one gold one. So Waldo could afford to kill or simply take two thousand people.

The people of the countryside were not considered slaves, they were serfs. They were bound to the land and required to work it. They were not allowed to leave their villages without permission. They were not allowed to own the land. When they died they were usually not even permitted burial or cremation. They were not given ANY rights under the law.

Still, they were much better off than the slaves who lived in the cities. For one thing, many were not under the eye of the families. Every city had at least one branch family living in it, most had several. The serfs tended to live longer lives. They also enjoyed much more real freedom. Each fall they were expected to hand over half their crops and a certain percentage of their livestock. They were allowed to keep the remaining half to sustain themselves and to plant for the following spring. They could choose which crops to plant and how best to take care of their flocks and herds. They could marry whoever they wanted (within their village) and raise their families as they saw fit. So long as they produced the food Alteroth needed they were usually left alone.

Of course, if a branch family resided in the village, or if a member of one of the families was passing through as Waldo was, they were completely subject to any whim. Refusing, or in any way harming a Dark Mage, would mean death for all of them. He could sleep with any girl who caught his eye or take anything he wanted. Waldo noted that whenever he stayed at one of the villages there was never a pretty young girl to be seen. The only women were too old or unattractive to be of interest.

Waldo saw nothing wrong in any of this or in the dread he inspired. He was used to looks of fear from those who served him. Even the slaves he'd been kind to had always looked at him in that way. To Waldo it was natural, nothing more or less than a sign of proper respect.

XXX

For three weeks he went north this way. Sleeping in a village Inn or Hall when he could, camping out under the stars when he had to. During the long hours of the day, he would study the map until all three stops were burned into his memory. There were just three 'X's' in three cities. He had only Enver's promise that there were Great Monsters waiting for him. What sort of monsters or under what circumstances they lived he had no clue.

If they were real he would track them down. Waldo had a detection spell that would help with that. Along with memorizing the map he was using these hours to study his spellbook. His sister's words had convinced him to go this way, but he was not certain what he would find. From what he'd heard and read, Lothas wasn't a pleasant place for Dark Mages. It only made sense to be as well prepared as possible.

As he traveled he imagined giants roaming about and vampires prowling hidden lairs. The closer he got to Lothas the more he tried to work out various scenarios for capturing these Great Monsters. Along with spells he was also going over the binding ritual that would make them his servants.

The very first town marked on his map was a place called Stratford that was right on the border. If he really could capture a Great Monster right at the start things would be easier. That monster would help him capture the second and then he would have two of them capture the third. Then he would have three powerful creatures bound to him, he would quickly defeat the first knight he ran into and would have passed two of the conditions set for him.

81

Simple. What could possibly go wrong?

XXX

At long last he reached the river Mainz that separated Alteroth from Lothas. It was fast flowing and about seventy yards wide. A single wooden bridge spanned it. As he approached it there was a merchant train of six wagons led by oxen crossing over to Alteroth. The Lothasians hated his people, but not enough to decline their gold and silver. The merchants and the wagon drivers bowed their heads as they passed him, but did not slow down or call out greetings.

When Waldo stepped onto that bridge he finally left Alteroth.

On the other bank was Stratford, a good size city of perhaps ten thousand. Unlike the villages he'd visited where everyone lived in simple thatch huts the buildings across the river were of wood and brick and every one was brightly painted. Most of the walls were whitewashed and the slanted roofs were made of red and brown tiles. Some of the houses were deliberately painted bright colors to attract the eye; yellows, blues, reds.

The effect was jarring, he didn't see the point. Alter, which was his model for beauty, was a city built of black volcanic rock. From the castles down to the paving stones everything matched. The streets were all the same width and all ran perfectly straight. Every city block covered the same area and every building had the same rigid architecture. There were no twisting roads or confusing cul de sacs or dead ends. There were no vacant lots or buildings that stood out from their neighbors. Alter was a monument to order and to uniformity.

Even from a distance Stratford's buildings looked to have a bewildering assortment of sizes and styles as well as colors. It was as if people had deliberately decided not to make any two look exactly the same. Many of the houses were somewhat similar but one was slightly taller or wider or had a slightly

82

different framing or had a steeper roof. Some of the houses were pressed right up against each other, others had yards between them and in still other places was nothing but empty ground that stood out like a gap in a row of teeth.

To Waldo it spoke of poor planning and chaos. It might be interesting to look at but how could such a place even manage? Life here had to be pure anarchy.

On the other end of the bridge was a guard house where a dozen soldiers wearing chain mail and carrying an assortment of swords and axes. Casually they stood around and watched him as he approached. Waldo was surprised at their lack of discipline and the way these common soldiers were looking straight into his face. Hadn't anyone ever taught them how to show respect to a superior?

As he came to the end of the bridge and set foot on the damp ground the oldest of the guards came shuffling up to him. He did not bow or bend his neck, but stood there and spoke as if the two of them were equals.

"Welcome to Lothas stranger, all visitors are welcome here and free to do business. Just remember to follow our laws. We don't put up with folk breaking them, especially foreigners."

"Do you know who I am?" Waldo asked feeling offended. He could not believe a commoner would talk to him this way. Even public slaves had better manners!

The soldier looked him up and down. "I'm guessing you're a black wizard, we've seen your kind before." By his tone he might have been referring to cow droppings. "Don't cause trouble or you'll regret it. Now move along."

Waldo stood there for a moment in simple disbelief. Some ordinary soldier was giving him orders? There were so many things wrong with that he could not even count them all. He was tempted to explain to this man exactly who he was and the sort of respect he was due.

The hostility of the other guards made Waldo change his mind. He was going to have to fight men like these, but he needed it to be on his own terms. Once he had a Great Monster bound to him he would be able to deal with rude idiots. First things first.

He headed down the dirt road and into the city as the guards watched him go.

XXX

If the guards had been suspicious and rude the people were openly hostile. They stared and gawked at him and hurried to get clear of his path. A couple old women spat in his direction and made hand signs that he recognized as rudimentary curses.

In an odd way he preferred this sort of treatment to how the guards had acted. The guards' behavior had smelled of contempt, while these folk were obviously afraid of him. Mother had always said that fear was the best sort of respect. They were however sadly lacking in good manners. None of them bowed or bent their necks. Even the ones who spat and cursed him looked him brazenly in the eye.

"What an uncivilized folk," he muttered.

Well he hadn't come here for their company. Motioning his hands in a specific pattern he spoke one of the spells he'd memorized. The people stared as he did so and several fled. *"Taranos evel monstri desu noratal est aki est avaratos."*

When the detection spell was completed he was surprised to see four distinct targets appear. To his eyes there were now four sources of reddish light glowing. None of them were right at hand; two were to the north, one to the west, and one to the east. So there were four monsters living here. Most importantly the

84

one to the east was giving off light akin to a bonfire whereas the other three were lamps.

"Enver was actually telling the truth." Waldo said. Up until this moment he had more than half expecting to find nothing, but it looked like his efforts were going to be rewarded. He turned in the direction of that beacon and began to head towards it.

Behind him people were whispering to one another. Some ran off while a few followed behind Waldo.

Chapter 5

I Have Come To Make You Mine

In the middle of the river Mainz was a small outcropping of bare rock about sixty yards long and twenty yards across at its widest. On it was a single building. An old foot bridge connected it to the rest of Stratford. The building was two stories high with a slanted roof and a dozen shuttered windows packed together up on the second floor. It was trimmed all in fiery red and had a wooden sign that depicted a snow white dove with black smudges on its wings.

This was the Inn of Lost Sighs. It was a place where a man could enjoy a good meal or a drink or a woman's warmth. The women who worked here and occupied the rooms up on the second floor were politely referred to as 'Soiled Doves.'

The less polite called them whores.

It was not the only place of its sort in Stratford, but it was certainly the best known and most popular.

The first floor was the common room. It had tables with wooden chairs as well as a bar that ran the length of the far wall. The kitchen entrance was located behind the bar. Here the customers would eat and drink and relax, and the women would sit and talk to them and try to separate them from their purses.

On the side opposite from the bar was a set of stairs that led up to the second floor. Twelve doors led to twelve rooms; there was an open walkway with a railing so that everyone downstairs had a clear view of the upstairs. Men could peek up and see girls draped along the railing smiling and inviting them up. When a man went upstairs it was always to cheers and jealous shouts.

Nancy Sanders was not surprised to see the place empty when she came downstairs. The only other person was the owner, Elsa, who was standing behind the bar. It was noon and they had just opened. This was their slow time. Things would start to pick up around sunset and they would be busy until the early morning. All the other girls were still in their rooms sleeping. They would get up some time in the afternoon and wander downstairs or simply stand by the railing on display. Elsa didn't care, so long as everyone was working by the time things started to get busy.

Nancy, seventeen and the youngest of the soiled doves, managed with less sleep and was more than happy to get first dibs on any early visitors. She was five foot tall with auburn hair and freckles, she had a small bust and short legs. The customers found her cute and friendly and she did well enough at her work. Nancy knew how to please and how to get a man's attention. She'd put on a long skirt that was slit down one side to show off her smooth legs. She had a lacey top that revealed her belly as well as her shoulders. Outside the Inn women didn't reveal more than their ankles. A lot of men got excited just at seeing so much of a woman's body. She had also colored her face with blush and painted her lips. Outside the Inn that too was frowned upon.

Nancy strolled across the vacant common room. The wooden floor had been swept and mopped. All the chairs were in place and all the tables as well as the bar had been wiped clean. No matter how neat the place was there was always the same odor hanging over everything; a stale mix of ale and sweat and cheap perfume.

"I see Alice has cleaned up," Nancy said as she leaned over against the bar. "Where is she right now?"

"In the kitchen helping," Elsa said.

The rotund woman was the owner of the Inn of Lost Sighs. She was a thick, plump woman with more grey in her hair than blonde. Her arms were ham hocks and her breasts shapeless masses of fat. Looking at her now it was hard to imagine she had once been a beauty, but she'd made enough money on her back to buy the Inn and had made a healthy profit with it. Every meal and mug of ale that was served was a coin that went straight in her pocket. The girls were allowed to bargain for their services and charge whatever they pleased, but every time a man went upstairs the accompanying girl owed Elsa thirty copper traks. On top of that, the girls had to pay a monthly rent for their rooms. Elsa loved to tell people she had never lost money on any deal.

"So the slave is in the kitchen is she?" Nancy asked with an impish grin. "Any chance she can stay back there?"

"We don't keep slaves." Elsa said. "She's an indentured servant."

"What's the difference?"

"They're less expensive but more trouble."

Nancy chuckled at just how seriously Elsa had answered. "I really wish she could stay back there."

Elsa shook her head slightly making her double chins wobble. "Better for you, but not for me."

"I don't see what's so special about her."

"In that case you're the only one."

"She's just the barmaid. Why does she get so much attention?"

"You know the answer to that." Elsa sounded bored. "Just be grateful she's too stupid to put that body of hers to proper use. There's food ready, do you want to eat now while we're empty?" Elsa charged her girls full price for their meals too.

Nancy was considering it when the front door opened and their first customer of the day arrived. He was dressed in work clothes and a pair of worn leather boots. He was clearly not a big spenders. The Inn of Lost Sighs got its share of commoners who could afford a girl's services perhaps once a month. They would mostly come by just to look and drink.

Recognizing the man, Nancy straightened up and offered him an inviting smile. His name was Harold Brauer, a cooper who owned his own shop and employed a few workers. He wasn't rich by any means, but could afford to share some of his silver with a pretty girl now and again.

This was the reason Nancy liked to get up early.

Harold closed the door behind him and walked up to the bar. His eager eyes went right past her. "Is Alice here?"

The simple question soured Nancy's mood. *Every damn time! It never changes!*

"Alice!" Elsa shouted. "We have a customer! Come out and serve him!"

"Coming!" A voice answered from the back.

Harold jutted out his chest, sucked in his gut, and did what he could to wipe off the sawdust from his work clothes. It made Nancy want to scream.

She slid over to him and fanned her fingers over his chest. She leaned in and asked huskily, "Don't you know Alice won't do anything for you? Why not spend your time with me instead? You won't regret it. I promise."

Harold pulled away from her, and took a couple steps along the bar, as if afraid of being caught. "No, it's all right; I just want to see Alice."

"Of course you do," Elsa said with a knowing smirk. "Who can blame you?"

The kitchen door swung open and out stepped the twenty year old Alice. She was dressed as a barmaid, with a proper skirt with a hem down to her feet, and a plain cotton blouse that seemed to strain just to contain her large and magnificently firm bosom. Her clothes did not expose any skin, but fit tight and revealed a set of shapely curves. She had long straight hair the color of fire and eyes the color of amethyst. Her skin was alabaster, and her face almost angelic in its flawless beauty. She wore no makeup of any kind. Her hips swayed slowly and rhythmically with each step and her tread was utterly smooth and graceful. Alice was simply stunning, with a figure and face that put Nancy, and every other girl who worked here, to shame.

Nancy stood on the tips of her toes, arched her back, and flounced her hair, it was still not enough to distract Harold as his eyes gorged on the barmaid. If she suddenly burst into flame she doubted Harold would notice.

Alice smiled with perfect white teeth and spoke with a warm lilting voice. "What can I do for your darling?"

"Marry me," he said sounding only half joking.

Alice gave a low playful laugh and lightly patted his arm. (Nancy noted that he didn't try and get away from her touch.) "I'm sorry darling, but I'm not free to marry. I have an owner."

"Employer not owner," Elsa said. "She is indentured and can't marry or leave my employ without permission."

"What would I have to do to get her away from you?"

"Be richer than Sir Lancel Griffinheart."

Harold's eyes widened at the mention of that name. The Griffenhearts were related to the ruling family and among the richest and most powerful nobles in Lothas. Harold made a good living and earned about a hundred silver dalters a month; or the equivalent of five gold ducats. Sir Lancel could spend that in a single night and not even notice.

At the mention of Sir Lancel Alice gave an involuntary shudder.

"Haven't you heard?" Nancy said brightly. "Sir Lancel has visited us a few times and he has his eyes on our barmaid."

"You mean he wants to marry her?" Harold's voice was heavy with disappointment.

"Marry?" Nancy chuckled and shook her head.

Alice cleared the matter up. "Sir Lancel doesn't want me for a wife. He wants me to be his mistress, he has six or seven already. All he wants is to put me up in some nice house out of the way where he can visit me when he likes." She shut her eyes and another slight shudder passed through her.

"What's so wrong with that?" Nancy demanded. "You'll have a large house with servants and beautiful clothes and an allowance to spend how you please. And all you'll have to do is lie on your back or get on your knees maybe once or twice a month. That sounds like a pretty sweet life to me."

"I wouldn't be loved."

"Yes you would, in all sorts of ways."

"Lust isn't love," Alice said primly. "The things you do upstairs have nothing to do with real love. Devotion, caring, and selflessness... that's what real love is."

"What would a virgin like you know about real love?" Nancy demanded. "Have you really grown up here? How can you still have such silly notions? You don't know anything about what happens between men and women."

91

"I know enough. The Inn has always been my prison, and I know what men are like."

"I would call it your home and your place of employment." Elsa said with a grunt.

"When you are never allowed to leave it's a prison."

"If you want to leave so badly pay me what you're worth." Elsa said.

XXX

Alice lowered her head. She'd been working here since she was old enough to walk. She'd started with small errands and tasks. Then worked in the kitchen; stoking the fires, chopping, cutting, washing dishes, and learning to cook. She would sweep and mop and wipe down tables and clean out the privy. When someone vomited she would take care of that too, all without pay. An indentured servant got food and a place to sleep; nothing more.

When she had turned thirteen, puberty had struck hard and her body had started to fill out. The men had started to notice, and though she was still young Elsa tried to turn her into a Soiled Dove.

That had proved to be a horrible mistake.

Elsa had been forced to make her the barmaid instead. Men, such as Harold, came just to stare at her and try and talk her into taking their silver. She always refused, and despite Elsa's threats, never took a man upstairs or offered anything more than a smile or kind words.

She had started to finally earn money though. Customers would tip her in hopes of winning her affection. Elsa actually permitted her to keep those tips, as they helped motivate her to be as charming as possible. Alice had saved up quite a bit of money, but nowhere near enough to buy her freedom.

"If you would just open your legs up you'd earn enough gold in a few years." Elsa said.

Alice felt her stomach turn. Growing up here she'd known what kind of animals men could be. They were filled with lust and treated women as nothing but meat. There was nothing special in it at all, nothing beautiful. To Alice what happened behind the closed doors was vulgar and ugly.

When her body had filled out they had turned dirty eyes to her, followed by dirty hands. The thought of being used like that disgusted her. The first time Elsa had tried to force a customer on her Alice had fought back viciously. Though just a thirteen year old girl, she had left the man with a broken jaw.

Elsa had beaten her for that, and locked her in her room for three days without food. Elsa had threatened to whip her and let her starve. Alice had still refused to become a soiled dove.

What Alice wanted was to be loved. She wanted a man to cherish her and care for her without only wanting her body. Alice wanted to be someone's wife and to leave this place with her husband and always be with him. When she made love she wanted it to matter and not have the act reduced to simple commerce.

She dreamed of someone declaring his love for her without demanding she also provide him certain services.

Alice could still remember last spring when Robart Connors had come in holding a batch of wildflowers in his hands and walked right up to a startled Risa Sanders.

"I've come to make you mine!" He declared loudly and held out the flowers to her.

Risa had hesitated, but finally taken them from him and answered. "I would gladly be yours."

Rob had then taken her into his arms and kissed her. Just like that he and Risa had been married. In Lothas that was all that was required. A man made his declaration and offered a woman flowers. If she accepted them and they kissed they became husband and wife.

Oh but Elsa had been furious! Risa had been one of her most popular girls. Sadly for Elsa though Risa hadn't been indentured. She walked out with her new husband and never returned.

To leave this place behind with a husband who loved her, that was Alice's dream.

It was never going to be more than a fantasy of course. She'd had plenty of men talk about marrying her. Somehow they all seemed to have a problem with the concept of doing things in their proper order. All of them wanted to have the wedding night first and then marry. When she mentioned the problem of Elsa owning her (whether you called it slavery or being indentured it was the same thing) they all either ignored the problem or talked about running away together.

As if I could run away.

She'd tried it when she was fourteen. The city guards had gone after her with tracking dogs and wound up bringing her back tied in ropes. Elsa gave her nothing but water for a week; she would have whipped her too but did not wanted to ruin Alice's soft skin.

Elsa had given her a warning.

"If you ever do this again girl I'll tell everyone your secret. Do you know what will happen to you then?"

"No," the fourteen year old had answered.

"The same thing that happens to the goblins that run away." Elsa said grimly. "You'll burn."

Goblins and other monsters were property. They didn't bother pretending they were indentured. Monsters had no rights; they were treated just like cows or horses. If a monster ran away, or so much as disobeyed, an owner had the right to do whatever they pleased. In Lothas the usual punishment was to have the offending creature burned alive at the stake. The locals typically turned such executions into little festivals and would gather to watch and cheer as the creature burned.

Alice did not doubt that Elsa would do exactly as she promised. Alice was only treated as well as she was because everyone assumed she was human. Harold, and all the other men who hungered for her so shamelessly, would have been disgusted and horrified to know what she really was.

Elsa had bought her for five gold ducats from a knight who had found her as a baby after slaughtering her mother. The knight had likely spared her only because he'd expected to be able to sell her. Elsa had paid such a high price, and put up with dealing with a baby, expecting to make a handsome profit one day.

Elsa was the only one who knew the truth. She held the secret over Alice's head and it worked better than steel chain in keeping her bound to the Inn.

The only mollifying factor was knowing that the truth would ruin Alice's value, so Elsa could not use it to force the girl to let men stick it in her.

It would also kill the chances of Sir Lancel buying her.

Sir Lancel Griffinheart had visited them for the first time three months ago. He had spotted her and immediately chosen her for a trip upstairs. When she'd explained to him she was only the barmaid and didn't do those sorts of things he'd laughed, assuming she was joking. When it became clear she was serious he'd offered her a gold ducat for her services for the night. A silver dalter would have been plenty to have gotten that from any of the girls who were working. He was offering Alice twenty times that.

Elsa had hissed to her to take it. Alice had shaken her head and still refused.

The half dozen heavily armed men who rode with the knight had been angered at her refusal and for a moment things had threatened to turn ugly. Sir Lancel however had merely laughed.

"I like a challenge," he had told her. He'd wound up taking a couple other girls to bed for the night along with paying for women for each of his men. His eyes though had remained on her all through the evening.

He came back again a couple weeks later and that was when he began talking about taking her as a mistress. When he found out about her status as an indentured servant he'd started haggling with Elsa.

"He offered me twenty ducats for you girl." Elsa had told her the next morning. "These high bloods are a strange lot, they'll spend gold coin like copper for a night's pleasure but they expect to get bargains on other things. I will get fifty ducats from him at the very least. See if I don't."

Since then the offer had gone up to twenty five. Alice had no idea how long it would take, but she was sure that sooner or later Elsa would get her price and she would be sold. Sir Lancel would then cart her off to some country estate and expect her to do whatever dirty things he wanted. He was richer and better mannered than most, but he would still treat her as nothing but a piece of meat. She would never be married. She would never be loved. If she ran away she would either be tracked down or killed. She was trapped.

No one was coming to save her.

XXX

That was when the door opened and the second customer of the day entered.

Alice, Elsa, Nancy, and Harold all turned and were startled to see a young man dressed in black robes standing there.

His eyes met hers. She was startled by them, they were the soft, pure yellow of a sunflower. Just as unusual was the way he was looking at her. There was obvious desire, but nothing lustful. Whoever he was he had a handsome face, young, but very attractive. Alice felt a sudden ache in her chest and her hands quickly smoothed out the front of her blouse.

Remembering her duties she smiled wide for him and called out a friendly greeting. "Welcome to the Inn of Lost Sighs darling. What can I get for you?"

The stranger in the black robes strode right up to her without a second's hesitation, his eyes never wavering from hers. When he stood across from her he spoke loudly and clearly. "I have come here to make you mine."

Alice's jaw dropped. *A marriage proposal?* "What?"

Calmly he repeated himself. "I have come to make you mine, and I will not allow you to refuse."

Chapter 6

Huh?

When he was still just a child, Waldo had once asked his mother why they had to go out on their quests all alone, without servants or guards.

"Because," his mother had told him. "In this world only the strong can rule, and the best way to know your own strength is to face things alone."

He hadn't really understood it back then; he thought he was beginning to.

Just walking so many miles, with his backpack weighing him down, he had grown stronger. His back ached and his legs and feet were always sore, but he was getting used to it. Waldo hadn't realized just how soft he'd grown living in the castle with servants taking care of his every need.

Now if he could just capture a Great Monster and bind him with a contract.

Waldo had memorized the ritual while on the road, he could recite it backwards and forwards while in his sleep. What worried him was how exactly to subdue the monster long enough to perform the binding. The beast did not have to submit willingly. (Enver was forever complaining about that fact and of how his mother had forced him into her service.) What was required though was physical contact.

How exactly was he supposed to hold a Great Monster in place even for just seconds?

His spellbook had several paralyzing magics. "If only I could use any of them."

It was always the same problem. He could work protective wards and healing magic, everything else though was a monumental struggle.

How was he supposed to capture this Great Monster without offensive spells?

"I suppose I could at least start off by asking him to join me."

He hated the weakness of the idea, but it was not totally without merit. A master was responsible for the feeding and care of his familiars. They were also under his protection. Some monsters thought that a good bargain, and it was not unheard of for them to submit willingly.

Of course… those were usually weak monsters who struggled to survive on their own.

Powerful monsters like Enver would fight fang and claw to stay free.

I'll just have to try and convince him to serve me. If that doesn't work I'll have to try and use my magic and take my chances. No matter what, I can't leave here with hands empty.

Despite the obvious problems Waldo was excited. This was his first real chance to prove himself. If he could do this, then maybe this quest wasn't as impossible as it seemed.

As he walked along, there trotting towards him was a bulky creature with pasty grey skin. It had short stubby legs, thick muscled arms that hung almost to the ground, and a turnip shaped head with tiny black eyes and a slit of a mouth that ran from one side to the other.

Goblin.

Simple minded brutes who were barely capable of speech. They were among the most common sort of monster, and good only for physical labor of fighting. This one had a leather harness tied about his chest. He was pulling a wooden cart weighed down with sacks of flour.

Waldo moved to the side of the narrow street to let it go by. To Waldo the goblin was giving off a reddish light, just enough to outline it. He wondered how much it would cost to acquire. Goblins had their uses. Maybe he would try to acquire it later. Comparing that flickering glimmer to the blinding radiance he was moving towards Waldo picked up his pace. It was clear what his priority was.

As he hurried along Waldo never thought to turn around and look behind him. His spell would alert him if a monster approached. It would never occur to him to actually worry about ordinary people.

About fifty paces behind him a small crowd had formed and was carefully following.

XXX

Eventually Waldo came to a building was sitting right in the middle of the river. To his eyes light was pouring from it, what he sought was definitely inside.

There was a simple wooden foot bridge, just wide enough to allow two people to cross side by side. It had waist high railings that were worn and faded. When Waldo took his first step onto its planks there was a very slight creak.

He hesitated.

Before coming here he had never seen a river, and had no idea how to swim. Looking at the water rushing past he imagined falling in. His knees grew a bit weak and he put a hand on the railing.

Then he glanced at the building that was just a short walk away.

100

"There is no place for cowards in this family," his mother had told him.

Taking a deep breath he let go of the railing and took another step forward. He did his best to ignore the creek he heard and placed another foot in front of the other. Keeping his eyes focused he walked quickly across, all the while wondering why people would build something in the middle of a river.

When he made it to the other side and his feet stepped onto rocky ground he let out a relieved sigh.

The two story building took up most of the little island. He saw the edges of it were surrounded by weeds and that the red paint was cracked and flaking off. Above the door was a sign with some bird that had black streaks on its wings.

Light was spilling out of the doorway. A powerful monster was just on the other side. This was the reason he had come here, no matter what he had to acquire this Great Monster. Waldo took a deep breath to steady himself and squared his shoulders. He opened the door and walked inside.

As soon as he entered four faces turned to him. He ignored all but one of them. It was some sort of tavern, and behind the bar was a woman who was absolutely glowing! From the intensity he thought she might well be an equal for Enver. Could she be a vampire? That would be too perfect. Whatever she was he wanted her. Waldo needed this power, and would claim it no matter what it took.

Their eyes met. Hers were the most unusual shade of violet. When she spoke her voice sounded as sweet as morning sulfur. "Welcome to the Inn of Lost Sighs darling. What can I get for you?"

"*Nunc*." He whispered, ending the spell.

Waldo took a closer look at her. She was quite a beauty, with long red hair and both a face and a body to attract any man. Her eyes gave her an exotic appearance. It was a definite plus that she was attractive, he was already thinking about how that could use that. He strode towards her.

"I have come here to make you mine."

He saw her mouth fall open. "What?"

"I have come to make you mine, and I will not allow you to refuse."

The girl just stood there staring.

"Hey now! Who do you think you are?" The man at the bar spoke.

Waldo had not bothered to take note of the others. There was a man in faded grey tunic and trousers, a young girl in somewhat revealing clothing, and a large mid aged woman standing just behind his monster looking on.

"I am Waldo Corpselover, heir of the Corpselover family, one of the Seven Great Families of Alteroth."

The man mouthed the word 'Corpselover' with obvious disdain.

"Great family?" The brown haired girl asked. "So are you like a lord or something?"

"There are no lords in my country, we have no kings or nobles. There are Seven Great Houses that rule Alteroth and my family is one of those seven."

"But you're rich right?" The girl slid over to him. "Would you like to relax and enjoy my company?"

Having grown up with slaves whose lives depended on pleasing their masters, Waldo had long since learned to recognize false affection.

"I am not here for company or for play." He turned all of his attention back to his potential familiar. "I am here for you. I want you to come with me and be mine."

Her cheeks blushed and one hand ran nervously through her long hair. "Well thank you darling, I am flattered, but you don't even know my name."

"What is your name then?"

"Alice."

"Just Alice?"

Her eyes avoided his. "I don't have a last name."

The other girl was only too eager to supply the reason for that. "She's an indentured servant; so she doesn't have a family name."

Waldo glanced at the girl who had just spoken. "I'm not familiar with that word. What exactly does, 'indentured' mean?"

"It means she's a slave."

Alice stared down at her feet. "Technically I'm not."

"I don't care about that," Waldo said.

"You don't?" Alice frowned and crossed her arms across her chest. "I suppose you're hoping to bed me first? If you are, then I need to tell you I don't do that."

"Do you think that's why I want you?" Waldo shook his head.

"I came here all the way from Alter just for you. Even though we have never met, you are incredibly important to me. I want and I need you."

XXX

Alice could feel her heart racing and was suddenly very hot. She couldn't count how many times men had tried to tell whatever they thought she wanted to hear. She'd heard every sort of false promise, every kind of endearment. The words were always tender and spoken with passion.

They were always lies.

The men were always the same. They would tell her anything to try and get what they wanted from her. None of their gentle words ever touched her.

Until now.

The way he was looking at her and the frankness of his declarations made Alice really believe him. Though it made no sense at all, she really did think he wanted more than just her body.

"Why? If it's not to sleep with me, why would you want me?"

He smiled at her and she thought her heart was going to melt.

"Well because you're a monster obviously!"

Alice stepped back and put both hands over her mouth. "How did you..."

"Hey! How dare you!" Harold shouted. "Who the hell do you think you are you black wizard?!"

"I've told you who I am. Weren't you listening? You are very rude."

104

Harold had about three inches and at least fifty pounds on Waldo. His hands were fists and he looked like he was ready to start beating the wizard.

"Please don't do anything stupid Harold," Elsa said with an annoyed sigh. "I'd rather not have to put someone in the stocks so early in the day."

"But he just called Alice a monster!"

"I know, I was here when he said it."

"Why wouldn't I call her a monster?" Waldo asked. "She is one."

"Don't call her that!" Harold shook a fist in Waldo's face.

Waldo just stood there, seemingly unafraid. "Are all the people in this country really so rude? If this were Alteroth your head would already be on that floor."

"This aint Alteroth you damn black wizard."

Alice could see Harold was about half a breath from hitting him. "Darling, maybe you should go."

Harold nodded in agreement. "You heard her wizard, get out of here and don't come back."

"I believe she was talking to you." Waldo said.

"I was." Alice confirmed.

"You want me to go? Harold asked. "But I was defending you."

"I know, and I appreciate it, but I think it would be best if you leave."

105

Elsa stepped forward. "That seems like a fine idea. I think I'll close the Inn for a bit. Come back later and I'll give you a free meal and ale."

"But…"

"Go." Elsa said firmly. "And please don't tell anyone about any of this."

"But…"

"Please go Harold," Alice asked him. "It's all right."

He wavered. "Are you sure?"

"I'm sure."

"Fine." Before going he sent Waldo a hard look. "You better not insult her again."

"How is calling her a monster an insult?"

Harold tensed.

"I wonder if the worst thing about the stocks is spending hours bent over or having everyone see you in them." Elsa said. "Or spending all those hours without any food or water. What do you think?"

He muttered something foul and left the Inn slamming the door behind him.

"Well that was fun," the other girl said. "What are you going to call her next? A troll? A hag?"

Waldo gave Alice a speculative glance. "Are you a troll? I didn't think they could disguise themselves as human."

His question made Alice look uncomfortable while the brown haired girl started to laugh.

"Nancy," Elsa said. "Why don't you go back up to your room and make yourself look pretty?"

"I'm already pretty."

"Then make yourself prettier."

"Hmmph, fine!" She slid off her seat. Padding over to Waldo she expertly slid her modest breasts against his arm. "It was a pleasure meeting you. If you would like to have a little fun I'm upstairs in room five."

"You shouldn't be so forward with someone you just met." Waldo told her. "It makes you sound like a whore."

Nancy blinked, and then burst out into fresh laughter. "You really are too much!"

She headed up the stairs and to her room.

"Why was she laughing?" Waldo asked. "I was just telling her the truth."

"You might want to do a bit less of that." Elsa said.

Waldo nodded slightly. "Yes, lying is a skill I need to improve in."

"How did you know about me?" Alice finally burst out.

"A vampire told me. How he knew I have no idea."

"A vampire? But how would…" She stopped and swallowed. In the end, how he knew didn't really matter. "Doesn't it disgust you? Knowing I'm not human? All the men who want me would be sickened if they knew what I really was."

107

"Then they're all fools. Being what you are makes you special. It's because you're what you are that I came here. If you were just a pretty girl I wouldn't be interested at all."

She stared at him. *He knows and still wants me.*

Alice felt a torrent of emotions. He didn't care that she was a monster or that she was low born. He wasn't trying just to sleep with her. Here was the handsome prince come to save her and take her far away just like she's always imagined.

She'd never once dreamt he would have black robes, but she thought he was cute and could tell he was kind. She thought she could be happy with someone like him.

Is this what it feels like to fall in love?

"If you came all the way here for Alice then I'm afraid you've wasted your time." Elsa said.

Those words brought Alice's momentary hopes crashing down. Even if he was serious it didn't matter. She was still trapped.

"Why is that?" Waldo asked.

"It's because she isn't free to just leave. She is my indentured servant and I don't intend to let her go with you."

"I see. So you're her owner?"

"The correct title would be 'employer' but close enough. Do you even know how much trouble you've caused me? I doubt anyone will actually believe Alice is a monster. They'll just think it's a dark wizard being insulting. Even so, word of this will definitely get out. There's no way Nancy won't talk about it no matter how I threaten her."

"I don't understand. Just how have I caused anyone trouble?"

108

"No one else here knows I'm a monster, darling." Alice told him. "The men who like me wouldn't want anything to do with me if they knew."

"But you have monsters here." Waldo stated. "I saw a goblin pulling a cart and I could tell there are others in this city."

Elsa waved her hand. "We also have oxen and donkeys. Most men don't want to sleep with them though."

"You have a prohibition against being intimate with non-humans? How close minded."

"So… so you really don't find it disgusting?" Alice asked, her hopes rising despite the circumstances.

"Of course not. Obviously no one would ever want to touch a goblin, but elves? Vampires? In Alteroth we believe a person should take pleasure wherever they find it."

"Then you can also love someone who isn't human?"

"Well of course."

Alice gave a heartfelt sight. "You really are a sweet, kind man aren't you?"

"There is no reason for you to be insulting."

Alice opened her mouth and didn't know what to say.

"Enough of this," Elsa declared. "People here don't much care for your sort. It's time for you to leave and move on."

"Fine. How much?"

"How much for what?"

"Alice, obviously." Waldo shrugged off his backpack and put it on the floor. "As I've already said I came all this way for her. I am not leaving without her. Since you're her owner I will buy her from you."

"I've heard that before. There is no way you could afford the price."

"How much?"

Elsa rolled her eyes. "One hundred pieces of gold, by coin or by weight."

"Fine." He opened up his backpack and rummaged through it.

Alice stood there certain she must have heard wrong.

"What did you just say?" Elsa asked.

Producing the leather purse his mother had given him, he opened it up and let all those beautiful coins spill out onto the bar.

"One hundred pieces of gold, by coin." He smiled eagerly at Alice. "You belong to me now."

She couldn't believe it.

He was literally giving up a fortune… for her.

He was her hero, her savior…

Her husband.

"Darling!" In one easy move she leapt clear over the bar and landed at his side. She wrapped her arms about him and hugged him, mashing his face into her massive breasts. "I'm so happy!"

Waldo's arms jerked about. "You're… crush… ing… me."

"Oh! Sorry!" She immediately let go of him. "I'm much stronger than I look."

He staggered and gasped for breath. She was really strong. He also noticed that she was also about a head taller than he was. "It's fine. I'm glad you're so robust."

He is so cute, she thought. "Normally darling, I don't like being touched by men, but of course you can touch me as much as you want." She put her hands together and twisted about girlishly. "Though, ah, could we wait a little while to have our wedding night? I'm sort of shy about those things, so could we hold off just for a while?"

XXX

Wedding night? What is she talking about? It wasn't as though he was marrying her. He just assumed that was how the locals here referred to the first time being intimate with someone. She was certainly very beautiful and he had no problem believing lots of men wanted her. Waldo though was not worried about losing his virginity. He had much more important things on his mind. He still needed to acquire the other two Great Monsters and continue his quest.

"That's fine," he assured her. "Like I said, I didn't come here just to try and sleep with you."

"Do you really mean that darling? You don't mind waiting?"

"No, of course not."

XXX

She sighed contentedly. He was just too perfect. He'd paid a fortune to free her and didn't even demand a husband's privileges. He was treating her with respect and care; the way you would treat a wife rather than a mistress. Now he was going to take her far away from this place.

111

He was everything she'd dreamed of.

Well except for him being an evil wizard, but then we all have our faults.

Everyone knew that the people from the south were evil to the core. They were savages who murdered and stole almost from birth. She'd met some merchants and wagon drivers from the south; they had seemed no better or worse than the people who lived here. Alice had never met a Dark Mage before though, and her new husband certainly didn't seem anything like the stories.

When she really stopped to think about it maybe it was *because* he was a dark wizard that he was so accepting. No ordinary man would have been so generous and compassionate. There was no comparison at all between him and Sir Lancel. The knight would have spent money on her, but she would have been nothing more than his property. Alice was sure he spent plenty on his mounts and his armor as well.

"I will definitely make you happy, you will never be sorry that you chose me." Alice said.

Rubbing his ribs he nodded. "I have no doubt."

"I am a good cook and can sew and take care of the home. I also promise to be a good mother to our children."

"Our children?" Waldo echoed sounding confused.

Alice began to twist about again. "Let's just take our time though, there's no need to rush."

While all this had been going on Elsa had been counting out the coins. She bit a couple of them just to confirm they really were all gold. She also checked to make sure none of them were shaved. Most were ducats, but there were also denari, lions, and gleks mixed in. All the coins were minted to the standard weight, which was all that mattered to her.

Elsa could find nothing to complain about.

When she finished counting out all one hundred coins she quickly slid them into the small chest she kept behind the bar.

"You belong to him now Alice." Elsa announced. "Go gather up your things. It was a great pleasure doing business with you Sir Waldo. If you ever grow bored with her please feel free to come back and enjoy the services of our other girls."

"My proper title is, 'Master' not, 'Sir.'" Waldo said. He turned back to Alice. "Now that you are mine we need to perform the ceremony that will bind you to me."

"Right now? Right here?"

Waldo nodded. "I insist on it, I refuse to take any chances of you being parted from me."

Hearing him be so decisive and manly just made her want to melt. "Oh! Darling, is this the ceremony they perform in your country?"

"Well yes, though as far as I know all mages use it, not just the ones from Alteroth."

"Then wait just one minute please!" She ran out the door.

"Hey! Where are you going?"

"Just one minute darling!"

Outside the Inn Alice scanned the weeds clumped about the stony ground. She tore some of them up and then quickly ran back inside.

"Here!" Alice pressed them into Waldo's hands.

He had half a dozen white and yellow plants. "What are these?"

"Have you never seen daisies before?"

"Well, yes, on my way here. I've seen a lot of different plants since I left Alter. Why are you giving them to me though?"

"It's so you can give them to me darling!"

"You gave them to me so I could give them back to you?"

"That's right."

He closed his eyes and shook his head.

"Very well, here." He handed the daisies right back to her.

Alice accepted the flowers from him. "Now please say what you said before."

"What I said before?"

"What you said when you first saw me."

He stared at her dumbfounded. "You are making no sense at all."

"Oh please! I don't mind performing your ceremony, but I've always dreamed of this so please let's do it the proper way first!"

"I have no idea what you are talking about, but if I do this you'll let me perform the binding ritual without any more delays?"

"You call it the binding ritual? That's not very romantic."

"Romantic? It's not meant to be romantic, it's simply meant to bind you to me."

Alice was a little disappointed. Some people, particularly nobles, had that view of marriage. Overhearing Lancel talk to his men it was obvious he felt nothing at all for his wife. Waldo was also a nobleman, or something similar, so she supposed it was only to be expected he see it that way too. But calling a wedding a, 'binding ritual' seemed a bit much.

"Please say it darling, it would mean so much to me if you would."

Waldo shrugged and took a moment to recall what it was he'd said. "I have come here to make you mine."

"I would gladly be yours." Alice felt her knees grow weak and was trembling. It was really happening. All her dreams were coming true. "Please kiss me now, and I will be yours forever."

"Well that's true."

He reached out and took the hand that was not holding the flowers. To make a contract it required they be in physical contact as he recited the spell. To Elsa the words were in the language of magic and completely incomprehensible. To Alice, who was being bound, they were clear as day.

"Until the moment of my death, or the moment of your release, I bind you to me. Your life is one with mine. You shall obey me and do me no harm. You shall answer my summons. You shall never be parted from me or be hidden from my sight. This is our contract."

He leaned forward and got up on his toes, he touched his lips to hers completing the spell.

For both of them this was the very first kiss.

To Waldo there was nothing at all emotional to it. He thought of it simply as a necessary component to performing a magical spell; no different than motioning your fingers or using some basalt or mandrake.

Though he couldn't help but notice that her lips were very soft.

For Alice his kissing her represented a promise. That he was her husband and she was his wife. The words he had spoken were a little bit extreme and not at all loving. She supposed that was just how nobles did things. It was fine though, marrying a foreigner you had to accept strange ways. The important thing was that she was now properly married.

When he touched his soft lips to hers she felt a flash of heat rush through her body from head to toes. All her strength left her and she actually fell on her butt right in front of him.

Sitting on the floor she looked up at her new husband in amazement. "I... I never knew a kiss could be so amazing darling!"

"Well it's done now." He held a hand out to her. "You're mine."

Blushing she took it and got back up to her feet. "Yes I am darling. I'm your wife!"

"Huh?"

XXX

Outside the Inn, on the other side of the foot bridge, a crowd had gathered and waited for Waldo to come out.

Chapter 7

The Wrong Thing To Say

"So where will we be going? Will I get to meet your family? How many children do you want to have? There is so much about you I want to find out!"

"Wait! Wait! What are you talking about?"

"I just want to find out what you plan for us. Not that it matters; now that we are wed I'll be by your side no matter what."

"I believe there's been a misunderstanding here. You are my servant, my familiar, not my wife."

Alice frowned. "That's not very nice. I don't know how things are in your country, but here you don't treat your wife that way. Calling me a servant is just plain rude."

"You are not my wife." Waldo told her flatly.

Alice tilted her head slightly. "You change your mind quickly. You've married me, before gods and men. Marriages are until death, so even if you decide different you can't unmarry me."

"She's right," Elsa said from behind the bar. "Marriage is for life here, and just so we are clear, even if you decide you don't want her I don't give refunds."

"I'm starting to get a headache." Waldo muttered.

"Would you like me to massage your temples darling?"

He shook his head. It wasn't as though she was trying to oppose him the way Enver did with his mother. She seemed willing to do whatever he asked. It was just her being confused about the situation. As her new master it was his responsibility to make her understand.

"All right, obviously I've somehow failed to make things clear to you. The ritual I performed just now, the binding ritual, is just that. It binds you to me as master to servant."

"That's a very cold way to see it darling. Even if you are from a lordly family, it's insulting." She crossed her arms underneath her ample breasts. "Of course I'll be happy to do things for you, and take care of you. It's only proper that a wife care for her husband, but you can't expect to treat me like hired help. I want to be loved and cared for. I definitely won't put up with just being ordered around."

"Yes you will! It's part of our contract; you have no choice but to obey me!"

"You've obviously never been married before." Elsa commented with a chuckle.

"I am not married!"

"Yes you are darling. We are twice married in fact, once your way and once mine."

"Huh?"

"When you gave me the flowers and made your declaration, I accepted and then we kissed; in Lothas that is all that is required to wed."

"What? Don't you at least need a priest or some sort of official?"

Alice and Elsa shook their heads.

"Cannassa, goddess of the home, family, and childbirth teaches that all a marriage requires is the willing heart of the man and woman." Elsa said. "We are a practical folk here and we don't worry too much about ceremony."

Alice nodded. "She is one of our twelve gods, and the only one who doesn't have any temples or priests. She asks for no rituals or offerings, just for devotion."

How barbaric, Waldo thought. The Dark Powers had no temples or priests either, but they demanded offerings, not devotion. "So you're telling me she and I are really married?"

"That's right," Elsa confirmed.

"Well that's… interesting, but it doesn't really matter."

"What do you mean it doesn't matter?" Alice gasped. "How could it not?"

"The important thing is that you are bound to me as my familiar. If I accidentally performed some other ceremony I wasn't even aware of, so what?"

XXX

For a second Alice's eyes tried to bulge out of their sockets. He didn't think getting married was important?

She did not understand. Less than ten minutes ago, he had stormed in here proclaiming that he wanted her. Wanted her in a pure and chaste way. He had handed over a fortune in gold to Elsa to free her and then performed not one, but two, wedding ceremonies Followed by a kiss that had literally brought her to her knees.

Now he was pretending none of that had happened and that they weren't married.

"I don't understand you at all."

He opened his mouth to say something but she continued giving him no chance.

"But it's all right. You are my hero and my savior and I… I like you." Her cheeks blushed and she twisted about. "Even if you are strange and say rude things, I promise to stay at your side and take care of you. I can tell you are a very sweet and kind person. In time we will definitely love each other."

"You think I'm sweet and kind?"

"I do!"

"There is no reason for you to be insulting you know."

Alice's mouth hung open for an instant. "It's going to take me awhile to understand you isn't it?"

XXX

Waldo stood there and just shook his head.

She thought *he* was the strange one?

When had he ever said a word about marriage or wanting her as a wife? From the start he'd made it clear that he wanted her because she was a powerful monster. She'd been the one to grab the flowers and trick him into performing some bizarre marriage rite.

What she did not realize, was that as a member of the Corpselover main family he could not take a wife without the approval of the head of the clan. Until, or unless, his mother acknowledged the union he was not married under Alterothan law. What the locals here believed didn't matter to him in the least.

Now that he knew what she was talking about he stopped and really examined her. Physically, Alice was a stunning; no man

120

could possibly have any complaints there. Her being so much taller than he was, was a bit annoying but not a real issue, neither was the fact she was clearly older. As he'd said, he did not have any aversion to being intimate with a non-human. While it was much more common to have them as lovers, it was not completely unheard of for someone in the seven families to actually marry one; particularly among the Blooddrinkers. He even found her wish to delay being intimate rather appealing. (He was used to having the pretty slaves offer themselves to him in hopes of gaining his favor.) Despite her weird ideas she certainly sounded eager to take care of him.

He didn't find the thought of her being his wife distasteful; it was just inconvenient.

All that mattered was completing the conditions of the quest and eventually returning home. Alice was the first, and most important, step in that. With her help he could acquire the other two Great Monsters. What he needed was for her to behave like a proper familiar.

I need to start acting like a Dark Mage,

Alice was now bound to him by their contract; that meant she could not harm him and he could compel her to obey his every command. She needed to understand her proper place. The sooner she got this silly notion she was his wife out of her head the better.

"From now on you will refer to me as master."

She gave him a beautiful smile. "No."

"What? You are under a contract! You have no choice but to obey me! I order you to call me master!"

"No, you have some strange ideas about married life, I am not going to play into them. I will call you darling or sweetheart or dear or cutie pie or…"

121

"Stop!"

"Yes darling?"

"I ORDER you to call me master! I COMMAND it!"

"No, darling."

"Master!"

"Darling."

"Master!"

"Darling."

"Oh how cute," Elsa said. "You are already having your very first fight. You are starting to act like a real married couple."

Alice twisted about hugging herself. "I know! Isn't it wonderful?"

Waldo stood there at a complete loss. All his life he had seen just how total the power of a contract was. Familiars had leeway to act as they pleased, but not when there was a specific command. His mother had once ordered Enver to dance for her and the family. He cursed her for it, but had still twirled around the dining room floor until she finally told him to stop. From everything Waldo had ever seen, or been taught, the power of a contract was binding and absolute. Alice should have been calling him master whether she wanted or not.

Did I make a mistake casting the spell? He wondered.

If he had the Dark Powers knew it would not have been the first time. He'd gone over it constantly on the way here and was sure he'd performed it correctly. Not that performing it properly always mattered; he'd lost count of the number of spells where he'd been technically perfect only to see the magic either fail or work improperly.

He was sure the binding ritual had been at least partially successful.

That was because in his mind he could now sense Alice's presence. If she were to wander off he would be able to close his eyes and point in the direction where she was.

A partially successful contract was not a good thing. If she was free to ignore his orders, and even worse, do him harm, he might be in serious peril. She didn't seem to be dangerous, but he would need to be careful with her until he figured out just what had gone wrong. It wasn't as though he could afford to release her and just leave.

"So darling, where are we going?"

"Huh?"

"Where are we going?" Alice repeated. Despite their short argument her manner was still friendly and open. "Will we be going back to you home now?"

"No, our next stop is Middleton."

"Middleton? That's a mining city. Why would you want to go there?"

"There's something there I need to acquire." Until he figured out what was going on, Waldo thought it would be best not to tell her he was going to acquire two more monsters. He also thought it would be wise to keep quiet about their real marriage status. "I am on a quest, so I will have to do quite a lot of travelling before I can return home."

"A quest? You mean like knights go on? Are you going to find a relic or save a village?"

"In Alteroth our definition of a 'quest' is a little different."

"It sounds like fun. Going from place to place on a heroic journey and seeing the world. I've been trapped here my whole life so I've always wanted to travel."

"Your luck is in then." Waldo also intended to avoid the subject of dragon's eggs and how many years they might be on the road.

She laughed and was practically jumping in place.

"You should gather your things so we can be going."

"Yes darling!" Catching him by surprise Alice planted a warm kiss on his cheek. "I'll be just a few minutes!" She flew up the stairs and raced to her room.

Waldo put his hand to where she had kissed him. He wasn't used to that. Open, honest affection hadn't been that common in Castle Corpselover. It felt kind of nice.

"You're a virgin aren't you?" Elsa asked with a smirk.

"That is none of your concern."

"Which means you are one." Elsa told him. "You're very lucky you know. If you'd come much later she might have been gone."

"Really?"

Elsa nodded. "I was planning to sell her to a knight. He was very interested in her."

"So he knew she was a monster?"

Elsa choked out a rough laugh. "Hardly, if he'd known what she really was he'd have cut off her head. He just wanted to sleep with her."

"What a waste then. You can always find beautiful women. A monster that can tear people apart, that's a real treasure."

Elsa stared at him. "Are all black wizards as strange as you?"

"No, some are actually pretty odd."

XXX

In her room Alice tossed her few possessions on top of her bed. They consisted of a handful of dresses, shoes, combs, brushes, and various assorted items. Unlike the other girls she had never bothered with buying pretty things. She got far too much attention as it was. Alice pulled up the corners of the blanket and tied them together making an impromptu sack.

With one hand she lifted up her bed and moved it over a few feet.

There was a loose floor board that she removed. In the space beneath was a leather purse that was bulging with coins. These were the tips she had received over the years from all the men trying to get her to like them.

She carefully tied the purse onto her skirt and then tossed the sack over one shoulder. It never crossed her mind to say goodbye to any of the girls. None of them had ever tried to be friends with her. She was eager to leave this place behind forever.

Despite his bad manners (honestly, he expected to be called master?) Alice had no second thoughts about being with Waldo. No matter how strangely he acted, she could tell there was no cruelty in what he said or did. A kind husband who was a little odd, was so much better than belonging to someone who only wanted to use you.

Peculiar as he was, she really did like him. He didn't look at her like she was just a piece of meat. He knew her secret but didn't think less of her; actually he thought more of her for it. When he looked at her she felt wanted without feeling dirty. Thinking about the way he'd kissed her made her bring her knees together and slowly twist from side to side. She wanted more of his kisses. Just thinking about him gave her this tingly warm feeling deep in her chest. Alice didn't know if it was love, she only knew that she liked it and hoped she would always feel it.

XXX

Alice hurried back down the stairs, more than ready to leave.

She gave Elsa a final heartfelt farewell. "I hate you and I hope I never see you again."

"That's fine, it was all just business. You were nothing but trouble to me, but I made my profit."

"That's good, because money is the only thing you will ever have." She then turned to Waldo. "Can we go now darling?"

He nodded. "Yes, let's be on our way." They headed out, him with his back pack and her with her blanket / sack slung over one shoulder. "So what sort of monster are you?"

"Why do you ask me that? I thought you already knew what I was."

"I know you are a Great Monster, I don't know which sort though." He opened the front door and exited, she followed on his heels.

"You can't ask a girl something like that."

"Why not?"

"It's very, very personal."

"Are you a vampire by any chance?"

"A vampire? You mean the sort who drink blood and sleep in coffins? Ick! No."

"They don't actually sleep in coffins. Well some do, but it's a lifestyle choice." As he approached the foot bridge Waldo noticed a mass of people waiting on the opposite bank. "I take it this tavern is very popular."

There were at least a hundred of them. They were not trying to cross the bridge. Rather they were all crowded in front of it on the other side. They were staring at the two of them without anyone calling out a greeting.

Alice did not like the looks on their faces. "We get our business late in the day and in the evening. I don't think those are customers. Maybe we should go back inside for a bit."

"Why?"

"They don't look friendly to me. It might be best to wait before we cross."

"They're just commoners. They wouldn't dare cause me any trouble." He set foot on the bridge and began to cross it. As before there was an unsettling creak with every step. Having gotten across safely once before he ignored his concerns and stepped quickly.

"I have a bad feeling about this." She followed quickly after him.

XXX

Waldo was not blind to the looks being directed at him or to the mutters running through the crowd. But all of his life experiences had shown that ordinary people would not touch someone of his rank. It was not like they could actually be dangerous to him.

As he neared several voices called out mocking him.

"What are you doing here you damn black wizard?"

"Don't think about stealing our children!"

"Everyone knows what your sort does!"

"Get out of here!"

"We don't like your kind."

A man pushed his way to the front and began to point.

"You see?" Harold Brauer yelled. "It's like I said! He's come to steal Alice! He's going to make her his slave!"

Alice could see the already ugly mood of this mob being incited by Harold's words.

"That's not so! He and I are married now and I'm going with him because I want to."

"So he really is kidnapping you!" Harold shouted.

Others began to shout, hearing only what they wanted to and ignoring Alice's words.

"You can't take her!"

"We won't let you steal poor Alice!"

"Get out of here right now and don't come back!"

Waldo stood there trying to do his best to look down his nose at them. "My familiar and I will be more than happy to do just that as soon as you get out of the way."

"You're not taking her with you!" Harold yelled,

Members of the crowd began to creep closer.

Waldo held his ground. "Stand aside. Do you people know who I am? I am a Corpselover!" Back home that would have sent all the commoners bowing and declaring how honored they were.

There was a moment of stunned silence. Then…

"Disgusting!"

"Monster!"

"Sick!"

"Wicked!"

"He does that with dead people?!"

"He's going to kill Alice and do that to her!! Get him!"

When they surged forward a dozen hands grabbed onto Waldo.

"What is wrong with you people? Didn't you hear me? I'm a Corpselover! A Corpselover!" Too late he tried to grab for his wand. Strong hands were gripping his arms and shoving him about.

"Stop! Leave him alone!" Alice screamed.

"Throw him in!" Someone shouted and there was a roar of approval.

Before he knew what was happening Waldo was tossed over the railing and into the river.

His backpack pulled him down into the water.

Chapter 8

The Real Alice

The sheep do not rule over the wolves.

That was a common saying in Alteroth, and one Waldo knew well. He'd been taught over and over again, that it was the duty of the strong to rule the weak, and that the weak existed only to serve the strong. His entire life he'd known servants and slaves. Some tried to win his sympathies, while others tried as best they could to go unnoticed. Disobedience was rarely seen in Castle Corpselover.

There was good reason for that.

Slaves were cheap and very easy to replace. Not only his mother, but every member of the family could get rid of a slave for any reason or no reason. Even Enver, who was just his mother's familiar, could kill a slave and walk away. No slave would dare to so much as speak a defiant word to him, never mind lay a hand on him. Waldo was taught to rule over the sheep; not to fear them. Knights, White Mages, and monsters were dangerous. Ordinary people, mundanes, could never harm someone like him.

So it didn't occur to him he might be in danger until they actually grabbed him.

"Throw him in!"

There was a roar of approval and before he even knew what was happening he was flung up and over the railing and into the river.

As soon as he splashed in he was caught in the current and sent rushing downstream. The weight of his backpack caused him to sink like a stone. The cold water was a shock. He could feel it pouring down his nose. Instinctively he panicked and began to kick and flail about wildly. This did him no good at all. He sank deeper and deeper towards the river's bottom.

I'm going to die, he realized.

He fought to somehow reach the surface. The part of his mind that was still rational searched for a spell that might save him, but nothing he had memorized would be of any help. Staring up into the watery blue he could feel his lungs aching and the water still flowing down his nose. There was nothing he could do.

I don't want to die like this. Mother, I'm sorry.

XXX

Alice watched in horror as her husband was tossed by the crowd into the river. She saw the large splash and he was just gone.

The people gave a huge cheer.

Harold was the first to rush to her side. He put an arm around her and tried to pull her into his embrace. "It's all right Alice. You're safe now. He wo…"

Her fist smashed into his face with a loud clear 'crack' as his jaw bone broke and teeth spilled out of his mouth.

"WHAT HAVE YOU DONE?!!"

In fear, in rage, in panic, she lost all control and unleashed her power.

XXX

"Never show what you truly are," Elsa had warned her long ago. "All those people who like you would hate you for it. If they ever knew what you really were they would put you to the flames."

XXX

132

All of her life Alice had lived in fear.

Afraid of the day people would find out what she really was. Afraid they would see her as ugly and horrible. Every single moment was spent hiding, even (especially) when surrounded by admirers. All she'd ever truly wanted was to find someone who would love and accept her as she really was; someone who she could feel safe with. She just wanted to stop being afraid.

That was why Waldo was so amazing to her even if he was strange. He'd sought her out knowing what she was. Told her he wanted her despite the truth. Touched her, kissed her, and made it feel so incredibly right. When his yellow eyes looked at her she didn't feel strange.

She felt like she was something precious.

Waldo was the one she'd been waiting for her whole life. To Alice he was the answer to every secret prayer. Seeing him murdered right in front of her filled her with an unimaginable fury.

In her rage she finally let her true self come out.

XXX

The crowd turned their attention her way.

The immediate reaction was surprise, both at her outburst and at seeing her hit Harold so viciously.

Some of the men took half a step towards her and then stopped. She was looking at them with such open hate.

"HOW DARE YOU?!!" She shrieked as her body shook. "HOW DARE YOU HURT HIM!"

She tossed aside her sack and twisted about in pain.

There were cries and gasps from the crowd as they heard the sound of clothing, skin, and muscle tearing. As they watched, black leathery wings sprouted out of Alice's back. They spread out and stretched at least twelve feet from tip to tip. A long, slim, lizard like tail appeared and thrashed back and forth furiously. Her fingernails extended into razor sharp talons. Above each ear a short curving horn grew.

The rest of her remained as lovely as always, but in just a matter of seconds she had revealed herself for what she truly was.

"Monster!" Someone screamed.

In an instant the crowd that had been so angry and hostile was shoving and trampling each other as every one of them tried to run from her. Those who were too slow to move were pushed down and run over. They were all screaming for help.

She recognized many of them. Men who'd flirted with her and paid her all sorts of unwanted attention. Just one look at the truth set them fleeing in blind panic.

Slapping her wings down she launched herself into the air. This was the first time in her life she'd ever released her true form. She'd never once dared to, not even when she'd run away. The fear of being discovered had always been too strong to overcome. Now though, the only thing she could think of was trying to save Waldo. Everything else was tossed aside.

To her immense relief she discovered that all of her natural instincts made flying as easy as walking. She flew high into the air as swiftly and gracefully as a hawk. The feeling of it, of defying gravity and rising up into the sky, was exhilarating. She didn't have time to appreciate it though.

Shifting her wings she swung over the river and looked straight down searching for him.

All she could see though was the light shining off the water.

Somehow though she knew where he was. Ever since he'd given her that magical kiss she'd had a sense of him in the back of her head. When she'd been up in her room she had been certain of the exact spot he was downstairs. She didn't know what this was exactly, but she took it as a gift from him. A way to make sure they were never parted.

Pulling her wings in she dived down towards the water.

XXX

He stopped flailing.

It was useless. He was going to die and there was nothing he could do about it. He wondered if when his brothers and sisters had died if it had been like this. Had their deaths also come as such surprises? Had they also thought about the sheer unfairness of it? He had never thought to ask Walter or Gwen.

It didn't look like he'd get the chance to now.

Well maybe mom will bring me back as a spirit or something. She wouldn't get to recover his body so being a zombie was out.

Good, he thought. *I'd hate to end up like Walter.*

His lungs were aching and he was about at his limit. He wondered if drowning would at least be quick.

He was still staring up at a watery blue above him. He thought he saw a winged figure coming. Despite his impending death he wanted to laugh. *An angel coming for me? Figures I managed to screw up even this.*

He'd failed to notice the sense of Alice approaching him.

Just before she hit the water Alice pulled her wings in completely and stretched out her arms. She hit the water in an almost perfect dive.

Her eyes spotted him and she kicked her legs and swam over to where he was. She could see him turn his face to her and was relieved that he was still alive. He was almost all the way to the bottom. His robes and his pack were pulling him down.

With her powerful body she was able to swim right down to him.

XXX

Waldo got a good clear look at her. He saw the horns and the folded up wings and the whip like tail. He recognized what she was.

Succubus.

Her left hand grabbed tight about his collar and her right rose up, claws ready to strike.

She's going to kill me? Wouldn't it have been easier just to let me drown?

Her right hand slashed down. Once, twice, three times in quick succession. Just that quick Waldo felt the weight pulling at him vanish. Both her arms wrapped around him and they were rising to the surface.

He held his breath to the very last second and then opened his mouth when he just couldn't hold it any longer.

He coughed and choked, and gratefully breathed in the air.

Chapter 9

I Can See You're Happy

When they broke the river's surface Alice heard him gasp and choke.

"Darling! Are you all right?"

Waldo needed a minute just to breathe and fill his lungs. "I'm… fine." He managed between gasps as he coughed up water. Alice was holding onto him tight as they were being swept downriver.

"Hold on to me and I will get us to shore." Keeping one arm around his chest Alice used her legs and other arm to fight against the current and push them towards land.

Having no idea how to swim, and having just nearly drowned, Waldo wrapped both arms around her waist and held on tightly as she pulled him along. Through their new bond he could sense that she was worried for him. She had rescued him because she genuinely wanted to.

That wasn't how it normally went.

He knew most familiars would have been happy to just stand by and watch as their master died. A contract prevented a monster from physically harming a master, but if there was no direct order to help they were free to just allow things to happen. With the master's death the contract was dissolved and they were free.

Alice could have just let him drown and then walked away able to do anything she liked. Instead she had saved him, of her own free will.

I guess I'm lucky she's so odd.

XXX

Alice finally got them to the muddy shore. She dragged him out of the water and carefully set him down. Still breathing hard Waldo just lay there, staring up at her.

"Are you really all right darling?"

Waldo found it strange to hear concern from anyone other than his mother or Gwen. "I'm fine," he reassured her. He then said something he'd never expected to say to a servant. "Thank you for saving me Alice."

This brought a wide smile to her face. She hugged herself and began to twist from side to side. "You are more than welcome. I'm your wife after all. Just knowing you are all right makes me really happy."

"I can tell."

"Really?"

Waldo nodded. "I can sense your emotions through our bond. Also your tail is wagging."

"What?" Alice looked behind herself. Sure enough her three foot long tail was wagging just like a dog's might. Not knowing how to make it stop she grabbed onto it with both hands and spun herself around a little.

Seeing Alice literally chasing her own tail Waldo couldn't keep from chuckling.

Alice looked back at him mortified, while still holding on to her tail and being bent around. "Don't laugh at me! It's not funny! Why do I even have a tail?"

"It's just a part of normal succubus physiology, there's nothing unusual about it. Your tail is as natural as your wings or claws or horns."

Alice let go of her tail and stood there with a look of disbelief.

"What?"

There was a puddle of still water near her. Alice looked straight down into it so that she could see her reflection. "I have horns!!!" She put her hands to her head and tried to cover them up.

"What's wrong?" Waldo could feel her distress in the back of his mind. He could not read her thoughts or feel everything she felt, but strong emotions were easy to pick up.

"What's wrong? I'm... I'm... ugly!" She quickly turned her back to him. "I look hideous!"

Waldo noticed her tail was now drooping and lifeless.

"No man would ever want to be with someone as repulsive as me!"

"You're acting like you're surprised by how you look."

"I am! Before today I'd never taken on my true form. I was always afraid to. But when I saw you in danger I didn't think about it. Now that you see what I really am you must be disgusted. You probably don't even want to touch."

Waldo sat up and stared at her back. *I wonder if this is because she is a succubus or because she's a woman.* He knew how a proper Dark Mage would deal with a situation like this. A typical master would order his familiar to stop behaving so foolishly. The relationship between master and servant was based on authority and obedience. A Dark Mage didn't waste time dealing with his familiar's childishness.

For some reason though Waldo could not bring himself to be so harsh to her. She had just saved his life, and even if she was just his familiar, he didn't think it would be proper to simply order her to behave.

He got up and walked over to her, not sure what he was going to do.

On instinct he put his arms around her back and embraced her. Her folded up wings pressed into his chest and he could feel her tremble.

"What are you doing?"

Not knowing what the right response was he just said the first thing that came to mind. "I think you're beautiful, like this or in your human form."

XXX

Alice normally hated being touched by men, but his arms felt comforting. *How did he know just the right thing to say?* She slowly leaned back against him. She liked the warmth of him, the feel of his body pressed against hers.

"Do you really mean that?" Alice asked in a small voice. "You don't think I'm ugly?"

"No, you're lovely no matter what form you are in."

"Th… thank you. It makes me happy to hear you say that."

"I know, your tail is starting to wag again."

"Aaaah! Don't tell me that! It's so embarrassing!"

Waldo just couldn't keep himself from laughing.

Chapter 10

A Surprising Question

When Waldo eventually stopped laughing Alice was able to calm herself.

"I don't even know how I changed. It all just sort of happened." She was staring at her claws. "I don't know how to turn back."

"It shouldn't be hard. Enver would transform automatically with sunrise or sunset, but he could also change forms just by concentrating."

"Who is Enver?"

"He's a vampire who serves my mother."

"Your family has a vampire? Really?"

Waldo felt a certain pride. "My family has all sorts of monsters and undead as both members and servants."

Alice shook her head slightly. "You come from a really strange place don't you darling?"

"No, where I come from is normal, it's this place that is strange. Anyway, just concentrate on how you want to appear and you should change back to your human form."

"Just concentrate?"

"Try it, relax and think of your original self."

XXX

Not having anything to lose Alice shut her eyes and tried to picture the way she normally looked. After a moment she felt a

141

slight ache creep over her skin and muscles. Her wings collapsed inwards and melded into her back. Her tail seemed to be reeled in until it vanished from sight. Her horns and claws turned to a powdery dust and were blown away. In less than a minute she was back to looking human.

Opening her eyes Alice saw her fingernails were back to normal. She patted the side of her head and then looked behind her. She gave a relieved sigh and turned her attention appreciatively back to Waldo.

"Thank you darling, I was really afraid I wouldn't be able to change back. How did you know what to do?"

"I'm a member of the Corpselover family. I have had an extensive education on many subjects, but I am particularly knowledgeable in the fields of monsters, magic, and the undead. I likely know more about succubi than you do."

"Well since I don't know a thing you probably do. I mean except for being an embodiment of lust and all that. Elsa made sure I knew that much."

"Well actually, something you may not realize is that succubi are a... a..."

"A?"

"Aachoo!" Waldo sneezed. "Excuse..." he sneezed twice more. "Ah excuse me." He rubbed his nose.

"Oh! We need to start a fire and dry these wet clothes or we'll both come down with a cold!"

"We shouldn't really need to. It's a warm summer day and the horrible ball of fire is hanging above us."

Alice blinked. He certainly has his own way of talking. "I know the sun is out darling and that it's warm, but we're both soaked to the bone and our clothes are wet. Getting a chill is nothing to take lightly. I'll get a fire started."

XXX

The river had swept them a good distance from Stratford and there didn't seem to be any farms or homes nearby. They were stuck in the middle of a forest by the river's edge. Alice began to gather up dried leaves and grass for tinder. She then stacked up fallen branches and sticks around them. She then took two sticks and began to rub them together.

"I used to take care of the kitchen fires all the time," she explained. "But there was always a flame already lit." She rubbed the sticks together furiously. "I think this is the way to do it though."

"Here, let me." Waldo knelt down beside her. "*Pyro.*"

A small flame came to life on the tip of his index finger. Waldo touched the tinder and kindling and the fire caught.

"That's amazing!"

"Not really." Waldo negated the spell and the fire vanished from his finger tip. "Even with my spellbook there were a lot of spells I couldn't manage. All I have now are the ones that are memorized."

"It's still amazing, I mean you can do magic. What else can you do?"

"Right now? I could create fire, levitate a book, cast a detection spell, repel the undead, heal someone, and I know a number of wards and trap spells. It's not much."

"What do you mean? Don't you know how amazing that is? How many people can use magic? It's like something right out of a story. That you can do so much only proves how talented you are. I can already tell you are going to do incredible things and I am glad that I will be there to help."

"Thank you Alice, I hope I can live up to your expectations." *Thanking a servant twice in one day. Will wonders never cease?*

"You're welcome." She glanced at the camp fire that was now burning well. "Please take off all your clothes now."

"Huh?"

Staring at the fire she began to tug at some of her hair. "We both need to take our clothes off to let them dry."

"I see, well I suppose that does make sense."

"But you have to keep your back to me! I mean, I know we're married, but I want to wait until my heart is ready. You don't mind do you? You said you would wait."

Waldo wondered if now would be a good time to tell her about the half-naked sex slaves that were just part of the scenery in Castle Corpselover, or about the things that happened on the Summer and Winter Solstice. Or about the fact that with her blouse wet he could make out the exact shape of her breasts.

He decided to save all that for another day.

Turning his back to her he began undressing. "No, I don't mind."

Alice stood there silently watching as he took off his shirt, then his boots and socks, and finally trousers and small clothes. Though she had grown up at the Inn and Elsa had done everything in her power to turn her into a soiled dove this was actually the first time Alice had laid eyes on a naked man.

Unlike most of the big burly folk she was used to, Waldo was scrawny. He had pasty white skin and arms and legs that were

144

sticks. He had delicate hands that were the opposite of the beefy paws she was used to. Alice thought he was cute and adorable.

She especially liked his tight little ass.

Her face blushed as she felt the sudden urge to clutch and squeeze with both hands. What would he say if he knew what she was thinking right now?

"So are you going to grab these?" Waldo asked.

"What?"

"My wet clothes." He held them out with one hand while keeping his back to her. "Do I give them to you or do I put them by the fire myself?"

"Ah, I'll take them darling." Feeling embarrassed she took his clothes then quickly removed her own. She spaced them by the fire so they would dry as quickly as possible.

They both wound up sitting down in the grass with their backs to each other as they waited.

"I hope you're not feeling ashamed because I've seen you in your skin."

"Not really," Waldo told her. "My family doesn't have any issue with nudity."

"If you don't mind my asking, why are you and your family so open minded? I mean is it because you're mages or because you come from another country? I've known some noble bloods and I can tell you they are really traditional about things. They expect everything to be a certain way and won't put up with anything else. Why are you so different?"

"It's because I'm a Corpselover and an Alterothan I suppose. We have our own standards as to what is proper and acceptable."

145

"The people here, the nobles especially, would say that makes you barbarians."

"I don't much care what Lothasians think about civilized behavior. In my country commoners wouldn't dare talk back to someone of my status, never mind assault me. If this had happened in Alteroth this entire city would be laid to waste."

"Well, to be fair, the folk here wouldn't ever do that to a knight or a lord. It's just that there are a lot of stories about Dark Mages."

"What sort of stories?"

"Well," Alice tried not to offend him. "People say they steal away children and virgin girls. That they rob merchants, cast curses, raise the dead, and summon evil souls to serve them. That they kill all those who anger them or get in their way."

"That's not wholly correct."

"Really? Oh I am so glad to hear that."

"Mages, even dark ones, very rarely use curses except when they're on their deathbeds. The laws of magic demand too high a price."

"Ah, what about the rest of it?"

"Oh the rest is pretty accurate. Take slaves, steal, raise the dead, kill; that's what we do."

Alice turned to look back over at him. "Even you darling?"

"Of course, I am a Corpselover. I intend to make a great name for myself and make my family proud."

Alice frowned as she looked at the back of his head.

"Wouldn't you rather just be a good man?"

"What do you mean?" Instinctively he turned his head around.

He was rewarded with a clear view of her magnificent chest.

"Aaah! Don't look!" Covering herself with both arms she turned back around.

"Sorry." Waldo quickly turned back around as well. *Wait, why am I apologizing to her yet again?*

"It's... it's all right, I'm not angry."

Waldo felt relieved to hear that. Then he felt annoyed with himself for feeling relieved. Why should her opinion matter? His mother never cared what Enver thought or felt.

There was a long uncomfortable moment of silence.

"Are you really going to do those things? Stealing and killing and all that?"

"Yes."

"Why?"

"It's expected of me; it's what a Dark Mage does."

"Is that the only reason?"

"It would make my mother proud."

"But is it what you want to do?"

That was a question he had never asked himself. He had always struggled to meet the expectations of his family.

"What I want is to be worthy of my family."

"But do *you* want to kill and steal and all that?"

"If it will make my family proud, then yes."

He heard Alice give out a long sigh. She asked him no more questions.

Chapter 11

Why He Missed His Black Robes

Sitting in the grass with his back to Alice, Waldo slowly turned a thin knife in his hands. He was not strong physically, but at least he'd been blessed with long nimble fingers. Waldo could handle a dagger surprisingly well. He held the tip of the blade between thumb and forefinger and slowly turned it around and around.

Along with the clothes that were drying right now, this and one other knife, were all he had. Waldo's spellbook, wand, maps, spell components, other clothes, travel supplies, and even his robes were all gone now; lost somewhere in the river.

When the euphoria of still being alive passed, he thought about just what to do now.

During the weeks spent on the road he had burned the destinations on the map into his memory. Taking the dagger he drew the names of three cities into a patch of dirt.

Stratford.

Middleton.

Norwich.

With deliberate care he drew a line through, 'Stratford.' The map hadn't provided any more information than just their locations so it was no loss.

The wand had always been pretty much useless. (Though he would miss it, as it had been a gift from his mother.)

All his coin had been spent to acquire Alice.

His other daggers, clothes, waterskins, and most else in his backpack could be replaced. It had always been his intention to steal whatever he needed on a daily basis. That was only sensible as it would both provide him good practice as well as help him save.

The items he would really miss would be his spellbook, his various components, and his robes.

A spellbook was every magic user's most prized possession. It contained all his acquired knowledge. So long as you had one, and time to study, dozens or even hundreds of spells were available to you. For Waldo many of the spells had still been useless. There were however pages and pages of defense, healing, and general use magic that would have been valuable. He would need to keep reciting the few spells he had memorized over and over again. If he forgot them they would be lost as well. Recipes for potions were also lost now, though he thought he might be able to recall some of them.

Getting his hands on a new spellbook was going to be difficult. Very few people in the world had the ability to use magic. That was the reason Alteroth was feared and respected, even when the whole world hated her. It was also the reason why the nations feared Avalon though the wizards of the Misty Isle tried to act as advisors and diplomats. Magic was a rare and wondrous sight outside of those two lands. That meant the chances of his finding a replacement spellbook were very slim.

He missed his black robes nearly as much. That was not due to any pragmatic reason; the robes did not grant him any sort of magical power or protection. They were tailored silk, nothing more. They just represented who and what he was. Without them the mundanes wouldn't know he was superior to them.

"The clothes are dry now darling." Alice said from behind him.

"Good." He stood up, careful not to turn his head around. He kept facing away as she handed him his clothes and as he got dressed.

"Is it safe for me to turn around?"

"Yes darling, its fine."

When he did so he saw her in her tight fitting white blouse and long skirt. She was shifting from foot to foot and tugging at her long red hair with one hand. Looking at her Waldo felt an annoying mix of emotions. He was deeply grateful to her for saving him. He felt pride in having a genuine Great Monster as his familiar. Despite her bizarre ideas he found that he genuinely liked Alice. Her simple devotion and protectiveness were endearing as was the faith she had in him.

At the same time…

She just did not have the right attitude.

She spoke to him freely without even a trace of fear. Assumed they were equals and refused to even acknowledge him as her master. Asked him questions and brought up issues that bothered him in unexpected ways. Despite having been that fat woman's slave Alice was shockingly bad at it.

"So what do we do now?" Alice was still shifting from side to side.

"We'll head to Middleton. From what I remember from my map it should be north of here."

"You talked about going there before darling. It's a part of your quest isn't it?"

Waldo nodded.

"Well if it helps I still have my money." She patted the bulging leather pouch tied to her hip. "I lost everything else but I held onto this."

"You have money? Slaves aren't allowed to own anything."

"Elsa let me earn and keep tips. She believed it would motivate me to work harder."

"Really?" Waldo said in surprise.

"Yes, I hoped I could eventually buy my freedom so it did make me work hard."

"Hmmm, well that's interesting."

The idea of rewarding slaves for good behavior was not totally unknown in Alteroth.

Only members of the Seven Families were considered to be free citizens. Everyone else was a slave or servant; that did not mean they were all treated exactly the same. The serfs who lived in the countryside and raised the food could not leave the land they were bound to, but were lightly supervised. So long as they produced the food required, they were usually allowed to live, marry, and raise families however they pleased.

In Alter and the other cities were a large number of skilled workers; masons, carpenters, blacksmiths, weavers, glass makers and other such. They worked in the business district assigned to their profession making not only whatever their owners needed, but filling orders for others as well. Everything still belonged to the family that owned the worker; slaves were not permitted to own anything, not even their own bodies. However, they also did not have to pay for rent or food or clothing or anything else. Their needs were all provided for by their masters, and if they were especially skilled and productive it was not unusual for them to receive special comforts or be granted certain indulgences. Such as being allowed to choose who to marry, or being permitted one day in ten to rest.

Unlike the serfs, the skilled workers were not permitted to marry as they pleased, and had to get permission from their owner. The children were automatically slaves and valuable property, so marriage and the raising of family was as much a matter of commerce as anything else. It was extremely rare for a worker to be permitted to marry a slave with a different owner. When it did happen one owner usually bought the property of the other. This avoided problems with ownership of the children.

Like the serfs, the skilled workers, or artisans, were not permitted to leave the city where they labored or go into a different profession. All the children were expected to be taught the same trade.

Serfs and skilled laborers could, of course, be sold or whipped or killed like any other slave. But in general, unless they had committed some heinous offense, it was considered wiser to simply leave them be. They had a role to play in the economy and replacing them was usually considered more trouble than it was worth.

The ones who had it worst were the castle slaves and the manual laborers; the unskilled slaves. They were the class most likely to be abused and killed. The former because they were in close contact with their masters, the latter because brute labor could be done better and more cheaply by undead. So they were normally worked to death, raised, and kept working. The castle slaves were taught to be especially obedient and pleasing because any member of the ruling family could kill them at any time.

Maybe that's the problem. Waldo thought. *Alice is used to being treated like a skilled worker slave not a castle slave.*

Familiars were actually treated very indulgently, far better than most any other servant. They were valuable and extremely hard to replace. But that didn't mean they got to put on airs and pretend to be equals. There were limits to how indulgent you could be. He planned to treat Alice well, but she needed to understand her proper place.

"Want to see how much I have?"

"What?"

Alice shook the purse. "Want to see how much I have? I never bothered to keep track. I just kept it hidden away."

"Certainly."

Kneeling down Alice carefully poured the coins out into the grass. Waldo noted there was no gold. There was the reddish glint of copper along with flashes of silver here and there.

Alice's hands moved quickly, with practiced ease. She first separated out the silver and then began silently counting out the copper ones and stacking them into one pile after another. When she was done sorting everything out she announced what she had. "Fifteen silver dalters, two silver wolves, twelve hundred and twenty three copper coins; mostly traks."

"So you have the equivalent of twenty nine silver pieces and twenty three copper, or one gold piece, nine silver, and twenty three copper."

Alice stared at all the coins. "I have been working and saving all my life and this is what I have to show for it."

"Well considering how low your station was its actually very impressive."

Alice frowned. "Really?"

"What? You were a slave. Having anything is a surprise." He held his hand out. "I'll take possession of them now."

She began scooping them back into the leather pouch. "No."

"Alice, as my familiar, whatever you have automatically belongs to me."

As she tied the purse back to her side, she gave Waldo a shake of the head. "As your wife, I consider this to be our money now, but I will decide how we spend it."

"You have the wrong attitude."

"What do you mean? Men are always horrible with money. They waste it without a second's thought. I've seen men spend a whole month's wage on one night of drinking and whoring. So I will be the one who decides how we spend our coin."

"This is not how the master, servant relationship works Alice."

"Well I am pretty sure this is how it works with husbands and wives."

"You are supposed to obey me without question."

Alice sighed. "That's cute. So, Middleton?"

Waldo was at a loss. Since he could not compel her with their contract there was nothing he could do. *I can't even get her to call me master.* "Yes, we're going to Middleton. Unless you know of somewhere I can pick up a new spellbook."

Alice blinked. "Oh."

"Oh?"

"Well I'm not sure, but maybe there is a place."

"Really?" Waldo asked suddenly very interested. "Tell me more."

Chapter 12

White, Dark, And Independent

"Well, as a barmaid I got to hear lots and lots of different stories from folk from all over Lothas."

Waldo nodded.

"One of the stories I'd hear would be about this old hermit by the name of Roger who lives near the village of Bittford. They say he could make it rain or make the sun come out. That he could always tell when someone was lying. That he could cure sheep and cows. That he could find lost children. There was even a story about some bandits who came to Bittford. He drove away when Walton summoned a dragon!"

"A dragon?" Waldo repeated dubiously.

Alice nodded her head. "That's what the stories say."

"Well if that's what they say then I'm sure it's true."

Alice narrowed her eyes. "Lots of people told the same stories about him. An old hermit living in the woods who carried a wand and wore brown robes. People would come to him and ask for cures or help with crops or herds. He hardly ever leaves his home so folk who need his help have to seek him out. I don't know if he could help with a spellbook, but I thought you would want to know."

"Well, I have my doubts about summoning dragons. Otherwise, he sounds like a hedgewizard to me."

"What's a hedgewizard darling?"

"It's what we call magic users with no formal training and no connection to a powerful house or patron. They're also called local mages or unschooled mages. They're the weakest sort of independent mages."

"Independent mages?"

Waldo sighed. This was basic information, at least for someone like him who was born into one of the Seven Great Families. He was going to need to teach her quite a number of things. "In the world there are three types, or schools, of mages; White Mages, Dark Mages, and Independent Mages. White Mages come from the Misty Isle of Avalon. Dark Mages, like me, come from Alteroth. Independent mages can come from any other country."

"Oh! I've heard stories about the White Mages of Avalon! They go around helping people and giving advice to kings and lords! They aid knights on quests and protect the common folk! Everyone says they are very powerful and very wise."

"They're idiots."

"So they're not good with magic?"

"No," Waldo admitted. "They're very skilled. In their own way they are as well taught in the mystic arts as my people. They're idiots because of their philosophy."

"I thought they just liked helping people."

Waldo nodded. "They do, that's what makes them such idiots."

"Darling, you're doing it again."

"What?"

"Talking and not making sense."

"All right, let me explain. The White Mages of Avalon have a philosophy based around, 'Unity, Justice, and Peace.' Their ultimate goal is to unite the Shattered Lands into a single nation and rid the land of strife and injustice. They dream of returning to the days of the Amoran Empire, before the Shattering."

"That's wonderful."

"No it's not! Can't you see what they're up to? It's obvious!"

"Helping people?"

"It's a plot to dominate the world! Those idiots go around telling people they're serving a higher cause. They go preaching about, 'Unity, Justice, and Peace' pretending to have no ulterior motives. They offer advice to local rulers and help the subjects, all the while telling people about their ridiculous ideas and trying to convince them how much better the world would be if they would only join together under Avalon's leadership! It's all just one vast conspiracy to take over the world and destroy Alteroth!"

"Ah, could it be they just want to help make the world a better place?"

"Don't be naïve, who thinks that way?"

"I do, I like helping folk."

"You're not a mage. Wolves don't go around protecting sheep. It's unnatural. It's obviously all part of a conspiracy to secretly take over the world."

"Darling, no one thinks the White Mages would do that. They're just good people." She paused. "Well, I have heard a few nobles and merchants say they shouldn't be trusted."

"Which only proves how effective their conspiracy is. They have almost everyone fooled."

"People think it's the Dark Mages who want to rule the world."

"That's just propaganda," Waldo waved the idea away. "We're actually happy with things just as they are. Conquering more land would just mean the seven families would be at each other's throats over how to divide up the spoils. We don't want to conquer the world, we just want the world to think we want to conquer them so they don't try and conquer us."

"Darling, you sound paranoid."

"How is it paranoid to think the White Mages and everyone else are out to get us?"

Alice gently patted his arm. "It's all right, I promise to protect you from the scary White Mages."

Waldo sent her a hooded look.

"They don't sound so bad to me."

"Did I mention they would put you to death if they could?"

"What? Why? What did I do?"

"You were born a succubus."

"So? I'm a good person!"

"That's not the point. They want to create an ideal world; one without war, injustice, or strife. They also want a world without evil, which means no undead, no Dark Mages, and no monsters."

"What do you mean no monsters? What would they do with all of us?"

"Didn't you hear me say they would kill you if they could?"

"But… but… how is that just? Killing people simply because they weren't born human? Isn't that evil?"

Waldo shrugged. "Not to them. They are only interested in justice for their own kind. Their ideal world has no place for people like us."

"I can't believe people could be that cruel. It makes what Elsa did seem almost merciful by comparison."

"In any case, my original point was that magic users are divided between White, Dark, and Independent. In general we and the Whites are the strongest because we are the most thoroughly trained and have access to libraries filled with arcane knowledge. By comparison, most magic users from outside Alteroth and Avalon rely on the apprentice system. How well trained they are and what spells they have access to vary wildly. A lot of mages will actually join us or Avalon of their own free will, just to get access to our knowledge. The weakest sort of Independent is referred to as a hedgewizard."

"Most magic users will try to find a wealthy patron. They typically end up in some court or in the employ of someone rich. Hedgewizards, on the other hand, choose not to serve any particular master. They live on their own, often in the same place where they were born, and usually deal with only the locals. Often they are never even apprenticed and are self-taught or only acquire a few spells from occasional meetings with other mages. Since they lack any formal training, and aren't in a position to acquire spells or arcane material, they are usually very weak. It's not unusual for a hedgewizard to only know one or two rudimentary spells or how to brew potions or have a small talent for telling fortunes. In Alteroth we don't see them as real mages. The very idea that someone like that could summon a dragon is ridiculous."

"Well it was just an idea darling. If it's no good that's fine."

Waldo looked unhappy. He considered for a long moment.

"How far away is Bittford?"

"Not too far I think. I never left Stratford, but it should be about a couple days walk to the west of here."

That was going away from Middleton. Going there would add a few days to his journey.

"I suppose it's worth looking into. Okay, we'll go there first and then head to Middleton."

"Really? I thought you said he wouldn't be a real mage."

"I'm not saying he is, but even a hedgewizard will have a spellbook, or even just a few scraps of vellum."

"Vellum?" Alice had never attended school, but felt like she was in one now.

"It's a special sort or parchment that you can write magical inscriptions on. If you write them on ordinary paper they will light on fire when you read them."

"Really?"

"Yes. Even if this Roger character is as useless as I think, it would still be worth visiting him just to get my hands on some vellum. At the very least, I could write down the spells I still have memorized and make a temporary spellbook. That's worth a few days delay."

Chapter 13

Second Best

They were trudging through the forest away from the river. There was no path and they were walking through bush and high grass. Waldo's eyes kept darting about the underbrush and the branches overhead with ever 'chirp' 'squawk' and 'caw.'

"What a savage place this is."

"There's nothing to be scared about darling. This close to Stratford there are no wolves or bears."

"I am not scared." Waldo said with great dignity as he stepped around a tree root. "I am a Corpselover and I fear nothing."

"Of course."

Though I'd rather not run into anymore of those horrible creatures with those deformed long ears. "I wish I still had my map. Are you sure this is the way to get back to the road?"

Alice nodded. "So long as we keep going away from the river we're sure to run into it."

Waldo grunted. So far the quest had been very much a mixed result. On the plus side he had actually succeeded in making a contract with a Great Monster. Something almost unheard of for a First Quest. Were the circumstances normal he would have turned right around and headed home. Returning with a succubus in tow would be plenty to cover himself in glory.

On the negative side he'd very nearly been killed by a bunch of commoners and lost practically everything, including his spellbook and wand. Almost as bad, he'd needed Alice to save him. A Dark Mage's servants were supposed to fight for and protect him, but he was never supposed to be vulnerable.

162

He tried to imagine his mother under similar circumstances.

What came to mind was a picture of a whole lot of skeletons and zombies munching on raw peasant. That was how a Dark Mage was supposed to deal with things.

Whenever he tried to compare himself to his mother it made him feel utterly unworthy. His mother had always said he had great potential. She had actually told him that of all her children he was the strongest raw talent. The ability to use magic was a rare trait in human beings; perhaps one in ten thousand were born with it. Each individual blessed with that precious gift was also born with the capacity to wield a certain amount of mana and with a particular 'talent.'

Mana was a measure of magical energy. Every spell required a certain amount of mana to be worked. The greater the effect of the spell the more mana it required; no different than the amount of muscle needed to move an object. The amount of mana needed to lift a feather was less than that needed to lift a book which was less than what was needed to lift a boulder. Though the spell remained exactly the same different results required different amounts of energy.

The amount of mana a magician could wield varied from one person to the next. There were some who would never be able to do more than work the most basic cantrips and minor spells. While very few had the potential to work the deeper magics. A magic user could recover his strength with rest. He could train and study in order to reach his full potential. But in each was an inborn limit that could not be passed. The amount of mana a person could wield was determined at the moment of your birth and there was nothing you could do about it. Magical items like wands and staffs could strengthen the effect of your magic; much as a lens could focus light. Rings and scrolls could help you cast a particular spell. But the blood in your veins decided where your limits were.

163

Along with a limit, each magic user was born with a particular 'talent.' There were always certain spells that just came more naturally and easily. His mother's talent was in necromancy. His brother Walter's had been in summoning.

Waldo's was in healing and protective magics. In other words, his talent was in white magic.

The Dark Powers have a sense of humor, Waldo thought. He was born into the Corpselover family with massive mana reserves and powerful talent. He should have been a prodigy, recognized as one of the strongest in his generation. But his own talent ran counter to everything that was valued by his people.

He was useless at necromancy and barely competent in most of the other schools; elemental, summoning, illusion, evocation, invocation, and divinization. For all his potential he had always been viewed as a failure.

XXX

Alice was walking alongside of Waldo.

She saw a faraway look in his eyes and could sense he was brooding about something. Not only her eyes but the feel in the back of her head told her so.

"You don't need to worry you know." She said quietly.

"What?"

"I said you don't need to worry darling. Things may seem bleak right now but everything will work out fine. So please don't be gloomy."

"I am not being gloomy."

"It's all right if you are, just so long as you know things will be all right."

"I am not being gloomy."

"Of course."

Waldo picked up his pace slightly. Alice had no trouble keeping up.

"Uh, darling?"

"Yes?"

"There's something I was wanting to ask you about."

"What?"

She was walking alongside him tugging at some of her long hair with both hands. Alice was trying to come up with the least embarrassing way she could to bring this up.

"What is it you want to ask me?"

Feeling uncomfortable she averted her eyes and spoke in a half mumble. "Before, by the fire, you saw them didn't you?"

"Saw what?"

"My... my breasts." She got her question out in a rush before she lost her nerve. "What did you think of them?"

"They were nice."

XXX

He went another ten steps before noticing she was no longer at his side. Stopping he turned back around and saw her standing there, mouth hanging open, fists planted on hips, she was just glaring at him.

"Is something wrong?"

"NICE?!!" She exploded. "Nice? Is that all you have to say?!"

"What's wrong with nice?" He asked not understanding her reaction. You would think he'd insulted her.

"My breasts are not nice! They're wondrous! Amazing! Men have been staring at them ever since I was thirteen! I've had men come to the Inn and spend entire evenings just ogling them! They have ruined marriages! I once had a traveling bard compose a song for them! You are the first man to ever actually see them and all you have to say is that they're nice?"

Waldo thought for a moment.

"They're very nice."

"Aaaarrgh!" Alice shouted in frustration.

She stormed off in a random direction.

"Hey! Where do you think you're going?"

"Away from you!"

"What are you upset about? It's a compliment! If I said that to any of the sex slaves they'd have been flattered!"

Waldo saw her stumble and almost fall. She turned about to stare at him in disbelief.

"Sex slaves? You mean there were soiled doves in that castle of yours?"

"Soiled doves? The only birds kept in the castle were ravens."

"I don't believe it! I actually thought I was going to be your first and only and instead it turns out you've been with other women? Just how many women have you had?"

"If you're asking me about sex the answer is none, I am a virgin. I had never even kissed a girl until I contracted you." He didn't bother to explain that the reason for that had nothing to do with virtue or a desire to remain a virgin. It had been the fact that any girl he picked out would have been killed by Enver. He didn't understand why Alice was reacting this way. In his family sex was nothing more than a past time for both the men and women.

Alice was looking at him with obvious doubt. "Most men who have seen a woman's breasts aren't still virgins. Usually the one happens right before the other."

Waldo shrugged. "If that were true in my case I would have stopped being one a long time ago."

"Hearing that does not make me happy."

 "Would it make you feel any better if I told you they were the second best breasts I've ever seen?"

Alice's jaw dropped.

"SECOND?!!"

"I'm guessing that was the wrong thing to say."

"I am a succubus! My body is made to enthrall men! Who could possibly have better breasts than me?"

"My mother," Waldo answered primly. "Hers are spectacular."

Alice just stood there unable to even speak. Her mouth kept opening and closing without any discernable sound.

"If it makes you feel any better I'm not the only one who thinks so. My mother has had songs, poems, and entire stage plays dedicated to her."

"Aaaarrgh!!" She stormed off into the forest and away from him.

"Alice! I order you to come back. Hey! It's a compliment! If you'd ever seen them you'd understand!"

Waldo chased after her.

Chapter 14

Not That Obvious

She could run very fast and was quickly gone from sight. With their bond he knew exactly in what direction she was going. He ran after her as fast as he could, even as he sensed her getting farther and farther away. He ran and he ran; following her even as he wondered to himself why he was doing so.

He finally came to a stop, doubled over and panting. Through their bond he could tell she was still moving away from him at full speed.

"Enough… of… this." Without making hand signs or initiating a proper spell he just spoke a single word or magic. "*Concalo.*"

Instantly Alice appeared directly in front of him.

Running at top speed.

Her eyes widened in obvious surprise at seeing him but there was no way for her to stop her momentum. She plowed right into him knocking Waldo down hard.

"Ow!"

Despite knocking him over Alice was able to come to a halt without falling herself.

He stared up at her from his spot on the ground. "I'm starting to wonder if Enver was doing me a favor."

"Are you all right?"

"I'm fine," he grunted.

"How did you suddenly appear in front of me? Was it magic?"

169

Waldo slowly got to his feet and rubbed his lower back. "Well I certainly didn't outrun you. I didn't appear in front of you, that would require teleportation which is one of the deeper magics. I used a summons to bring you to me."

Alice looked at him blankly.

"Summoning magic is used to bring living beings to you. Humans, animals, monsters can all be summoned provided you know the correct formula."

Usually, he thought, recalling his own many failed efforts. "It's one of the more complex forms of magic and one of the most difficult to master. It normally requires a summoning circle and a magical inscription meant to represent what you are summoning. However, if you make a contract you can automatically summon your familiar without bothering with those."

"Are we back to that again? I'm your wife, not your servant or familiar." She began to deliberately stomp away.

"Where do you think you are going?"

"Away from you! Don't chase me anymore."

"Alice! I order you to stop and come back here right now!"

She sent him an icy glare from over her shoulder and kept right on walking.

I really did screw up the contract. Even so he was in no mood to have her defy him like this. "*Concalo.*"

Suddenly she was standing right back in front of him face to face.

"Stop doing that! I don't feel like talking to you right now!" She turned around and started walking away from him yet again.

170

"I can keep summoning you back to me all day if you like."

She continued to walk away.

"*Concalo.*"

She once more appeared in front of him.

"Will you stop that? I really don't want to talk to you right now!"

"I don't understand why you are upset. What did I say that was so terrible?"

"How can you even ask that?"

"Obviously I am asking because I don't know!"

"If you don't know I am not telling you!"

Waldo's mouth opened and closed. His back was still hurting and he was starting to get a headache. Through their bond he could tell her anger was rising though he still had no idea why. "You do know that makes no sense at all don't you?"

"I thought our special connection was supposed to help you to understand me."

"Obviously magic has its limits."

Her back stiffened and her eyes blazed. She was looking down at him and he got the very clear sense she was wondering just how far she could send him flying.

"If you bring me back one more time I am going to kick you... hard."

With that she left, at a slow deliberate pace, as if daring him to do it.

As she walked out of sight he did not try to bring her back.

XXX

In Castle Corpselover

Enver opened a single weary eye in response to the pounding on his door.

"Open up vampire! I want to talk to you!"

It would be him. Enver thought wearily.

The windows to his quarters were bolted tight, but Enver knew it was still daytime. His body was sluggish and longed for sleep. He wanted to stay right where he was, in his nice warm bed.

The pounding on the door did not let up.

"Open up! You damn blood sucking leech! I'm not leaving until you answer me!"

Enver sighed. When the idiot got something lodged in his teeny tiny little mind he never let it go. *I wish Lilith would let me kill him and have done with it.*

Tossing the blankets aside he slid out of bed and smothered a yawn as he shuffled to the door. He didn't like dealing with people during the daytime. Vampires were considered among the most powerful creatures in the world, but they had one glaring weakness. During the daytime they were unable to access their full strength. They were vulnerable and lethargic. Contrary to certain folk tales sunlight was not lethal to a vampire. (Not that sunshine was anything to worry about in Alter.) Enver could still transform into his vampiric form if he wished, but he would remain weaker than normal and sluggish. Like most of his kind he tried to remain hidden during the day. Unfortunately, some people refused to leave him be.

172

Enver opened the door. There was an irate zombie standing on the other side. "What do you want you walking piece of rotted meat?"

Walter glared; he was almost always angry these days. "I want to know why you helped him."

Enver smothered another yawn. "Who?"

Seeing Walter become angrier was amusing. Enver understood the zombie was here now because he thought it gave him some sort of advantage. They both knew the vampire could easily tear him apart when it was night time. Even at this moment Walter could not do anything. Enver's room had been warded by Lilith. Walter could not enter without being stuck in place like a bug in amber. He could snap his jaws but he couldn't bite.

Enver found him to be pathetic; loud, annoying, and pathetic.

"Don't play with me. You know who I mean. Why did you help Waldo on his quest?"

"Isn't it obvious? I want him to return. After all, how can I eat him if he dies in some far off place?"

"If he makes it back somehow I will blame you."

"How terrifying." This time when Enver yawned he did not bother to cover it. "Why are you so excited? The Council sent him off on a fool's errand; there is no hope for him. He will either die or realize his cause is forlorn and settle down somewhere. He will never come home again. Your mother knows this, though she has not said so out loud."

"If he's doomed why help him at all then?!"

"Because it cost me nothing, and as I said, I would like him to survive though I certainly do not expect it." The frail, human

173

looking vampire, narrowed his eyes thoughtfully. "Why do you care so much?"

"Mother makes me sit to her left. She keeps the seat to her right empty. That means she still considers Waldo her heir."

"So?"

"So until he dies she won't acknowledge me. I need his death to secure my future."

"Your future?" He cackled. He laughed right in Walter's face. "Your future! Ha, ha, ha!"

"What is so funny?"

Wiping a bloody tear from one eye Enver let the chortles die down before answering. "The idea that you have a future. You really believe it though don't you? That your mother will elevate you to heir, and that one day you can be head of the clan. Listen to me you walking corpse. There is no future for you, none. You only exist now because even a woman as cruel and wicked as your mother loves her children."

Shaking his head he continued.

"The dead cannot rule the living. You know that don't you? It's one of the lessons every member of the Seven Families is taught. Your chance to rule the family died with your body."

"If Waldo is gone mother will have to choose me!"

"Are you really that self-deluded? 'If the tree dies plant a healthy branch.' There are other branches of the Corpselover family and other candidates she could choose from. All of whom would be better than a walking corpse like you. Forget leading the family; it will never happen. Go torture and eat a few slaves and settle for that. That's as much as a hunk of rotting meat like you can hope for."

"You're wrong. Mother will choose me."

"Keep telling yourself that. Don't bother me again." Enver slammed the door shut and headed back to bed.

XXX

Waldo finally found her shortly after the horrible ball of fire had left the sky and it was beginning to darken. Alice had another camp fire going. There were two skewers over the flames, each with a small animal speared through. The scent of the cooking meat was making his mouth water.

Alice was just sitting by the fire as he approached her. Waldo was not picking up any emotion from their bond. He couldn't tell if she was happy or still upset, only that whatever she was feeling now was not felt strongly.

"I knew you were coming, I could tell right where you were, like when you were in the river."

Waldo nodded. "If it weren't for the bond I don't think I would have found you at all."

"I suppose it's a good thing we can always find each other."

Waldo came to a stop ten feet away from her.

She was just sitting there in the tall grass eying him. She didn't look or sound angry; she also didn't seem very pleased to see him.

"I don't know how to deal with you. I've seen the way my mother handles her familiar and I thought that was proper. I thought I was treating you well, but you acted as though I was insulting you. I would like us to have a good relationship, but I am not sure how to manage that."

175

"I guess that's fair, I'm new to this too and I suppose I'm not sure how to handle you either. I want us to be close too darling." She motioned toward the fire. "Are you hungry? The squirrel should be about done."

"Sure."

He took one of the skewers. The animal appeared to be staring back up at him. Having been at a dinner table with Walter however he did not have a squeamish stomach. He bit into one of the legs and tore off some of the flesh. The meat was a bit chewy, but tasted good. As hungry as he was he was just glad to be able to eat something.

"It turns out it's very hard to make a fire. It was much more trouble without your help."

"Then next time I'll be sure to help."

The two of them ate together quietly.

"Please don't compare me to your mother," Alice said between bites. "No woman wants to hear that."

"My mother is the most powerful necromancer in Alteroth as well as one of its greatest beauties. Comparing you to her is no insult; on the contrary you should feel honored."

"That is not the point. What girl wants to think her husband is matching her against his own mother? It's completely embarrassing. Please don't do it again."

"All right."

Alice fidgeted a bit. "When I asked you before about… you know. I was just hurt by what you said. That's all. To be told by your husband that you are not beautiful, I wasn't expecting to hear that."

"When did I ever say you weren't beautiful? The only thing I said was that your breasts were nice."

Alice narrowed her eyes and Waldo felt her anger rising again through their bond.

"How do you expect me to act when you say such hurtful things? I happen to be a succubus, the incarnation of lust! I am willing to give myself to you completely and forever. Can't you at least pretend to find me attractive?"

"What are you talking about? Of course you are beautiful to me! You are as lovely as a river of fire flowing through blackest night. Your beauty is so complete and obvious I didn't think it needed to be commented on."

She blinked. "That's... very sweet of you to say. Do you mean it?"

"I do. I think you are lovely. Isn't it obvious?"

"From a lot of men, yes. From you, no."

Waldo shrugged. "I apologize for not being as apparent as most men."

For some reason Waldo could not begin to understand that bought a giggle from her. "That's all right darling, I like that you're different."

She got up from where she was seated and came over to him. Without warning she placed a kiss on his cheek and settled in next to him, laying her head on his shoulder and wrapping herself about his arm.

"You really are very strange," she whispered. "But I like you."

She felt warm and comfortable snuggled up against him.

"I like you too Alice."

In response she squeezed his arm a little.

"Let's try and find the road again tomorrow."

"Yes darling."

Chapter 15

Different Dances, Different Offerings

That night Waldo fell asleep with Alice by the fire. They had no blankets, so the two of them simply laid down in the grass. She'd put her head on his chest and rested against him.

"We need to keep each other warm. We're married so this is all right. It's normal."

It was summer time and the night was warm. With the fire going it was actually pleasant.

Awkwardly he slid an arm around her. "I suppose it is. Good night Alice."

"Good night darling."

He closed his eyes and fell into a deep and peaceful sleep.

XXX

In Castle Corpselover

Walter was seated in his usual place, to his mother's left. Directly across from him was an empty chair.

On his plate was a live suckling pig with its legs and snout tied with twine. The animal struggled and twisted against its binds. Even with its mouth tied shut it gave off high pitched squeals.

Normally this would have added to Walter's appetite. He enjoyed seeing the terror in his victims, whether it was a pig or a human slave. Tonight though, all his focus was on the empty seat in front of him.

"Is something wrong?" Lilith asked. She was calmly eating a steak and lightly sautéed mushrooms. She was used to Walter's eating habits and the helpless animal's cries bothered her not at all.

"Why am I still on your left?"

Lilith took a sip of red wine before answering. "I think you know why."

"Waldo is never coming back, he is a dead man."

"A dead man? Interesting choice of words considering the source."

"Are you making fun of me mother?

"No, I just think you should be a little less certain about things. Your brother is alive and well, and I have every hope he will return one day. Until then, or until I am certain he is gone, that seat," she nodded to her right. "Belongs to him."

"When Waldo dies, what then?"

"Don't ask stupid questions. The answer is obvious."

Walter directed a furious glare at his mother. She had no trouble at all meeting it.

"You won't choose me will you? Even though I would be your last surviving child, you won't make me your heir."

Lilith gave an annoyed shake of her head. "The dead cannot rule the living. You know that. There are laws that even I cannot break."

"Would you if you could?"

"You are starting to annoy me."

"You broke one of the rules for Waldo. You're not supposed to give someone coin when they set out on their First Quest. You didn't do it for me but I know you did it for him."

"I didn't do it for any of my other children either. You and the others went out on normal First Quests. Since the Council cheated I did too. I did the best I could for Waldo like I did for you and the others."

"That's not true! You could give me what I deserve, what's mine!"

"Lower your voice when you speak to me."

Walter sat back and obediently did so. "Yes mother."

Lilith spoke quietly while checking her own mounting anger. "I did the best I could for you. When I found your body I sewed up the hole in your chest where your heart had been torn out. I washed your corpse and wrote the runes on your skin with my own blood. I offered up a sacrifice and called upon the Dark Powers to return your soul. I saw you open your eyes and live again. You are still able to use some magic and retain most of your memories. You can think and feel. You are a superb zombie, but you are a zombie all the same. You cannot father a child. You cannot work the deeper magics. You cannot take my place upon the Council. I have already given you all that I could; do not ask me for any more."

Lilith returned her attention to her meal.

Walter got up from his seat and left.

XXX

When Waldo woke the next morning Alice was no longer at his side.

181

She had the fire going again and a couple fish already speared and cooking.

"Good morning darling." She said cheerfully. "There's a little stream over in that direction if you're thirsty or want to wash up."

"Morning," he said yawning. He could see the horrible ball of fire was already up in the unnatural blue sky. "I think I'll do just that."

Wandering off about fifty feet he found the stream. It was only five feet wide and could easily be walked across. Kneeling down he cupped his hands and drank as much water as he could and then washed his face.

I don't have any waterskins so I can't bring any water with me. He also didn't have a blanket if the night was cold. He didn't have any spare clothes. Not to mention he felt almost naked without his robes.

When he came back to the fire he and Alice sat down together and began to eat.

"We need supplies." Waldo told her. "If we're going to travel we are going to need more than just the clothes on our backs."

"That's true enough. There are plenty of stores back in Stratford, but by now I'm sure everyone is talking about me." She gave a slight shudder. "I don't think we should go back there."

"No, that wouldn't be wise. Where would be the next closest place?"

"There's a small village about five miles up the road from Stratford called Fall River. We may be able to buy what we need there."

"Buy or steal."

"Steal?" Alice said scandalized.

Waldo nodded.

"Do you really want to do that sort of thing?"

"Don't be ridiculous. I'm a Dark Mage, of course I steal. In a sense that's the whole point of going out on quests; to take all that you can and bring it back with you."

"I always thought quests were about facing danger in order to perform noble deeds. Slaying dragons, rescuing princesses, recovering holy relics, you know, that sort of thing."

"Knights may have those sorts of quests, though I'm willing to bet they're not as altruistic as they pretend. For us the quests have nothing to do with noble deeds. They are about proving your strength and bringing back treasure."

"Then why did you give Elsa all that gold to save me?"

"It seemed simpler than trying to overpower her and steal you away. I was bringing you with me no matter what. In any case, you are much more precious to me than a hundred pieces of gold."

Alice's cheeks blushed slightly. "I think that is the sweetest thing anyone has ever said to me."

She began twisting from side to side.

Waldo saw her reaction and felt a sense of pleasure through their bond. If she was happy he was glad, though for the life of him he couldn't guess why.

"We should set out to find the road." He glanced about. "So which direction should we go?"

"West."

He paused and looked around again. "Which way is west?"

"Can't you tell just by looking at the morning sun?"

"No."

Alice snorted a laugh.

"This is not funny."

"I'm sorry darling; I'm just surprised that someone so smart wouldn't know something so obvious."

"I can tell you about monsters of all types and about various forms of magical theory. I am well versed in history, math, and the sciences. I can explain to you why the sun circles the earth. I can make a love potion guaranteed to steal away any heart or make a ward strong enough to hold back an army of the undead."

"You just can't figure out which way is west."

"Navigating through the wilderness was not a part of my education." He said with as much dignity as he could muster.

"Might have been good to learn before going off on a quest. It might help with not getting lost in the woods."

"I had a map."

Even a map needs you to know which way is north. Not wanting to hurt his feelings she decided not to say that aloud and pointed. "West is this way."

Together the two of them started to make their way through the wood.

"Darling, there's something I'm wondering about, though I'm almost afraid to ask."

"What?"

Alice began pulling on her hair. "Ah, the other day, when you compared a part of my body to your mother's. You've, ah, never actually, I mean except when you were a baby of course, you haven't really…"

"Alice what are you trying to ask me?"

"You've never actually seen your mother's breasts, right? I mean not directly, right?"

"Well that's a silly question."

She breathed a huge sigh of relief.

"Of course I've seen them."

Waldo went another seven steps before realizing he was on his own. Turning around he saw Alice standing there with her jaw open and a look of horror on her face. "WHAT?"

He sighed. "You're not going to run away again are you? I only saw them during the holidays."

Her lips twisted. "Holidays?"

"What? Don't your people celebrate the Solstices?"

She just stared at him. "What do the summer and winter solstice have to do with you seeing your mother's breasts?"

"How do you celebrate them?"

"What does that have to do with anything?"

"Please just humor me."

"For the summer solstice we have an outdoor festival with feasting and games and we have a special dance around a pole with long strips of ribbon attached to it."

"Do you dance naked?"

"Who dances naked in public?! Even soiled doves only do that sort of thing behind closed doors."

"I see, so your culture has a prohibition on nudity; very close minded. What do you do for the Winter Solstice?"

"We build a bonfire and sing to the Earth Mother Terrasa, beseeching her to return and bring life back to the land. We also bring offerings to the graves to remember the dead. Well most folk do, I don't have any family so I never had any graves to visit."

"Offerings," Waldo nodded. "We do that too. So you brought criminals to be offered up in sacrifice?"

"Criminals? What are you talking about? We bring offerings; bread, cakes, nuts things like that."

"I see, well it's a good idea to feed the undead, however they prefer flesh. Especially if it's still living. If you're not going to give them any criminals you should bring pigs or goats."

"There are no undead! Ick! It's symbolic! It's a way to show the spirits that they have not been forgotten."

"It just sounds like a huge waste of food to me."

Alice didn't appreciate his mocking the customs she had grown up with. "Well what do you do?"

"Well for the Summer Solstice our traditions are a bit similar. Each of the Seven Families gather together and have a feast that includes special ginger cakes with ground wolfsbane mushrooms."

"Wait a minute! Wolfsbane is poisonous!"

"Only if consumed raw. If you boil them the mushrooms give you a powerful mind altering effect. They will take you to places you never imagined. The very first time I ate the ginger cakes I imagined I was a raven flying free high above the castle. It was amazing."

Alice did not know what to say.

"After the feast we would go into the courtyard and light a bonfire. We would then undress and have the slaves cover us in oil and paint ceremonial images on our skin. Then they would play drums and chant as we danced about the fire crying out like savages to the night. Our minds and souls completely free and one with nature and the darkness. You cannot begin to imagine how liberating it is! Casting away the civilized mask and returning to the primal. That's when I saw my mother naked, as we all danced about the fire howling like wild beasts."

"You danced around naked?! Where people could see you?" Alice was scandalized. Not even Elsa and the women who worked for her would ever go that far. Even soiled doves had their limits.

"It's very liberating. Especially when you've had the ginger cakes and your mind has been opened."

"It sounds absolutely barbaric."

"Which is what makes it so much fun."

Alice closed her eyes and shook her head. "What would you do for the Winter Solstice?"

"Again, our custom is a bit similar to yours. We would make an offering to the Dark Powers to renew he land. We would force any criminals or prisoners we had to fight each other to the death until only one remained."

"You made men kill each other?" Alice asked horrified.

"They were only criminals and would have been executed anyway. This way their deaths had some meaning."

"I suppose you at least let the last one go free right?"

"Don't be ridiculous. Who would set a criminal free? The survivor we fed to the zombies, they deserved a treat too. It was a holiday after all."

Alice just stared at him.

"So I hope everything is cleared up now."

"I think I'll stop asking questions for a while."

XXX

They again set off in search of the road.

As they went Alice spotted something from the corner of her eye. It was a color that did not belong in a summer landscape.

She saw a tree whose bark and leaves were white as snow.

Instinctively she stopped and drew a circle above her heart.

"What is it?"

Alice pointed out the solitary tree. "A soulwood."

188

Following her finger he immediately noticed it. Waldo's reaction was he opposite of Alice's. "How interesting."

To her utter consternation he headed straight towards it.

Chapter 16

A Question Of Trust

Waldo walked right up to the soulwood as Alice held back.

"You shouldn't go near it." Alice told him and again drew a circle over her heart.

Waldo stopped right in front of the soulwood and got a close look at it.

The bark was white as bleached bone, as were the drooping tear shaped leaves. Except for the color the tree was anything but impressive. Its trunk was slender enough that he could have wrapped his arms around it and easily clasped his hands together. Only five branches stretched out like frail fingers from a withered hand. From each branch the large flat leaves hung limply. There were too few leaves, and so the tree had a bare look to it even in the summer. From the ground to the highest tip of the tallest branch was only about fifteen feet.

The soulwood's trunk was twisted like a man trying to stoop though a mine shaft. Rather than growing straight it twisted to the right with one of the branches growing parallel to the ground, the other four reaching to the sky.

There were many knots and divots in the bark that resembled faces. Seeing a soulwood up close for the very first time it was easy to understand why the uninitiated believed the stories that they did.

He took out one of his two slim knives from a boot. He began hacking off some of the bark.

"What are you doing?!" Alice cried aghast.

"Soulwood bark can be used in a number of mind control potions. Outside of Avalon these trees are exceedingly rare. There's no way I'm missing the chance to collect such a precious ingredient."

"But everyone knows that the souls of the condemned are trapped inside of them!"

"That is superstitious nonsense,"

"You don't believe the souls of the dead can be called back to Earth?"

"No, as a matter of fact I know that can be done. However it requires a special ritual, a sacrifice, and the assistance of a Greater Power. It also requires a container for the soul such as the original body, a doll, a suit of armor, or a mirror. Souls have to be forced back to this Earth; they do not return naturally or by choice. This tree has some magical properties, but so does wolfsbane or mandrake; it has nothing to do with human souls."

To Alice everything touching a soulwood or the summoning back of souls was forbidden. That Waldo not only knew about such things but found them mundane made her worry. "Darling when you talk like that you scare me."

He stopped and looked back at her over his shoulder.

"Thank you! It makes me happy to hear that!"

He went back to carving off some more bark and stuffing the strips into his pockets.

"By the way, when I get my hands on a vial or glass container with a stopper I am going to need to make you cry." His pockets were filled to bulging. He carefully began to exam the stunted branch that was near the ground.

"Why would you want to make me cry?"

"The tears of a succubus are the core ingredient to making an incredibly powerful love potion."

"…"

Satisfied, Waldo took his knife and began sawing through the branch.

"What are you doing now?"

"I am going to make myself a new wand."

XXX

In Castle Corpselover

Walter carefully inspected the runes he had chalked into the floor. It was a complex enchantment, but not one that required a large amount of mana. When he'd been alive this had been child's play. Now it represented the absolute limit of his magical abilities.

If Walter had allowed himself to just stop and consider the situation honestly, he would have to admit that everything his mother had said to him was true. She had done the best for him that she could. As a zombie, still having most of his memories and the ability to work any magic at all was verging on the miraculous. After his death, being granted any sort of existence was a mercy he certainly did not deserve.

If he could have admitted this to himself, he might have tried to find satisfaction in the small pleasures his situation granted him.

But Walter had never been one for introspection even when he was alive. Now that he was mostly dead he didn't want to see things rationally. He wanted to hate, and to blame, and to pretend he could still get the thing he wanted most.

"Grandfather, will you come and talk to me?"

The chalked runes gave off the slightest glow.

Walter felt strength drain from his body. Even this minor spell was demanding for him.

The runes were drawn around a circle. The air a couple feet above the floor shimmied and warped. The barest outline of a skull took form. Its shape was made of shadow and was just visible. If you looked away and looked back you might not see anything there at all.

"Is that you Walter?" The skull's jaw moved and a rasping voice could be heard.

"Yes, it's me grandfather."

"Well this is a surprise. I haven't seen you since I ripped out your heart and ate it."

"I remember."

"How are you?"

"I'm a zombie."

The shadowy skull nodded. "Yes, I'd heard that. How is your mother?"

"Same as always I suppose; clever, powerful, and ruthless."

"Ah, it makes a father proud, though I still do have hopes of eating her someday."

"If you tried she would destroy you."

"Yes, likely she would."

Walter glared hatefully. "I should curse you for what you did to me."

"The dead cannot cast or be effected by curses."

"I hate you."

"I'm not surprised; I did eat you after all."

"Why did you betray me? We had an agreement. I gave you access to the castle so that you could kill mother for me."

"That plan was never going to work. Unlike you, my daughter was never a fool; the castle certainly has other defenses against me. I could never have taken her by surprise."

Walter stared hard at the mocking skull. "Then... from the start? You were planning to betray me from the very start?"

"Why are you so surprised? You were planning to betray your mother. Did you think you were the first in the family to ever do something like that? Do not complain. We all deceive and betray to get the things we want. I was just far better at it than you."

"I trusted you!"

"For that alone you deserved your fate."

Despite his anger Walter knew that was true.

'*Trust is a dagger pointed at your own heart.*' One of the many sayings he had learned growing up. He had never been one to trust others, but Walter had also never had much patience. He'd been forced to wait as all those in front of him had died and he was heir.

Being heir though was not enough. His mother was at the height of her powers and looked to have many, many more years ahead of her. He had been impatient and unwilling to bide his time.

194

Walter had also been too aware that he was not powerful enough or devious enough to remover her on his own.

So he had contacted his grandfather and made a pact with him. He was to arrange for him to enter the castle and eliminate his mother. In the end though Walter had been the one betrayed.

"I should have been head of the family."

"You were never strong enough or clever enough for that. Just as importantly you lacked patience. Your mother would not have removed you. You had time to grow your strength and lay your traps. You should have waited for your moment, even if that meant waiting for years. That is how a true Dark Mage would have acted. Instead you turned to me to solve things for you. You trusted me and put yourself in a position of weakness." The skull shook from side to side. "You were never fit to rule the family."

"I will rule the family!"

The skull's jaw opened and closed in laughter. "Even in death you remain a fool. I see you have learned nothing."

"I've learned a few things grandfather. For instance I know where Waldo is questing, the last living child of your daughter Lilith. Would you be interested in that information?"

"So that's why you contacted me. Once again you want me to do what you are too weak to."

"Do you want the information or not? Your last grandchild is wandering about vulnerable."

The shadowy skull chuckled.

"Tell me."

XXX

Tramping through the woods Waldo was patiently whittling down a foot long piece of soulwood.

"Is that really safe darling?"

"No ghosts are going to start haunting me if that's what you mean."

"You're really not afraid?"

"A Dark Mage is never afraid."

"You know you're not a good liar darling."

Part of making a contract meant being free to share truths with your familiar that you wouldn't with anyone else. Even if they hated you, the binding meant they were yours.

Usually, Waldo thought.

'Trust is a dagger pointed at your own heart.' Trust did not come easy to him, but she had saved his life and was bound to him. It was hard, but he would try and be as honest with her as he *could*.

"All right, I fear a great many things. Carving a wand isn't one of them though. White Mages prefer to use soulwood for their wands. While it's not as good as using a thigh bone it should be a decent substitute for now."

"Your old wand was from somebody's bone?" She asked with obvious revulsion.

Waldo nodded. "It was a birthday gift from my mother, she carved it herself."

"Don't expect anything like that from me."

Chapter 17

The Greater Evil

"Alice Corpselover. Mrs. Alice Corpselover. Mrs. Corpselover. Lady Corpselover."

"What are you doing?"

The two of them were on the road heading north. They had already gone a few miles and it was getting towards midafternoon.

"Practicing, I never had a last name, I wanted to see what it was like. I always dreamed about getting married and taking my husband's name. Though I have to admit I never imagined it would be something like Corpselover."

"Corpselover is a proud and honored name known in every corner of Alteroth."

"Of course it is darling, and when we are in your country I will be more than happy to use it. Until then though maybe we should go by something else? It might make things a little easier if you didn't tell people you were a Corpselover."

Alice saw his back stiffen and knew instantly what his answer would be.

"No."

"Is it because you don't want to be dishonest?"

"Don't be ridiculous, if anything I need to practice that. Telling convincing lies is a very important skill."

"So you actually want to be a liar?"

"No, I want to be a *convincing* liar. Any idiot can tell the truth. It requires skill, a good memory, and a talent for improvisation to invent a story and make people believe it."

"Everyone lies darling, but I don't think I've ever heard anyone be as enthusiastic as you."

He shrugged. "We all have room for improvement."

"Well since you don't object to lying why don't you just give people a fake name?"

"I want them to know who I am. I want the name Waldo Corpselover to fill my victims with dread. When I return home I want to leave behind a reputation, not only for myself, but for my clan as well."

"I see." She let out a sigh.

"What?"

"I didn't say anything."

"You obviously want to though."

She smiled at him. "You're starting to sound like a husband."

"I am your master not your husband."

"I will remember you said that the next time you need directions."

"What are you thinking?"

"Well… I was just wondering why men always want to pretend to be something they're not. You talk about doing terrible things but you're not that sort of person. You don't have an ounce of cruelty in you."

"What a terrible thing to say! How can you even say that when we've only known each other for two days? There are a lot of things about me you don't know."

"That's true darling, just like there are things about me that you don't know. Being a barmaid though, you learn how to see through the lies and empty boasts people love to spew. Every barmaid is an expert at separating the real from the fake, and I can see clear to a man's heart. Most men pretend to be what they're not. Cheaters want to tell you how faithful they are, even as they're trying to get you into bed. Cowards talk about being brave. The dishonest will thump their chests and swear they are truthful." She smiled at him warmly. "You always want to talk about how evil you are."

"I am evil! I am evil to the core!"

"Of course you are."

"You are making fun of me."

"Am I?" Alice asked sounding much too innocent.

"I am a Dark Mage. Obviously I am a frightening and horrible man."

"No you're not. Even if I have only known you this short time, it's obvious that you are kind and gentle and very, very caring. You are a good man."

"I can't believe you would say something that terrible to me."

Alice sighed and gave a weary shake of her head. "Fine then, since you are so evil just how many people have you killed?"

Waldo looked about. "None."

"What sort of things have you stolen?"

"My family is the richest in Alteroth. All my needs were attended to and I had a host of servants to look after me."

"In other words you have never stolen anything in your life."

"Well… not yet, but I am going to."

"You mentioned before that you can't do, ah what was it, necromagic?"

"Necromancy," he corrected. "And no I can't, I have no talent whatsoever for it."

"Right, so even though you are a Dark Mage and all, you have never made skeletons or undead or anything like that. Right?"

"True."

"I think we've established you're not much of a liar. So just what is the most evil thing you have ever done?"

Waldo was surprised by the question and needed a moment to think.

"When I was a child I cared openly for some of my servants."

"How is that evil?"

"It caused Enver, the vampire I told you about, to kill them right in front of me. Causing the deaths of servants isn't much of an evil I know, but it's the worst I've done so far."

"Did you do it deliberately to try and have them killed?"

"No, and once I understood it would always happen I stopped being kind to any of them."

"Did you… did you enjoy seeing them killed?"

Despite it having been so long ago the memory made his stomach turn. "No, I never enjoyed it. I have never liked seeing anyone die, not even the slaves or the sacrifices. It's one of my weaknesses. Mother has told me that it will be different when it's someone I hate. She swears it is one of the great joys in life." He paused. "I think I would enjoy killing Enver."

"My darling, please don't take this the wrong way, but your family sounds monstrous."

"Thank you."

"That wasn't a compliment! Can't you see that you're a good man and that everything you've been taught is wrong?"

Waldo shook his head. "I like you Alice, but you know nothing of what it means to be a Dark Mage or one of the Seven Great Families. You cannot raise a wolf to be a sheep. I was raised to be a wolf that preys upon the sheep. I will admit that I may be a poor wolf, but that doesn't mean I want to be a sheep."

"What if you were born a sheep though and were raised as a wolf?"

"That is not the case. I am a Corpselover and we are all wolves."

"But what if…"

She was interrupted when a small furry brown creature with long deformed hears hopped out onto the road.

"Gah!" Waldo leapt back and took another couple steps away from the horrid little thing.

Seeing his reaction Alice laughed. "You're kidding right? You're scared of a rabbit? Some wolf you are."

"I am not scared! I just think it's a disgusting beast with its ears and twitching nose."

The rabbit was patiently waiting in the middle of the road eying them both.

Alice dropped slowly to her knees and motioned towards it. "Come here little bunny, come here cute little mister bunny."

"Alice what are you doing?"

The rabbit hesitated before hopping over to her.

"That's a good Mr. Bunny!" She expertly picked up the rabbit and held it against her chest with one arm and she slowly petted it with her free hand. "What a good bunny you are."

"Alice we are not keeping it as a pet."

"Oh, I know that darling."

She put her hand by the rabbit's neck and gave a sudden sharp twist.

There was a clear snap. The rabbit gave a twitch and then went limp.

"I just took care of dinner. The pelt will also be worth at least five copper traks."

Waldo stared at her in surprise.

"Do you not like rabbit? It's good meat."

"You just killed it."

"So? I also killed the squirrels and fish we ate. You know, since you've never killed anything, does that make me more evil than you?"

"I guess I'm surprised that you could kill so easily."

Alice smiled at him. "It's just a rabbit. I think you'd be surprised at the kinds of things I am willing to do for you. A good wife takes care of her husband even if it means doing things that are unpleasant."

Waldo took a good look at the lifeless rabbit.

"Good to know."

Chapter 18

Shopping Trip

Alice borrowed one of his knives.

She slit open its belly then reached in with her hand to yank out its guts and other organs. Alice then skinned it and hacked off its head. When she was done she tied the animal's carcass to her hip.

All the while singing a happy tune.

Waldo was no stranger to bloodshed or sudden death. The fact Alice had killed an animal disturbed him less than the casualness of it. Somehow, given her shyness and innocence, he had come to assume she would have a very delicate nature about such things.

Clearly he'd been wrong.

As they continued down the road he whittled the piece of soulwood as his mind wandered. Even if it had surprised him, having a succubus who didn't mind killing could only be a good thing. There was no doubt that there would be killing in his future. That was something every Dark Mage took for granted. He was unusual in that he had never taken a life and never felt the desire to do so. (With the exception of Enver.) That didn't mean he was unwilling. He wouldn't take any pleasure in it, but he would do it when it was called for. Just as he was willing to steal should the opportunity arise.

As his knife sliced off another thin sliver of wood he thought about just what it would be like and how it would happen.

The spells currently at his disposal were a long way from lethal. Even if he still had his spellbook and his full complement of magics it would not have been much better.

That meant he would have to use Alice as his weapon. He remembered the long lethal claws she'd displayed when in her true form. Recalled just how easily they had sliced through his robe and straps. He could easily imagine what they would do to flesh.

"You're really good at that."

"Hmmm?"

"Your carving, it's starting to look like a wand. How did you learn to do that?"

"Making magical items is another of the skills I was taught growing up. It's really not hard, so long as you have a steady hand and patience. I have always been very good with my hands."

"Maybe I'll have you help me in the kitchen some time."

"Kitchen work is for servants."

Alice pretended not to have heard him. "So will you be able to make it work? Even though you don't have your spellbook will you be able to make it work like a regular wand?"

"Probably, wands are just focus items. They don't require a specific enchantment to activate."

She looked at him questioningly and it was obvious she had no idea what he meant. Sighing he began to explain.

"Most magical items are divided into two types; focus and effect. Focus items such as wands, rods, and staves act as an extension and magnifier of a mage's own power. They focus magical energy much the same way a lens will focus light. They tend to become very personal after a long period of use. They will match their master's mana exactly, so that another mage may not be able to use the item at all, or else use it only a fraction as well."

"Sort of like having a favorite carving knife that fits perfect in your hand?"

"I suppose. The same way only certain people can use magic, only certain materials can be used as a focus." He frowned at the piece of wood in his hand. "To be honest, I'm not sure why I'm even bothering with this. Soulwood is ideal for White Mages. They say in Avalon they keep whole groves of soulwood trees just for that. I could barely use the wands my mother gave me, so I don't imagine I'll be able to use this at all."

"Why are you making it then?"

"A mage is supposed to have a wand, just as he should have robes and a spellbook. Even if it's worthless, I'd at least want it for appearance sake until I can make a proper replacement. That may take a while, until I can get my hands on the necessary material."

"Is it hard to get?" Alice asked. "As hard as soulwood?"

"In Alteroth no, here it might be more difficult."

"What is it you need to get?"

"It requires a bone from someone who was able to cast magic, preferably a thigh bone."

"Ick! You use human bones?"

"Usually, but not always, any creature able to cast magic will usually work. Elven, half elven, okuri bones will all work just as well. Obviously sprites and fairies are too small to be practical. It has to be a creature able to actually cast spells, monsters with magical abilities like medusa or unicorns won't work. Wands made from dragon bone though are said to be the most powerful of all."

Alice stared at him. "The wand you had before. Where did it come from?"

"My mother gave it to me as a gift, she carved it herself. It was made from the thigh bone of Caston Poisondagger. He was an old rival of hers and she saved his bones especially to make wands for me and some of my siblings."

"And you were all right with that?"

"Why wouldn't I be? He was a powerful wizard and his bones made excellent material."

"But… but… how could you be okay with touching a dead person's bones? Didn't it disgust you?"

"Doesn't it disgust you to have a corpse tied to your hip?"

"This is just dinner."

"Well it was just a wand."

He went back to carving.

Alice did not think to ask him about the other sorts of magical items.

XXX

At last they arrived at Fall River.

To Waldo it reminded him of the villages he had passed through on his way to Stratford. The main difference was that the locals here did not show him the reverence he was due. Most of them were staring at Alice and didn't seem to notice him at all. Since he wasn't in his robes he could understand that.

There were a few dozen homes scattered about like toadstools. He recognized an Inn and a blacksmith shop slapped up against it. Near it was a squat store front with a faded front porch and a sagging straw roof. In front of the door was a crude wooden sign with no words but the images of a barrel and hammer carved into them.

Alice promptly pointed to it. "That will be the general store. I'll go and buy what we need. I should be able to trade my rabbit fur while I'm here too."

"Taking care of the supplies is the master's responsibility." Waldo held out his hand. "Go ahead and give me the coins and I will take care of this."

Alice smiled at him.

"No," she said flatly. "Darling, don't take this the wrong way, but you're not very good with people, and I don't think you'd know how to bargain. I'm used to dealing with all sorts of folk. Just wait here and I will take care of this."

"But I..."

"Don't talk to anyone, and for goodness sakes don't tell anyone that you're a Dark Mage or what your last name it. The river here isn't too deep, but I'd rather not have to rescue again."

"But I'm the..."

"Just stay here and don't cause any trouble, I should be right back."

"But..."

Alice began to sashay towards the store, putting a very deliberate swing to her hips. The men who were out all stared at her, oblivious to all else.

208

"But I'm the master." Waldo said to no one.

XXX

He waited for about twenty minutes or so.

A couple men came up to him and politely inquired about the woman he'd arrived with. When he told them that she belonged to him that pretty much ended their interest. Waldo managed to keep his annoyance under wraps and to avoid telling anyone who or what he was.

When Alice at last came back out she was half buried under a pile of goods. She had bought two back packs, a pair of blankets, water skins, sacks, rope, smoked meat, nuts, and other travel food.

"Did you get any vials or glass bottles?"

"They didn't have anything like that; this is just a little village after all. I was lucky they had as much as they did."

She gave a heartfelt sigh. "This cost me two silver dalters and twenty copper traks, but it was worth it. The store owner tried to charge me five dalters, damn thief, but I smiled and told him how handsome he was and I got the price lowered as much as I could."

He wasn't familiar with what things cost, but he had to admit she'd gotten most of the things they needed and if she had paid less than half of the original price she had done well. *Of course it helps being able to Charm.*

"Good job, I suppose you can make the purchases from now on."

"You're too generous darling. Can I also do all the cooking? Please?"

"Most familiars would be more appreciative when their master grants them a privilege."

Alice rolled her eyes. "Oh, but here's the best part, they had a wizard's robes!"

"What? In a place like this?"

Alice nodded. "A travelling mage left them here to be mended and never came back for them! They are in great condition and I am sure they will fit you!"

Reaching into the pile she had brought out she produced them. Sure enough, they were clearly a mage's robes and about his size too.

They were also as white as snow.

"What do you think?"

He looked at her. "From now on I am doing all the shopping."

Chapter 19

A New Name

They had stopped and made camp a little ways off from the road. Alice had gone through the woods and found some rosemary and sage. While she'd been in the general store she had also bartered some salt. She borrowed one of his knives again and cut the rabbit into pieces and then massaged the herbs and salt. She found a couple flat rocks, set them on the edge of the fire, and put the pieces of rabbit on top of them. The rocks heated up and cooked the rabbit quite nicely.

The savory scent made Waldo's mouth water and he devoured his share. Alice ate hers just as quickly and licked her fingers after she was done. "Walking all day sure builds up an appetite. I'm still hungry."

"That's not because of the walking," Waldo said absently.

"Hmmm?"

Not paying attention to her reply Waldo reached into the pile of supplies and pulled out the robes Alice had bought for him. After a careful inspection he could not deny their quality. The robes were made from wool rather than silk. They would be a little big on him, but not be too bad. Even so he was frowning and held them at arm's length.

"How could you buy me white robes?"

"I'm sorry darling; it must have slipped my mind since they had a huge selection for me to choose from." She shook her head. "It was amazing they had even one! I was sure you'd be happy, what with you complaining about not having robes and all."

"But it's white!"

She pointed to the wand he was still whittling. "Didn't you tell me you were making that because a wizard should have a wand? Even if it doesn't work? I thought robes would be the same. I know they're not perfect, but I figured they were better than nothing."

"This is completely different."

"How?"

"Only another magic user would notice what sort of wand I have. Everyone will notice the color of my robes."

"If you'd been wearing those back in Stratford you wouldn't have gotten tossed in the river."

He opened his mouth to argue, but found he didn't have a basis to. "That's probably true."

He continued to hold the robes out at arm's length.

"Didn't you say you wanted to be a really good liar? Wouldn't pretending to be a White Mage be good practice for that? You can go around fooling everyone and being deceitful, that's pretty evil isn't it?"

That gave him pause. Completely fooling everyone he met would be rather useful. "It might be," he said, dragging out the words. "The issue isn't lying. The problem is that I want to return home with a terrifying reputation. I can only imagine what the other houses will say if they find out I went about in white robes."

Alice smiled at him.

"What?"

"Nothing, I just think it's cute you're scared about what the other evil wizards will say about you. Men are all like that, from the playground to the grave. You never want the other boys making fun of you."

"It's not like that!"

"Of course."

"A Dark Mage's worth is based not only on his abilities but on his personal reputation. Those who never do anything of note are not feared or respected."

Alice nodded. "Sounds like how the ten year olds are always daring each other to go into the woods at night to prove how brave they are."

"You're comparing my interest in building a great reputation to childish games."

"Am I?" Alice asked sounding far too innocent.

"I can just imagine the sort of stories they would tell if they found out."

"You know, you keep going on and on about how evil you are, but from all I've seen and heard the worst thing you've done is dance around naked."

"It's because I haven't done anything that I need to build a reputation."

"Is it really that important? Couldn't you just lie about what you did?"

Waldo shook his head. "Whenever someone returns from a First Quest they are required to go before the Council of Seven and tell of their deeds. You can't lie to them; they will compel you to speak the truth."

"Well is there some rule that you have to wear black robes the whole time?"

"No, and others have gone on their quests in disguise."

"Well that's great! Then there's no problem."

"The people who do that are considered weak. A powerful Dark Mage would never stoop to hiding what he is."

"I see, and you want all the other boys to think you're brave."

"Don't mock me."

Alice brought her hands together in front of her and offered him a most gracious smile. "I wouldn't dream of it, but it seems to me that you could use the robes the same way you want to use that wand. It's not perfect, but it will do. Won't it be easier for you to do all these evil things you have in mind if you can sneak up on folk? Can't you just tell this council of yours that it was a matter of tricking people?"

He thought about it. "I wore white robes to help deceive those whom would be my prey. Hmmm, I could say that truthfully."

He paused and considered. No one was expecting him to survive. So long as he fulfilled the conditions the Council had placed on him his reputation would be made. How much would it really hurt to be in disguise? Even if he was found out, it would not take away from the glory of returning home with a dragon egg.

"I suppose I could wear them," he finally admitted reluctantly. "However, I'll need to change my name. It would be humiliating to tell everyone who I really am while dressed up in this."

"I think that would be a fine idea. Any thought what you'll call yourself?"

He considered. It could not be an ordinary name. It had to be something to call up disgust. A name that would make a powerful impression, something memorable.

Then it came to him.

"Yes, I will take a name that will inspire fear in all those who hear it. A name to terrify and fill common men with dread." A cold hearted smile crossed his lips. "Until I return to Alteroth my name shall be… Waldo Rabbit!"

Alice blinked and only just managed to not snicker. "Waldo Rabbit? Seriously?"

"Too scary?"

With a single finger Alice tapped her chin and pretended to think about it. "Actually darling, I think it's perfect for you."

Chapter 20

Pounce

Following dinner Waldo sat by the fire carving while Alice excused herself and went off into the woods. When she strolled back into camp he glanced up at her.

"You were gone for a while." He started working on his wand again.

"I just felt like taking a short walk."

"We spent the entire day walking. It wouldn't have been for something else would it?"

"Don't be silly. What else could I have been doing?"

"Hunting. You were still hungry and so you went out to find more food."

"That's ridiculous."

He stopped carving. "You have dried blood splattered all over your mouth. I'm guessing whatever you found you ate raw."

"What?" She hurriedly ran back into the woods.

When she returned about fifteen minutes later her face was washed clean.

Alice sat down next to him by the fire. "Don't you dare make fun of me."

"Why would I? The instinct to hunt when hungry is a part of every predator."

216

"Please don't talk about me like I was some rabid dog. Before we met I'd never turned into my true form or killed anything larger than a mouse."

"Did you eat the mouse?"

Her eyelids lowered and Waldo could feel a sharp rise of anger through their bond.

"Forget I asked."

"The worst part is that I am still hungry! I ate half a rabbit and a hedgehog and my belly is still not full!"

"You ate a hedgehog?"

"Don't judge me! I never knew walking all day could build up such an appetite. When I was working at the Inn I would just have a couple small meals each day and that was always enough. I can't help that I need to eat more to make up for all the exercise I'm getting."

"It's not the walking that is giving you your appetite, and no matter how much you eat the hunger will not leave you until we stop in a village."

"What do you mean?"

"You're a succubus." He said simply.

"Yes, I know, wings, tail, horns, and claws; but I've always been one and I've never felt this hungry before."

"That's because you were always surrounded by men."

"What does that have to do with it?"

"You really know nothing about succubi biology do you?"

She was starting to get aggravated. "Look darling, I already told you that I was raised by Elsa, and the only thing she ever said to me about being a succubus was that I was one. Since I don't know anything at all about my race I figured you'd know more. No need to prove to me just how smart you are, so if you know why I am so hungry all of a sudden could you please just tell me?"

Waldo shrugged. "Lust."

"Excuse me?"

"Lust," he repeated. "The reason you have a sense of hunger is because you are no longer the object of lust for a number of men."

"Wait, what? I'm hungry because there aren't men staring at my chest? That doesn't make any sense."

"It does once you understand that you are a succubus and not a human. Different species have different nutritional needs. A wolf cannot survive eating grass and a sheep cannot digest raw meat. On occasion Enver would sit down and eat at a table with my family, that does not mean he could survive on that sort of food. As a vampire he is biologically designed to derive nutrition from blood, and only blood can satisfy him. A Will O the Wisp feeds off of human fear and Blossom Fairies off of human feelings of love or happiness. Succubi feed off of male lust and sexual desire. You can eat food from the table, but just like a vampire without blood, you won't be able to survive long term with only that."

"You mean all those horny guys were actually serving a purpose? Who would have ever guessed?" A thought occurred to her and she looked at him in horror. "Does this mean I'm going to die?"

"Of course not, a human being doesn't up and starve to death just because he missed a few meals. It takes weeks. The same applies to you."

"So I'm going to die, but it's going to take weeks?"

"You're not going to die. We'll stop by some villages or towns along the way and stay long enough for enough men to stare at you until you get your fill."

"Wait, so you want strange men ogling at me? Shouldn't you be more protective of your wife?"

"Familiar, and isn't that better than having you starve?"

Another thought occurred to Alice.

"Why aren't you able to take care of my needs? Isn't a husband supposed to do that for his wife?"

Waldo shrugged. "I guess I don't feel that way towards you."

Alice's jaw dropped.

"It's not that you aren't beautiful," he amended quickly. "It's just that I grew up with sex slaves constantly about, so I'm kind of immune to that sort of temptation. You are very attractive and very important to me; I just don't have those sorts of feelings."

"So you're saying you don't want me?"

"I do. You are more important to me than anything. It's just that I don't look at you as just a sex object."

"Not even a little bit?" She sounded hurt.

"I thought you didn't like being looked at that way."

"Not from strangers, you're my husband; I want you to want me."

"Didn't you specifically say you wanted to wait for us to consummate things?"

Alice's cheeks became rosy and she pressed her index finger together. "Even if I ask you to wait to have the meal I don't mind if your mouth waters."

"I do look forward to it, from what I've seen it's very enjoyable. I just have other things on my mind."

"I see."

Without any warning Alice pounced.

She jumped onto him, knocking him back into the grass. Waldo suddenly found himself pinned to the ground with her holding his wrists. Her tongue had slipped into his mouth and was licking and teasing his own. Her breasts were pressing onto his chest and she was rubbing them back and forth and around.

With her knees she forced his legs wide apart and settled the lower part of her body between them. She was grinding against him. Her whole body was rubbing and pressing on him producing the most delicious sort of friction.

His initial reaction was to tell her to stop, but after a moment he found himself enjoying it and all thoughts of resistance fled his mind.

There had been scantily clad sex slaves in Castle Corpselover; but because of Enver he had never taken advantage of their services. He had also been so devoted to trying to become competent with magic it had left little time for other interests.

Alice's surprise attack was threatening to change all that. She felt very good and he began to want more.

Then, after just a few minutes, Alice let go of his wrists and popped back up to her feet. She was looking down on him with a self-satisfied little smile on her lips. "Well, I'm full now. Good night darling." She ambled off to her blanket.

Still sprawled out on the grass and not sure what had just happened he managed to answer. "Uh, yes, good night."

Waldo was not completely certain, but he suspected Alice might be toying with him.

Chapter 21

We All Have To Start Somewhere

He blew off a bit of shaving and put away his knife. "It's done."

"You finished your wand darling?"

He nodded. "I'm not sure how much good it will do me, but I have a wand now at least. I will still need to sand down the edges a bit and carve some words of power into it."

"What are those?"

"Wands are very personal magical items. It helps to carve words or names into them with a special connection to the user."

"Did your old wand have words carved in it?"

"Yes; 'Corpselover,' 'power,' and 'pride.'"

"How… sweet. Why did you choose those?"

"I didn't. My mother chose the words."

"Will you use the same ones?"

He slipped the wand into one of the deep pockets sewn in his nice white robes. "Probably, but I'll decide for certain later. After we get to Bittford and meet this hedgewizard."

XXX

The two of them reached Bittford early the next afternoon.

Bittford was a fair sized village with close to a thousand people. That made it much smaller than a city like Stratford, but far larger than Fall River had been. At the village center there was an Inn, a couple stores, a smithy and a simple temple. The houses were of lumber or mud brick with thatch roofs. They were unpainted and of a similar, basic design, but looked to be in fair condition.

There were plenty of people out and about and as the two of them came walking down the muddy road folk stopped and stared.

"Interesting," Waldo said.

"What's that darling?"

"The way they gape at me now isn't much different from when my robes were black. I expected them be falling on their knees crying out in adoration."

"Well, even if you have these on, you're still a magic user. It's only natural that people be a little wary."

"So long as they don't form an angry mob that will do."

They went directly to the Inn. No one greeted or approached them. Everyone kept a safe distance. When they stepped inside there was a portly Innkeeper behind a bar and three men in muddy work clothes at one of the tables. All four of them stared at the newly arrived couple.

Waldo cast his eyes about.

"Are you looking for something?" Alice asked.

"I thought all the Inns in this country had women with revealing clothes."

Alice blushed slightly. "We won't ever be visiting a place like that, and please don't ever mention it again."

"Why not?"

"There are just certain things best left in the past."

"You mean like how your breasts are not the equal of my mother's?"

Alice sent him a look of complete disbelief. He could sense a spark of anger rising in her through their connection.

"Can I help you sir?" The Innkeeper asked cautiously from behind his bar.

"My correct title is, 'Master' not, 'Sir'."

The Innkeeper raised an eyebrow.

"Please ignore him," Alice said. "He wants everyone to call him that."

Waldo shot her an annoyed glance. "I don't suppose you have wine here by any chance do you?"

"We have ale," the man answered.

Waldo made a face, one more hardship. "We'll have some then and a meal."

"We have mutton and potatoes and wheat bread."

"That will be fine." Waldo said and sat down at an empty table.

Alice sat down beside him as the Innkeeper went to the back to tell someone to ready the food, before filling two large tankards with a foaming brown liquid.

As this was going on Alice glanced over at the table where the three men were staring.

"Looks like I won't have to worry about being hungry later."

"That's nice," Waldo said absently. He stared down at his drink. The color reminded him of muddy water and it had a wheaty smell to it.

"Could you at least pretend to be upset that there are men lusting after me?"

"That would be like being upset about a wolf wanting to devour a lamb. A sensible person should accept the natural order of things."

"Well it's natural for a husband to be jealous when strangers are eying his wife."

"Shouldn't I take that as a compliment? It's not as though I would be upset if people admired the horse I was riding."

"Now you're comparing me to a horse?"

"It's just an example; obviously you're worth a lot more to me than any horse."

Alice sat there and just stared at him.

"You're planning to kick me aren't you?"

"I am thinking about it."

Waldo frowned at her. "Do you want me to kill them for looking at you?"

"Who said anything about killing them?"

"Well that's a relief. I would have had to use you for that. Killing people for me is a part of your duties as my familiar."

"Wife. Darling, I am not asking you to murder anyone. I don't even expect you to beat them up."

"Glad to hear that."

"I just want you to be jealous."

"So you want me to be jealous, but not to actually do anything about it?"

"Yes."

"Well that's pointless. It's like being thirsty but not trying to take a drink."

"It's not about doing anything; it's about showing that you care."

"By feeling jealousy?"

"Yes."

"Isn't the fact I bought you proof of that?"

"I'm going to kick you now."

XXX

A few minutes later the Innkeeper came to their table with two plates filled with hot food.

"Is there anything I can help you with sir?"

"Can you tell me where to find Roger the hedgewizard?"

"Why?"

"My reasons are none of your business. Do you know where he is or not?"

Alice saw the man stiffen.

Whack!

"Ow!" Waldo began rubbing one of his shins. "You kicked me!"

"Did I?" Alice asked sweetly. "Must have been an accident." She sent the Innkeeper an indulgent smile. "Please forgive my husband's rudeness. There is an important matter we need to meet with Master Roger over. It would be a huge help if you could tell us how to find him."

She looked intently into his eyes.

The man's cheeks turned cranberry red and he tried to suck in his gut. "He lives in the woods a quarter mile west of the village. There's a little path that will take you straight to his door, so you should be able to find it. I can tell you though that he won't go with you. The other two didn't have any luck and you won't either."

"Other two?" Waldo asked as he rubbed his bruised ankle.

"I always heard you White Mages knew what all your sort were about. Two others came to visit him; last one was a couple years ago I think. They wanted to invite him to Avalon but he turned them down. Roger is one of us, and he's not one for putting on white."

Waldo smiled triumphantly at Alice. "See? I told you they weren't to be trusted."

"They?" The Innkeeper asked.

"The other White Mages," Alice said quickly before Waldo could answer. "There are different groups, and ah, uhm…"

"Factions," Waldo provided seeing what she was doing. "We have different philosophies on how to achieve our ultimate goal." Smiling he lowered his voice conspiratorially. "We're trying to conquer the world you know. You shouldn't trust any of us."

"As you say sir." The man replied nervously and scuttled back to his bar.

"Why did you say that?" Alice whispered. "That's only going to cause trouble for us."

"That's fine, so long as it causes trouble for Avalon too. I intend to make the name Waldo Rabbit is feared throughout the land by the time I'm done."

"And you're going to do this by spreading rumors in bars?"

Waldo shrugged. "We all have to start somewhere."

With a shake of her head the two of them began to eat.

Chapter 22

Roger The Hedgewizard

"Will you look at the tits on her?" Edwin said quietly.

He and his two friends were at the Inn, having a few tankards of ale, when a white wizard and his woman came in. They had made a bit of a scene but were now just eating. The three men had trouble taking their eyes off of her.

"Ought to be careful," Marcis said. "I heard her say she was his wife. Don't want to mess with no of them sort."

"Roger's not so bad." Edwin pointed out.

"He is a local sort, not one a them white ones." Marcis said. "Them sort is wise and quick to anger."

"I wanna grab dem tits," their friend Joster slurred. He'd already downed four tankards of ale and his eyes were swimming. He was a big man and used to getting his way.

"Go ahead then, I dare you." Edwin said.

"Ah no." Marcis said softly.

"You dare me fooker?" Joster got up on unsteady legs. "I'll show ya." He began to stumble towards the table where the White Mage and his woman were seated.

"This be a bad idea." Marcis said

Joster paid no attention though and Edwin was clearly anticipating what was about to happen.

The couple didn't notice Joster's lumbering approach until he leaned over and clamped down both hands on the girl's shoulder.

229

Her reaction was immediate.

"Eek!" She yelled at the top of her lungs and smashed a fist into his chin. Marcis and Edwin watched as their beefy friend was launched off his feet and into the air to land in an unconscious heap.

"She took him down in one punch?" Edwin said disbelieving.

"Now that be a healthy gal!" Marcis sounded impressed.

The wizard was still seated with a forkful of food halfway to his mouth. He lifted a hand in the direction of the Innkeeper. "We'll be going now."

XXX

The two of them were headed out of the village in the direction where the local magic user Roger was supposed to reside.

"Did you really have to hit him that hard?" Waldo asked.

 They'd been forced to shovel the rest of their meal down and quickly leave. While Waldo was all for committing crimes to build his reputation, he would rather do so without inciting another mob.

"He grabbed me!"

"I know, but couldn't you have been just a bit more reserved?"

"How would you like it if some fat hairy oaf suddenly grabbed you?" Alice demanded.

"I wouldn't. Well, unless he was a masseuse."

Alice sent him an ugly glare.

"The point is you didn't need to go that far. You are a succubus, even in this form you are a lot stronger than an ordinary human being."

"I can't help it! I have always been that way when men tried to touch me. As soon as my body started to develop Elsa tried to make me one of her girls. When a customer would start to touch me my instinct was to beat him off."

"That's not normal for a succubus."

"Well pardon me for not wanting to be molested! I grew up seeing men as beasts and I didn't want any of them doing those sorts of things to me!"

"You didn't react that way when we first met."

Alice's face blushed slightly. "Well of course not darling, you were my savior, and you wanted to marry me. I'm fine with you touching me; it's just all the other men in the world I can't stand."

"I feel honored. You mean to say whenever a man touches you this is how you react?"

"A woman has a right to defend herself."

"How did you manage working where you were then?"

"Everyone who worked there was a woman. The regulars knew better than to grab. Occasionally there'd be a customer who would grope me, but he never did it more than once. Elsa always threatened to whip me for causing trouble, but the men all still liked me."

"Makes a certain amount of sense, we always want what we can't have."

XXX

They had no real trouble finding the path that led to the hedgewizard's home. It soon took them to a plain cottage with an expansive garden near the edge of the village.

"This must be where Roger lives." Alice said.

"It is." Waldo said with certainty, as his eyes glanced about.

"Something wrong darling?"

"I can sense him inside. All magic users can sense each other. That means he can sense me as well, he should have come out to greet me."

"I'm sure that's…"

She was cut off by a monstrous roar.

Out of the forest a massive green lizard, at least thirty feet long and fifteen feet high, came stampeding. Black smoke puffed from its nostrils, it bore a mouthful of foot long sharpened teeth, and snapped its tail around furiously.

"Is that a dragon?" Alice immediately jumped in front of Waldo to place her body between him and the monster.

"It certainly looks like one." He replied calmly.

"Run darling! I'll protect you!" She was about to transform.

"It's all right. *Descoros.*" Waldo spoke a single word of magic and made a sign with two fingers of his left hand.

Immediately the giant lizard's form began to blur, its roar was muted and as it continued to charge it grew more and more indistinct. Then it was gone.

Alice stood there gaping at the suddenly empty wood.

"Damn it, I was hoping that would scare you off." Out of the building stepped a balding, middle aged man with a wide gait. He was dressed in dirty trousers and an over shirt that was half tucked in.

"The hedgewizard Roger I presume?" Seeing his appearance made Waldo's opinion of him drop even further. "A dragon? Why not something more subtle? Like a giant or an army of goblins"

"It worked on a bunch of bandits." The balding man said with a frown. "Hedgewizard? There's no need to be rude you know, just because I'm not from Avalon doesn't make me less of a magic user than you."

"Sorry, I'm a White Mage, so I always think I'm better than everyone else."

Roger grunted. "First time I've ever heard one of your kind admit to that."

"Uhm, excuse me?" Alice waved her hand to get their attention. "What happened to the dragon?"

"I dispelled it." Waldo said.

"What does that mean?"

Roger gave her his full attention, his eyes slid up and down her figure and then halted on her chest.

"The dragon was an illusion, I was hoping to scare you off. Of course, that was before I got a good look at you. I am Roger the Magnificent, what is your name lovely lady?"

She crossed her arms and made a point to stand behind Waldo. "My name is Alice Rabbit, and this is my husband Waldo Rabbit."

"Husband?" He spared Waldo an envious glance. "You are a lucky man."

"I know, being a White Mage."

Roger raised a perplexed eyebrow while Alice shook her head.

"Well since you are both here why don't you come inside?"

XXX

The inside of Roger's home was no more impressive than the outside. There was a fire pit for warmth and cooking. There was a rickety table with four stools and a pile of furs that served as a bed. The floor was dirt with some straw scattered on top of it.

The slaves in Castle Corpselover live better than this.

When the three of them sat down about the table Roger sat as close to Alice as he could. He kept openly staring at her chest.

"Your illusion was quite good." Waldo said.

"Not good enough obviously. How did you know it was an illusion?"

"It was a dragon."

Roger gave another sour grunt. "Do you even know how to talk to someone without insulting them?"

"No, comes from being a White Mage. By the way do you know we're plotting to take over the world?"

Alice shook her head.

"You're a lot more direct than the other whites I've met. So is this where you start in about, 'unity, justice, and peace'?"

"Do you want me to?"

Roger narrowed his eyes. "I've met two White Mages before, and they both tried to convince me to go to Avalon and study with them. All they would talk about was unity, justice, and peace. They went on and on about how wonderful the world would be one day, once everyone was on their side. No more war, no more poverty or crime. Get rid of all the monsters and all the Dark Mages and everything wrong with the world will be fixed."

"Why do you have to get rid of all the monsters?" Alice demanded.

Roger looked at her in surprise. "You're married to a White Mage, hasn't he explained their philosophy to you?"

"I've tried but she is not very smart. Honestly I just keep her around to warm my bed."

Thump.

Waldo managed to not shout in pain as he was kicked beneath the table.

Not noticing Roger nodded. "Lucky man."

"Yes, that's me, I'm drowning in luck." Waldo tried to rub his shin without making it too obvious.

"If you've come here to try and recruit me the answer is still no. I'm happy right here."

"Really?" Waldo pointedly looked about the cramped, dirty interior. "You obviously have some skill. Why not find yourself a patron who can properly reward you?"

"Because this is my home, and these are the people I've grown up with. I like being able to help them. Just seeing them happy is reward enough."

"No, seriously, why do you stay here?"

"That is the reason."

"Do you rule over them and make them do your bidding?"

"Of course not! They are my neighbors, my friends, when they need my help I am there and they pay me whatever they can. When outsiders come here I'll charge them, but the most important thing to me is the welfare of my village."

"So what you are saying is you take care of these villagers without demanding anything more than the bare minimum from them in return? That you see their wellbeing as your true reward?"

"That's right."

Waldo sighed. "Fine, don't tell me."

"Darling, you're being rude."

"Me being rude? He's the one lying to my face, and not even doing a good job of it."

"You know the other two White Mages who came here were pretty haughty, but you outdo them. I swear you're almost as bad as a Dark Mage!"

"Thank you."

"Are you mocking me?"

Alice saw their host was about to throw them out. Though she loathed doing it, she put a hand gently on top of one of Walton's

236

sweaty paws and smiled sweetly at him while leaning forward just a bit to give him a better view. She was okay with touching men, so long as they did not use it as an excuse to grab onto her.

"Please sir, my husband meant no offense."

Roger's eyed darted to the top of her breasts and he calmed noticeably. "Well I can forgive him lovely lady, but I am still not going to Avalon."

"That is not the reason we came here." Waldo pulled the soulwood bark and shavings from his pockets and placed them on the table in front of Roger. "I am afraid I lost my spellbook. Would you be willing to sell me a couple pages of velum, along with a quill and some ink, so I can write down the spells I still have memorized?"

"You lost your spellbook?" Roger asked with a chuckle. "Only an incompetent would do that."

Waldo frowned. "That's as may be, will you trade me some velum for this soulwood?"

Roger shook his head. "I have some spare velum, but I also have plenty of soulwood too."

"All right, will you sell it to me then? I can pay in silver and copper."

Alice sent her husband a sharp look. They didn't have that much money, and what they had *she* had earned. She was willing to spend some of it for his sake, but did not like the way he was offering to just toss it away. Later on they would have a very long talk about bargaining and negotiating and about just who would handle the money.

It would not be him.

"I don't really need coin, I have enough. Anyway, the people here supply me with the basics." Roger said cautiously as his eyes drifted back to Alice's chest. "I might be open to trade though."

Alice had been dealing with lonely men for years and she immediately caught the tone of his words. She took her hand away and scooted her chair closer to Waldo.

"I have nothing more valuable than the soulwood."

"Well there you have it." Alice said quickly. "We don't have anything else to trade. How about you sell us this stuff? I'm sure we can negotiate a fair price."

Roger swallowed and faced Waldo without meeting his eyes. "Let me have one hour with your wife and I'll give you five pages."

Alice jumped to her feet. "That's disgusting! My husband would never agree to anything like that!"

Waldo nodded and stood. "Done, have your way with her."

"WHAT?!!"

"It's just one hour. Is it asking that much?"

Alice stood there gaping like a fish.

"Enjoy yourself." Waldo gave Roger with a friendly nod, and exited.

XXX

He waited just outside the door.

It took less than half a minute.

"Eek!"

He heard a 'smack' followed by a loud thump. Waldo went back inside, and was not surprised to find Roger laid out like a rug. Alice was standing there glaring at him murderously; from his connection to her he knew she was furious.

"Good," he said cheerfully and went over to the bed and began tossing aside furs. "You search him and I'll start here. He should have a spellbook along with magical supplies and he said he had some money too. We need to go through every inch of this place as quick as we can."

"What do you think you are doing?

"I am robbing him, obviously."

"I don't care about that! How could you agree? He was going to... to..."

Waldo sighed. "Alice, I saw what happens to a man who tries to touch you. I knew what was going to transpire and that there was no chance of anything unwanted occurring."

She blinked. "Oh! I understand! You would never actually let another man have his way with me!"

"Well not for five sheets of velum, he would have to pay a lot more."

"WHAT?!!"

Waldo could feel her rage roaring to new heights. *You would expect a succubus to be more open minded.* "I am kidding of course."

"You had better be." She growled.

"Now could you please search him Alice? We need to rob him and be long gone from this place by the time he wakes."

As he searched there was a smile on his face. The fearsome legend of Waldo Rabbit had begun!

Chapter 23

Stealing For Fun And Profit

They spent about twenty minutes ransacking the place before fleeing. Waldo had insisted they head into the woods to avoid the locals and any possible pursuit Roger might send after them. Tramping through the woods Waldo was humming what sounded like a funeral dirge.

"You know darling, I don't think I've ever seen you in such a good mood."

"Well I never knew just how much fun robbing someone could be." To emphasize the point he held up his newly acquired spellbook. "We should definitely steal more often."

"I'm glad you enjoyed taking everything a man had."

"Yes."

It had been quite a haul. He had discovered jars filled with mandrake, wolfsbane, lotus blossoms, devil's grass, sulfur, ground obsidian, and more soul wood. With those he could make a few potions when he had the time. Almost as valuable, he'd found glass vials with wax stoppers.

"By the way, I still need you to cry."

"Not this again. I am not going to cry just because you tell me to."

"Don't be selfish. Do you have any idea how valuable love potion is?"

"I am not crying."

Waldo stopped and thought for a moment. "You're fat."

"What?"

"I don't think of you as my wife. Your mother probably never loved you. I've always preferred dark haired women."

Alice stared at him.

"Do you feel like crying now?"

"No, but one more word and I'll hit you."

Waldo stopped talking.

He could always make her cry later.

Along with the jars and vials there had been a coin box. You would never have guessed it, but Roger had actually had a lot of money. Not a one of the coins had been gold; the vast majority were copper traks, but there had also been silver dalters, ribs, and wolves. Alice had quickly and expertly counted and separated the coins. The secret hoard had contained one hundred and eleven silver coins and two thousand two hundred and ninety copper ones. It was the equivalent of six gold coins, thirteen silvers, and ninety coppers. (Twenty silver coins to one gold one and a hundred copper coins to one made of silver.) Alice had then put them all in a separate purse and buried it inside her back pack.

On Roger's person they had found a wand. Waldo had seized it and made it disappear into one of his pockets.

The most useful, and to Waldo the most valuable, thing they had taken was the spellbook. It was bound in sturdy brown leather and its pages were all made of yellow velum. More than a third of it was still blank. There had also been pens and ink. When they stopped to rest for the night Waldo would write down all the spells he still had memorized.

In the meantime, he was reading it to see what sorts of spells and formulas it held. Roger's hand writing was a bit sloppy, but not unreadable. As with most spellbooks it contained not only enchantments but also recipes for brewing potions. Listed were cures for minor ailments and pain relievers, a potion of disguises, and a potion of truth telling that looked interesting. Sadly, there wasn't one for making love potion.

The spells themselves were a disappointment.

There was not a single offensive spell listed, nothing that would harm another person, never mind kill them or slowly drain the life from them. What self-respecting magic user went without combat spells? From what he could see almost all of Roger's magic was based around illusion, healing, and weather control. The healing spells would be easy to memorize and might be useful. Creating illusions could come in handy as well. But weather control? How utterly worthless!

Still, since this was the spellbook of a hedgewizard, he was just grateful that it contained anything at all. It would be good to get back in the habit of learning new magic. He would study all of it when he had the time, even the spells he did not expect to ever use.

"Are you really happy about it?" Alice asked.

He closed the spellbook and stopped in order to put it in his back pack. "About what?"

"Stealing. I mean he wasn't a very nice man, but he wasn't much worse than most of my old customers. Was it really right for us to just rob him like we did?"

"I am not sure what you mean. He had what I wanted and so I took it from him. What could be wrong with that?"

"I mean it's wrong to steal. Especially when you take everything someone has."

"So it would have been fine to only take half?"

"Well… no, that would still be wrong, but not as bad as taking everything. I mean don't you feel even a little bit guilty"

Having put the spellbook away he put the back pack on again and started walking. "You haven't forgotten who I am because of my brilliant disguise have you?"

"Trust me darling, that wouldn't be possible."

"Then you should understand that this is what I am here to do. I can't go home again until I have completed all the conditions of my quest. If robbing someone helps me with that then it's what I'll do. Besides, it's fun!"

He really did look happier than she'd ever seen. "Don't you feel even a little bad for Roger?"

"Why would I? This is what Dark Mages do, we take what we want. The whole point of the First Quest is to prove your strength by doing whatever you please. For us, 'do as thou wilt' is the whole of the law."

"Darling, I know what you are and what you believe. A few of the things you've told me have really worried me, but in spite of that I've seen that you're a good man. Have you ever stopped to think that things would be better if you didn't do things like steal?"

"I have a spellbook now, along with a wand, spell components, and all the coins we found. How exactly would I be better off by not stealing?"

"All right, let me try and explain it this way. In this country thieves get whipped and sent to work in the mines."

"Which is why we're going to avoid the roads for a while, I only intend to do things I can get away with."

"Well that makes it all right then."

"Exactly!"

XXX

The two of them were swinging wide around Bittford. Alice had found them some squirrels and they'd already eaten. They were currently sitting around a fire as Waldo was writing in his new spellbook. He'd already written down the spells and potion recipes he clearly remembered.

He was writing a final entry under the heading; Love Potion (?). He knew he had most of the formula correct. If one or two ingredients were missing he thought he could 'improvise'. Even in Alteroth love potion was highly sought after and extremely valuable. In a backward place like this it would be worth even more. Once he got the key ingredient he would definitely try and brew some.

But how do I make Alice cry?

"So where do we go now darling?"

"Middleton. That's where the next part of my quest is." Waldo finished the recipe and carefully blew on what he'd written to help the ink dry.

"So what are you going to do there?"

Waldo glanced at her consideringly. He hadn't told her any of the specifics about his quest yet. Once they arrived she would have to be told. Since there was no way to keep it secret much longer he thought now would be a good time to tell her.

"Part of my quest requires that I make a contract with three monsters. That was the original reason why I came to Stratford and sought you out. There are two more powerful monsters in Lothas that I mean to find and make a contract with."

"What do you mean? When you say make a contract I know you can't mean…"

"I am going to try and find two more familiars who will help me with the rest of my quest."

Alice did not look happy. "You're not going to do the same thing with them that you did with me are you?"

"Yes, I am; I will perform the binding ritual with each of them. I am going to make a contract with them and make them my familiars."

"You can't do that! You're not allowed to have more than one wife! I definitely won't share you."

"Alice, I can't return home without three monsters bound to me. There are also other conditions to my quest; having three Great Monsters serving me will make achieving them easier."

He didn't intend to tell her about those other conditions for a while yet.

Sitting next to him by the fire Alice began to fidget just a bit. "I don't see why you need anyone else. The two of us have done pretty well haven't we?"

"Except for my almost drowning, yes."

"You can't have other wives."

"I've already told you that the binding ritual is not a marriage ceremony, and I promise I will not give anyone any flowers this time."

246

Alice slowly nodded, that did help. It meant he was not going to marry these other monsters. But that didn't completely satisfy her.

The truth was Alice was really enjoying this strange new life of hers. Despite the bad moments she found she really did care for her husband. He accepted what she was, and made her feel normal in a way she never had before. In the short time they'd been together they'd been on the move constantly, traveling and having adventures. She still thought he was very, very strange, but he was a good husband. In his own peculiar way.

What worried her was the thought of things changing with strangers joining them. She did not want other people coming between them. Alice most particularly did not want his attention wandering to any place it shouldn't.

"What sort of monster is waiting for us in Middleton?"

"I don't know." Waldo replied as he took out Roger's wand to give it an inspection. "All I know is that there are two more Great Monsters out there for me to claim, and one of them is in Middleton. Until I met you I wasn't even sure that Enver's map was real."

"Are either of them women?"

"I have no idea."

"Could one of them be a succubus?"

"It's possible I suppose."

"I don't care how beautiful or willing she might be. You better remember a man only gets to have one wife."

In this country maybe. "I will keep that in mind."

He slowly rotated the wand in his hands. There were fifteen words of power carved into it, and all of them looked to be names. He hadn't seen that before. In his family words of power tended to reflect the ambitions and desires of the caster. 'Death,' 'power,' 'strength,' 'cruelty,' and 'mercilessness' were all good examples of what his family would use. The thought of using the names of the people who mattered to you was a radical concept.

With a flick of his wrist he tossed the wand onto the fire.

"What are you doing?"

"Wands are very personal magic items. Even if I had real skill I doubt I would be able to get it to work for me. All magic users know how wands work so it wouldn't even be worth trying to sell."

"Then why did you steal it in the first place?"

"Because Roger could use it. Why would I leave someone I just robbed his wand?"

"Good point." She began fidgeting again. "So, what will you do if it is another succubus we meet in Middleton?"

"I will bind her to my service with a contract, like I did with you." *I will also try and make this one work properly.*

"Does that mean you'll kiss her?"

"That is part of the ritual."

Alice looked at the fire.

When she imagined her precious husband kissing another woman it made her feel surprisingly sad. She didn't want anyone else to ever kiss him.

Without even realizing it she began to cry.

When Waldo saw that he quickly tore open his backpack to pull out the glass vial and stopper.

XXX

In Castle Corpselover Lilith stood before her bedroom mirror and watched as her son tried to capture the succubus's tears as she threatened to hit him.

Lilith couldn't keep herself from laughing. "My son, you really do need to learn how to handle your women."

Chapter 24

A Day At The Office

Lilith had watched each of her children when they had gone out on their First Quests. None of them had ever known, it was important they believe they were on their own. (Which they were, all she could do was watch.) She had seen her eldest and strongest, Roland, die with a sword through his chest. Watched as Gwendolyn had her throat cut. She had begun watching one day to see Kara's body lying stiff and abandoned on the side of a road. Her daughter had been murdered sometime in the night, who had done it and how Lilith never knew.

She never tried to avenge her murdered children, that was not her way. If someone died on their First Quest it was a sign they had been too weak or too careless.

When she had sent Waldo off she held hope that he would return. Despite what most people believed Lilith had always understood that Waldo had strength in him, and a great deal of talent. Hope was not certainty though, and she could not pretend that the odds were not set very heavy against him.

She had been watching when he was thrown into the river and had feared it was the end. Lilith thought she was about to see her last child die. Then she had witnessed the miraculous rescue by his succubus. Since then she had been watching his actions with even greater interest.

"The terrible White Mage Waldo Rabbit." She snorted with a laugh.

Her son had certainly come up with some… unique solutions to his problems so far. The fact he was going about disguised as a White Mage would be looked down upon by the Council and others. Ideally a Dark Mage was supposed to go around openly, relying on his intelligence and his magic to keep him safe. It had however been done before, and there was no rule against it. So far as Lilith was concerned, her son was entitled to use whatever trick he needed to survive.

The fact he had already made a contract with a succubus was a tremendous accomplishment. If this were an ordinary First Quest that by itself would have been plenty. Waldo's familiar had already proven herself extremely useful. She had saved his life, provided his meals, and helped him rob that fool of a hedgewizard.

Lilith did have a few concerns about her though.

Waldo had clearly botched the binding ritual. The succubus was at liberty to refuse direct orders and even physically assault him. Normally that would mean instant disaster. Alice though appeared content to serve.

Lilith found the fact the girl really believed herself to be his wife amusing. No matter what ceremonies Waldo performed in the outside world he would not be married under Alterothan law unless she gave consent. Her son was entitled to take multiple wives, and there was no stigma against taking a monster as one. If her son really wanted this girl to be his wife Lilith would permit it, but Alice was being quite presumptuous to believe a few words spoken in a whorehouse made her the wife of the Corpselover heir.

All that was for the future though, for now all that really mattered was that her son was not only still alive, but actually making progress. Maybe there really was hope.

In the mirror she saw her son rubbing his backside where his 'wife' had just kicked him after collecting some of her tears. With an amused smile Lilith waved her hand before the mirror. The image rippled and vanished, leaving her staring at her own reflection.

"Stay safe Waldo."

XXX

The following morning she had business with the Council.

Enver, as usual, preferred to stay hidden within his room. Walter had been avoiding her for the past few days. No doubt he was roaming through the castle torturing and feeding on some of the slaves. She would leave him be until his mood improved.

The only company she had before setting out were her servants. Most of them, of course, did not dare speak a word to her unless spoken to first. They bathed her, dressed her, and served her breakfast with an absolute minimum of conversation. Some of them were new; some had been in her service for years, yet none of them felt comfortable around her. Their movements were eager and swift, clearly longing to please, constantly anxious to escape her presence.

They were always afraid.

Lilith was happy to see that in the people around her. It was pleasing to know she inspired dread. So far as she was concerned it was the sincerest form of respect.

When her breakfast was complete and the plates and utensils were cleared away her steward approached her. He had been serving the family for over thirty years. He had originally been in the service of her father, back when he was still flesh and blood. Hollister knew her as well as almost anyone, and had served her faithfully for the entire time she had been in power. She trusted him as much as she trusted anyone, which was not very much. Even with him there was no familiarity. He did not presume to joke or act in a friendly manner. He was respectful and formal at all times. He never forgot that no matter how useful he might be to her, he was never anything more than a servant.

"The meeting of the Council is scheduled to begin in half an hour's time Mistress."

Lilith gave a slight nod. "Is my escort ready?" It was a pointless question. She knew they were.

"It is Mistress." He began going over the new business of the day. "We have received an invitation for a wedding to be held in Castle Wormwood in two months' time."

She never attended the weddings of the other houses, they were painfully tedious affairs. The others all knew that of course, but an invitation was expected. Appearances had to be maintained. "Send them my sincere regrets. Who in that brood is getting married anyway?"

"Sygor Wormwood, who is the third son of Gawreth and his third wife Ellen is to marry Tasha Wormwood, daughter of Adam Wormwood and his wife Natalia."

Lilith recognized none of the names. Gawreth was just marrying off another of his sons to some girl in one of the branch families. If you were a member of one of the Seven Great Families you either married someone from your own extended family or someone from one of the other houses. That was one of the ways the Great Families kept exclusive control over everything. If you were not born into one of the houses there was almost no chance of ever gaining entry. The exception was if you could use magic, in which case you could expect to be adopted into one of the seven.

Lilith thought for a moment about her son and his pretty little succubus. Except for the Blooddrinkers, it was rare for an heir to marry a monster. The Blooddrinkers were obsessed with breeding though, and followed their own traditions. It was fine for members of the main families to marry non humans, but it was considered tradition for the designated heirs to only take human wives. She laughed to herself just imagining the uproar it would cause among some of the more conservative families. It might be worth doing just for that.

253

Her laughter caused Hollister to look at her questioningly; he did not however ask her about it.

"There was a cave in at gold mine six last night. The entire work force was likely lost. Early estimates are that it will take at least twelve months to restore production."

Lilith frowned. The loss of the workers meant nothing to her. All the mines used undead; they could stand up to the conditions far better than living men and worked without rest. For simple physical labor like mining, the dead were always much better than the living. (Work that involved any sort of judgment or skill was best left to the living.) It was not even the loss of the gold production that annoyed her. She owned many other mines and Corpselover was far and away the wealthiest of the seven houses.

"That's the mine Poisondagger has been trying to lay claim to."

"It is Mistress."

"That little worm did this, Dante. He's been trying to get me to share the rights. This is his doing."

"There is no proof of that Mistress."

"I didn't think there would be, he is a competent little fuck."

"Do you intend to respond Mistress?"

One of the few drawbacks to how things worked in Alteroth was that if she did want to respond it would mean acting on her own and perhaps intensifying the feud between Corpselover and Poisondagger.

Alteroth was less a country than it was the private property of the Seven Great Families. They were the only authority, and the law was whatever they said it was. It was meant to apply to those beneath them, not to those who ruled. When it came to disputes among the families themselves there was no authority they could turn to. The uninvolved houses did not like to intervene, so as to keep their own freedom of action as well as avoid making an enemy. So what wound up happening was that whenever two or more families had a dispute they were left to solve it on their own.

This tended to turn any problem into the cause for a long simmering vendetta. The families did not war on each other openly; that would lead to civil war and complete ruin. They would instead snipe at each other from the shadows. There would be smear campaigns, thefts, destruction, sabotage, and even assassinations. Often these feuds would stretch out for years.

Knowing what was scheduled later today Lilith let a faint smile cross her face. "I already know what to do. I am going to get my pound of flesh from Poisondagger."

Hollister looked at her and raised an eyebrow.

"I mean that figuratively."

Her steward nodded. "I would also remind you Mistress that your cousin Andris Corpselover will be coming to dinner tonight."

"Good, I need to talk to him about an important matter."

XXX

In the courtyard a hundred armed skeletons waited. They moved in answer to her will. When the drawbridge was lowered they shuffled out ahead of her. Undead surrounded her, matching her pace as she set off for the Council's Hall.

The sky was the color of ash, and though it was mid-morning it was no brighter than twilight. As always the sun was hidden by an iron sky. As she walked Lilith breathed in the air, ripe with the scent of fresh sulfur. You had to try and notice it, it was a constant that people grew used to and ignored. As she and her escort traveled the people in the street very quickly cleared out of the way. Lilith saw their scurrying forms and smiled.

When she arrived at the Hall the ten skeletons nearest the front entered with her while the rest waited where they were. Each council member was allowed to bring in ten guards, which was what they had all agreed to.

Inside the guards from the other houses all stood apart. There was always tension when the Council of Seven came together, suspicions were plain on every living face. Among the other guards were mages, ogres, trolls, a vampire, and a half dragon. At the first sign of any sort of trouble they would tear into each other without mercy.

When Lilith arrived with her escort all the others focused on her. Having only brought skeletons her force was easily the weakest of those assembled. The eyes being directed at her were cautious, not because of her guards, but because they all new she could summon hundreds more in an instant. Her wand was tucked into a hidden pocket, where it was in easy reach. A second was in a stocking beneath her robes. Even without bothering with a wand she could recite the necessary spell in just seconds. One always had to be prepared.

She pushed open the doors to the inner chamber and then shut them behind her.

XXX

Five of the seven seats at the round table were already occupied. Elven maidens were busy serving wine and the quiet conversations were momentarily disrupted as attention was turned towards the door. Lilith noted immediately that Dante Poisondagger was at his regular place. The despicable, shrunken, old man with rotten teeth grinned at her and lifted his goblet in a mock salute. He felt safe to slight her because they were here inside the Hall. To strike at him here would be to attack openly and begin a war between Corpselover and Poisondagger.

The day would come when blood would be spilled here in the inner chamber. Lilith was certain of it. They were all enemies, only their fear of the outside world held them together in their tenuous alliance. There was too much hate, too much distrust, too much anger for it not to erupt one day.

It would not be today though. Lilith returned Dante's gesture with a wave and a false smile before taking her usual seat. She motioned to one of the elves and a goblet of red wine was immediately brought to her. Lilith looked about at the faces at the table.

"I see Loram is running late today. A little odd, usually Blackwater is among the early ones."

"Are you jealous that you're not the last one to arrive for once?" Poisondagger asked.

"I'm willing to concede the honor from time to time." She answered.

"I heard there was an accident at one of your mines last night. Quite catastrophic, if what I'm told is right, it will take a long while to reopen, a great shame." Dante said.

"Your sources are surprisingly well informed. It's nothing more than a very minor inconvenience. My vault is bursting with gold and silver. It's not as if my house is short of funds. Now that would be rather sad, don't you think?"

Poisondagger had a sour expression as he muttered. "Certainly."

Among the seven families it was common knowledge that Poisondagger was the poorest. They owned none of the mines near the Forge and the incomes from their lands and skilled workers never came close to being enough. This was because the family head had a taste for the expensive and the exquisite. His castle was filled with rare books, marble statues, paintings, pieces of art imported from all over the Shattered Lands, and only the most beautiful and delectable slaves. Dante was perpetually in search of more revenue. It was no secret that his support was always available to the highest bidder.

A large reason for the hard feelings between Poisondagger and Corpselover was that Lilith had never felt any need to buy him off, despite having vast sums. Lilith had never thought him worth a single copper knuckle. Dante had always resented her for that, and over the years their conflict had grown only more bitter and acrimonious.

As she waited for the arrival of Loram Blackwater, Lilith listened to the side conversations going on around her.

Xilos Soulbreaker was trying to convince Baldwin Blooddrinker to sell him a particular seamstress. Apparently one of Xilos' silver smiths had fallen in love with the girl and wanted to marry her. Skilled workers were valuable, and depending on who owned the mother the children would either become smiths or textile workers. Xilos was offering five gold skulls for the girl, but Baldwin was demanding twenty. He was however willing to allow the silversmith to marry her, as the children would be his property. Xilos was unwilling to agree to that.

It looked like the poor silversmith was going to have to find someone else to marry.

Gawreth Wormwood was complaining about the harassment his merchants were suffering in Lothas and the other northern kingdoms. He felt they were treated with suspicion and forced to pay higher prices.

"They expect anyone from Alteroth to be a murderer or a thief!"

"Shocking," Lilith said in a sympathetic tone. "Clearly those northerners don't know us at all."

"Just so."

If they really understood us they'd build a wall along the border and kill anyone who tried to cross it.

"It's because of those damn White Mages stirring things up!" Darius Heartless shouted, loudly adding his opinion. "They go around everywhere spreading their lies and building their conspiracies against us! All the suspicions we face are because of the secret plots being hatched in Avalon! We'll never be safe until every last White Mage is dead!"

Lilith and the others all turned annoyed faces his way. This was a *very* familiar refrain. Avalon was Darius' personal hate, and everything that was wrong with the world could somehow be blamed on the Misty Isle. He argued constantly that all their problems could be solved by laying waste to the island and putting every last White Mage at the sharp end of a pike. Never mind that Avalon was far away and Alteroth had no shoreline. Never mind that the White Mages had a massive fleet and were a great power. Never mind that openly attacking them would likely bring many nations into the conflict on Avalon's side.

No one denied the White Mages were a problem, or that they would have to be dealt with. It was just that they were not the sort of problem that could be solved directly. They needed to be opposed with subtlety. The best way to defeat them was to damage their credibility and reputation.

When Lilith thought that she also thought of her son and what he was up to. She smiled slightly, what a wonderful justification this would make for his going about in white.

"Oh give it up Darius," Gawreth Wormwood said snidely. "You're the only one here stupid enough to talk about war with Avalon seriously."

The two men openly glared at one another. Wormwood and Heartless were in the middle of a long running vendetta. It was the sort of blatant hostility that kept everyone on edge at every meeting.

"Did I say we should declare war on Avalon? If we can't strike at them directly let's instead bring down one of their puppets! Let's invade and conquer Dregal!"

Five faces stared at him blankly.

"You really are an idiot." Gawreth chided.

Before Darius could yell some reply Xilos also spoke. "War in the north would be too costly."

"I agree," Lilith added. "If we invade Dregal the other northern kingdoms will come in against us."

"So what? Let them! We'll crush all three and take all their lands!" Darius looked around the table hoping for any backing.

"I think it is an interesting proposal." Dante said in a voice that oozed sympathy and understanding. "We should discuss it."

Hearing someone else side with him only made Darius puff out his chest and look even more determined to push his view.

Lilith sent an exasperated glance at Dante. She had spoken up in the hopes that it would be enough to end the ridiculous debate. Lilith was certain that the only reason Dante had voiced his support was because it meant opposing her. He didn't give a damn whether or not they went to war; he just wanted to inconvenience her.

"Fine then," Xilos sighed. "Let's talk about it. Keep in mind that Loram still isn't here."

Darius came to his feet and put his shoulders back, making every effort to look imposing. "We have a quorum and it only takes four votes. The reason why we need to crush Dregal should be obvious! While all the northern kingdoms are infested with White Mages, King Doran keeps one as his closest advisor and talks of bringing Dregal into the Alliance! He is nothing but Avalon's puppet! If we do nothing then it will be an invitation for them to strike at us!"

"You've been saying that for years now." Gawreth pointed out. "We all know how much Doran loves the whites, especially his pet Ramiel. Nothing you're telling us is new."

"And yet we have done nothing as Doran plots to sell his country to Avalon!"

"He wouldn't dare," Xilos said wearily. "He knows we would never tolerate an Alliance nation on our border. They know what we would do to them."

The Alliance of Mist, or more commonly just the Alliance, was a league of several countries dominated by Avalon. The member states all kept their own governments and were, in theory, independent and equal. They were however required to adopt the laws of Avalon, allow free and open trade to Alliance merchants, and come to the aid of any member who was attacked. In member countries all monsters and non-humans were killed on sight, only White Mages were permitted to practice magic, slavery was forbidden, necromancy was forbidden, and all merchants from Alteroth were denied access.

The Alliance nations were far away, and except for Avalon weak and insignificant. But the White Mages could be found in every country spreading their lies and trying to seduce those in power to join them. Doran was the most obvious example, but far from the only one.

"Most of the nobles distrust the whites as much as they do us." Lilith said. "They can all see that joining the Alliance means submitting to Avalon."

"Doran is an exception! He's been fooled by Ramiel's sweet lies! I tell you he intends to join!"

"Fine," Gawreth said. "Then when he does bring up the motion again and I will gladly choose war."

"You would have us look weak then?" Dante asked.

"No one cares about small wars." Lilith answered him. "If we invade Dregal then Wylef and Lothas will certainly fight, others may decide to join as well."

"Let them!" Darius said. "They are all scheming against us, plotting with Avalon to destroy us! If they want to fight us so much the better! We'll just get rid of them all and add their lands to our own! What can their little armies do to match our power? We'll crush them all in a month!"

There was some truth to that.

Alteroth was much larger than all three of the northern kingdoms put together. If the seven houses put their full effort into it they could raise armies (of living and dead soldiers) five or six times as large as what the three kingdoms could. Defeating the knights and their levies though was not the main concern.

"What happens when we face an Alliance army with a hundred White Mages leading them?" Gawreth asked.

"Why do you think I want to attack Dregal in the first place? It's so we can draw out the whites and bring them where we can actually deal with them!" He looked around the table. "You say it's impossible to attack Avalon. Fine then! Let's force them to come to us! Let them send a hundred White Mages! Let them send a thousand! Once we destroy them in battle that will be the end of the Alliance and of all their plots! No one will dare join them after that! Even if we can never invade Avalon their power will be broken!"

262

"Or ours will." Gawreth said quietly.

Darius glared at him. "You doubt our strength?"

"No, I wonder about Avalon's. Their mages are as skilled as ours and even if they lack monsters and undead their armies are not to be despised. Their knights are the finest warriors in the Shattered Lands and fearless. They also have something we don't, allies."

Now Gawreth too stood up so that both he and Darius were on their feet staring one another down.

"The entire world hates us, and no matter how strong we are we will never be strong enough to fight them all. We prosper; we survive, for only two reasons; because they are divided and because they fear us. Should they ever lose their fear, or should they ever unite, we are doomed. What you are suggesting will cause our enemies to unite against us behind Avalon's banner! Can you not see that you loud mouthed fool?"

Darius's face turned even redder than it already was. "They are already doing that! Every day their influence grows stronger! They are turning all the countries against us! If we do nothing we'll find ourselves surrounded by armies of knights and White Mages! The only answer is to attack now, before it's too late."

"And start a war that may destroy us?"

"The whites have to be annihilated! There is no other course!"

"There is a third choice," Lilith said in a soft voice. As she knew they would, all eyes turned in her direction. "Instead of attacking them directly why don't we attack their reputations? Lies can be even more effective weapons than swords. They thrive by making people see them as just and heroic. Strip that away and people will see them for what they truly are; power hungry extremists. That would be enough to destroy their efforts without risking such a dangerous war."

263

Darius and Dante frowned at her proposal. The others appeared interested.

Before Darius could rail against the suggestion they were interrupted. The doors to the inner chamber were opened by a man in black robes. They all turned towards the door expecting to see their last member. He had the familiar curly black hair and cleft chin of Loram Blackwater, but his face was much newer and unfamiliar to them.

"Who are you?" Darius demanded. "You are interrupting a meeting of the Council of Seven!"

The young man smiled confidently and entered. "I am Tiberius Blackwater, second son of Loram Blackwater and his third wife Amyla. It grieves me to have to announce the tragic passing of my beloved father. As his heir I claim leadership of the Blackwater family and its place upon the Council of Seven. I ask you to acknowledge me."

Loram must have let his guard down and become sloppy. Lilith thought. He had been in perfect health at the last meeting.

"You're not the heir." Xilos pointed out. "His son Farris from his first wife is."

"Sadly, my brother Farris suffered a tragic accident, as did a few others."

Oh ho, this one bears watching. Lilith thought.

Within the seven families it was not unusual for the head of the household to suffer an 'accident.' It was accepted that there was no place for the weak and that the strong were entitled to take what they could. (Which only made Dante's continued survival all the more infuriating.) What was unusual was for anyone but the designated heir to arrange that sort of accident. If this Tiberius had managed to eliminate not only his father, but all his rivals in one fell swoop, he was clearly someone with great ability and an iron nerve.

"You might at least pretend to be sorry your father and brothers are gone." Gawreth said in obvious annoyance. He and Loram had gotten along fairly well. "There is such a thing as civility you know."

"I apologize." Immediately Tiberius's face became a comic extreme of sadness, with downturned mouth and lips quivering. "Is this better?"

Dante snorted a laugh while Gawreth's eyes narrowed.

"Be careful boy, you don't want to make an enemy of me."

"I should hate to make an enemy of any of you. I hope we can all be the best of friends." He came to a halt before the only empty chair at the table. "Before I take my seat, I would like to be formally acknowledged by the Council. That is only proper after all."

This was normally just a formality. When someone seized control of one of the families the others usually just accepted it.

Darius took them all by surprise by being the first to speak and actually managing to not sound in a rage for once. "I acknowledge you as a member of the Council and as head of the Blackwater family. I sincerely welcome you and hope we can work well together."

"I thank you for the warm welcome Darius Heartless. I wish for the same."

"I acknowledge you as a member of the Council and as head of the Blackwater family." Dante said quickly, making sure he was second.

"I acknowledge you as a member of the Council and as head of the Blackwater family." Lilith said.

"I acknowledge you as a member of the Council and as head of the Blackwater family." Baldwin said.

"I acknowledge you as a member of the Council and as head of the Blackwater family." Xilos said.

"I acknowledge you." Gawreth said.

With that Tiberius Blackwater was a member of the Council of Seven. He gave Gawreth a nod before pulling out his father's chair and sitting down in it. "It feels comfortable."

"It might not always." Gawreth said.

"Well, this has been interesting." Dante Poisondagger said. "However, let us get to the actual reason for our meeting."

Chapter 25

Punishment Is Its Own Reward

Dante motioned to one of the elven servants.

"Have my grandson brought in."

"Yes master," the girl said with an obedient bow. She then hurried out of the chamber.

All of the earlier events had certainly been entertaining, but the original reason they had been called together was for a simple confirmation.

As they waited Lilith noted that Darius had given up trying to continue the debate for war. That was unusual. Normally he would press his argument until the Council either told him to shut up or they actually went through the trouble of voting him down. Seeing Darius be reasonable for once was both a relief and a bit worrisome. He was making polite conversation with Tiberius and, amazingly, doing so in a civil manner.

It was all too obvious what Darius was playing at. Loram Blackwater had been an associate of Gawreth's and had steadily opposed all of Heartless' efforts. He was clearly trying to bring Tiberius into his camp.

XXX

It took a few minutes before a young man in black robes strode in. He was of average height and weight, with horsey teeth. Standing before them he bowed.

"I am Nunca Poisondagger and I have come in answer to the summons of the Council of Seven."

There was a sheen of sweat on his forehead. Despite trying to look calm his eyes darted about. Lilith saw them come to rest on her. Seeing exactly where his eyes were going she deliberately leaned forward a bit while sitting on her robes.

"We have summoned you to confirm you have completed your First Quest." Dante pointed to a spot on the other side of the table. "Stand within the Circle of Truth and answer all questions put to you by the Council of Seven. I warn you to speak only the truth."

The young Dark Mage immediately walked around the table to the far side of the room. There, etched into the stone floor, was a circle. Surrounding it was a complex formula of runes and magical symbols. As soon as he stepped inside, the markings, as well as the circle itself, began to glow with a murky bluish white light.

Whenever someone was brought here to deliver a report, be questioned, or to be tried they were made to stand within the circle. The enchantment carved into the floor did not actually compel anyone to speak the truth. Rather it inflicted pain on those who spoke any sort of falsehood while inside its confines. The Council had discovered long ago, that truth spells that forced subjects to speak could be defeated simply by making irrelevant statements that just happened to be true. It also tended to cause its subjects to resist and reveal as little useful information as possible. By comparison, this method permitted a person to lie, but the lies were obvious and were instantly punished. Whereas speaking the truth was rewarded. It encouraged subjects to be more revealing.

Once he was inside the circle and the carvings were glowing at his feet Nunca tried very hard to appear calm, but the way his eyes kept darting to the floor gave his true feelings away.

"There is no need to be nervous grandson," Dante said in a soothing tone. "Confirmations are routine and nothing to be feared. Simply speak the truth; you will only suffer if you lie.

Each member shall ask one question, all you need do is answer truthfully. Should you lie we will know and the council member will be free to ask an additional question. Once you have answered seven questions you will be a true Dark Mage of Alteroth. Do you understand?"

"Yes," Nunca said with only a slight shake to his voice.

Nodding Dante looked about the table inviting someone to be first. All council members were equals and no one was permitted to act as leader. The questions would be asked in no particular order. It was tradition though that the head of the candidate's family would be permitted to ask the final question. Each member was free to ask anything they wished, but was limited to a single inquiry unless lied to.

"What is your name?" Darius Heartless asked.

"Nunca Poisondagger." He answered with obvious relief.

"Where did you travel to?" Xilos Soulbreaker asked.

"I went into the Barrens in northern Rutenia, near the Kyrtos Pass."

"Did you kill anyone?" Baldwin Blooddrinker asked.

"I killed three shepherds who crossed my path."

The idiot actually sounded proud of that. As if killing poorly armed shepherd boys were any sort of accomplishment for a Dark Mage.

"Did you take any spoils?" Gawreth Wormwood asked.

"Yes, there were no coins but I took five iron daggers from my victims along with a coat I liked."

269

Typical Poisondagger, Lilith thought. *They just want to survive the damn quest, they don't care at all about coming back with a reputation.*

"What is your favorite color?" Tiberius Blackwater asked with a straight face.

Nunca blinked before answering. "Black."

That was five.

Lilith smiled affectionately at the young man. "Do you like staring at my chest?"

"What?" Nunca said startled. "No! Of..."

His denial was cut off by a sudden shout of pain. The runes and symbols throbbed an angry red and sparked, sending energy into the fool's body. He instinctively tried to get out, but ran into an unseen barrier at the circle's edge. Seeing the look of startlement on his face as he bounced off brought a few unexpected chortles from around the table.

The punishment lasted only a few seconds, then the aura changed back to a tranquil bluish white.

"Obviously you were not paying attention when your granddaddy explained to you what would happen if you lied." Lilith informed him, trying to be helpful. "What you just suffered was the minimum punishment the Circle will inflict, if you tell another lie the pain will grow worse, and it will continue to increase with each additional lie. Tell enough lies and it can even be fatal."

Nunca looked down fearfully. He then bowed his head. "I apologize, please forgive me."

Lilith just sat there and smiled.

As she did so the sweat on his forehead began to shine.

"Well, since you did not answer me truthfully I am permitted to ask you another question. Tell me, has your grandfather ever said he would like me dead?"

A look of terror covered the boy's face. "No!"

The light bathing him shifted to red and there was a crackling as magical energy coursed painfully through his body. It lasted noticeably longer, perhaps for fifteen seconds or so. When it ended he was bent over and his legs were shaking. They could all hear him gasping for breath.

Lilith waited patiently to allow him to recover. "Would it make you happy to see your grandfather with his throat slit?"

His gaze jerked from her to Dante, his fear obvious. "No! I wou…"

Once more his words were swallowed by howls of pain. His body twisted and spasmed, his arms and head jerked about like a string puppet in a child's hands. It drew laughter from all around the table, from everyone save Dante.

"He doesn't learn very quickly does he?" Tiberius quipped.

"Well he is a Poisondagger, you know." Gawreth said.

The light remained red for perhaps half a minute.

This time when it stopped poor Nunca dropped to his hands and knees. Tears were leaking from his eyes and there was a stream of drool from a corner of his mouth. The way he was trembling Lilith half expected him to start begging.

Lilith turned her attention over to Dante. His expression was utterly blank.

"Is this really the grandson you were bragging to all of us about?" Lilith asked him. "The one you said was brilliant?"

He said the same about all his children and grandchildren. Dante refused to acknowledge that anyone with a drop of his blood could be anything less than exceptional.

"Brilliant?" Tiberius turned to Dante. "Did you actually say that?"

Dante answered as if each word were being dragged out of him. "I may have been mistaken."

"Obviously," Tiberius said with a chuckle.

Dante turned those cold eyes towards him. She wondered if a brand new feud had just been started between Poisondagger and Blackwater.

Dante then shifted his gaze towards her. She just smiled back. It gave Lilith the deepest satisfaction to know just how much this had to be hurting him.

Revenge really was sweet.

The fact this would only worsen the problems between their two houses did not bother her at all. She didn't want to make peace with him. She only wanted to injure him as much as she could, before one of his children finally got up the nerve to stick a knife into his back.

She had to wait about five minutes for Nunca to finally climb back to his feet.

"So, do you think your grandfather is a vain, greedy, small minded, petty, vindictive ass that the family would be better off without?"

The poor boy turned a frightened face to his grandfather and opened his mouth.

"Just answer the question truthfully you fool!" Dante snapped.

Nunca shut his mouth and nodded obediently. "Yes."

The light surrounding him remained tranquil.

"Amazing, who would have thought a Poisondagger could actually learn something?"

That produced a fresh series of laughs.

Dante sat rigid in his chair, eyes locked on his grandson. When the laughter finally died down he asked the final question. "Do you know you are a disgrace?"

The young man lowered his head. "Yes grandfather."

The aura remained unaffected.

"It's over," Dante said voice hollow.

Nunca flinched.

The council members all quickly agreed that Nunca Poisondagger had indeed successfully completed his First Quest and was now a Dark Mage of Alteroth. The newly recognized Dark Mage was given leave to go and did not waste a second. Shortly after that the meeting was adjourned. Dante was the first to exit, storming out without a word.

Lilith was in a fine mood, humming and singing all the way home. It had been years since she'd enjoyed a council meeting half so much.

XXX

When a couple days later it was announced that Nunca Poisondagger had suffered a fatal accident Lilith was anything but surprised. The news made her a bit sad.

After all, getting rid of such an obvious incompetent would make Poisondagger stronger.

Chapter 26

A Favor

"I take it the meeting went well Mistress?" Hollister inquired in a respectful voice.

"It was surprisingly entertaining."

Her steward did not ask for details. "I wish to remind you that Andris will be attending dinner tonight."

"I haven't forgotten. Is Walter still sulking?"

"He is somewhere in the north tower. He killed one of the slaves and is likely eating her."

"So long as it was one of the general slaves and not one of the staff it's fine. He should be out of the way at least."

Many of the slaves in Castle Corpselover had no specific task and were essentially here to be eaten or killed off. Walter, Enver, and certain others were free to do with them as they liked. Other slaves like her steward or her cook or her maids were off limits. It kept her from having to replace important servants and also kept the slaves divided. The ones who knew they were safe were not inclined to help the others.

"I want Andris to enjoy his visit."

Hollister bowed low to her. "It shall be done Mistress."

XXX

No one in Alter ever saw the sun rise or set.

When the day ended twilight simply bled away until there was only blackness.

There was no moonlight or stars, no street lights, and most windows were shuddered tight and gave off no flicker. The only illumination came from the Forge.

Lilith sat by one of the open windows high up in the south tower. She looked out into the blackness and felt at peace. She was a creature of darkness as much as her father or Enver.

For a moment she wondered about Waldo. He was not like her. No matter how hard he tried he would never belong to the darkness. She had known that for a very long time. It had surprised her that rather than make her despise him, it had only made her love him that much more.

He truly was his father's son.

Lilith had loved all of her children, but Waldo had always been especially dear to her. Was it because when she looked at him she saw his father? Or was it the natural affection a mother felt for the child who was different from all the others? She couldn't tell the reason; she only knew that she would do anything to assure his survival.

When Walter had died Lilith had realized that Waldo would need a great deal of help if he were to survive as the next head of Corpselover. If any of her other children had lived she would have found a nice quiet place for him where he could be the head of his own branch family. He would visit for the festivals and weddings, but otherwise be forgotten.

When he became her last child things became much more complicated. She could not have set him aside in favor of someone else even if she had wanted to. Any relative she elevated to replace him would have had Waldo killed the moment she died. Waldo would have a stronger claim to be head

276

of the family than anyone else. He had to become head or else perish.

If he were going to rule Corpselover and sit on the Council he would need a great deal of help. That was why Lilith had come up with her plan. The Council's action in sending him on his fool's quest had forced her to begin things years sooner than she'd wanted. There was no helping it, she would begin to put things in motion.

Plots within plots, wheels within wheels, I'll tear all of it down if I have to. My son will rule after me no matter the cost.

Out in the darkness she saw a light approaching from down below.

It was bright enough to reveal several forms shuffling through the empty streets. It had to be Andris and his escort.

"Is someone coming to dinner?" A playful voice spoke.

Lilith continued to look out the window without bothering to turn around. "You do know it's pointless to sneak up on me when I always know where you are."

"Forgive me, you know how I am."

"Yes. Be grateful you are so useful or I would be rid of you."

"Such cruel words for your most devoted servant."

Lilith laughed softly. Devoted? Except for kind or maybe merciful she couldn't think of a word that described him less.

She didn't hear his approach but could sense it through their bond. "The servants tell me someone is expected for dinner but they don't know who. Found a new lover have we?"

"I am a little too busy for lovers at the moment."

Enver stood just a few feet behind her. Their bond had grown very sensitive over the years and they could both pick up the other's emotions easily.

"I can feel that little spark of excitement you have whenever you start a plot. What is it you are scheming?"

"You don't actually expect me to tell you do you?"

"Of course not, but one can always hope."

"Never mind who is coming, I expect you'll get the information from the staff soon enough. I'll have a task for you soon."

Enver did not look pleased. "Is this going to be one of those pointless errands you like to annoy me with?"

She shook her head. "What I have in mind will be important."

"Like the treasure map I provided your son?"

Lilith nodded.

Enver gave her a bloodless smile. "Will I at least get to kill someone? Slaughtering helpless slaves gets boring after a time."

"Oh yes," she promised.

"Well that is pleasing to hear, but it hurts that you won't share your plans with me."

"I will tell you your part, that is all you need know."

"Walter has been very upset with you lately. His mood has been black as night."

"I know."

"He killed one of the sex slaves, pretty little thing, name of Deena or Deelia I think. He beat her to death. Probably taking out his frustration; probably imagining it was a certain other woman."

"If he is unhappy it is because he wants more than he can have."

"Well don't we all?" Enver leaned a bit closer to her. "Why don't you end him? There is no happiness for him you know. His entire existence is pathetic. Why don't you put him out of his misery? Or were you hoping Waldo would do it? Was that your plan? Did you bring Walter back just to teach your youngest how to hate? How to kill? It would have worked if Waldo had any sort of spine. Too bad your last child is such a coward."

No one else would ever talk to her like this. Enver loved to mock her and point out her failings.

"Kneel."

His legs trembled as he tried to resist. They soon bent, he kneeled before her on the stone floor.

"Beg my forgiveness and ask me to punish you for your rude tongue."

His lips twisted and she could feel his resentment through their bond.

He clasped his hands together and bent his proud neck. "I beg your forgiveness Mistress. I beg you to punish me for my insensitive remarks."

Lilith knew he didn't mean a word of it.

"Remain exactly as you are for the rest of the night, and thank me for my compassion."

He clenched his teeth before speaking clearly. "I thank you for your consideration Mistress."

She walked past, leaving him to remain there on his knees until the dawn.

XXX

Andris Corpselover was dressed in black robes and was being guided by the castle's steward.

Within his heart a tiny portion of fear mixed with excitement and expectation. He was the head of one of the many, many branch families of Corpselover. His family lived on a small estate about twenty miles from Alter. They would visit for the Solstices and if there was a wedding in the main family. Lilith would spare him a few moments for some idle chatter and a polite question or two, before moving on to the next family and doing the same. Nothing at any of the get togethers had ever suggested she held him in any sort of special esteem. So when he'd received this invitation he'd been taken by surprise.

"Did my cousin say why she wanted me to come here?"

"The Mistress did not share her reasons, nor did I inquire." Hollister replied stiffly.

Andris nodded and continued to follow in silence.

Any unexpected summons by the main family was always cause for some trepidation. It was not unheard of for visiting family members to simply disappear. Usually though, that only happened in response to some sort of significant blunder. Since he'd not committed any he felt reasonably sure he would survive this. Andris suspected the reason he'd been called to dinner, his suspicions filled him with eagerness.

The branch families held a unique status within Alteroth. Being members of the ruling houses they were all citizens. Most of them could practice magic and they were not required to go on First Quests. They had the freedom to travel and could go to foreign countries without asking for permission. They had the freedom to marry whoever they chose and to choose their own profession and make their own money. (They were permitted to be married to only one spouse at a time though. Only members of main family were entitled to multiple wives.) Many of them were merchants or overseers or officers within each family's military. Some travelled far and wide offering their magical services to the highest bidder. Each branch family was provided their own home, normally outside of Alter. They also had the right to demand a meeting with the head of the main family. (A right seldom used.)

Compared to most of the people they were very well off.

However they had no political power, and remained at the mercy of the main family. They could earn money and have personal property and livestock; but they could not own land. Their homes were gifts from the main family and could be taken from them on a whim. If the family's troops were assembled they were expected to serve and fight. They were citizens, but unless they left Alteroth permanently, they remained pawns of the main family and could be killed at a single word.

The family gives and the family takes. Was a saying Andris knew well.

When he was at last brought to the dining hall Lilith was there waiting for him. Rather than the usual black robes she was dressed in a simple red dress that covered her from neck to ankles. There were settings at the head of the table and to the immediate left. She was making a special effort to honor him.

"Cousin, it is good to see you again." Lilith greeted. "I've missed your company."

That was a lie, but it was a welcomed lie.

Andris bent his head slightly as a sign of respect. Dark Mages rarely bowed, even to each other. "It also pleases me to be in your company again cousin."

Lilith motioned to the table and nodded graciously. "Let us catch up over dinner."

As soon as they were both seated the servants appeared with the appetizer; freshly baked bread with honey and butter. For the main course there were a variety of dishes placed before them. Succulent roast pig, baked chicken, slices of beef, baked potatoes, stewed vegetable, and loaves of white bread. For dessert there were cakes and pies and sweet puddings. To wash it all down was strong red wine. It was a sumptuous meal that would do any kitchen proud.

As they ate Andris was careful not to do more than sip at his cup. He wanted to keep all of his wits about him. They talked of family and of magic and of things unimportant and harmless. She asked him about his travels as one of her merchants. He shared a few stories and won some amused smiles and even got a few laughs from her.

It was all meaningless.

She wanted something and was simply trying to soften him a bit. He was flattered to have the head of the family go to so much trouble. Darius Heartless, for example, was known to simply give his extended family orders when he wanted something from them. Lilith had the good graces to at least frame her wishes in the form of requests.

When the meal ended and they had both had their fill the servants took away all the dishes and plates. Leaving them only their goblets and the wine. Andris observed all the servants withdraw from the dining hall to leave them alone.

Lilith leaned back casually in her seat and balanced her goblet at the end of her fingers, carefully swirling the wine about. "Cousin, I need a favor."

Here it comes. Andris thought, the moment he'd been waiting for since receiving her invitation. "How can I be of service to you?"

She looked at him over the lip of her goblet. "By now I am sure you have heard about my son being off on an… unusual First Quest."

The dictates of the Council were supposed to remain secret, but they never were, not for trivial matters like this.

Andris cautiously nodded, her words stoking his hopes. "I have."

"As you know, Waldo is my last living child. The Council's actions have made the situation more difficult than it needs to be, and I am forced to take certain precautions."

"I understand." He was very careful not to let his eagerness show. Lilith knew that her son was doomed. Ever since the news of his First Quest and its impossible requirements had gotten out, every one of the branch families had started to guess whom she might choose to be her new heir. Rumors had been flying that this candidate or that one was about to be selected.

"If you would agree to send me one of your children I would be deeply grateful to you."

It had actually happened. He let out a breath of relief and allowed himself a wide smile. "My son Erebos would be more than honored to be adopted into your family, and to act as heir should anything occur to dear Waldo."

The edges of Lilith's mouth turned down. "No."

Andris was caught off guard. "I beg pardon cousin, what do you mean no?"

283

"I mean no, I am not asking to adopt your son as my heir. Waldo will succeed me, no one else."

"I don't understand. You just told me that you needed my son."

Lilith closed her eyes. "I know what sort of rumors have been going through the family. I do not doubt that all of you have already buried my son. Well, unbury him, Waldo will survive to return home, don't doubt it. It may take many months, but he will return, so I have no need for a new heir. For ten generations this line of the family has held power and I will not see the line end with me. He is my last child and he has my blood. I mean to see him rule this family after me and I will do whatever it takes to ensure that."

That certainly made things clearer. He felt the sudden need to take a long swallow of wine. His dream of becoming part of the main family had been realized, and then crushed, within the same conversation. He took the bottle and began refilling his cup. "Then why do you need my son?"

Lilith sighed. "I don't."

"What?"

"I want your daughter." Lilith said, spelling it out for him. "The child I was referring to was your daughter not your son."

"You want to adopt Hera?"

"You really do jump to conclusions don't you? I never mentioned adoption."

Andris looked at her dumbfounded. His daughter was sixteen and already very talented in the Dark Arts. However she had certain issues. He had planned to give her a few more years to mature, before taking her under his wing and teaching her about being a trader. "I don't understand. What do you want with Hera?"

284

Lilith stared into her wine. "The Council sees my son as a fool. That will not change no matter what he does on his quest. Once I am gone they will simply try to use him or arrange an accident for him."

She looked up from her wine and her dark eyes stared into his. Andris shifted uncomfortably in his seat, the intensity of her gaze was unnerving.

"I know what you and the others think of him. No matter what you may believe, Waldo is strong and has great talent. One day, I promise you, all of you will see him as I do. You will see his power and tremble."

Andris could only nod; he didn't dare to so much as make a sound.

"Until that day comes though, he will need someone at his side the Council will fear. If they will not respect him then they must respect someone close to him. That is the only way he will survive long enough."

To Andris's relief she turned her focus back to her wine.

"I will take your daughter on as my apprentice. I will instruct her not only in the deeper magics, but also in the ways of politics and show her what it really means to rule over others. I will bring out her full potential and make Hera someone to be feared."

He was trembling slightly. The hopes that had been raised and just as swiftly dashed were rising again. Members of the Council very rarely took on apprentices outside of their own immediate family. When they did so, it was always a sign they'd found someone of extraordinary ability. His daughter's future was suddenly looking very bright. Andris was not about to bring up his concerns and risk damaging Lilith's high opinion.

XXX

Lilith stared into the wine and imagined her son's reaction when she told him. She knew of Hera's faults and doubted she could fix them completely. Lilith didn't expect Waldo to thank her, or be very happy about what she was planning. The fact was this was what he would need to continue once she was gone. If a foul tasting medicine would save you then you held your nose and forced it down.

"When my son returns he will need a proper wife, to guide him and start giving him children with suitable blood. Someone who can point out the hidden dangers, someone the Council will respect. I think your daughter would make a fine wife for him."

She drank the wine and thought it tasted a little bitter.

Chapter 27

<u>The New Apprentice</u>

It was the nose.

One couldn't help but focus on it.

It wasn't just big, it hooked. It looked like some sort of fleshy beak. When you looked at her face your eyes were just drawn to it.

Poor girl, Lilith thought. For a woman there were few things worse than to be ugly.

Lilith considered the girl's features with a critical eye. She was small, just barely standing five feet and very much on the thin side. Even in black robes it was obvious her chest was as flat as a boy's. The rest of her features were bland. If she had been blessed with a cute little button nose, she still would still have been plain.

What was more interesting was her posture. She stood straight with shoulders back and eyes returning Lilith's scrutiny. Her face was not defiant, but there was nothing submissive there either. Despite the situation and how much was at stake for her, she seemed confident and calm. Lilith was quite skilled at reading people, yet she could not be certain whether the girl was as relaxed as she appeared or hiding her natural anxieties.

Either way it was a promising start.

"Welcome to Castle Corpselover Hera. I trust your father has explained why you were summoned?"

"Yes Aunt Lilith, he told me I was to become your apprentice." The girl bent her neck ever so slightly. "I am deeply honored and will work hard to prove myself worthy of your selection."

Technically, Hera's father was a fifth or sixth cousin to Lilith. It was tradition that within the extended family older relatives were referred to as uncle or aunt, younger relatives went by nephew or niece, and those close to the same age were simply cousin. This made things less confusing.

"Did your father tell you anything else?"

"He said that you wanted me to marry your son, and that you very sure he would return from his First Quest."

"What do you think about that?"

Small shoulders gave a small shrug. "If that is the price for being apprenticed I will pay it."

Lilith lifted a single eyebrow. "You don't like the idea of being married to Waldo?"

"I like the idea of becoming your daughter. Even more I like the idea of becoming your apprentice. I don't have any special interest in being married."

"Just with Waldo or with anyone?"

"I have no wish to be married to any man."

"Well I was never married, but that was because I would have no longer been head of the family. I always had my lovers though."

"I have no use for men. Except for my father, I have never met a single man that I liked."

"Oh," Lilith said after a slight pause. "It's like that then?"

"It is."

Lilith was not shocked. Hera had a reputation for hostility and rudeness, especially towards men. For a Corpselover such behavior was fine, when it was directed towards those beneath her. It became a problem when it was aimed at other members of the family, or at members of the other houses.

As for her personal preferences, those were unimportant so long as they were limited to the sex slaves. In Alteroth all pleasures could be indulged without fear.

"That is fine niece; I have some lovely slave girls I keep for just that sort of thing. You are free to indulge your tastes." Lilith saw the girl lick her lips ever so slightly. "However, when the time comes, marrying my son and giving him children will be part of your duty."

"I have already said that I understand Aunt Lilith, and will do what I have to."

"My son has a very likeable personality. You might actually enjoy being his wife."

"I doubt it."

Well that's fair, I doubt Waldo will much enjoy being your husband. "I am sure once you have some children you will come to love them and be happy with your new family."

"If you say so Aunt Lilith. What really matters to me is the chance to learn more magic. I want to be a powerful and feared necromancer like you. I want you to teach me everything."

"My, my, so young and filled with ambition. Do you want to know why I chose you?"

"Certainly."

"It's not because of your talent for necromancy, though that was an important element. It's also not because of your intelligence

289

or your vast potential. Obviously, it wasn't because of your looks or your sweet disposition."

Hera did not look either pleased or upset.

"I chose you because I needed someone who was ruthless."

Hera grinned. "Thank you."

"Tell me, what happened to your younger brother Malcor?"

"He had an accident."

Lilith smiled knowingly. "An accident?"

"Yes Aunt Lilith. He fell down the stairs and died."

"When you just happened to be the only one with him?"

"Accidents happen my aunt."

"Oh they certainly do. Though usually not until after a child has earned the black robes and can protect himself. Your brother was, what, six at the time and you were fourteen?"

"That's right."

"Did you really think he was so dangerous to you? Were you afraid he might be a threat some day?"

"No. I just didn't like him."

There was not even a hint of guilt.

Yes, Lilith thought. *I picked the right one.* "I think you and I will get along splendidly my niece."

"I think so too Aunt Lilith."

"There is just one thing I need to make clear to you first though."

"Yes?"

"My son Waldo will not suffer any accidents."

"Of course not," Hera assured her. "I would never…"

Lilith cut her off.

"Yes you would. It's obvious. I am sure you are already calculating how long you would have to wait and what the best method would be. You probably wouldn't dare while I am still around, but I will not live forever. Frankly my dear niece, you wouldn't be the person I need if you weren't already thinking about it."

Hera considered for a moment, and then nodded. "Do you blame me? You say I will have to endure being married and having some screaming children tear their way out of me. Very well, if that's the price I will pay it, but why would I suffer it longer than I have to?"

"Because within one hour of my son's death you will know your own."

Hera's eyes widened.

"Do you know what a Death Seal is Hera?"

The girl nodded.

"Before you marry my son I will place one on you connecting your life to his. I did not bring you here because I need an apprentice. I brought you so that you could act as my son's advisor, and do the things for him that he cannot do for himself. You will live only for his sake, and all your strength and knowledge will be placed at his service. You will be a proper wife to him Hera, whether you want to be or not."

"I see, so the price for my apprenticeship and joining the main family is not only my freedom, but eventually my life as well. That seems rather high."

"Oh it's higher than that still. The sort of power you seek always demands a very heavy cost. If it is more than you are willing to pay say so. You can return home and learn how to be a merchant or a common mage for hire."

As Lilith was speaking Hera noticed the fingers on her aunt's left hand were trembling slightly.

"The kind of power you are offering is worth any cost."

"I thought the same once."

"Are you trying to tell me it's not?"

"What I am telling you is that you are very young. The day may come when you regret some of your choices."

A smug grin blossomed beneath Hera's nose. "I doubt it Aunt Lilith. So long as I get what I want I don't care what it costs me."

The words called up a memory.

XXX

For an instant Lilith imagined she could taste the salt air and could feel the warmth of Gawayne's arms wrapped around her.

"Are you sure this is what you want?" He'd said to her so tenderly.

"Yes, I don't care what it costs."

She could still remember how he'd looked at her with those mournful, honey colored eyes. She'd understood that it had never been for his own fate, but for hers. He really had loved her.

As she had loved him.

XXX

"May you always feel that way." Lilith said. "Now come with me and I will begin your instruction. There is much you need to learn and time is short."

XXX

Hera was striding through the halls as though she owned them.

The Dark Powers smile upon me. She had just had her initial lesson and was filled to bursting with excitement. Hera had only just glimpsed the possibilities and they were whirling through her head. Teleportation, transfiguration, polymorphication, transference, material evocation, and all the other deeper magics; Lilith knew about all of them! The power to twist the universe and bend it to your will. How marvelous it was, how exciting! With such knowledge anything was possible.

Aunt Lilith was all that Hera had imagined her to be and more. She had met Lilith twice during the summer solstice celebrations. Hera had just been one in a long line of relatives to greet her and exchange a few words. How she had longed for more, but it had not been possible. She'd wanted to confess how she admired her and yearned to be the same. Hera recalled eating the ginger cakes and having a vision of being Lilith; of having the power to make everyone kneel before her. The power to condemn with just a word and to have the living and the dead obey her.

It had been such a vivid dream. She hadn't been able to get it out of her head. Now here she was, apprenticed to her beloved Aunt Lilith, about to learn all of her secrets and become like her.

293

In Alteroth power was what mattered most, and women could have quite a lot of it. Even here though they were not quite equal to men. Lilith had never married because her husband would have immediately become head of the family. In an enlightened society like theirs, a husband's penis still trumped all the intelligence and ability a woman possessed. Women could learn magic, have careers, and earn their own money; but having children was still seen as their primary duty. Men came first, and they wanted their women to be beautiful and obedient.

In Hera's eyes Lilith was everything a strong woman should be. She ruled the Corpselover family with absolute authority. The Council readily acknowledged her as their strongest member. While she was a stunning beauty Lilith used her looks to her own advantage, she went through lovers like a fox through a hen house, and was not above turning a man's passions against him. She had expanded the wealth and influence of an already great house, and was as ruthless in business as she was in politics. Lilith really was everything Hera wanted to be.

The only thing that kept this from being a dream come true was the fact she was going to have to marry Waldo.

Thinking about that soured her mood, but only slightly. She had seen Waldo at the festivals and been anything but impressed. Whether dressed or undressed he had looked timid. To look at him one would certainly never guess he was heir to the richest and most powerful family in Alteroth.

Within the extended family there had always been talk about Waldo. He was the disgrace of the main line. Weak, with abilities that centered around healing and defensive spells. Within his veins was the blood of Avalon, and the color of his eyes proclaimed he was no true Dark Mage. Growing up she'd heard whispers questioning why someone like him was allowed to exist. The talk was always kept very quiet though, no one wanted rumors reaching Lilith.

When Walter died, the unthinkable happened, and the talk grew noticeably louder. No one wanted Waldo to be the next head of Corpselover. For the only time, there were doubts as to Lilith's leadership. People wondered if she were somehow blind to all her son's glaring faults or if it were just a simple matter of pride.

Again, no one in any of the branch families dared speak their doubts aloud. None of them would risk her wrath. They all feared Waldo becoming family head, but the general consensus was that Lilith would remain in power for many years yet. Waldo was unlikely to ever actually inherit. Even if she refused to arrange an accident, six of her children had already died, every one of them a respected magic user. What were the chances of an incompetent surviving?

During this time Hera had been upset. The idea of a fool man one day succeeding the great Lilith and ruining all she had built was infuriating. The sheer injustice of it was sickening, but of course there'd been nothing she could do.

When the news of the Council imposing their First Quest had come out there had been a unanimous sigh of relief. The Council had stepped in and done what Lilith should have done years before. Everyone assumed Waldo would never return and that Lilith would now select a proper heir.

"Instead we have this." Hera said to herself. "Well it doesn't matter."

No one besides Lilith believed Waldo was coming back. For even a skilled Dark Mage the conditions would have been near impossible. What chance did the idiot stand? As brilliant as she was, her aunt clearly had a blind spot where her own children were concerned. Well it didn't matter; Hera was willing to do anything for this opportunity. For the sake of entering the main family, and learning the deeper magics, she would even agree to be permanently chained to an incompetent and unworthy male.

Now that she'd had time to think about it though, she realized the terms were not near as bad as they appeared. Regardless of what Aunt Lilith believed Waldo was not coming back. Even if Lilith held onto her delusions for years, so what? She would be groomed to be the heir. Hera would master the necessary spells and learn everything else she needed to, to run the Corpselover family every bit as well as her aunt had. Sooner or later Lilith would accept the fact her son was not returning home and name her the heir.

Once that happened she could either wait for her time to come, or arrange an accident for her aunt. Either way, Hera was never going to be married or have children. She would rule with unquestioned authority and make her house even mightier than it was now, and when the time came she would find the best female candidate from among the branch families and adopt her as heir.

A wonderful future with unlimited possibilities awaited. Hera was headed towards the slave quarters, to pick out a couple young girls to help her celebrate her first night in the castle. As she was going a figure came around a corner up ahead. It was dressed in faded and tattered black robes with grey skin and jaundiced eyes. One look was enough to confirm the being was undead.

Seeing this did not concern Hera. Castle Corpselover was filled with undead; squads of them patrolled the halls and the outer courtyard. As a necromancer it was no more terrifying than a roach skittering across the floor. She barely even noticed until it deliberately moved to block her path and addressed her.

"Who are you?" It demanded.

Hera came to a halt about ten feet from the undead. "Oh, a zombie, I thought you were just another walking corpse."

Her lack of concern made it scowl. "I asked you who you were. You have robes so you must be a mage. What are you doing here?"

"You have independent thought? You can feel anger? That's astounding. Most zombies have limited mental capacity and can't feel emotions. You are a wonderful piece of work. I can't wait for Aunt Lilith to show me how she made you."

"You had better watch that mouth of yours you ugly scab or you're going to die." The zombie growled. "Now tell me who you are."

"Ugly scab?" Hera's left hand came up with three fingers bent. *Mixataros.*

The zombie's body suddenly went rigid and could not move.

"I take back what I said, a zombie insulting a necromancer is about as stupid as stupid can be, and if you think I'm ugly you need to look in a mirror. Now, shall I rip you apart or burn you?"

"Do you know who I am?"

"You are a defective undead soldier who is about to be unmade. I think I'll just tear you to pieces. Maybe my aunt and I can look you over and figure out what went wrong. It might make a good lesson."

"You can't destroy me! I am Walter Corpselover! The family heir!"

"Oh, yes, I've heard about you. You were the one killed by your grandfather inside the castle and Aunt Lilith brought you back. I can see she put a great deal of effort into it."

"That's right! I am her son and the family heir! Now release me immediately!"

"Despite the obvious quality of her work you don't have a strong grasp of reality or of logic do you? Well that's not surprising, even with someone as skilled as Aunt Lilith there are limits to what you can do with dead flesh. Still, you are a magnificent zombie. I really hope I am able to make something as good."

"Stop talking to me like I was just a servant! I am the family heir and if you do not release me right now I will see that you suffer a slow and painful death!"

A similar threat would have left any of the human servants shaking in terror.

Hera laughed at it.

"You are going to kill me? Really? I never imagined a zombie could tell jokes." She continued laughing.

"Stop mocking me! I am the heir! Do you understand what that means?"

She let out a couple more guffaws before speaking again. She had to make an effort to keep from giggling. His anger was just too amusing.

"You are not the heir. The dead cannot rule the living. Whatever you were in life all you are now is a zombie. Perhaps you can give orders to the slaves and the other undead, but not to me."

"Just who are you?"

"Hera Corpselover, daughter of Andris Corpselover and his wife Bianca. I am Lilith Corpselover's new apprentice."

"You lie! My mother would never take an apprentice! Never!"

"Yet here I am."

"My mother would have told me if she were planning to bring a new mage into the castle!"

"Why? Does she need your permission?"

Walter glared at her hatefully and she had to struggle to keep from laughing again.

"Well, as fun as this has been I think I'll be going now." She slashed her left hand through the air.

There was a sound of meat and bone being chopped. His right arm was torn from its socket and landed on the floor with a thud. Black blood dripped down from his open wound.

"That's for calling me ugly." Hera said as she walked right past him. The severed arm was in her way so she gave it a light kick. "Don't ever do it again or I will unmake you. The only reason I don't do it now is because there's a chance Aunt Lilith would be unhappy with me."

"You will die for this! Mother will never forgive you for attacking me!"

"The only person I was forbidden to harm was Waldo. Aunt Lilith never even mentioned you, and anyway, you're just a zombie."

Hera left him there, still unable to move, without a second thought.

XXX

In an empty corridor of her castle Lilith stood before a mirror with no reflection.

She felt a tremor run through her left hand and it shook just slightly.

Lilith grabbed it with her other hand and forced it to stop. *It's all right, I still have time.* When the tremor passed she let both hands fall to the side.

299

"Daughter, will you come and talk to me?"

Lilith waited patiently as colors swirled about and an image slowly took form. Gwendolyn appeared before her, throat cut and leaking fresh blood.

"Hello mother," she rasped.

"Hello dear, how are you?"

"Still dead."

"Yes I know, I mean has anything changed since the last time we talked?"

"Nothing ever changes on this side. It's very boring. That's why I would like to pass on."

Lilith felt a twinge of guilt at those words. When she had originally bound her daughter's soul to the mirror she had believed she was doing Gwendolyn a great service. Instead all she had done was consign her to a different sort of purgatory. Neither alive nor dead, she was a spirit trapped here between two worlds, unable to enjoy life but unable to move on to whatever awaited her.

"I am sorry my precious daughter, but I can't let you pass on yet."

"I know mother, you need my gifts for Waldo's sake. You must make one child suffer for the benefit of the other."

"Do you hate me for that?"

"No, I love my little brother and want to save him too. Besides, I am dead, I can wait."

"All I wanted was for all my children to be happy."

"No. What you wanted was power, we were an afterthought. You only started to care when most of us were gone."

I had too many enemies. Everyone on the Council was trying to control me. The branch families were trying to pressure me into taking a husband. They all feared my father and brother and thought I was nothing back then. I had to fight! I had to get power! I did what I had to!

It was true, but saying so would sound like a pathetic excuse. "Is my plan still on its course?"

"Plans within plans, wheels within wheels, you travel down the road that will bring you to your chosen end."

"In other words yes."

Gwen chuckled. "I see everything that I told you before, but as I have warned you, things can be changed. I see what will be, but also shadows of what still can be. Life is filled with choices and with possibilities; it's so very different from death."

"So even with your help nothing is guaranteed?"

"It will rain tomorrow, the sun will rise and set without being seen, and lava will flow around the Forge. Those things I will guarantee."

"Wonderful, can you tell me anything I can use?"

Gwendolyn sang in her gasping voice. "Three wives he will have, one painted with fire, one of gold, and one of night. One who loves him, one who follows him, and one who hates him. Each shall be bound to him, by marriage and by magic."

Lilith's eyes widened. This was new. "I see. Well I can already guess who is going to love and hate him, but who exactly is this third one?"

Gwen smiled playfully. "You will find out."

Lilith knew that Gwendolyn's prophesies always came true, just as she knew her daughter never revealed everything. "I really wish you could just tell me what you know without obscuring it."

"You must let me have my fun mother; it's very boring where I am."

"Well, I thank you for this knowledge."

Gwen nodded as her image began to fade away. "For what it's worth mother, all your children loved you, even Walter."

Lilith waited until the mirror was once again empty, then turned and walked away.

Chapter 28

A Matter Of Justice

It was a bright and sunny day as Melissa Cornwall strolled into Bittford. The last time she had been here was a couple years ago. She had returned to have another go at trying to recruit Roger.

The last couple of years had been spent tramping all over the north. She had visited several nations, preaching about unity, justice, and peace. Melissa had been received by royal courts and spoken directly to various rulers and noble families. She had used her magic to carry out requests from lords and wealthy merchants. There had also been charitable acts for the common folk, all done without any sort of reward or payment.

People needed to understand that the Order was different from the Independent Mages, who were out for themselves, or the Dark Mages who were simply evil. The White Mages served a higher cause. They wanted to restore the Shattered Lands and bring peace and order to them. To bring back the tranquility the world had known in ancient days under the Amoran Empire. Her order sought to purify the world and rid it of all its corrupt elements. White Mages could be counted on to help the weak and to always keep their promises. It was the duty of every single one of them to represent the ideals of Avalon and make all people, high or low, know they could be trusted.

It was a heroic crusade against the forces of chaos and darkness.

She was proud to be taking part in this valiant struggle. Melissa saw herself as a crusader helping to bring light to those in darkness. It was a war, but not every battle in it demanded bloodshed. Sometimes what was called for was a little kindness and help for those in need. If you could win over the hearts and minds of the people you could bind them to your cause.

Melissa was here to once again try and convince Roger the hedgewizard to travel with her to the Misty Isle. Once most independents saw the groves of soulwoods, the Great Library, and the Hidden Lady they were overawed and more than willing to join the Order. Even those who refused returned home to spread stories of the wonders of Avalon.

Right now the Order had a great deal of interest, not only in Roger, but in Lothas in general. There were hopes Dregal might soon join the Alliance. If Lothas could be enticed to join as well it would give them a long common border with Alteroth. They could begin cutting off trade routes and building up depots and bases for the inevitable war. So far as Melissa was concerned that day could not come soon enough. Every time she visited a royal court and told them about all the advantages of joining the Alliance she would always hear, 'but what would the Dark Mages do to us?' Avalon was far away, while Alteroth was close by. The thought of armies of undead lead by black robed mages could unnerve even kings.

Melissa's eyes swept southward in the direction of the enemy. The Dark Mages sabotaged everything they did. They had undermined the Alliance's growth and opposed all of Avalon's noble ambitions. Alteroth's very existence was intolerable. They had to go and would go; it was only a question of when. It pleased Melissa to know her efforts here were one small step toward that glorious end.

XXX

Walking through Bittford Melissa noted the less than friendly reception the locals were giving her.

People stared and made sure to keep their distance even when that meant crossing to the other side of the street. Children ran away or hid behind their parents. Some of the adults drew circles over their hearts. She waved to the villagers and called out greetings. Her efforts though only seemed to make the people more skittish. No one returned her greeting or even approached her.

The reaction was not a total surprise. Most people, especially common folk, feared all magic users. To many a wizard was every bit as terrifying as a troll or a vampire. That was part of why Avalon put so much effort into establishing their reputation with the people. Melissa had run into this sort of suspicion before and it did not particularly bother her. What was surprising was that these people were used to seeing magic and had a magic user living among them. She clearly recalled the people being much more receptive and friendly during her last visit.

I wonder if anything has happened.

When she sensed a fellow magic user nearby, she soon spotted a balding man in brown robes heading up the street in her direction. Melissa smiled and approached him. Running into him in the middle of the village was good luck; it would save her time.

"Hello again Roger, I bring to you the blessings of Unity, Justice, and Peace." She offered him a bow, something normally only reserved for those of noble birth.

"Hello." He did not return her bow, and made a point to keep his distance from her.

She was surprised by his reaction. The last time she had been here he had insisted on buying her drinks and trying to get as close to her as possible. In the end he'd shown no interest in visiting Avalon or converting to her path, but he'd had plenty of interest in her. She had expected a far warmer welcome from him.

"My name is Melissa; I tried to recruit you two years ago. We had some very lively debates about magic and how a mage can best serve the people. Perhaps you have forgotten?"

"I remember you. What do you want?"

She continued to smile. "Perhaps we could go to the Inn and talk a bit over some ale. As we did the last time we met. I have some interesting stories to tell you and I was thinking I could offer you some assistance if you'd like."

"What sort of assistance?"

"If you'd like I could add some spells to your spellbook and offer you some magical ingredients." That was a normal practice when trying to recruit others into the Order. You gave without asking for anything in return. It helped to build up trust, and it put the person you were recruiting into your debt.

The offer was not always accepted, but she had never seen it spark anger before.

"I see. So first you rob me, and then you offer to give me back what you've stolen. Is that the way of it?"

"Robbed you?"

"That's right; one of your kind stole everything that I had! My spellbook, my wand, all my magical supplies, and all my money too! He was a white like you who came here with this beautiful girl named Alice he said was his wife. He just used her as a distraction to knock me out from behind and then take everything!"

Melissa's spine stiffened. "You must be mistaken. White Mages do not steal. I'm sorry if someone stole from you, but it could not have been a member of my order."

"He was a magic user, and he wore white robes, so what does that make him?"

"An imposter," Melissa answered without missing a beat.

"Because White Mages are all paragons of virtue? I never believed your sort were as pure as you claimed. When a man talks about how honest he is you need to keep a hand on your purse."

"We do not stoop to criminal acts for personal gain." *When we commit crimes it is always for the cause.*

"Does that mean you would if it were for a greater purpose?"

"We serve the cause of Unity, Justice, and Peace. When our cause comes into conflict with local laws or with petty officials, we are sometimes forced to take action for the sake of the greater good."

"So you admit your kind will break the law if it's for the good of Avalon?"

She frowned at him. "You are twisting my words."

"No. I am calling you out on what you just said; you're fine with breaking the law if it's for a greater good."

"What I am referring to is punishing the guilty and protecting the innocent. No member of my order would ever commit theft. Such things are beneath us."

"What about forcing someone to join your order? I lose all my money and magical items, then lo and behold, another white shows up offering to help replace what I lost. But at a cost I'll bet, like say my agreeing to visit Avalon with you?"

"That is ridiculous. I had no idea you had been robbed and I certainly was not going to demand anything in return for my assistance. My offer was made out of an honest desire to help a fellow magic user."

"How convenient."

Melissa took a deep breath. She had grown a thick skin during her years. He was hardly the first person to be rude to her. What was much harder to swallow were abuses aimed at Avalon and at the reputation of her Order.

Roger hocked and spat on the ground in front of her feet as some peasant woman might have. "That is what I think of all you damn White Mages! You talk about honor and all that but then you'll use dirty tricks to get what you want. Do you think me a fool? You expect me to believe its coincidence that one of you assaults me and leaves me with nothing just before you show up offering me your help? Some things are too obvious to be denied. You knew I would never agree to leave my home, so you did this to force me. Well it won't work. My friends and neighbors will help me get by, and I would rather give up magic all together than join your kind."

"Roger, I give you my word that whoever it was that did this was not a White Mage. Did this man tell you his name?"

"He said he was Waldo Rabbit, and the vixen he was with said her name was Alice Rabbit."

Melissa lifted an eyebrow. "He said his last name was Rabbit? Honestly? Come now, that's a false name if I've ever heard one! What did he look like?"

Walton crossed his arms over his chest and narrowed his eyes as he answered. "He had white robes, like yours. He had golden hair, like yours. He had yellow eyes, like yours. He had pale white skin, like yours. He had the *look* of the Misty Isle. I've met two of your sort before and he would have fit in perfect with the both of you. He was a White Mage, no question!"

The description was a problem. Most of the folk in Lothas and the surrounding lands tended to have dark hair and eyes of brown or green. Blondes were exceedingly rare in this part of the world. Yellow eyes were unique to the people of Avalon.

"Could he have been using an illusion?"

Walton snorted. "I'd have sensed it."

This was becoming more and more troubling. She had assumed this person was an imposter. The physical appearance argued against that. Could he be a deserter? It did happen from time to time. The Order made many demands of its members, and some lacked the commitment and strength of will needed. Abandoning your sacred duty was a crime punishable by death. The first thing deserters normally did was throw away their robes and flee as far and as fast as they could. Lothas was pretty far from the isle. Could some deserter have come here thinking he would be safe? Possibly, but why keep your robes in that case? It was like flaunting your crime to the entire world and asking the Order to come and hunt you down.

Whoever this man was his actions had hurt the reputation of Avalon and all White Mages everywhere. That could not be tolerated.

"This Waldo Rabbit is no White Mage, I promise you. I will find him and punish him, not just for his theft but for the far greater crime of impersonating a member of my order. I will return with his head and with all that he stole from you."

"I don't believe a word of it."

"I don't tell lies."

"That's what a liar would say."

The way he glared at her it was obvious nothing she said would change his mind. So she offered him a bow, said a pleasant farewell, and walked away.

She was sure when she came back with this imposter's head in a sack that would convince him.

Chapter 29

A True Knight

This was the time she liked best, early evening. It was summer, so there was no need for the fire place. Torches along the wall provided all the light needed. The Inn of Lost Sighs was filled with customers, almost all of them regulars. Her girls were working. They were either sitting with customers here on the ground floor or else satisfying their desires up in their rooms.

Elsa watched as her soiled doves interacted with her patrons. They smiled and laughed and gave the men they were with all of their attention. Her girls rubbed sore shoulders and caressed arms and legs. They made the men who came here feel wanted in a way their wives or girlfriends never could. It was a feeling every man hungered for.

It was a game, an illusion, a slow seduction.

Except for the youngsters, all her customers knew that none of it was real, but that didn't make their pleasure any less. Here every man could pretend to be handsome and strong and charming. He could talk to a beautiful woman without fear of being rejected or mocked.

Many of her guests came here just for that, the chance to enjoy a woman's company. To pretend the interest she was showing him was real and not part of an act. They would spend their coins on ale and food and were satisfied.

As Elsa watched, Nancy leaned over to her customer and whispered a suggestion in his ear. The man gave an eager nod and hurriedly finished his ale. Nancy then took him by the hand and led him towards the stairs. A couple of his friends lifted their mugs and shouted at him to ride her long and hard.

Elsa chuckled. Yes, some of her customers were happy with a meal and some drinks, and a little attention. Others just wanted spread a woman's legs open and slip inside. Well, either was fine, so long as the customer had the coin. Every meal, every drop of ale, and every trip upstairs brought her profit. The Inn of Lost Sighs wasn't simply a whorehouse, it was a place that catered to the wishes of its customers, and strove to make each one happy.

Given how busy they were she estimated her take from all the sales would come to between fifteen and twenty silver dalters. A good sum, no complaints. Of course it paled beside what she'd made about two weeks ago when that black wizard had suddenly shown up and bought Alice. In one transaction she'd made about three months income. All the trouble she'd put up with from that girl had been more than worth it.

Though there was still one more issue to deal with there.

In the immediate aftermath, when that stupid wizard had gotten himself killed, Alice had revealed herself. The fact Elsa had, had a succubus working for her had threatened to ruin her reputation. In Lothas people, especially those of the upper classes, looked down on brothels and prostitutes. They were however more or less accepted as necessary. Men had needs after all.

Lusting after a monster though was another matter entirely. That was bestiality; a sin against all things decent and against nature itself. Any man who would fornicate with a monster, even one as lovely as Alice, was considered disgusting and beyond contempt. No self-respecting man would ever admit to being attracted to a monster, that would be like confessing you wanted to have sex with a cow.

So given the fact that half the men in Stratford had been hungering for Alice, her suddenly exposing her true form had been a serious problem. If anyone had thought she'd known the truth Elsa would have lost everything. She would have been lucky to escape with the clothes on her back and a whole skin.

Fortunately, she'd always had a sharp wit and a sense for sudden changes in the wind. Elsa had immediately joined in with the crowd shouting about her horror and shock at the discovery of what Alice really was. Sweet dear Alice a monster? How horrible! Who could have guessed? Since no one else had known the truth, and since so many had been fooled, everyone had just accepted that she had been tricked as well. After the initial shock people quickly decided to not speak of it any more. By mutual consent Alice was to be forgotten and no one would ever mention her again.

Elsa had soon recruited a new fourteen year old girl to serve as the barmaid. Mossa was pretty and cheerful and worked hard at her new job. She was friendly to all the men who came here and got along well with the staff. Unfortunately she was also flat and a bit on the plain side. The customers had no complaints about her, but none of them wasted much time on her either. Certainly none of them were coming here just to stare at her all night.

Her girls were actually pleased by the change; they had always resented Alice's charms and the way so many men had fawned over her. Elsa's soiled doves had welcomed plain faced Mossa with open arms and made her feel right at home.

Elsa was satisfied, and in a couple years, if Mossa blossomed, would make her a soiled dove. Alice was gone, but she had made a hundred gold pieces from her. The chaos caused by her revelation had passed and things had returned to normal. Her business was running smoothly and she was content.

She had only one worry.

As if summoning him, the door to the common room burst open and in he strode; Sir Lancel Griffinheart. As he always did, he entered with head held high and with a confident air. The way he walked with shoulders back and with long easy strides, it was clear he expected people to get out of his way. He was the heir of the Griffinheart family and all of its vast lands and wealth, a superb horseman, skilled with the lance and the sword, the possessor of the magical blade *Steeltooth*, the slayer of the troll of Red Rock, a distant relative to the royal family and nineteenth in line for the succession. In short he was one of the richest and most powerful men in Lothas.

Everyone in his way quickly moved. They bowed and murmured words of respect and deference. If Lancel even heard them he paid no mind. He was wearing steel plate armor with his family's crest emblazoned on its front. Holstered by his side was his magical broadsword along with a dagger and a fat purse. Following in his wake were six men at arms, all in chainmail and with long swords and daggers of their own. Wherever Sir Lancel traveled he always kept his loyal men close by.

Lancel was a tall, muscular man with a rugged face. It was a handsome face, but the features were all rigid. There was not an ounce of softness to it. One look and you were certain that this was not a man to cross. His grey eyes were especially unnerving, they seemed to always carry a threat of malice, even when he smiled or pretended to be charming. Sir Lancel could be most chivalrous when he chose and most generous. Just so long as he got what he wanted.

Elsa watched his eyes darting about the common room. He spotted Mossa in her barmaid's uniform and instantly dismissed her. He continued looking about. Elsa knew who he was searching for. Her stomach was queasy and she felt a sliver of fear making its way up her spine. Dealing with Sir Lancel was always a delicate matter. He was not used to hearing the word 'no' and did not like the sound of it. He did however care about his reputation and tried always to guard it.

Elsa had played on his personal pride by pointing out how poor it would look to steal Alice by force. He had agreed to negotiate with her to avoid any black mark to his good name. Elsa had aimed to get fifty gold ducats from him. She had always understood though that there were limits, and that it would be dangerous to push too far. Now she would need to very gently give him the bad news that the object of his affections was gone.

At last the knight stopped looking all around and focused his grey eyes on her "Where is she?"

He strode over to stand on the other side of the bar across from her.

Despite her girth Elsa managed a smooth bow. "Welcome back Sir Lancel. As always, your presence in my establishment greatly honors me."

"I am sure that it does, now tell me where she is." From his belt he removed his purse and tossed it down on the bar. "I have had enough of waiting. That is twenty five ducats, much more than she is worth. Wherever she is bring her out, I mean to have her tonight and take her with me when I leave."

Elsa made no move to touch the purse. Instead she dipped her head in apology. "I am very sorry Sir Lancel, but I am afraid Alice is no longer available."

"I am in no mood for bargaining or delays. Twenty five is all I'll pay, and it is more than generous. I have been hungering for her all this time, and I mean to have her tonight. Now where is she?"

"Gone, I am afraid."

"What do you mean gone? She was indentured to you. Are you saying she ran away?"

"No," Elsa replied cautiously. This had to handled very, very carefully. Men filled with pride and lust could be extremely dangerous, and that was when they weren't carrying magical swords. "Someone else paid to take her off my hands and married her as soon as he did."

His smile withered and his eyes narrowed. "That someone would want to marry her on sight I believe. What I have trouble with is imagining you agreeing to it. You certainly had no trouble rejecting my offers."

No trouble?! It was like fighting off a rabid wolf with a stick! "I would never think to refuse you Sir Lancel." She again dipped her head. "I am a woman of business; I merely sought a proper price."

"What you are is an old whore."

"That too."

He snatched back his purse and tied it once more to his belt. "So tell me, why did you agree to sell her after refusing me three times?"

"He asked me my price to free her. I told him it would cost a hundred gold coins. He paid it, without even batting an eye." She spread her hands. "What could I do?"

"A hundred gold ducats? You could buy a keep for that. No woman is worth so much."

"To this one man she was. As I said, he saw her and immediately declared he wanted her for his wife. He paid to free her, offered her flowers and made his declaration. She accepted and they were husband and wife. I admit I was quite amazed, in all my years it was surely the most romantic thing I had ever seen. Like something from a tale of old."

Elsa hoped the image of such a romantic union would salve Lancel's pride and help him accept his loss.

"Is this some sort of lie? If it is you will regret it."

"I would never lie to you Sir Lancel."

"Who was this man? If he was as rich as you say I would know him."

"I am certain you would Sir Lancel, if he were from Lothas. He was a foreigner though, a mysterious one, he appeared without warning and left with his beloved just as suddenly. I never saw his face before that day and do not expect to see it ever again. I do promise you Sir that what I say is true. I would never have freed her had he not paid me a fortune."

Every word Elsa had spoken was true. She had censored the events of that day to spare his pride. There was no way Lancel could be happy to have lost Alice. She didn't need to make him happy though, she just needed him to accept the fact. The image of some foreign prince riding in and swooping up Alice in a moment of passion would make it easier. As would the thought he had spent more than the knight himself would ever dream to.

Lancel turned from her and instead faced the men and women sitting at their tables or standing near the walls. "Is what she says true?" He demanded. "Is Alice really gone? Did some stranger really claim her as his wife?"

As she'd known they would, all her customers and girls nodded their heads.

"Aye, it's true."

"She is gone."

"Yes."

"It's so."

"She left."

The common folk steered clear of nobles as much as they could. When they had to deal with them they had enough sense not to say or do anything to upset them. Elsa could see that Lancel remained furious, but that he was starting to believe that Alice was truly gone. She was just beginning to relax when she heard harsh laughter coming from one of the tables.

The sound drew Sir Lancel's full attention. There at one of the back tables was a man in plain work clothes bent over an empty pitcher laughing so hard he looked in danger of falling out of his chair. He was with a couple friends who were whispering to him urgently.

"You find something funny?" Lancel slowly walked across the room to the table.

The Inn was abruptly silent. The only sounds were of the man's laughter and of the knight's steps as he crossed the floor. Every eye watched them. No one dared to move or even to breathe. At the table the man's companions sat there motionless, obviously terrified of what might happen. If a knight felt like slitting a commoner's throat he could do so and walk away from it with hands clean.

Lancel came to a stop in front of the table. "Why are you laughing?"

Harold Brauer needed a moment to stop. When he was done he was splayed out half in his chair and half on the table. Elsa wished the man had not paid a healer to repair his jaw. He was smiling drunkenly at the knight towering over him. "I am laughing because you don't know the truth."

With those words Elsa felt a chill flow through her. "Please ignore him Sir Lancel. He's just a drunk and…"

An angry wave of Lancel's hand silenced her. "What truth are you speaking of? Are you saying Alice is still here?"

"No, no, she flew away." The words made Harold burst out into laughter again. His friends and many of the others looked away uncomfortably.

317

Lancel did not miss the reactions. "What do you mean? Did she run away? Was she taken? Tell me the truth or you will regret it."

"The truth?" Harold answered as his laughter died away. "I can tell you the truth, I was there, and I saw it happen."

"Then tell me, I am not accustomed to being the source of so much mirth. Depending on what you say I may forgive your presumption."

"Well she was married all right, like Elsa said, but she left a few things out."

"Shut your lying mouth or I'll never let you back in my place!" Elsa yelled.

Lancel turned back around to look at her.

The fury she saw made Elsa want run and hide. "He... he is drunk and will only tell you lies."

"Then you have nothing to fear. Now be silent, I want to hear what he has to say." He turned back to the table. "Speak, was Alice married or not?"

"She was, she married a black wizard."

"A black wizard? You mean a Dark Mage from Alteroth?"

Harold nodded drunkenly. "He was dressed all in black and he said he was from another country. Said he'd come here just to take Alice. He put a spell on her and made her fall in love with him. She never would have married him otherwise, I know it."

Lancel again turned back to stare at Elsa. "You sold her to a Dark Mage? Have you no shame at all? Everyone knows the sorts of things they do. How could you sacrifice her like that?"

"His gold was real enough, and it spends as well as any other."

"What was this wizard's name? What direction did he leave in? How many days ago? I will track him down and cut him to pieces. I'll save Alice."

This brought another round of laughter, this time it was tinged with bitterness and mockery. "Don't bother. When we saw him trying to take her we threw him in the river. He is gone."

"He is dead?" Lancel asked in surprise. "Then what happened to Alice?"

"She flew away."

Lancel frowned. "Have a care with your tone, drunk or not you should be more respectful. If Alice ran away you might have mentioned that from the start. I will find her."

"Don't bother Sir Knight, she's a monster."

"What did you call her peasant?" He placed a hand on the hilt of his sword.

Harold looked back at him, too full of ale and sorrow to care. "She's a monster. When I say she flew away that's just what I mean. I saw it; we all saw it, right there on the bridge. She grew wings out of her back, big black leathery wings, like a bat's but a hundred times bigger. It wasn't just wings either, horns and claws and a tail. I saw it clear as day. Beautiful Alice was a monster. I saw it, and then she flapped her wings and shot up into the sky like an arrow."

"You lie." He began to draw his sword.

"He doesn't lie sir!" One of the man's companions burst out. "It's the truth I swear it!"

"It is true sir," the man's other friend spoke nervously. "We all saw it, ask anyone."

Lancel hesitated and did not pull out his blade. He looked about the common room. All around him, at every table, he saw men slowly nod their heads. No one spoke, they looked ashamed and fearful, but they nodded.

He turned his attention to Elsa. She gave a single quick nod before lowering her eyes.

"Are you saying that all this time I was trying to take a filthy monster into my bed?"

He was met with silence.

Sir Lancel paused and gathered himself.

"Alice never existed. None of you are to speak of her ever again. You will not mention me either. I have never visited this place. Should any of you spread any tales I will come back here and turn you into dog meat. Now all of you get out."

Everyone hesitated and looked at each other.

"I SAID GET OUT!"

The men and women moved, knocking over chairs and tables as they stampeded toward the door. Both of Harold's friends grabbed an arm and got him to his feet. From behind her bar Elsa hurried to join them. As soon as she was out from behind it Lancel roughly grabbed her.

"Not you," he growled.

Lancel motioned to his men to clear out the kitchen and upstairs as well.

"You knew, didn't you?" He tightened his grip.

320

"No! No, never! How could I?"

"How could you not?!"

From upstairs a customer ran down wearing nothing but his breeches, he had a tunic and his boots in his hands. Right on his heels was a young girl who had nothing on but a skirt.

"Please Sir Lancel! I am innocent I swear!"

"What would an old whore like you know about innocence?"

"I know I did nothing wrong! I never knew I swear it! I swear it by all the gods!"

His grip tightened like a vice and made her whimper.

"You lie."

"I don't I swear it! Please! You are hurting me!"

"I aim to do much worse to you. You always loved gold didn't you? That was all that mattered. You sold Alice for a hundred pieces of gold. Tell me, how much is your own life worth to you?"

"Everything! All that I have! Please don't kill me!"

"If you were a man I already would have." He let go of her. "Out of my sight!"

Elsa ran as fast as her fat body would take her. She ran outside and into a crowded foot bridge.

Lancel reached into the bar and pulled out a couple bottles of spirits. He opened the bottles and poured the contents out onto the wooden floor. He then went over to the nearest torch and pulled it out of its hold.

"She said her life was worth everything. This is still better than she deserves." He calmly dropped the torch into the spilled liquor. The flames caught and spread across in a flash. Much of the common room was burning as Lancel led his men outside. Before stepping onto the footbridge he took a moment to look back at the Inn.

"I am much too merciful."

Chapter 30

What A Husband Would Do

Waldo blew the last bit of shaving from his wand.

Carefully examining his handiwork he gave a satisfied nod and put his knife away.

"It's done."

"It is?" She was at his side almost instantly, her head craning over his shoulder. "So can I finally see what you carved?"

"No," he replied. "A mage's wand is his most private... hey!"

Alice snatched it out of his hand and was looking it over.

"Give that back to me right now." He tried to grab hold of it, but Alice simply held it up out of reach.

"I'll give it back to you in a minute. I just want to see what you wrote."

He tried to jump up, but could not get high enough. He felt like a child being denied a sweet.

"Alice I command you to give me back my wand."

"In a minute."

He tried jumping again, only to have her dance around him.

"You are the worst familiar! You are supposed to obey my direct commands."

"I keep telling you darling, I am your wife not your familiar."

Waldo silently cursed his botched binding spell and swore to get it right next time.

Alice managed to get a good, close look at the wand. There were three names carved.

Lilith. Gwendolyn. Alice.

She handed the wand back to him. "I know Lilith is your mother, but who is Gwendolyn?"

He slid it into one of the many hidden pockets in his robes. "Why do you ask?"

"Just curious, it's not like I care." She paused a beat. "So who is she?"

"The only one I have ever loved. Besides my mother of course"

Her mouth fell open. "What? Loved? Seriously?"

"Is it really such a surprise?" He was annoyed by her reaction. "I am human after all."

"Well, when you put it like that, I suppose not." Alice shook her head as if to get rid of some bad images. "So what is she like?"

"Clever, sarcastic, and with a very dry sense of humor; she could see something funny in almost anything."

"Could? You're using the past tense."

"She was killed on her First Quest, she's mostly dead now."

One of Alice's eyebrows quirked. "Mostly?"

"She's a ghost."

Alice stood there for a long moment, perhaps expecting him to tell her he was joking. "You really mean it."

"Why would I not?"

"So, what, does she haunt the castle or something?"

"No. Her soul is bound to a mirror. I can see her whenever I want, but she's not as much fun as she used to be. She's always complaining about how boring it is to be dead and trapped between worlds."

Alice opened her mouth, and then closed it and gave a slight shake of her head. "Well I'm sorry for your loss."

"Thank you."

Alice began looking at her fingernails. "So was she prettier than me?"

"Why would you care about that?"

"I am just curious. So was she?"

"No, she was pretty, but you are a true beauty."

Alice sent him a relieved smile. She might have stopped with that, but apparently felt the need to ask one more question.

"You never did anything with her did you?"

"What do you mean?"

"When you kissed me you said that was your first. So that means you never kissed her… right?"

"On the lips?" He shook his head. "We only ever kissed on cheeks or foreheads."

"That's all right then."

"Though when we bathed together she would give me little kisses on my neck some times."

"Grrrrkkk." Her mouth was twisted and she was making a half wheezing half choking sound.

"Alice are you all right? Did you swallow a bug or something?"

"You, you took baths with this girl?"

"Yes I did. Normally I would have slaves bathe me, but Gwendolyn enjoyed washing with me." He smiled fondly. "I miss those times."

Alice's jaw moved but she couldn't say anything.

"So you saw her naked?"

He glanced at her in confusion. "Well of course, do people here take baths with their clothes on?"

Alice shook her head.

"So what else did you do? Did you sleep with her too?"

"Every once in a while."

"What?"

Waldo nodded. "Sometimes when I had trouble sleeping I would go visit her bedroom. She was always happy to let me slide under the covers." He sighed wistfully. "I always slept peacefully when I was in her arms."

Alice put both hands to her face. "I really need to stop asking you questions about your past. So just who was she? A slave? Another magic user?"

"She was my sister."

"Wait a minute! She was your sister? Your sister!"

"Did I not mention that?"

When she smacked him in the back of the head and stormed off muttering to herself Waldo couldn't begin to guess what the problem was.

XXX

After the little exchange their evening was routine. They made a fire, had dinner, Alice assaulted his virtue to satisfy her appetite for male lust, and then they went to sleep.

Despite the occasional punches and head slaps Waldo was getting used this new life. With a spellbook and wand he was feeling more at ease. Granted the spellbook had little useful magic in it, and he didn't expect this wand to work any better his others had. Still, just having them made him feel like a proper mage again.

And, despite her constant defiance, he was glad to have Alice by his side. She provided his meals, acted as guide, and gave him a sense of security. No matter her appearance, she was a succubus, a Great Monster, just having her with him meant he was protected.

Things had not gone as he had originally planned, but now they looked to be back on track. He went to sleep easily, looking forward to the next day.

XXX

All magic users had the ability to sense magic.

It was something they were born with along with the ability to access and shape mana. A mage would always know a magical item when he touched it or sense a ward. Mages could sense each other as well. It was impossible to hide what you were from a fellow magic user.

Waldo's ability to sense the undead was different. It was a unique trait that he had inherited from his mother. When undead were in the area Waldo would get a feeling of cold. Whenever Walter would try one of his ambushes it was as if there were a chill breeze blowing. He would be able to sense him and about how near he was based on how strong the cold was.

As he was sleeping he felt a sudden freezing, like plunging down into ice water. His body shook with the chill.

Waldo came completely awake and sat bolt upright. He tossed off his blanket and scrambled to his feet. Grabbing his spellbook Waldo rushed over to Alice and shook her roughly awake.

"Huh, what?"

"Quiet," he hissed. "Hurry and get up." He grabbed her arm and got her to her feet.

"Hey, what's going on?" She blinked and looked around. "Why are you so scared?"

"We need to run." He took her by the hand and began to lead her through the darkened woods.

"Wait, but our things…" she had her purse always on her, but everything else was being left behind.

Waldo was carrying only his spellbook and the various magical items in its many pockets.

There was a half-moon out and the stars, but it was still very dark. He dragged her through the bushes and tall grass, ducking

328

beneath tree limbs that he could barely see. He was stumbling, tripping over the uneven ground, trying to keep his balance and keep going.

"Darling what is going on? I can feel your fear."

"There is something behind us." He kept running, praying he would not trip and fall.

"What is?" She glanced back over her shoulder but there was nothing.

"Something very bad," he panted.

Alice did not understand, but she held onto his hand and ran with him.

As he tried to lead them to safety Waldo could feel the icy presence keeping up with them. They had gained a little distance, but not much, and it was following. It would not stop chasing them until it caught up. Waldo knew well that the dead never tired.

As they ran he caught his foot on a tree root. Stumbling, he lost his balance and fell.

"Darling are you okay?" Alice quickly got him back up.

"This isn't going to work." Waldo panted. "We can't run away." He looked at her. "Alice I need you to transform and fly us out, as far from here as you can."

She hesitated, he knew she didn't like to transform in front of him. Alice could sense his fear through their bond though, and had to know how desperately he wanted to escape.

"All right darling."

Closing her eyes she breathed deeply. There was the sound of tearing flesh. Large leather wings ripped out of her back. Horns, claws, and tail all appeared.

She wrapped her arms around him.

"Hold tight."

Her wings stretched out then flapped down. Waldo felt the jerk as they lifted up off the ground. When Alice flew on her own she was as swift and graceful as a hawk. When she carried him her movements were more like a lame vulture's. They rose sluggishly and topped the tree line.

Alice was just starting to take them away when Waldo heard a sharp crack.

From down below a bolt of lightning shot up and struck Alice right in her side.

"Aaaaahhh!!" She howled.

She lost control and they began to tumble out of the sky. Her wings spread and slowed their descent, but they still came back down to earth hard and fast.

XXX

His ribs and back hurt like hell, each breath sent a stabbing ache into his side. He got to his hands and knees, glad just to be alive. What worried him was what was in the back of his head; fear, confusion, and pain. Alice's emotions were a jumbled mix and they were coming to him weakly. He knew what direction she was in. He staggered to his feet and went to find her.

She had landed about twenty feet from him and was on her side, moaning. The air was filled with the smoke and the smell of burnt meat. He could see a horrible burn wound on her side.

There was some blood, but the lightning had mostly sealed the wound. The danger was in how badly hurt she might be internally.

"Alice." he whispered.

Her eyes were half open, and she struggled just to turn her head in his direction. She spoke just one word, but he heard it clearly.

"Run."

Waldo took a deep breath that sent pain stabbing into his side.

She could not even stand right now. In her present condition she was worthless to him. Waldo knew what any Dark Mage would do in a situation like this. If your life was in danger and your familiar could no longer fight or help you escape, you saved yourself and abandoned her.

That was what his mother would do.

If he did that Alice would definitely die. Their short flight had gained them some space, but it was coming. If he ran it might be satisfied with her and allow him to escape. In a sense this was what a familiar was for; they were supposed to serve and protect you and sacrifice themselves if necessary. She would simply be fulfilling her purpose.

"Please... go..." she gasped. There were tears in her eyes.

Through the bond he could sense worry, and it was for him. Lying there in the dirt, helpless and in such pain, she was thinking about him.

"It's going to be okay Alice." He told her as gently as he could.

Her tear filled eyes stared up at him.

"After all, a husband has to protect his wife."

He could tell his words startled her. After the initial surprise though she managed a slight grin.

There was very little time. He knelt down beside her and gently placed his hands by her wound. The flesh had been charred black, with the edges raw and tender. Despite being as gentle as he could she still winced.

"This will hurt, but try and bear with it. I need you to not cry out."

"I understand."

With that he summoned up his mana and began a healing spell. *"Noxtoros est corpus desral venti est dostri."*

His hands glowed with a pale, silvery light.

Alice gasped and twisted, he had to hold her down and keep his hands on her.

As the energy flowed from him into her, the spell began to repair what had been damaged. Blood vessels were made whole, muscles reformed and knit back together, the body regenerated what had been destroyed or lost.

"It hurts," Alice cried, trying her best to stay quiet.

"I know, and I am sorry, but it can't be helped. Your body is doing something it shouldn't be able to. The pain is part of the price. I can heal you, but I can't make it painless."

She nodded and clamped down her jaw. Her claws dug into the earth.

Waldo focused on the spell and set everything else aside. Alice's pain and the approach of the being who was hunting them were unimportant. He needed all his concentration for the magic.

332

This came naturally to him. The words spilled from his lips and he could feel the mana flowing easily through him and into her. This was the one thing he had always excelled at, his gift. No matter how he struggled with the more important magics, no one had ever doubted his ability to heal.

So many times he had despaired because his talent was in an area that no one valued. How he had longed to be able to summon monsters or call down fire or animate the dead. Abilities that were prized.

Right now though he was glad that this was his talent.

His spell mended her from the inside out, repairing the most serious damage first. Alice was lucky that none of her organs had been damaged. He could have still healed her, but it would have demanded far more time than he had now. As it was she would be whole again without even a scar. The last thing the spell healed was the skin, the blackened flesh cracked and peeled away, leaving raw, tender, pink skin.

"I've healed you." He got up, wiping the blood and black bits from his hands. Taking his wand out he drew a large circle in the dirt surrounding her. "You'll be fine."

Alice slowly sat up, she cautiously rubbed her side. "You're amazing."

"No I'm not. If I were we wouldn't have had to run away."

Inside the circle he was drawing arcane runes and symbols from memory. There were ninety nine arcane symbols, each one with its own specific meaning and significance. Just as putting together the right combination of letters would create words and sentences, if you wrote out the correct combination of symbols you could create permanent or long lasting magical effects. But only if you had the exact formula. Protection was a word, portection was nothing but the same letters in the wrong order.

He *thought* he had the right formula. At that moment Waldo would have gladly traded five years of his life to have his old spellbook again. Of course he wasn't sure he had five years to trade.

When he finished he stuck two fingers in the circle. "*Loratos.*" He sent a flicker of mana into it. Before his eyes there was a subtle glimmer from the runes and circle and he could sense the ward now active and radiating magic.

He gave a satisfied nod. There were a few things he was actually good for.

"What are you doing?" Alice asked.

"This circle will hide you from what's chasing us. Stay inside of it until I summon you, or until the ball of fire rises. If I haven't summoned you by then, you're free." It was a rather unnecessary point, the bond would tell her.

She drew a sharp breath and tried to reach for him.

"Goodbye Alice."

He ran from her, careful not to step on what he had drawn.

"Waldo!"

Ignoring her he ran towards the thing that had come for him.

XXX

As he ran towards the danger, rather than away from it, Waldo understood just what he was doing. Every step was likely bringing him closer to his death. His mother would have been

334

very disappointed in him. Not necessarily for what he was doing, but for the reason behind it.

When he could feel the presence growing near he stopped and looked about for a patch of clear ground. When he saw some he hurriedly drew a circle with the same runes and symbols inside of it.

"*Loratos.*"

The ward activated. Standing inside the circle it would give him some protection. He took out his wand and faced what was coming.

It would not be long now.

XXX

Only a couple minutes later he saw a figure step out of the darkness and into the pale moon light. Tattered black robes fluttered and swayed with the evening breeze as it detached itself from the shadows. The hood was pulled up, but Waldo caught a glimpse of what was there.

A grinning skull with yellowish light emanating from its eye sockets.

He was able to make out the hands at the end of robe's sleeves, they were skeletal with greyish, mummified skin.

The being came to halt about twenty yards from him. It simply stood there.

After a slight pause the robed head nodded. "Hello grandson."

"Hello grandfather."

Chapter 31

Grandfather

Waldo was surprised when he heard a chuckle.

"You know I kept track of all of you, and I know what people said about you in particular Waldo. I assumed it was all just meaningless venom. Yet here you are, dressed in snow white robes. Maybe you really are a White Mage as others say."

"I am wearing these because of circumstances. My original robes were lost and these were the only replacements I could find."

That produced a soft rasping laugh. "So you had no choice? Yet the first time you leave Alteroth you are in white. The Dark Powers are playing with you."

"It wouldn't be the first time."

Waldo saw the hood shake as there was more scratchy laughter. "Well, you do have courage. That pleases me. You have no idea how disappointing it is to discover one of your grandchildren to be a coward. Just standing there you have already surpassed your brother Walter."

"Thank you."

"I dare say you may actually have some real talent. I was most surprised to find you had a succubus in your service. Had you been just a little further away you might have escaped me. Did I kill your pet?"

Waldo couldn't keep from snarling at the mocking tone. "Yes, she's dead."

There was a momentary pause. Waldo could see those sickly orbs staring out at him. They made him feel defenseless.

"How interesting," his grandfather stretched out the words. "You are lying."

It extended a boney hand and pointed in the direction Waldo had come from.

"I cast detection spells before coming here grandson. I know she is alive." There was another pause. "Could it actually be you are trying to save her?"

Waldo said nothing.

"It's very noble. Are you certain you are not a White Mage?"

"She doesn't matter."

"True, but I'll eat her anyway after I am done with you."

"Leave her alone, she has nothing to do with this!"

"Such anger. Your lifespan can be counted in minutes, yet you are worried about your little succubus. Tell me, is she your familiar?"

"Yes."

"Then why are you trying to save her?" There seemed genuine curiosity. "There is never any reason why a master should put his own life in danger for the familiar's sake. Didn't your mother at least teach you that much?"

"Yes, I know. She has already saved my life though, and done more for me than I probably deserve. I suppose I just want to do the same for her."

"Gratitude?" It mocked. "That's not something to be wasted on a servant. My daughter really was indulgent with you wasn't she? She always was weak, but she used to have standards."

"Weak? My mother is the strongest person I know! Everyone acknowledges her the strongest Dark Mage in Alteroth."

"The standards have really fallen then."

Waldo opened his mouth with a sharp retort, but held up. He stopped and analyzed the situation.

It is not even bothering to use a wand. His grandfather wasn't attacking him. The one offensive spell used had been to prevent his escape. This behavior was like that of a cat with a mouse.

"May I ask you something grandfather?"

"Certainly."

"Why are you doing this?" Waldo asked. "Not just with me, why did you turn on the family?"

"Because it was fun, and because family blood always tastes the sweetest."

"That's all?" Waldo asked incredulous.

"It's very boring being dead. You have to have your fun where you can."

That actually reminded him of Gwen. "I think most people would find some other way to pass the time."

Bony shoulders shrugged. "To each his own."

Waldo shook his head. "I hope you will forgive me if I don't indulge you."

The archlich waved a hand graciously. "I wouldn't want you to. It is so much more fun if you struggle. Do whatever you can to try and live just a little bit longer. It doesn't matter. When I was

338

alive I was the strongest necromancer in existence. I killed Fenlen Poisondagger just outside the Council chambers, and no one dared to so much as question it. I conquered the city of Bescan alone, with only my undead. In my day I was more powerful than whole armies. I am weaker now than I was then, dead flesh cannot summon mana as well as living. Your mother might be a match for me, perhaps, but with someone like you..."

It took a stride forward.

"What can someone as weak as you do?"

"Fight." Waldo answered. "*Pyro.*"

He didn't expect anything to happen, but it was the only offensive magic he had. None of his wands had ever worked, and they had been superbly crafted from the bones of mages. How could this one do any better?

Waldo found out. He felt the mana surge through him and into the wand. Saw it shine and felt it become warm in his hand. A massive stream of fire shot out. Waldo gaped. For the first time in his life he was working real combat magic.

The flames rushed and struck his grandfather in the very middle of its chest, billowing and spreading out.

For just a second Waldo's hopes soared. He had done it, he had won. Waldo expected to see the archlich burning up like a torch.

The moment of triumph ended as quickly as it had begun. The flames danced and spread, setting the grass on fire, but his grandfather was unaffected. Even his decrepit robes were unharmed.

"You look disappointed grandson. You didn't expect it to be that easy did you? I always cast protective wards." It stood where it was, making no effort to counterattack. "Feel free to try something else."

There was nothing else, he had no other offensive spells.

"*Repulso.*" He again felt the mana in him flow easily from his body into the wand. This spell worked specifically on the undead, if he could cast it strongly enough it might at least force his grandfather back.

The archlich's robes billowed and twisted as it caught in a light breeze.

Rasping laughter echoed through the forest.

"You actually expect such a minor enchantment to affect me? Is that truly all that you can do? I had no idea my daughter had grown so careless. How did she let you live to adulthood? For that matter, one of your siblings should have gotten rid of you long ago."

It casually held out its right hand, holding thumb and middle finger together.

"*Xatos ki.*"

Waldo hunched his shoulders and clutched his arms in front of him.

Nothing happened though. At his feet the circle and runes gave a fleeting glimmer.

"A protective circle? I would have sensed it when I was alive."

"It seems we are at an impasse."

"Hardly." It pointed to a tree. "*Levitaros.*"

There was the sound of snapping and tearing, as to Waldo's shock the tree was torn from the earth and lifted fifteen feet into

340

the air, roots and all. His grandfather had just done that using one of the most basic and rudimentary of spells.

"Are you beginning to understand now grandson? The vastness of the gulf that lies between us." It casually flicked its finger. "Catch."

The tree was sent flying towards him. Instinctively Waldo dived to the ground. It sailed five feet above him, crashing into the forest and tearing out a gouge in the forest.

His grandfather merely nodded. "You've broken your circle." Once more it touched thumb to middle finger. "*Xatos ki.*"

Before Waldo could even scramble to his feet he was hit by what felt like a stone wall. The air expelled from his lungs he was sent flying through the air. His ribs exploded in fresh agony and he could taste blood.

Ignoring the pain as best he could Waldo forced himself back to his feet. Somehow he had held onto his wand. Spitting out blood he steadied himself and took rapid shallow breaths, his free hand pressed to his side. His grandfather was still just standing there.

"Run," it commanded. "If you can't give me a good fight at least give me a decent chase, now run!"

Not having any better options Waldo decided to do just that.

XXX

As he stumbled through the dark, ribs hurting with every step, he racked his brains to come up with some sort of strategy. He had memorized everything in Roger's spellbook; illusions and weather magic. He also had various wards, defensive spells, and healing.

What good will any of that do me now?

When he'd put some distance between them Waldo stopped and healed himself. He hadn't wanted to waste the time or mana, but the pain was getting to be too much. Once that was done he tried to think rationally about his options.

Waldo could sense his grandfather approaching, but not quickly.

"Probably wants to enjoy the chase," Waldo muttered.

Just how was he supposed to fight someone so much more powerful than he was? Until now he had been used to thinking of undead as relatively harmless. They were dangerous to ordinary mundanes, but not to him. Waldo recalled all of Walter's pathetic attempts to kill him and all the different ways he had handled them. He thought of all the weaknesses of the undead.

It was thinking about Walter that led him to an idea. It was very basic, but it might work.

"Better than nothing."

Waldo began running again while keeping his eye out for just the right spot for what he had in mind.

XXX

What an interesting boy, Lucius Corpselover thought. *Almost a pity to eat him.*

He set out at a regular walking pace. There was no need to rush things. This would be the last time he would devour the heart of someone with his blood. Oh his bratty daughter was still alive, but no matter how poor a parent, she was a very competent mage. And unlike some of her children, she at least was no fool. Going after his daughter was far too dangerous, so sadly, tonight would be the last time he would have someone in his family for dinner.

342

"There are always the branch families I suppose, but it just won't be the same."

Lilith is not going to have any more children. I should have waited until I had great grandchildren.

Lucius really didn't think he was at fault, it wasn't as though he had been a glutton. Since becoming a lich he had only eaten three of his kin. His son and heir Tyver, his granddaughter Kara, and his grandson Walter. It wasn't as if he had set out deliberately to exterminate his line. A wolf doesn't kill all the sheep.

But the world was a dangerous place, and Lilith had obviously been incompetent in training her children.

"I should have eaten her and let Tyver live."

So now he was down to just one grandchild, the one everyone had seen as the family disgrace. And honestly, the heir to the Corpselover family going around in white robes? If this was what the family had come to it was just as well his line ended. At least someone from a branch family would not be an embarrassment.

The boy had courage, and was not completely incompetent like the rumors said, but he was much too weak. And he had bizarre notions. Risking your life to save a familiar? Where had he even picked up such an idea?

As he pondered that he noticed a mist rising all around him. In a matter of minutes it grew thick and filled the whole area with a dense fog.

Lucius could not sense magic, but this was obviously the result of a spell. Being undead his vision was also not as clear as it had been in life. He was effectively blinded. Going through the forest in this manner would slow him down. However it did nothing to interrupt the detection spell. He knew exactly how far away Waldo was and in what direction.

343

"Still, not a bad use of his limited abilities. Lilith should have done more with him."

He set out again at the same pace. The dead never tired. No matter how the boy ran there was no escape for him.

As Lucius went he nearly ran into a few trees. Even for an archlich navigating through this boundless fog was a hindrance. He could have easily dispelled it, but he decided to allow his grandson this tiny victory. Lucius wanted him to think there still might be hope.

It was soon clear the boy had stopped running. He was simply waiting up ahead. *Is he too tired to run any more or is he planning an ambush?*

The answer came in a stream of fire as he got within about twenty yards.

"*Pyro.*" His grandson said from somewhere in the mist.

As before the flames were deflected harmlessly away.

Lucius laughed. "I give you credit for having courage grandson, but is that the only spell you know?"

As if in answer another stream of fire came, it proved as useless as the others.

"This begins to grow tedious, either use a different spell or start running again."

"*Pyro.*"

A third blaze was turned aside by his protective wards.

Brave but stupid.

Lucius began walking towards him, if the boy wanted to die fighting that was fine. At least he was not ending his life on his knees crying and begging as Walter had.

It seemed Waldo really had chosen to make a last stand here. He was not moving, his grandson was holding his ground as yet another useless stream of fire lanced out. Lucius strode confidently towards him, excitement building within his decayed heart. The thought of ripping out his last grandchild's heart and devouring it before the boy's eyes filled him with delight.

This was why he had come to this miserable land and wasted so much time chasing after Waldo. It was for this feeling, this excitement, and this joy. Knowing what he was about to do made him feel alive again. To have this sensation pulsing through him was worth anything.

Lucius was within ten steps and the boy was still not running. Eight steps, six, four…

He ran into a wall.

Lucius bounced back. Had he run into a tree? He saw nothing in front of him and his grandson was too tantalizingly close now. Lucius stepped to the side to quickly skirt around the unseen object. To his annoyance he again struck some sort of barrier. He reached out with his hands and found the air in front of him as solid as stone. Quickly feeling around he soon discovered he was trapped.

Looking down Lucius saw he was standing inside a circle with runes written on the outside.

"*Nunc.*"

"That won't work," Waldo's voice called out unseen. "Look at the symbols."

Lucius did so. He took a moment to study the runes scratched out in the dirt. "I see, a containment circle for undead combined with magical suppression, a very complex formula. Did you have it written in your spellbook?"

"No, I just pieced it together."

Lucius was surprised, combining different effects in a single ward was tricky. Even for a competent mage it would normally require weeks of research and experimentation to figure out. "It seems you have some talent grandson."

"Thank you grandfather."

"Such a shame your potential was wasted, you might have actually been formidable one day."

"I still might."

"No you won't." Lucius said with certainty. Being within the circle had negated the detection spell, so he could no longer sense exactly where Waldo was. His grandson was so close, but out of reach. "It was a clever trick. Your attacks were never meant as anything but a distraction. You deliberately led me to this exact spot."

"I have a lot of experience dealing with undead grandfather. Whether you are a lich or a zombie all undead can be trapped and held within the proper ward."

Dead flesh slapped together as Lucius applauded. "Yes, it was well done, but it will not work a second time."

"I am satisfied that it worked once."

"Enjoy your victory, savor it, not many people have faced me and survived. Just know this will not hold me long."

"It will be long enough for me and Alice to get far away from here."

"Ah, so the succubus' name is Alice. I will be sure to introduce myself to her properly before I rip her to pieces. Tell me my boy, would you prefer me to kill her first or second? I can let you watch if you like."

"Don't threaten Alice." Waldo's voice was harsh.

"Your succubus is doomed now just as much as you are. You've stopped me, but this is only a delay, nothing more. I will hunt you down boy, no matter how long it takes, no matter if you run to the ends of the earth, I will never stop chasing you and your pet until I have ended you both."

"Good to know."

Lucius then heard the sound of Waldo walking away.

The archlich began to chortle, then hoarse laughter poured from him. He had not laughed like this since turning.

"This will be so much FUN!" Lucius howled and he tossed his head back and laughed and laughed and laughed.

Chapter 32

A Temporary Escape

As soon as Waldo had gone a safe distance he summoned Alice.

"*Concalo.*"

Instantly she appeared before him, lying on the grass at his feet.

It took her a couple seconds to realize what had happened. When she did she climbed up to her feet. "Darling! You're all right!"

She grabbed him and gave him a shuddering hug. Alice put her face against his neck, after a moment he realized she was crying.

Waldo slid his own arms around her and gently stroked her back.

"It's all right Alice, everything is all right now."

Though they needed to get going the two of them stayed that way for a while, holding and comforting each other.

XXX

They spent the entire night traveling.

In spite of her wounds Alice carried him through the air, eager to put as much distance between themselves and Waldo's grandfather as possible.

She did the best she could, but it was physically impossible to fly very far while holding onto Waldo. The extra weight was a strain; she could not fly much above tree top level and was as graceful and maneuverable as a boulder. They could cover about half a mile before she was forced to land and rest for a bit.

Each time they were back on the ground Waldo would ask her if she was all right. He would use some of his magic while rubbing her wings and shoulders. Unlike what he'd done healing her wound these were minor magics. His hands were gentle as he touched her. She would feel warmth soak into her body and a little of the exhaustion would vanish.

"Are you all right?" He would ask her over and over again as he soothed her aches.

And each time she would smile for him and tell him she was.

"Was that really your grandfather?"

"Yes." Waldo answered and continued to heal her.

"Why did he want to kill you?"

"Because it was fun, and to a lich nothing is sweeter than the taste of your own family's blood."

Alice looked away.

She didn't really understand, but it wasn't important. When it had mattered most he had risked his own life to save hers. Even if he didn't say the words she now knew he truly loved her.

"Thank you for saving me. I owe you my life."

Alice felt his hands tremble ever so slightly. Through their bond she felt a momentary surge of guilt and confusion.

"You don't owe me anything, you've already saved mine. I suppose we are even."

"I guess that's true, but I am still grateful. A husband and wife should take care of each other. I feel blessed."

"Blessed?"

Alice nodded. "We protected each other, and now you don't have to feel in any sort of debt. You don't need to feel guilty about what happened tonight." She turned her face back to him smiling tenderly. "I am just happy to know how much you care about me."

Through the bond she felt another sharp pang of guilt. His eyes avoided hers.

"Do you feel strong enough to fly some more? Or would you like more rest?"

She was as eager as he was to get further away. "I can go."

She wrapped her arms firmly around his chest so that his back pressed to her front. She spread her huge leathery wings and stretched them as far as they would go. With a grunt she flapped as hard as she could and the two of them staggered into the air. Alone she would have ascended easily and then simply glided along as she pleased. Carrying Waldo she was forced to continuously keep her wings pumping in order to keep them in the air. Before long she was sweating and her shoulders were aching.

She didn't complain though, and took them as far as she could before feeling exhausted.

They did this about two dozen times. They decided to stop only as dawn approached and with it the possibility of being spotted. They landed in a patch of woods not far from the road. Alice was completely spent. She reverted back to her human form and was quickly asleep.

XXX

Waldo was not as exhausted as she was, but he was tired. With all the spells he'd used he was almost tapped out of mana. For a mage using mana had a similar effect to performing physical labor. It used up your energy, and wore you out. It could be recovered naturally through sleep.

It had been a very long time since Waldo had felt as drained as he did now. He had poured all that he could into healing Alice and fighting his grandfather. It would take at least a couple nights of rest to fully recover, but sleep would have to wait a little bit longer.

"There is no rest for the wicked." He muttered to himself as he popped out a knife.

Alice had curled up in a patch of grass and was fully asleep. Waldo got down on his knees and stabbed his knife into the earth. Grunting with the effort, he hacked and cut and tore at the grass. Both hands on his knife ha dug out a line. He silently muttered and cursed at just how hard it was.

His forearms ached he was sweating. "I was never made for physical labor."

He glanced at Alice and thought about waking her to have her deal with this. Seeing her peaceful face he decided to just let her sleep.

As he struggled with his task he wondered at everything that had happened and at his feelings.

He had actually put himself into danger for her. He hadn't planned to, it had just sort of happened. When he'd heard her cry in pain and seen her wound, all he'd thought about was how to save her. He had made himself a target just to keep his grandfather away from Alice.

"Then why are you trying to save her? There is never any reason why a master should put his own life in danger for the familiar's sake."

351

His grandfather's words had been mocking, but truthful. What he did made no sense, but he was glad he'd done it.

He completed cutting a circle around where Alice was resting. He paused for a moment and rubbed his hands. Tearing out grass with a simple knife had been harder than he'd expected. He didn't allow himself more than a short respite before he got down on his hands and knees and began tearing out patches of grass inside the circle.

When he had set out from Castle Corpselover he'd thought of all the problems he would face. Capturing monsters, defeating a knight, and dealing with all the hazards of the road. Somehow though he had never thought about being attacked by his grandfather. That had definitely been stupid on his part. Grandfather had killed and eaten the hearts of two family members, it only made sense it would want to do the same to him.

That he had even survived the initial encounter was something of a miracle. His wand had worked better than he'd ever dreamt it could. Even with that all of his spells had proved useless. Waldo had only managed to trap his grandfather because he'd been underestimated. That would not happen a second time.

He tore up grass and tossed it aside. In the dirt he scratched out runes and magical symbols. When he was done he had created a Circle of Secrets. It would defeat all but the most powerful scrying magic. From this point on staying hidden would be a priority. It could not prevent his grandfather from tracking them down eventually, but it would at least make it much harder.

When all that was finally done he lay down beside Alice.

He looked closely at her sleeping face. He stared at her shut eyes and her lips. He would never deny that she was beautiful or that he cared for her. He wondered at these strange feelings. They couldn't possibly be normal for a master and servant. He'd seen how servants were treated. He'd had favorites, but his feelings for Alice simply didn't match.

He thought of his feelings for his mother and, to a lesser degree, for his sister Gwendolyn. Those seemed similar to how he felt about Alice. He couldn't accept they were the same though. He loved his mother and his sister; he couldn't possibly be in love with Alice. That was impossible. Love was a terrible weakness and no Dark Mage would be fool enough to fall in love with his servant.

Be affectionate with them? Certainly.

Be intimate? Surely.

Truly love them? No. Never.

With one hand he gently brushed aside a lock of hair that had slipped over her face. A thumb ever so softly caressed her warm cheek. Just being able to look at her and know she was safe gave him a sense of comfort.

As he shut his eyes and drifted into sleep he thought again how what he felt could not possibly be love.

Chapter 33

Something For Alice

They slept for several hours.

Alice was the first to stir awake. She opened her eyes to find her husband resting up against her. After everything they had been through, it was comforting just to see him alive and well.

She gently rolled him over onto his back, and was lying half on top of him. Alice placed a kiss on his lips.

His eyes opened immediately. His confusion and awkward stare only made him that much cuter. "You don't mind do you darling? I'm starving."

"No," Waldo aid. "I don't mind."

Alice was taken off guard when he placed a hand behind her head and pushed her back down. Her lips were on his again, but **he** was kissing **her**. For just a second she stiffened, not from opposition, just from surprise. Not only was he initiating this but he was kissing her very eagerly.

It felt wonderful.

She relaxed and leaned into his lips. One hand remained at the back of her head, as if to ensure she would not try to get away. The other was slowly running down along her back. His mouth eagerly played with hers. His desire was strong, and her hunger dissipated and quickly vanished.

Waldo had never done anything like this before; she was the one who always had to start things. Having him be the aggressor for a change was a bit exciting. She liked it. If his hands started to roam she wouldn't mind. Alice thought she might be ready to let him do whatever he wanted.

After several minutes of kisses and soft touches he stopped and looked up at her cautiously. "Are you full now?"

"Afraid not, still hungry."

"All right then."

They went back to their very eager kissing and touching.

XXX

Eventually they had to stop and get going.

"We need to reach Middleton before dark." Waldo said. "My grandfather will want to avoid entering a city if he can."

"So that means were safe now?

Waldo shook his head. "My grandfather is determined to come after us. He will never stop. I have a few wards that can keep us hidden, but he will track us down eventually."

"Then what can we do?"

"For the short term get into the city and find my second monster. For the long term we will have to keep moving until I can figure out some way to deal with him."

"All right darling, I trust you know best."

XXX

At long last they reached Middleton.

Waldo was pleased that the horrible ball of fire was still in the sky. There was still time to get everything done today. Depending on what sort of Great Monster was waiting for him their odds for survival would greatly improve.

"A vampire would be best," Waldo told her as they approached the city. "A really vicious, bloodthirsty vampire."

"As long as it's not another succubus it's fine."

"You understand that I will have to perform the same binding ceremony I used with you?"

"You're going to kiss her." Alice said unhappily.

"Or him, but I promise there will be no flowers this time."

"I guess that will have to do."

Waldo sent her a sideways glance. "I can't return home until I have three monsters bound to my service, defeated a knight, and found a certain treasure."

"I know darling," she said. "It doesn't mean I have to like it though."

They continued on for a bit when she turned to him. "What sort of treasure?"

"Something very precious and very well guarded, it will be the hardest part of my quest and I can't even begin to consider it until I have taken care of the other parts."

Alice nodded, apparently satisfied.

They entered Middleton through the south gate. The guards manning it were most respectful to him. They mentioned that the city gates shut at sunset and reopened with dawn. One of them offered to send a message to the Baron of his arrival. Waldo waved that away, the last thing he wanted was to draw more attention.

Twelve hills dominated the city. Each was surrounded at its base with a fortress wall with towers. Even from a distance one could see mine entrances carved into each hill, along with roads spiraled down from top to bottom. There was a steady flow of traffic going either up or down those long twisting paths.

From different sections of the city filthy, black smoke rose from multiple chimneys. There was a constant, never ending, ringing that filled the air. When Waldo first heard it he'd thought it some sort of bell. There was no order to it though, and no halt. The buildings here were a bit different from the ones Waldo had seen in Stratford. Nearly all were just one or two stories tall, and unlike in the previous city very few of them were painted. They were a mass of grey and brown stone, jammed together amid a confusing tangle of roads.

"What a depressing, noisy place." Alice said.

"It's disorderly." Waldo said in condemnation. "Who would design a city like this?"

"Cities aren't designed darling. They're like children; they're born and then they grow. No one can know how they will turn out"

Waldo shook his head. "Alter was planned out from the very start. The streets are all impeccably straight, and the buildings are all uniform. It's a place of perfect order."

"Then from what I hear it's probably the only one in the whole world like that."

"That's undoubtedly so. More's the pity."

"We'll need to find a place to stay and eat. We'll also need to replace everything we lost. That means backpacks, clothes, blankets, traveling supplies, and I suppose we may as well get a tent too." She put a hand protectively over her purse. "It's a horrible waste of coin, but I guess there's no avoiding it. Maybe I'll get a job to help pay for everything."

"All that can wait. The most important thing is to find my new servant." He began casting his detection spell. "*Taranos evel monstri desu noratal est aki est avaratos.*"

As soon as the spell was complete Middleton managed to give him another surprise.

Waldo took in a sharp breath. "Damn."

"What's wrong?"

"This is going to take longer than I expected." To his eyes Alice was now ablaze with reddish light. When he looked in the direction of the city he spotted hundreds, possibly thousands, of similar lights. Stratford had had a grand total of four! It had been very easy to distinguish Alice's signature from the much weaker lights being given off by the other three. The sheer number of lights he was looking at now made that impossible. There were some monsters in every section of the city, but most of them were concentrated within the various hills. Each hill was so flooded in reddish light there was no way to distinguish from a distance if one of them might be stronger than all the rest.

He quickly explained the situation to Alice.

"Why are there so many more monsters here than there were in Stratford?"

Alice shrugged. "How should I know?"

Waldo shook his head with helpless frustration. "I was hoping to find my new familiar right away, but there's no chance of that. We'll have to trek through this entire place until I can spot the strongest light." He glanced at the horrible ball of fire and estimated they had a couple more hours of daylight remaining. Searching at night would make the glows more distinctive, but it would be dangerous to wander about a city filled with uncivilized barbarians after dark. "Let's find a place to stay tonight. We can begin searching tomorrow."

"All right darling."

XXX

The reaction Waldo received was similar to that in Fall River. People would nod at him respectfully, but make sure to keep a safe distance.

He noticed that there were a great many more city guard here in Middleton than there had been in Stratford. They traveled the streets in groups ranging from four to ten. All of them looked to be quite well armed, wearing chainmail and iron helms. They mostly carried swords, though a few had spears or double headed axes. Perhaps one in three of the men he saw were members of the city guard. Even most of the commoners were armed, nearly every man who wasn't wearing chainmail had a long knife or even a short sword tucked into a belt or in a scabbard.

"The people here seem very well armed. Do they have bandits nearby?"

Alice frowned. "Not that I've heard of, the land is pretty safe outside of the marshes."

"Then why does everyone have a sword?"

"I have no idea. We would get merchants at the Inn all the time. They sold bars of wrought iron, tools, nails, and blades or they were passing through to someplace else. I can tell you the ringing is from all the blacksmiths working their forges, and all that smoke comes from the fires melting iron from the ore."

"You seem to know a bit about this place."

"Oh it's nothing; men always love to talk about their work and their homes. They call Middleton the Iron City because there is so much iron in the ground here. The blacksmith's guild is based here and there are hundreds of them working all day long, from sun rise to sun set. They say that if you live here you don't even notice the ringing."

"I find that hard to believe."

"They all told me it stops with sunset."

"I suppose I should be grateful for small favors."

"I bet we'll be safe as long as we're here." Alice said trying hard to look at the bright side. "Your grandfather wouldn't want to come into a place with so many armed men. Would he?"

"As a matter of fact, I don't think he will. Though I suspect he would be more worried about running into a White Mage than any number of city guards. I'm sure he'll wait until we leave to come after us again."

"Well, at least we're safe for now."

"We are never safe," he reminded her quietly.

"Don't worry darling, I'll keep you safe."

As they walked along a twisting street, a large cart with two shoulder high wheels came around a bend. The cart was piled high with sacks. It was being pulled along by a goblin. The creature wore a leather harness around its wide chest and an iron collar about its thick, bulbous throat. The collar was connected back to the cart by a thick chain that rattled with each shuffling step.

Walking beside the cart was a small man wearing a leather apron and holding a worn riding crop in his right hand.

"Keep moving you stupid beast." The man said. "We still have to make one more delivery after this."

To emphasize his words he struck the goblin on his arm with a loud audible 'thwack.'

The monster gave a slight grunt, but did not otherwise acknowledge being struck. He did not look back at his apparent owner or in any way hurry his pace. The common people walking along paid no mind, though Alice noted that the squad of soldiers who had just passed were watching.

Waldo didn't seem to pay any notice.

"Did you see that?" Alice demanded.

"What?"

"That man! He hit that defenseless goblin for no reason at all!"

"So?"

Waldo's rather indifferent reply earned him a sharp look.

It was clear she was upset with him, but he had no idea why. "I told you there were a large number of monsters in this city. It's not surprising they'd be used as draft animals. I saw a goblin pulling a cart in Stratford too."

"That would have been Noorook who works for John Millen. Mister Millen would never beat Noorook. Well, not unless he did something to deserve it of course. Just now though, that goblin was hit for no reason at all. It was like how some people will whip an ox or a mule to make it move."

"Then I suppose he was hit for the same reason."

"Goblins are different from oxen or mules."

"Very true," Waldo admitted. "So far as I know oxen and mules very rarely use swords or roast humans for a meal."

That earned him another sharp look.

"You know what I mean!"

"Actually, no, I don't. I have no idea what point you are trying to make."

"Goblins can talk. You can tell them what to do and they can understand you. You don't have to treat them as if they were animals!"

Waldo looked at her curiously. "And how should you treat a slave?"

"They aren't even slaves," she said unhappily. "Slaves at least are people. Goblins and other monsters really are just animals to most folk."

"Then I suppose it's lucky for them goblin meat tastes so bad."

"This isn't funny!"

"Who was joking?"

"What, you've eaten goblin?"

"Yes, but only once or twice, it's very chewy and tough. Still better than gremlin though."

"How could you eat a goblin?" Alice asked horrified.

"Fried usually, though it can also be baked."

"Really?"

Waldo nodded, still not understanding why she was so upset.

"Would you eat a succubus too?"

"Don't be ridiculous."

"Well that's a relief."

"Succubi possess immense mystical characteristics. Eating one would be a waste. You would chop the body up to use every bit for potion components."

Alice just stared at him.

"Please tell me you're joking."

"In my country we do not venerate the dead. The spirits go wherever the Dark Powers will them to go. The bodies are treated as a resource. If they cannot be used for food or spell components most are revived so that they can continue to work."

"So when you die you'll be a walking corpse?" Alice's mouth twisted with disgust.

"No, members of the Seven Families are never turned into common undead. It would be beneath our dignity. Our bodies are simply burned, but even for the heads of families there are no rituals or prayers, the body is simply disposed of."

"So they just burn you up like a log in the fire? You don't even have a funeral?"

"Everything that lives must one day die, even the gods must perish when the Long Night sets. That is a universal truth, and we accept it. We do not hold life sacred or make any ridiculous pretenses about it. You are born, you live, and one day you die, and unless you are called back you will go to whatever place is reserved for you. Funerals and rituals won't change that, so why bother?"

"Sounds very glum."

"Not really, knowing that life must end pushes us to do as much as we can while we are here."

"So I guess that means when I die I'm going to be chopped up." She sounded resigned.

"What would you like done instead?"

"I want to be given a proper funeral and buried somewhere the sun shines. There should be flowers and a grave stone with my name. I would also like you to mourn me for one year before you find a new wife."

"You've actually thought about this."

"Well naturally, people die all the time, of fever or the flux or in childbirth. I would have liked to have had a proper funeral and a grave. Its proof that you lived once, and that someone cared enough about you to do you that last service. But if I am your wife I suppose I'll have to accept your customs. I'll just have to try and live as long as I can before I end up in a bunch of bottles on a shelf."

Waldo stared at her for a long moment.

"If you die before I do, I will give you a proper funeral. I will bury you somewhere the horrible ball of fire blazes, and have a stone marker with your name placed there. I will bring flowers, and though I don't see the point, I will wait a year before marrying."

"Really?"

"Yes," Waldo hurried his pace. "Come on, let's find somewhere to rest."

Smiling, Alice quickened her step to remain at his side.

Chapter 34

The Inn Of The White Horse

The Inn of the White Horse was an unadorned and typical building on the Street of Nails. It was two stories, made of brown brick, jammed between a smithy to one side and a general store to the other. On the faded, weather beaten sign that hung outside the door, the horse was more grey than white.

The neighborhood was not one of Middleton's best. It belonged to the common folk; the people who lived and worked here stoked the furnaces and hauled in the wood for the fires of the smithies and forges. They loaded and unloaded wagons, brought water, made meals, and did all the little tasks necessary to keep the blacksmiths and the merchants happy. The people who liked to visit the Inn were hard folk who lived hard lives and liked to sometimes drink and talk and argue about all the things that were wrong with the world.

Tyrone Williams stood behind his bar listening to his customers shouts, and to the endless banging of hammer on anvil. He had long since learned how to ignore both. Thirty years he had been running this Inn, going from a young man to an old one. In that time he had buried his dear Inna (may the Terrasa grant her peace), and seen his two little girls get married and start families of their own. Tyrone had also seen himself slowly grow grey and fat. Those were the main changes. Everything else stayed the same.

He'd heard the same complaints, the same arguments, and the same stories repeated endlessly. The bosses were always loud mouthed idiots who never appreciated their workers, and never paid a decent wage. They complained about how the occasional noble would not even notice them, or worse, when they did. They complained about the women they wanted. They complained about the women they had. When they were young they complained about their parents controlling them. When they got older they complained about not being able to control their children. They complained about the rain and the snow and the summer heat and the winter cold. And on and on… The one thing that never changed was that there was always something to complain about.

Tyrone took out a rag and wiped down the bar. The wood was stained from countless spills, and there were cracks of varying sizes. The stone floor was always dirty and there was a layer of dust caked onto the walls. Every table and every chair was worn, and there was always the smell of cabbage, sweat, and ale. *Good enough*, he judged. Every table was occupied with customers eating cabbage stew and drinking ale. He knew his customers. They didn't come here to revel in cleanliness and brightly polished oak counters. They came to fill their bellies with cheap food and cheap ale and to talk free among their own kind.

They also like playing with the barmaids. He had two girls who worked for him, along with a cook and an assistant in the kitchen. Both Brienne and Nicola were sitting with customers right now, laughing and talking. He would have to yell to get them serving tables again. Long experience told him they would both have to be replaced soon. He always hired young, pretty girls. The men loved to look at and chat them up. They never lasted long; most of them were looking for a husband. The ones who weren't, and were serious about earning coin, always ended up moving on to a more profitable line of work. It was an inconvenience, but the customers liked having attractive, unattached girls serving them, so he dealt with it.

The rooms upstairs were usually empty, and the coins that filled his till were near always copper. He usually touched silver only once a month when he went out to make his stock purchases. In his life he had held gold only a handful of times. The bar was filled though, almost every night, and except during the riots things were more or less peaceful. There were the occasional drunken brawls, but he kept a wooden cudgel behind the bar for those times. And if things ever got out of hand the city guards were always there to crack a few heads and stuff them into stocks.

All in all, it wasn't such a bad life. Tyrone liked his customers and he liked being an Innkeeper. Really the worst thing about it was the boredom. There were always the same faces and the same voices. He just wished that now and again something interesting might happen.

That was when the door opened and a White Mage and the most beautiful woman he had ever laid eyes on walked into the bar. The customers who saw them were every bit as startled as he was and closed their mouths to stare. It got so quiet that the only sound was the banging of iron coming from outside the walls.

It was not unusual for there to be at least one or two White Mages in Middleton at any given time. However, they always stayed in the Baron's palace. Tyrone could not remember ever hearing of one visiting the working quarter. In the thirty years he had owned the Inn this was the first time any sort of wizard had ever entered it.

The mage stood there, just inside the doorway, calmly regarding the room. His straw colored hair and pale yellow eyes would have made him stand out even without the white robes. Just the presence of a White Mage made Tyrone nervous. They were good people and served a good cause, but some of them could be rather zealous at times. Rumors had it that the Baron, and even the King, dealt with them very cautiously. Bad things could happen to you if you made an enemy of one of them.

The woman who was standing just behind him received almost as much interest as the mage did. Her looks were every bit as foreign and exotic as his. She had long flowing red hair and eyes that were a shade of violet. She was wearing a plain white blouse and a long tan skirt, and she had a cloth sack over her left shoulder. Her clothes were a bit tight fitting and outlined a very tempting figure. He'd visited a few brothels in his time, but Tyrone had never once seen anyone half so captivating.

"Who is the proprietor here?" The mage asked.

The faces of most of the people turned to stare in Tyrone's direction.

"That would be me, my... lord."

"I am not a lord." The mage told him. "I am Waldo Rabbit. You may simply refer to me as Master Rabbit."

There were a couple startled laughs that were quickly covered up. Most of those present looked uncertain as to whether or not this was a joke. Since the mage appeared to be serious, they had to pretend to take him at his word.

Tyrone was just as uncertain, but decided to play along. "Well, how may I serve you Master Rabbit?"

Before the man could answer the woman put her sack down and stepped up beside him. "Darling," she said in a voice as sweet as honey. "Why don't you let me handle this?"

"Why? I can deal with the peasant."

At every table mouths tightened and eyes hardened. These people knew they were looked down upon, but they didn't appreciate hearing it from some foreigner in their Inn.

To the girl's credit she noticed the reaction, the mage seemed completely oblivious.

"Darling, be nice, or you might end up swimming again."

"What do you mean?" Master Rabbit asked. "I am being quite polite, especially considering he is just a peasant."

"Don't call him a peasant!" A burly workman at one of the tables called out.

"Would you prefer commoner?"

There were growls from several tables.

Tyrone glanced about nervously. The last thing he wanted was to have a brawl involving a White Mage. Mercifully the lovely angel took charge of the situation. She elbowed his ribs and shook a finger in his face.

"Don't say anything else or you really may go for another swim."

Not waiting for a reply she walked up to the bar.

'Walk' might not have really described it. Her hips swayed with every step. All eyes stared longingly as she crossed the room. Tyrone found himself mesmerized like every other man there. When she came to a halt across from him he had to remind himself to breathe. Staring into those captivating eyes he suddenly felt like a love struck boy again. Reaching across the bar she placed one hand gently on his arm, making his heart race.

"Please forgive my husband," she said in that soft lilting voice. "He didn't mean to be rude."

"Of course," Tyrone mumbled. "It's fine. You, you're his wife then?" Though it was ridiculous, he felt disappointed.

"Yes, I am Alice Rabbit; please feel free to call me Alice. My husband and I would like a room for the night and a meal please."

Tyrone nodded. Despite the foolish thoughts coursing through his brain he tried to remember he was an Innkeeper. "I have a room available; it costs fifty copper traks. Meals and drinks are separate, a bowl of cabbage stew is five traks and a mug of ale is one."

"Cabbage stew? Is that all you serve here?"

Normally, if anyone asked him that, his answer was to tell them to eat nothing. Hearing the hint of disappointment from her made him wish there was something else he could offer her.

"I am sorry Alice; I run a plain place for plain folk."

"Maybe they'd be happier staying in the Baron's castle." Brienne called out.

"You be quiet!" Tyrone said. Of course she and Nicola were the only ones not enthralled.

"I am sorry," Alice said holding up her hands. "I did not mean to complain. I am sure the stew is delicious, and it certainly is reasonably priced. But you see, my husband and I are trying to save our coin right now. So I was hoping you might agree to give us free room and board in exchange for my services?"

"Services?" He replied weakly. All sorts of thoughts were running through his mind. He was sure his dear Inna (may Terrasa grant her peace) would forgive him. She was dead after all, and he was still flesh and blood.

Alice nodded, and pretended not to notice where his eyes had drifted to. "I have experience as a barmaid. In return for free lodging and food I will work here for as many nights as we stay. I will get to keep my tips of course." She stared intently into his eyes. "What do you say?"

Feeling a little light headed Tyrone would have agreed to anything at that moment. "It's a deal."

XXX

The room upstairs was fifteen square feet. The only furniture was a plain bed pressed up against the wall, and covered with a single brown blanket. There was a small window that provided a view of an alleyway choked with garbage. The Innkeeper had insisted Alice begin working immediately. She had handed him the sack and simply promised to come up to their room once her shift was done. Shortly after he'd gone upstairs, one of the other barmaids had brought him a wooden bowl of green stew along with a pewter mug filled with a foamy liquid that was the color of dirt. Though dubious, Waldo was very hungry. He took the wooden spoon and dug into the soup. It certainly wasn't anything he would deliberately choose, but it wasn't actually too bad. Along with cabbage there were potatoes, carrots, and chunks of bread mixed in as well. Though not exactly fine cuisine, it did fill the stomach. He ate the entire bowl and wouldn't have minded a second. The ale tasted more like rye bread than anything else. He drank about half and then set the mug aside.

Through the door Waldo could easily hear the shouts and howls of laughter coming from downstairs. The noise somehow reminded him of yapping dogs in heat. Even he hadn't been able to miss how they had stared at Alice.

"Ignorant savages."

The idea that he, a Corpselover, would have to deal with such people as near equals was humiliating. That Alice would have to serve them was sickening. He was supposed to be the only one she served.

XXX

"What are you doing?" He had demanded right after she'd made her agreement.

With strangers watching she had stepped close to him and lowered her voice. "I am paying for our room and food. I am also going to make some tips too."

"You don't need to do that. We can just pay for our stay."

371

"The room would be half a silver per night, and you don't know how long we'll be here. The food and drink would be on top of that. The supplies we just bought were three dalters. I don't want to waste any more coin if we don't have to."

"We can afford it. I don't want you serving all these peasants."

"Aw, that is so sweet." She picked up the cloth sack with one hand and tossed it to him. It was heavy and he stumbled back a couple steps after catching it. "You don't need to worry, I'll be fine."

She began serving and he was forced to trudge upstairs alone.

XXX

He heard a fresh round of laughter coming from downstairs. Waldo considered going down and observing whatever was going on. He dismissed the notion almost immediately, as it would be beneath his dignity. It was also foolish. Alice was used to dealing with this sort, and if worse came to worse she was a succubus. It wasn't as though she needed his protection.

Waldo shook his head in mild frustration. What were these feelings? Why did the thought of those mundanes ogling her bother him so much? Why did he feel so possessive of her? He did not want her around other men.

Waldo knew these thoughts and feelings were not a normal part of the master servant relationship, but then what part of his connection with Alice was?

"I am wasting time," he said to himself. "Let me take care of the things I can actually fix."

Reaching into a pocket he took out his wand and pointed it at the bed.

"*Levitaros.*"

Just as had happened in the forest, he felt the mana flow through him and into the wand. The force of his spell was greatly magnified and the bed rose a foot above the floor. Levitation was one of the basics near every magic user could use. Before though, Waldo had never been able to lift anything heavier than a book. Now, with his wand, he could move something as large and heavy as a bed with almost no effort.

He remembered the streams of fire he had cast. Though they had been ineffective he had been able to really work destructive magic. His new wand really fit him perfectly; with it in his hand he was immensely stronger than he had ever been before.

The thought both pleased and worried him.

On the one hand, acquiring power was *everything*. Finally being able to use combat magic was a tremendous achievement. He was now a genuine threat, and if worse came to worse could fight on his own.

On the other hand, all this new found strength came from a soulwood wand. Such wands were used almost exclusively by White Mages. What did that say about him? What would the Council and others make of that? He was going around in white robes using a soulwood wand and acting as a White Mage. When all this was over, assuming he survived, what sort of reputation would he have?

Why is nothing ever simple?

He moved the bed to the center of the room and set it down. He then went over to the large sack that he had left in the corner. Before coming to the Inn they had stopped by the general store that was next door to it. There they had bought some spare clothes, blankets, a tent, and some equipment he would need.

From the sack he took out a piece of chalk. Getting down on his hands and knees he began to draw a circle around the bed. When that was complete he drew runes and symbols inside the circle. He also intended to put wards on the door and window to prevent the entry of any sort of undead. While far from perfect, he would do everything possible to protect both himself and Alice while they were forced to remain in this place.

XXX

The Inn of the White Horse was only about half the size of the Inn of Lost Sighs, it was also not as busy. At her old place more than two hundred men would sometimes pack in the common room. Here, Alice never counted more than about forty. This place was also nowhere near as clean or as polished as her old one. Elsa had always insisted that everything had to shine; she had always wanted things as close to perfect as possible. As long as the doors were open Elsa would always be there, riding her to make sure she was working. By comparison, Tyrone hardly said a word to her once it was clear she really was a barmaid. He was happy to just stay behind the bar mooning over her as she went from table to table. With three girls to share the work Alice found it pretty easy.

Two things remained exactly the same though; the other girls she worked with hated her and all the men wanted more than just her attention.

"Don't think you're special just 'cause you have a nice figure." Brieene had said to her almost as soon as they were introduced. "Your eyes are ugly and your hair is as pretty as a shep dog's."

That had gotten a squeal of laughter from Nicola along with a quick nod.

Alice had merely smiled. She had learned to ignore much worse. "You don't need to worry; my husband and I won't be here long."

"Who's worried?" Brieene snapped.

Alice continued to smile and gave up the idea of trying to make friends with the two of them. She had never had any female friends, just like always she was going to be resented.

Dealing with the customers had been just as challenging.

Alice was an old hand at serving men who were looking to grab her, or get a quick feel. She knew to always keep her eyes open and how to dance out of reach. In her old Inn the regulars all knew better than to try and clutch at her. Here all the men were determined to pull her onto their laps or get a squeeze.

Alice must have warned at least two dozen customers that she didn't like being touched. She was happy to talk to them and listen to their stories, but that was all. Of course none of them believed her. They all thought she was playing some sort of game, and as the night went on their efforts got more and more frenzied.

Eventually, a bulky blacksmith's apprentice named Makin succeeded in grabbing hold of her ass when she was looking in the other direction. Her reaction had been instinctive and instant. She'd 'eeked' and spun around, punching him in the face hard enough to knock him clean out of his chair.

The common room had erupted in laughter and cheers. Many of the men lifted their mugs to her. When his friends helped Makin back to his seat they all began to tease him mercilessly. He didn't seem to mind either. Makin ordered a few more mugs of ale and actually tried to grab at her again. If it had been a man that had punched him like that it would have certainly lead to a fight. Coming from a barmaid it was instead treated as something comic.

That was how her night went. She served bowls of stew and mugs of ale while enduring the open dislike of her co-workers, and trying to avoid a forest of grabbing hands. All the while smiling at, and playing up to, those very same grabby men. When one of them tipped her a copper trek she thanked them as warmly and sweetly as she could. It was long, tiring, boring work, but nothing she wasn't used to.

Since most of the men had to be at work the next morning, the place began to empty out well before midnight. Alice and the other girls were already cleaning up as the last customer sat at his table, slowly draining a final mug as he stared longingly at Alice as she wiped down tables.

Finally Tyrone came out from around the bar with three foot long sword in his hands.

"Come on Mathew, it's time for you to get home. Let me help you." The Innkeeper helped the managed up to his feet, and slid the sword into an empty scabbard. Everyone who came into the Inn was required to give up his sword.

Swaying slightly the man staggered over to Alice and held out a copper trek to her. "You was real sweet gal, hope to see ya tamorraw."

Alice took the coin from him gratefully. As she did so he tried to lean in to steal a kiss. She had no trouble stepping back to stay clear.

Smiling, she shook a finger at him. "Now, now I'm a married woman and my husband wouldn't like me kissing another man. Especially not one as cute as you."

His face lit up and he looked absolutely thrilled. "I wish Ida met ya first."

I don't. "That's sweet."

Mathew clearly wanted to keep talking to her, but Tyrone was at his back gently pushing him toward the door. Once he was gone the Inn was officially closed.

"He never tips." Brieene said sounding unhappy.

Alice slid the coin into a pocket sewn into her skirt. It jingled along with the other tips she had earned. "Then I am grateful he was in such a generous mood tonight."

The lighthearted answer only made the other girl look even more indignant. "Why are you staying here anyway? I always heard that White Mages stayed with the Baron when they visited."

"My husband has his reasons."

"You and your husband can stay as long as you like." Tyrone told her. "I am right honored to have you both here."

"Thank you,"

"Hmph." Brieene swept the floor with added fury.

"Can I ask a question?"

"Sure now, you can ask anything." Tyrone was eager to help her.

"Why do so many of the men here wear swords? I am from Stratford, and except for the city guard and the nobles no one else is allowed to have one."

"Oh," Tyrone sounded a bit embarrassed. "Well, that's on account of the goblins. Sometimes we have some trouble with them."

"Trouble?"

"Nothing you need worry about. They can get a bit bothersome is all."

"What does that mean?"

"They'll get it in their heads to just start killing people all of a sudden." Brieene told her with a smirk. "One will be acting normal, obedient as you please, then bam!" She slammed a fist down on a table. "They just go crazy and try to rip apart anybody close to them."

"Really? There are a few goblins in Stratford, nothing like that ever happened there."

Brieene shrugged. "We have thousands of goblins here; maybe you just got a few of the timid ones. They're always dangerous."

"No they're not," Tyrone said sharply. "There's hardly ever trouble."

"There are always some go crazy every year." Brieene insisted.

"A handful."

"But enough for most of the men here to carry swords." Alice noted.

"The baron's castle has plenty of guards." Brieene pointed out.

"It's safe enough here." Tyrone said. "The place is clean enough; you can go home now."

"Fine," Brieene said. She gave her employer a knowing look. "Try not to hurt yourself."

As his two other barmaids headed to the kitchen and the back entrance he turned to Alice. "There really is nothing to worry about. The goblins are just dumb animals. It's sort of the way from time to time dogs go mad. No one knows why, you just know to put them down when it happens."

"Goblins aren't animals. They can talk and think. Doesn't that make them people?"

"People? Goblins? I grant they can talk and do more than a horse or a dog can, but no goblin is more than a beast. I am right

378

surprised to hear you think that. You being married to a White Mage and all, don't they say we need to get rid of all the monsters?"

"My husband is very enlightened."

"I am right sure he is." Tyrone said uncomfortably.

"I am going up to my room now," Alice gave him a gracious bow. "Thank you for your great kindness."

"You are more than welcomes Alice."

XXX

At the top of the stairs Alice took out and counted what she had earned. Forty copper traks, almost half a silver dalter in just one night. That was not at all bad.

When she entered their room Waldo was already fast asleep. There was only a bit of moonlight coming in through the window. She could see in the dark though, and saw calk symbols scrawled all over the door, around the window, all over the floor, and much of the walls. The bed had a circle drawn around it with more symbols on the inside of it.

Waldo had explained to her about protective circles and seals. He had spent quite a bit of time doing all this to help keep them safe.

She smiled at him. Unlike the false smiles she had kept plastered on her face all night, this one was genuine. She shut the door and slipped out of her skirt and blouse, leaving only her small clothes. Alice went over to the bed, making sure not to step on any of the chalk on the floor. She pulled back the scratchy wool blanket and slid in beside him.

Alice wrapped her arms around Waldo and rested her head on his chest, careful not to disturb him. He was very warm. The sound

379

of his breathing was comforting. She closed her eyes and drifted off to a peaceful sleep.

Chapter 35

Protective Wards

When Alice woke the next morning she was alone in bed.

She sat up. "Darling?"

"Good morning." Waldo was sitting on the floor with a wooden bowl in his hands.

"What are you doing? Is that breakfast?"

"No, these are ashes mixed with a little water. "I need you to take your clothes off."

Alice's face turned beet red and she pulled the blanket up in front of her. "Oh, so you're done waiting and want to enjoy a husband's privileges? I… I guess that's all right. Please just be gentle with me though."

"Well of course I'll be gentle, I'm only going to use my fingers."

"Ah, really? Just your fingers? I… I don't mind if you use something, ah, bigger. You are my husband after all. I don't expect you to be *that* gentle."

Waldo blinked. "Alice, I am going to draw on your back to place protective runes on you. When we're outside this room they will help keep you hidden from any scrying or detection magic. They will also protect you from magical attack."

"Oh." She said feeling embarrassed all over again.

"Now take your clothes off and turn your back to me. The wards are temporary so we'll have to do this each morning."

"Every morning?"

"That's right."

"Well… if you think it's best."

She turned her back to him and pulled off her shift.

He sat down on the edge of the bed, and with one finger began to draw runes and symbols on her. As Waldo did so she couldn't keep from twitching.

"Stay still."

Alice was giggling. "Sorry darling, I'm ticklish."

What a fun way to start the day.

XXX

"Why are there so many monsters in this city?" Waldo complained. "They're everywhere! It's like undead in Alter!"

Alice looked about worriedly, but no one seemed to have overheard. One of the advantages of people all keeping their distance. "Darling, you need to be more careful with what you say."

They were walking along the endless, twisting streets of Middleton. Alice would not need to return to work until late in the afternoon. Right now it was getting on towards mid-day. She was accompanying her husband as he searched.

He looked over to her. "Why?"

"Would a White Mage know anything about that?"

"Oh. Right. That just sort of slipped out."

"You need to be more careful."

"I know," he turned away from her. "This place is annoying though. Everywhere you go you hear clanging, the air smells of smoke, there is too much light, and I don't just mean from the horrible ball of fire." He waved a frustrated hand at the road. There were two wagons coming up it, both being pulled by goblins. "My spell makes the whole city look tinted with red; it might as well be on fire. There's so much red light I can't pick anything out."

"I am sure you will find him eventually darling. There is no rush. I wouldn't mind if we had to stay here a while."

"Are you enjoying being a barmaid again?"

"I don't mind it, we're safe for now, and I am earning decent coin."

"Plus you have all those commoners lusting after you. Being what you are you must enjoy that."

"Are you jealous?"

"Certainly not, you belong to me."

She liked hearing that. "Yes I do."

"I am willing to admit it's convenient."

"I am glad you think so."

"Now you can get your cravings satisfied without attacking me."

"What?"

"You won't need me to satisfy your hunger for male lust. The way those men were staring at you I am sure you have enough to last you a month at least."

"Hey! You can't hold that against me. It's not like I want them to."

"I wasn't complaining. It's a relief not to have you constantly attacking me every night."

Smack!

"Ow!"

"Once again, you need to be more careful of what you say!"

As Waldo rubbed the back of his head the wagons rolled past. Each was being pulled by a single goblin in a leather harness and collar. The creatures thumped along without making a sound. One of the drivers poked his with the butt end of a spear.

"Move along." He growled.

The goblin kept going at the same pace. The human sitting in the cart did not seem surprised.

Why did he hit him then? "It's awful," Alice said. "Why must they be treated so badly just because they're not human?"

"How would you expect them to be treated?"

Alice frowned at him. "They're slaves in your country, right? Your people are just as bad, doing that to them just because of what they are."

"Everyone in Alteroth who is not a member of one of the Seven Families is either a slave or a serf. How well they are treated has nothing to do with whether or not they are human. In Alteroth the slaves receive different levels of consideration depending on how valuable they are. Unique and powerful monsters, like vampires, can actually rise to positions of great privilege. People with special skills, such as carpenters or engineers, are granted certain liberties. When a slave child is born who has the ability to cast magic, he or she will be adopted into whichever family owns them. If they prove strong enough in the Dark Arts, it's even possible to be adopted into one of the main families." Waldo looked proud. "In my country ability counts before everything else."

"What if the parents don't want their child adopted?"

"Why would that matter?"

Alice gave an annoyed shake of the head. "What about all the ones who aren't special?"

"They are put to work in whatever way best serves the owner's needs. Most goblins are trained to be soldiers. They are stronger and more aggressive than humans."

"Well that sounds a little bit better I suppose, but do any of them get to choose what they do?"

"Of course not. They're slaves. The only choice they are given is to obey or to die."

Alice was reminded of all the threats from Elsa. "Is there any place where monsters can just live how they want?"

"Certainly, outside of Avalon and their Alliance, almost every country has some wilderness that isn't fully controlled. In Alteroth there are mountains and highlands where monsters live outside our grasp. Here in Lothas, I understand they thrive in the marshes to the north. Almost every country in the Shattered Lands has some place where monsters flourish; where they get to live as savagely as they please. Go far enough to the east, past the last human settlement, and you will enter Ostagraad, the eastern wilderness. There the orcs, goblins, trolls, ogres, and all the other races live wild and free, and it's the men who have to hide and survive like animals."

"You mean there really is such a place?" Alice asked. "I always thought it was just a story to scare children with."

He chuckled. "It's as real as Dark Mages or succubi."

"I see."

Alice continued walking by his side thinking for a moment.

"In all those places, where monsters have power, how do they treat people?"

"About the same way you treat a nice fat suckling pig. So far as I know, none of the other races bother with keeping humans as servants."

"So everywhere in the world either humans abuse monsters or monster do the same to humans?"

"Of course, it's nature. The ones who have power always use the ones who do not."

"That's not how it should be. It isn't right and it isn't fair. Why can't we learn to live together in peace?"

"That's just foolishness."

"No it's not. I am living proof that monsters and humans can get along."

Waldo nodded sagely. "Yes, so long as the monster pretends to be human. It's only when people recognize you that there is a problem. What would happen if you released your true form right now?"

Alice didn't look happy. "That still doesn't make it fair."

"Well if it makes you feel any better, the world never has been, and never will be, fair."

"Thank you dear, that makes me feel so much better."

Waldo nodded. "Glad I could help."

XXX

As Alice and Waldo kept walking, neither of them noticed a seedy figure trailing a block behind them. He was a short, scruffy looking man in worn work clothes. He made a point to never approach too close to them, while always keeping them in sight.

XXX

When the two of them returned to the Inn of the White Horse, their shadow finally left.

The shabby fellow made his way through the city towards the merchant district. There he came to a modest home and knocked on the front door. A servant answered, recognizing him, and brought him into a den where his master awaited.

The home's owner was a middle aged man dressed impeccably and sitting behind a desk looking over some papers. The small room was filled with shelves and book cases, all crammed full of various tomes. He had hawk like green eyes and a very neatly trimmed mustache and goatee. Looking up from his reading material he glanced casually at his visitor.

"What have you to tell me Jonas?" He asked in a refined manner.

"I did like you told me to mister Varlos. I done followed them all day."

He gave a slight nod. "And what did our two guests do?"

"Not much, they just walked all over the place like they was looking for something."

"Did they make any stops? Did they speak with anyone?"

"Only time they stopped was at Millie's Place to eat. Didn't talk to no one that I saw, except to get their food."

"Millie's Place is near Stump Hill isn't it?"

Jonas nodded his head. "That's right sir, they went by all the hills like they was looking for somebody. Didn't talk to nobody though, they just kept walking."

"Did they approach the baron's palace or talk to any of the guards?"

The man shook his head. "Didn't go near the palace sir. They just went back to the White Horse, that's when I come here."

"I see." Varlos brought his hands together in front of his face. His eyes took on a calculating look.

Jonas fidgeted a bit and scratched himself. He didn't like when mister Varlos looked like that. It was like he went somewhere.

After a moment the eyes focused on his guest again. Reaching into a desk drawer the man produced a single silver coin and held it out. "Well done, I want you to do the same again tomorrow. Follow our white bird wherever he goes."

Jonas eagerly took the money and made it vanish. "What if the two go different ways?"

"The woman is not important, you follow the magic user. You can go now."

The man bowed and left happily. It wasn't often he did honest work, and it was even less often he got paid so good.

XXX

As soon as his agent left Varlos sat back in his seat and got the faraway look in his eyes once more. White Mages who visited Middleton *always* stayed with the baron. It was their common practice to stay with the local ruler or at least with one of the wealthiest or most influential.

They did not make it a habit to rent rooms in low end establishments or fail to announce their arrivals to the local authorities. For that matter they normally traveled alone, not with a beautiful wife in tow.

What was this one up to?

When White Mages did the unexpected it tended to make certain people very, very nervous. The whites were well known for their charitable and noble deeds, but they were just as well known for their political manipulations. Could this be some sort of new gambit of theirs?

He would have to keep a very close eye on this Waldo Rabbit.

Chapter 36

Alice Is Charming

He was struggling to breathe.

Waldo could feel weight pressing down on him. There was a vice like pressure all around him, tightening, squeezing, slowly constricting him and making it impossible to move or even draw breath.

XXX

He opened his eyes.

He was in bed, the blankets were half tossed aside, and there was predawn light coming through the window. Alice was asleep. Her head tucked comfortably on the top of his chest just below his chin. Her body was curled up, with her arms wrapped around his abdomen, and her long legs entangled in his. All of her weight was right on top of him.

She had on only her small clothes, as did he. Her breasts were pressed against him and he could feel them distinctly. Her long, fiery, red hair was a tangled mess. Though she was asleep Alice's embrace was like iron. Someone walking in might think it rather cute, sort of like a child holding a favorite rag doll.

To Waldo it felt more like a lion holding onto a future meal.

Her body was warm, and her skin deliciously soft to the touch. Unfortunately, not being able to move his arms and having to struggle to breathe kept Waldo from fully appreciating these facts.

"Alice," he gasped as loudly as he could. "You're crushing me again."

He had to repeat himself a couple more times before her eyelids fluttered open and she slowly lifted her head. Alice's light violet eyes gradually focused on him. A casual smile lit her lips.

"Morning darling."

"Good morning Alice, could you stop crushing me now?"

XXX

Waldo was downstairs sitting at one of the tables in the empty common room.

He gingerly rubbed his sides. "Every morning, I thought sharing a bed with a beautiful woman was supposed to be a pleasant experience."

He could hear Alice singing from the kitchen in the back. Despite their situation she was often in a cheerful mood. They had been here for a week.

A week!

Every day they had gone out through the streets searching. He slowly went blind staring at all the auras being given off by all the monsters who dwelled here. They would walk and walk and walk until it was time to head back to the Inn. He would get a meal and then head upstairs to study his spellbook before going to bed. Alice would also have something to eat and then begin her shift.

Waldo was frustrated and beginning to grow desperate. Somewhere out there his grandfather was still prowling. Just how long would his grandfather continue to wait? An army of ordinary men with swords would not deter an archlich. His grandfather had stayed away so far because there might be mages in this city. An archlich was nearly impossible to destroy with ordinary steel, but was hideously vulnerable to the right spell.

That was the reason his grandfather had waited, but its patience would not be unlimited.

His grandfather was far from the only threat.

He'd had Alice ask a few of the guard officers if there were any other White Mages in Middleton. Waldo had been relieved to learn that there weren't. In Alteroth all Dark Mages were taught certain stories that were never shared outside of the families. If two of their kind ran into each other in a foreign land, it was a standard practice to tell one of those stories. If the other one didn't know how it went it meant he wasn't a true Dark Mage. If the whites had a similar practice he would be found out.

Then there was the worry that one of the merchants Alice had met back in Stratford would spot her. He had not yet heard any rumors about a flying monster who had once been a barmaid. The news would not be long in arriving though; the two cities were too close to each other. If anyone connected Alice to that tale they could expect to have half the city guard come to arrest them both.

The longer they stayed here the more dangerous things became.

Alice came out of the kitchen with two bowls in her hands. She was in an annoyingly good mood, and was singing about a robin and a blue bird living together in sin.

She placed one the bowls, and a wooden spoon, in front of him. Alice then sat down in the chair next to him. "You should eat it while it's nice and hot."

Waldo eyed his food with a distinct lack of enthusiasm. "I hate porridge."

"That's not being appreciative darling. I worked over a hot fire to cook this for you."

"In my home," Waldo said wistfully. "The morning meal would be wheat cakes smothered in butter. There would be fresh fruits, nuts, eggs, steamed fish, bacon, and ham. Porridge was the sort of thing the slaves would eat."

"Sounds wonderful," Alice spooned up a mouthful and swallowed it down. "So who paid for all that?"

"My mother."

"I don't see your mother here now, and we don't have the money to spend on butter or bacon or ham. The porridge is free, and we're lucky Tyrone doesn't charge us for our meals. If you don't want to eat it I could make you a baked potato or some cabbage with carrots."

Waldo picked up his spoon. "I never said I wouldn't eat it."

Alice tilted her head slightly. "Why are you in such a gloomy mood this morning?"

"Because we've already been here seven days and I still have no idea where my second servant might be." He shoveled some food into his mouth and ate it reflexively.

"I'm sure we'll find who we're looking for sooner or later, and as long as it's a man or a really, really ugly woman everything will be fine."

Waldo frowned. Her relentless good cheer was grating on his nerves a bit. He hadn't shared all of his worries with her. There was nothing she could do about them, so there was no reason to burden her. Seeing her so relaxed and optimistic only made his own concerns weigh down even more heavily.

"Why are you so happy?"

"Why wouldn't I be? I am a free woman getting to have breakfast with her precious husband. There is nowhere else in the world I would rather be."

Waldo let out a grunt. Somehow her answer was both endearing and annoying at the same time.

The front door opened and the Innkeeper stepped into the common room. In his hands was a small clay jar with a cork stopper. There was a small back room where he stayed when there were guests. Most mornings he was up early helping Alice in the kitchen. Today it would seem he had gone out.

"Good morning Alice. I got this for you." He handed the small jar to her. "It's honey."

"Oh! That's so sweet of you! Thank you so much."

Tyrone looked like a puppy that'd just had his belly rubbed. "Well you mentioned yesterday how you wished you had some for your porridge."

Alice nodded. "I remember you telling me there wasn't any in the market."

"There wasn't, but there is a special herb shop that sells things you can't find at the regular market. They have all sorts of special foods and luxuries; they even have things for the local magic users."

Waldo's face immediately rose from his bowl.

"You really didn't have to go to so much trouble." Alice told him.

Tyrone puffed his chest out. "It was nothing. I don't mind a bit now so long as it makes you happy."

Alice was about to tell him how grateful she was when Waldo spoke up.

"Where is this herbal shop?"

Tyrone blinked, as if noticing he was at the table for the first time. "It's on the Street of Hammers near Baden Hill."

"Hurry up and finish eating," Waldo told Alice. "I want to visit this place." He began shoveling food into his mouth.

"Darling, don't you want to try some honey with your porridge?"

"No." He stuffed some more down. "Eat quickly or I'm leaving without you."

XXX

The clang of metal striking metal was everywhere. Waldo noticed it less than he had when they first arrived. That only meant it was less of an annoyance. What was annoying him now was the way Alice was dragging her feet.

"Come on, I want to get to this shop and see if they have anything useful. It would be nice to get something accomplished for a change."

Alice frowned and began moving even more slowly.

"If you don't want to come just give me the purse and you can go back to the Inn and let the Innkeeper fawn over you."

"His name is Tyrone, we've been staying there long enough for you to remember by now. And I've told you before that I will handle the money."

"Fine, but in that case move more quickly."

Alice came to a halt and crossed her arms.

"Now what?"

"You've been very rude today. Not just to me, but to Tyrone as well. I only mentioned wanting to get honey yesterday because you didn't like your porridge. Then Tyrone went out and found some without even being asked. You could have at least thanked him for that."

"Why? I didn't ask for any favors and he didn't do it for me, he did it to please you. He has been Charmed and will do anything for you."

"Well, I am very charming."

Waldo shook his head. "No, you didn't simply charm him, you Charmed him."

"Darling, when you use the same word twice it still has only one meaning."

Waldo glanced up and down the street to make sure no one was close enough to overhear him. The nearest person was a shabby looking man about twenty yards behind them. "When I say you Charmed the Innkeeper I don't mean with kind words or subtle suggestions you might let him enjoy your body."

Waldo completely failed to notice the sudden blush on Alice's cheeks.

"What I mean is the natural ability of a succubus to captivate and mesmerize a man. In short, you made him your willing slave."

"I would never do anything like that!"

"I'm not complaining Alice; it's one of the main advantages of having a succubus familiar. If anything, I would like you to do it more often. Once a man has been Charmed he will do pretty much anything for you."

"No, I can't do anything like that. I mean, I can get men to be nice to me, but that's only because they find me beautiful and I know how to talk to them. I've never done anything like make them willing slaves!"

"Are you sure? Haven't you ever had a man do exactly what you wanted?"

"Well… yes, lots of times in fact, but that didn't have anything to do with any special power."

"Uh, huh."

"It didn't," she insisted. "Gentle words from a pretty face are all it takes with most men."

"I'm sure that was the case often, but not every time. Charming requires you to look directly into your victim's eyes and desire him to obey you. Even if you were unaware, it would be instinctive for you. It's likely you have been doing it your entire life."

Alice shook her head. "No, I've never done anything like that."

"Really?" Waldo began looking at the blacksmith shops; there were three just in the immediate area. He pointed to one of them at random. "Go in there, go up to the owner, look him in the eyes, and ask him to give you a sword."

"What do we need a sword for?"

"It's just to make a point, ask the owner to give you a sword."

"Swords are hard to make, and even here iron doesn't come cheap, no blacksmith is just going to give me a sword because I ask."

"He will if you Charm him."

Alice gave an exasperated sigh. "Fine, I will do it just to show that you are wrong." She stomped over to the shop as Waldo waited where he was.

Less than two minutes later she came back out again, awkwardly holding a broadsword out in front of her.

The people passing on the street stared. It was common enough for men to carry weapons here, but a woman with a sword was a rare sight.

"I just looked him in the eyes and asked him if he would give me a sword." Alice was shifting her weight from one foot to the other and holding the sword out as far from her as she could. "He just nodded and agreed, like it was normal to gift a complete stranger with something like this. I mean he didn't even try to get me to do anything immoral! He just did what I told him to."

Waldo nodded. "That is how a succubus Charm works; it bends the victim's will and makes him completely obedient."

"Could you please not call him a victim? I feel bad enough as it is."

"Why? For you this is completely natural."

Alice turned her gaze to her feet. "I never knew I was forcing anyone to do what I wanted. When a man would do as I asked I always figured it was because he wanted to. I know what it's like to be controlled, and I don't want to do it to anyone else."

"Well that's a huge waste of your ability." Waldo noticed she was keeping her face down. "What are you doing?"

"I don't want to Charm you by accident. I would hate to think you were only with me because I was forcing you."

He chuckled. "You really are something special Alice."

398

She quickly glanced up, and then just as quickly looked down again.

"While I appreciate the concern it's not necessary. There are limits to the Charm ability. Women and magic users are immune to it, as are the blind. You cannot simply look at someone and affect them, there must be direct eye contact and you must feel the desire to have them do as you wish. Even then, if the vic… the person, has a strong will they can limit the influence the Charm has on them. The effect can be extended as long as you continue to be seen by the person. Once you leave, the Charm will wear off within a few days."

Alice looked back at him. "Well that's a relief. I would really hate to think you were with me because I'd made you."

"You have no need to fear then, I am with you because you are precious to me."

Waldo saw her blush again, he had no idea why.

"Ah, that's very sweet of you to say darling. So what do we do with this?" She swung the sword slightly from side to side.

"Well we could find a shop that sells leather goods and get you a free belt and sheath."

"I am not keeping it! What would I use it for? A sword is only made for killing."

"The same could be said about your claws."

"Those are a part of me, and no one sees them until I am about to use them. You're the man, why don't you wear it?"

"A mage carrying a sword on his hip? Barbaric. In any case, my wand is deadlier than any hunk of sharpened iron." That had not been true when he'd first set out, but it was now.

"So what do we do with this thing?"

Waldo pointed at a different black smith shop. "Go in there, look the owner in the eye and ask him to buy it from you. I'm sure you will get a very fair price without even haggling."

"I can't do that! Now that I understand my ability it would be like stealing!"

"So? I like stealing."

"I have a better idea." She turned around and walked back to the same shop.

"What are you doing?"

"I'm returning this."

"You mean for free?" Waldo sounded outraged.

"I am not going to just rob some stranger."

"Does that mean robbing people we know is all right?"

Closing her eyes and shaking her head she went into the shop.

Chapter 37

Please Stop Talking Now

"You're not allowed to be upset with me."

Waldo cast a stern glance back over his shoulder.

"You're not, all I did was return something that I had no right to in the first place."

"For free. You're the one who is always worried about how much money we have."

"That doesn't mean I want us to steal. It means I want us to earn what we can and spend carefully."

"You didn't seem to mind with Roger."

"That was different. He wanted to force himself on me."

"So it's all right as long as it's any man who wants to have sex with you? Good, that means we can still rob most of the men in the world."

"That's not what I meant!"

"I am just trying to understand where the line is. I want to know who you are willing to steal from."

"It's very simple. Stealing is never all right. Even stealing from Roger was wrong. I was just willing to help because of where he grabbed me is all. I think from now on we should follow all the laws and not cause any trouble."

"Have you forgotten who I really am Alice? Don't let this brilliant disguise fool you. I am Waldo Corpselover, an evil and black hearted mage. I am without mercy or compassion. The morals of ordinary men mean nothing to me. I am bound by no laws. I am a living, breathing, source of terror to all those who cross my path."

Alice suddenly pointed behind him. "Oh, is that a rabbit?"

"WHERE?" He jumped about and his head jerked from side to side as he tried to spot the horrid beast.

Alice snickered. "Evil and black hearted mage, huh?"

Waldo stopped panicking and narrowed his eyes at her. "That wasn't funny."

"Yes it was."

"You really do not have the proper attitude for a familiar."

"That's because I'm you wife darling, not your familiar or your servant."

Waldo decided not to bother correcting her as it would do no good.

"Why didn't you mention my being able to Charm before?"

"Why would I? I wouldn't try to explain flying to a bird, or swimming to a fish."

"But I told you before I didn't know anything about what I was."

"When I met you, you were working at an Inn. I simply assumed you were using your Charm instinctively. I was right. I just didn't realize you were ignorant of the fact."

"You don't have to be mean about it you know. You have been very rude to me this morning. I've only been trying to help you."

"Time is short," he grunted.

"What does that mean?"

"It just means I have a lot of problems to deal with. Now come on, I want to see if this herb shop has anything useful in it."

He picked up his pace.

XXX

Neither of them noticed the man carefully trailing after them.

XXX

The herbal shop was a crushing disappointment the moment Waldo entered.

In Alter there were three herbal shops that all specialized in providing mages with various spell components. They would have barrels filled with the most common ingredients such as mandrake, salt, and nightshade. On shelves would be jars with more select items such as wolfsbane, ground obsidian, elfroot, pickled goblin eyes, or ragweed. There would be supplies from all over the Shattered Lands. You could find cactus needles from the Zatarhn Desert, purple sea moss that only grew on the island of Lamos, ice peppers that only came from the far north, and all sorts of other difficult to acquire ingredients. They were expensive, but they were always available.

The shops also kept limited supplies of *truly* exotic materials locked away inside special vaults. Unicorn horn, dragon scales, vampire blood, medusa venom, and succubus tears were all worth more than their weight in gold. Such precious goods were not available in large quantities, but if you had enough gold you could usually find some in at least one of the shops. In Alter it was easy for a mage to acquire just about anything he might need for a spell or potion.

This was what Waldo thought of as the standard for what an herbal shop was supposed to be. So when he entered, 'Toppa's Herbs and Ingredients' he was taken aback. The very first thing he noticed was that of the several customers already inside, all of them were women, and not a one of them wore a magic user's robes. They all stared at him as though the presence of a mage were unusual.

Not a good sign, he thought.

As he began looking about his opinion was only confirmed. As Alice looked about her reaction was the exact opposite of his.

"Oh, they have fresh pepper! And sage and rosemary too! They have some nice onions and garlic!"

"They don't have mandrake," Waldo said in disbelief. "What sort of shop doesn't carry mandrake? It's the most basic ingredient."

"What sort of food do you use mandrake for?"

"You don't use it for food. You use it for all sorts of spells and potions." He was going through the barrels that lined the front of the shop. Flour? Beans? Barley? Nuts? "What is this?"

"Can I help you good sir?" A middle aged woman with black hair streaked with grey came up to him.

"Master not sir," Waldo said mechanically.

"I beg pardon?"

"My proper title is master not sir." He motioned at the barrels in front of him. "Where is the mandrake?"

"Mandrake sir?"

"Master not sir."

The woman stared at him uncertainly.

Waldo gave a frustrated sigh. "Where do you keep the mandrake?"

"We don't carry mandrake si... ah, master?"

"How can you not have any mandrake? What sort of shop is this?"

"Darling, you're being rude." Alice came over to his side. "Please forgive my husband; it's that time of the month for him."

Waldo glared at her while the shopkeeper's eyes tried to bulge out of their sockets.

"But... but... he's a man, how can he..."

"Well he's a wizard too, you know how they are, special connection to the moon's cycle and all that. Some months when we match we have to fight over the rags."

"Alice what are you doing?"

"Just explaining why you're acting the way you are. By the way, next week be ready to be on the receiving end."

The shopkeeper was twitching and slowly inching away. "I am sorry, but we don't carry mandrake. Was there anything else?"

"Rose petals, I need rose petals."

"We don't carry those either."

"Just what kind of shop are you?"

"We are a shop that sells herbs and ingredients for cooking. We don't sell things that don't flavor food. If you will excuse me." She hurried to a pair of customers who didn't appear to need any help.

"Just wonderful, rose petals are one of the key ingredients for making love potion."

"I don't know what you were expecting darling, none of the shops in Stratford carried those things either."

"I was expecting them to carry the basics of an herbal shop. Obviously I was expecting too much for this country of savages."

He did not bother to keep his voice down and was on the receiving end of some unpleasant stares.

"Maybe we should go," Alice suggested. "Before they gather their torches and pitchforks."

XXX

They stayed long enough to purchase salt and rosemary, then left.

"Well that was a complete waste. Calling that place an herbal shop is like calling a rabbit cute."

Alice sighed. "Whatever you say, oh, and sorry."

"Sorry for what?"

"This." She yanked up her skirt and delivered a swift kick to his backside which sent him flying.

A White Mage sprawled out in the street was a rare sight, and the people walking by burst out laughing.

"What was that for?" Waldo got to his knees and rubbed his rear.

"That was for the way you've been acting all morning. You have been very rude to me and to everyone else. That was a little reminder for you to behave yourself. You're usually very nice, so I don't know why you're acting this way."

Waldo's face darkened and he opened his mouth.

"I know, I know," Alice said wearily. "You don't like being called nice, though you **are** nice and I always mean it as a compliment." She held a hand out to him.

Scowling Waldo got up to his feet without any help. "Words like nice, kind, and merciful all imply weakness. I cannot afford to be weak; I am alone in a world filled with ignorant barbarians. I have enemies all around me and am always in danger. And despite my best efforts I haven't been able to move forward. Forgive me if I am not overly concerned with my manners."

Alice crossed her arms over her chest and began to tap one foot. "Darling, you are not alone. I am always going to be at your side. I am your wife until death parts us. I will never abandon you, no matter how much trouble you are in or how badly you behave. I have faith in you. You are clever and brave, and I know you will find a way to solve our problems no matter how bad they look. So try to be a little more cheerful, all right?"

"Fine then, I will try and sound more jolly." He began wiping some dirt off his not so pristine robes. "I suppose we may as well start searching again. At least we're in a good place for it."

The herb shop was located right near the main gate of Baden Hill.

Within Middleton the hills, all of them, were filled with iron ore. These hills provided easy access, and were all being mined heavily. Each of them was pockmarked with mine entrances, and roads had been dug into the sides, twisting all the way from top to bottom. Goblins worked in those mines, filling up carts with loads of ore to be hauled down to the forges.

407

At the base of each hill were brick penitentiaries where the goblins were crammed together. Except for those needed to pull wagons, none of them were every allowed to leave their dirty, overcrowded facilities. They labored until they died, and were then devoured by their hungry mates.

Surrounding these brick buildings was a wooden stockade, twenty feet high with several archers' towers rising a further ten feet. The towers were always well manned. At the first sign of any sort of revolt they would fill the ground below with arrows and shout the alarm. There were thousands of goblins, each stronger and more violent than any man, the people took the threat of an uprising very seriously. Each stockade had a single massive gate that shut every night from sunset to sunrise. Dozens of guards served it during the day time, and could shut and bar it in a matter of a few minutes.

Ringing the outside of each hill was a series of forges. All day massive fires burned, they took the ore and separated the precious iron from the useless rock. They made bars of raw iron that were then sold to the various blacksmiths all over the city, who turned them into swords, nails, horseshoes, and all other manner of goods.

Since most of the monsters in the city were to be found in the confines of these hills, they were where Waldo had focused his efforts. Each day, he and Alice would follow the same route, visiting every hill as they tramped all over the city. They would stand in front of the open gate and Waldo would peer in, hoping to spot a distinctive aura. With so many monsters though, it had been like staring into a bonfire. If there really was a Great Monster working among all those goblins it was impossible to tell.

"We'll start here today and go visit the others like we usually do."

Alice nodded. "I'm sure we'll find what we're looking for today."

"That would be nice."

"You said you would be merrier dear."

He turned to her and gave a wide, obviously false, smile. "Better?"

"I see someone wants to get kicked again."

He stopped smiling and just continued walking up to the open gate. Over the past week the guards at the various hills had gotten used to the sight of him and Alice coming by to peer inside. None of them had possessed the nerve to actually go up to him and ask what he was about. They had simply stood back and watched, most of them preferring to focus on Alice rather than him. People didn't try to converse with a White Mage if they didn't absolutely have to.

Waldo got to the gate with Alice on his heels. He was about to cast his detection spell when he saw something that took his breath away.

"Will you look at that?" He gasped. He stood there, rooted to the spot, his mouth hanging open.

"What is it?"

There before them was a creature standing at least eight feet tall and weighing five hundred pounds or more. His head was as bald as an egg and there did not look to be a single hair anywhere on his body. The only clothing on him was a burlap sheet that was tied about his waist and covered him to the top of his knees. His chest, arms, and shoulders were all exposed. His body was all hardened muscle and his pea green skin was glistening under the morning sun. The hands looked big enough to wrap around a man's skull. The face was flat and broad, with a big square jaw and a pair of floppy ears like a dog's. Two yellow tusks jutted out of his lower lip.

"An Ogre! The Great Monster I was sent here to find!"

Alice silently nodded, he was certainly that. There were shackles and thick iron chains on his neck, wrists, chest, and ankles. As he walked he pulled three ore carts linked behind him. During their search she had often seen individual goblins struggle to pull one when it had a full load. The ogre was pulling three of them; each piled high with ore, and didn't seem to be having any trouble at all. He looked to be as strong as he was ugly.

She was reminded of the stories she's heard about ogres. They were said to spit people and roast them over open fires. Their favorite treat was human skin, and they would peel people as if they were apples. They ate babies and children in single gulps and liked human intestines. Ogres could snap trees in half, and their hides were so thick and tough ordinary swords could not pierce them.

Given the stories she'd heard about Dark Mages and succubi, Alice knew the ones she'd heard about ogres were likely to be exaggerated. But the tales always had some truth to them. Were they really going to bring this beast with them? Would they be able to trust him? If he turned on them would she be able to protect Waldo? Such a monster would definitely help against a lich, but only if he could be controlled.

Waldo, for his part, did not have any doubts. As the dozen or so guards watched he ran right up into easy reach of the monster. The ogre came to a sudden halt as Waldo blocked his path.

"You're magnificent!" Waldo was waving his arms about jumping all around trying to look at the ogre from every possible angle.

"Your arms are like tree trunks! Your chest is like a brick wall. Your skin is beautiful; I don't see a mark on you. Show me your teeth."

The ogre's big grey eyes blinked. "Erk?"

"Your teeth, show me your teeth."

The ogre hesitated, but eventually did as he was told. He peeled back his lips to reveal a wide set of flat yellow teeth about his two tusks.

"Excellent, the teeth are good, that means the bones should be good as well." Waldo then pointed to the burlap. "And look at that bulge! You're filled with virility, absolutely made for breeding! When I get you home I will put you to stud and keep you rutting nonstop! I definitely want you! You must belong to me!"

The guards heard every word. One of them made a circle with one hand and quickly jammed a finger in and out of it. Several of them chuckled softly and whispered some jokes to one another. The only thing that kept them from laughing out loud and making some rude comments was fear of upsetting a White Mage.

Alice could feel her face going beet red. She was very sure there would be some new rumors going around town. "Darling what are you saying?"

"Don't worry Alice; I'm not going to use flowers this time. I'll just give him a kiss and make him mine."

"Erk?"

She closed her eyes and put a hand to her face. "Please stop talking now."

"What? Am I not being cheerful enough?"

The ogre grunted out what might have been a laugh. "Gronk like little man in white dress."

411

"These are robes, not a dress."

"Gronk like, they very pretty."

"Well I am glad you think so, not that it really matters." Waldo crossed his arms over his chest and tried to sound stern. "I am going to become your master and you will be my obedient servant. Your body will be mine and you will obey me without question. I will be hard on you sometimes, but I expect you to take it without complaint. In return I will see that your needs are taken care of."

The ogre gave a deep throated chuckle, while the guards struggled not to laugh out loud.

Alice shook her head. "Darling, people are going to get the wrong idea."

"How?" Waldo asked. "I just want to buy him and make use of that big, strong body. I already have lots of ideas of just what I can do with him."

"Wonderful, that's just what a wife wants to hear."

The sergeant in charge of the gate guards at last approached. Despite all the chains, Alice noted he made sure to keep well clear of the ogre. He gave Waldo an uncertain bow. "I beg pardon, but you need to step aside so that this beast can deliver his ore to the forge."

"Is his owner here?"

"Beg pardon?"

"His owner, is his owner here? I want to buy him."

"You serious? You really want to buy this thing?"

412

"Of course I am serious, do you have any idea just how valuable an ogre in his prime is? Bring the owner here so I can buy him."

"All right," the sergeant slowly nodded. "The owner lives nearby." He looked at the monster. "In the mean time you deliver your load. We'll see who you belong to."

The ogre gave a nod and grinned down at Waldo. "Gronk hope to belong to pretty man." He began heading towards the nearest forge again, the chains tightened and the carts began to roll along behind him.

XXX

As the sergeant left to fetch the owner Waldo took Alice aside to have a quiet conversation with her.

"All right, as soon as we meet with the owner I need you to look into his eyes and Charm him."

"What? No! I've already told you I am not going to do that."

"Then how are we going to acquire my new familiar?" Waldo asked reasonably. "You know how much coin we have. Do you think we can buy him? Do you think you can swoop down and carry him off in the middle of the night?

Alice frowned. They had a decent amount of money saved, but ordinary livestock (horses, sheep, and cows) were very dear. She didn't know the market price for monsters, but was willing to bet they cost even more. Just the thought of trying to lift that massive beast into the air and over the stockade made her back ache.

"There is no way we have enough to buy him, and you can forget about me flying him out. Even if I somehow managed it there would be search parties after us. You can't have an ogre go missing and expect people not to notice."

413

"Then what alternative is there? Alice, I need to have him by my side. When we meet my grandfather again, not if, when, having his strength at my command might be the difference between living and dying. The whole reason we came here was to find him. I am not leaving Middleton without that ogre."

She began to chew her lower lip.

He had a point. If they were going to face his grandfather again having such a monster might save them.

"Can you really trust him though? He's huge and frightening."

"Have you forgotten your reflection when you had horns, claws, and bat wings?"

"That's different," she said primly. "No matter what I look like, I have a sweet and gentle nature."

Waldo slowly rubbed his back side. "Yes, I was thinking that when you kicked me."

"You were asking for it. The difference is I would never chew on your intestines or peel off your skin for a snack."

No, Waldo thought. *You would just crush me to death as I sleep.* "Once I have bound him to me with a contract he won't be able to hurt either of us. A familiar cannot do any physical harm to its master or refuse any direct command."

Alice lifted a gingery eyebrow. "Is this the same one you used on me?"

"I obviously made a mistake with yours, I am sure I will get it right this time."

"That doesn't fill me with confidence darling."

"I will definitely manage to keep him under control. I can't leave here without him."

"Fine," she sighed. "I know how important this is to you, and I have faith in your ability."

"So you'll help me? You'll Charm his owner?"

"Yes, but just this once! I don't like stealing from people or controlling them. But since I don't see any other way I'll agree to do it this one time."

"Good. As soon as he belongs to me I'll perform the binding ritual. We'll get our things from the Inn and be on our way to Norwich."

"Fine, just remember not to make it a chaste kiss."

They waited fifteen minutes for the sergeant to return with the owner of Baden Hill and all of its workers.

"I understand you want to purchase my ogre." An old merchant woman said to him.

Waldo shut his eyes. *The Dark Powers hate me.*

Chapter 38

Negotiations

Carin Anders was the head of her merchant house. She stood just over five feet and did not weigh ninety pounds, her hair was completely grey and tied up in a bun. Carin had inherited the position when her husband had died seven years ago. As a product of the merchant class she had not a drop of noble blood in her veins. Carin had spent her entire adult life bargaining and making deals as she also raised four children.

While the nobility held a stranglehold on political power in Lothas it was the merchant houses that controlled the banks and much of the economy. There were many sorts and kinds of power. The power of the purse was not as highly respected as that of the sword. But it was real enough. Merchant House Anders was one of the richest in Lothas, with many holdings here and in other lands. Though she belonged to a lesser class, Carin Anders had more wealth and more influence than the majority of nobles. She still had to bow to them in public and acknowledge their superiority. In private though, they often came to her with hand extended begging for loans and favors.

Carin was sixty three, with eleven healthy grandchildren, and a position with more real authority than all but a handful of women in this land.

While not the sort to come running at a summons, when her sergeant had explained who it was asking for her she had decided to return with him.

The power of Avalon was very different from that of the local nobles or even of the King. There were all sorts of rumors about the White Mages. Their wealth and political influence were not to be despised, and that was not even considering what they could do with their magics. You did not make an enemy of a White Mage if it could be at all avoided.

So here she was, standing outside the gate to Baden Hill. Before her was a young man in white robes and a very beautiful red head, both with most unusual eyes.

"I understand you want to purchase my ogre?"

To her surprise he closed his eyes and there was a pained expression.

"Of course, it couldn't be that easy," he muttered.

"I beg your pardon?"

He looked at her hopefully. "I don't suppose there is a man I could discuss this with?"

She placed her hands on her slender hips and tried not to sound irritated. "I am the owner of all those who labor here. None of them may be sold without my permission, if you are uncomfortable dealing with me I can have one of my subordinates speak to you instead. However any agreement you come to with him will not be valid unless I approve it."

"Wonderful," he sighed.

Her eyes narrowed slightly. She had dealt with a few White Mages before. They usually demonstrated much better manners. "I am not in the habit of negotiating with strangers. It is customary to introduce yourself *before* trying to do business with someone."

"I am Waldo Rabbit," he nodded to the woman at his side. "This is my... wife, Alice Rabbit."

Despite the slight hesitation, his wife smiled radiantly and performed a graceful curtsey. "I am honored to meet you."

"The pleasure is all mine," Carin lied. "I am Carin Anders, owner and head of Merchant House Anders." She lowered her head respectfully to Waldo. "Now Master Rabbit, would you be more comfortable discussing this matter with a man instead?"

"That depends; if your man wanted to just give me the ogre at no charge would you allow it?"

"No, and if he did I would fire him. I run a business Master Rabbit, not a charity."

He nodded. "Then I suppose I will just have to deal with you. Do you know you are the first person in this country to call me, 'master' without being told to?"

"Some of us try to have good manners." Carin noticed his wife grimace but there was nothing from the husband.

"I agree, most of the people here are very uncivilized."

Carin quirked an eyebrow.

"Darling, you might want to get off this topic now."

"So what would be the price for the ogre?"

"Fifteen ducats and not a trak less."

The wife paled.

"Fifteen? That's all?" Waldo exclaimed. He turned to his wife. "I really overpaid for you didn't I?"

Smack!

Carin was amazed to see the White Mage slapped on the back of his head. They were usually figures of immense dignity and self-respect. You didn't expect to see one getting knocked about in public.

"Ow." He rubbed the rear of his skull. "Well in any case, that sounds reasonable." Waldo nodded to his wife. "Pay her."

"Darling, a word in private please?" She grabbed her husband's arm and physically began dragging him away. "Excuse us."

XXX

"What are you doing?" Waldo demanded when she finally let go.

"That is what I wanted to ask you."

"Isn't it obvious? Since you can't Charm her I will just pay her price. I was expecting it to be near what I paid for you. Having it be just fifteen is a bargain."

"Just fifteen? You can buy an estate for that! Darling, I know you come from money, but you really need to understand just how much gold is worth. Most folk never even touch a gold coin in their lifetime! They deal with silver and copper. If they have saved up enough to have the value of just one ducat they've done very well for themselves. The hundred gold coins you gave Elsa was a small fortune! A lot of noble families aren't even worth that much!"

"Really?"

"Yes."

"I really overpaid."

Alice narrowed her eyes.

"Not that I regret it."

"Keep that in mind."

"So how much do we have?"

Instinctively she put a hand to the fat purse tied to her waist. Their money was always with her, and she always kept a careful track of just how much there was.

"We have a bit more than eight and a half ducats worth in coin."

"That's all?"

"That's all?!" Alice screeched. "We could buy a nice house and a large farm with that, and have enough left over for some pigs and chickens and a couple cows."

He motioned for her to calm down. "All right, I understand, it's a vast sum. But we need more."

"Maybe not, maybe I can bargain her down some. I have always been good with dealing with people."

"I know, but that is usually with men who are staring at your breasts."

"Well I admit that helps, but I am good at haggling. Just don't say anything and let me handle things."

XXX

Carin watched as Alice strode back, her husband trailing behind. The girl smiled brightly and brought both hands together.

"Is there any possibility you could lower your price just a bit?"

"No."

"Not even for a White Mage?" Alice asked sweetly.

Carin crossed her arms over her chest. "White Mages always have lots of gold; I would think he would have no trouble at all with my price."

Alice spread her hands out before her. "Well even if that is true it doesn't mean he should pay such an extravagant amount."

Carin frowned. She was suddenly reminded of her many dealings with the, 'smith wives' at the market. They were the wives of the blacksmiths and iron workers. While their husbands concentrated on working their forges, it was the women who handled the money and all the transactions for the family. They were fierce negotiators who acted as though every trak they spent was taking food from their children's mouths.

"Iron costs," Carin quoted one of her favorite sayings. "So do healthy monsters. I have quoted you a fair price."

"Fair?" Alice sounded as if she were choking. "Fifteen is an absolute fortune! I would think five…"

"Five!" Carin barked. "That is an insult! A healthy, strong goblin would cost you at least three ducats. And an ogre is worth at least five goblins. Plus, I happen to know I have the only ogre in this city, maybe this country. They are very fierce in the wild and almost impossible to take alive. What is rare is always precious."

"I've seen him; he doesn't look that precious."

"If you want something pretty to gaze at I can direct you to a painter I know, he does lovely portraits. If you want raw muscle you can't do better than an ogre."

"Actually that's not true," Waldo put in. "Giants, vampires, and dragons are all stronger."

Carin gave a rude snort. "Good luck finding any of those. Better luck trying to buy them if you can't even afford an ogre." She peered at him more closely. "Why do you want this ogre anyway? I know you believe all monsters need to be gotten rid of."

"The reason doesn't concern you. We have our little conspiracies and plots that don't involve you common folk. By the way, we are trying to take over the world."

Alice sighed and put her hand to her face.

Carin felt insulted, but also a little bit unnerved. Some people claimed the whites had their own secret agenda. The ones she had met always declared they had nothing to hide. Meeting a white who was arrogant enough to actually admit to it worried her.

"Are you really a White Mage?" Carin asked.

In reply Waldo held out his hand. "*Pyro.*" Fire burst to life on his palm.

Carin took a step back from him.

Seeing the reaction made Waldo grin. He deliberately held his hand out towards her and took a stride in her direction. "We White Mages do not like to be questioned. Do you have any further doubt of what I am?"

"No! None, I apologize for questioning you Master Rabbit!" She quickly jumped back to keep the flames well away from her.

Waldo nodded. "*Nunc.*" The flames died away instantly.

To Carin, and to all the guards who had been watching, there was no doubt at all that he was a White Mage. They never even thought to wonder if he might be a different sort of magic user.

"So might we get a slight discount?" Alice asked. "I know my husband would appreciate it."

"I would."

Carin was torn between her desire to turn a profit and her inclination not to upset a White Mage. "Out of my great respect for your noble order I will lower the price to twelve. That is absolutely my best offer."

Alice held out her hand with index finger and thumb just barely apart. "Any chance you could drop it just a bit more?"

"No, that is already much less than I would normally accept. If he does not have twelve ducats then he cannot afford an ogre. If you like I could sell you some strong goblins at a good price instead."

Alice looked hopefully over to Waldo.

"I don't want any weak monsters, I want the ogre."

"Then the price is twelve."

"Could we work a trade?" Waldo suggested. "Would you like some soulwood? I could make it rain for you. If you have any people who are sick or injured I could see about healing them."

Carin shook her head. "I don't want or need any magic. If you have any gems or precious metals I would consider taking those. Magical weapons or armor are always valuable."

"I have none of that."

"Then we are back to gold. Twelve ducats and he is yours."

Alice came over to her husband's side. "Could we have a few days to try and work something out?"

"You can have all the time you wish. I don't expect to have any other buyers suddenly appear. Please feel free to contact me should you have the necessary funds." She gave Master Rabbit a respectful curtsy. "Good day to you."

At his nod she withdrew and hurried back to her home. Her guards would all have quite a story to share.

Chapter 39

Alice's Great Idea

"So what do we do now?" Alice asked.

They were on their way back to the Inn.

"We only need four more ducats. Then the ogre will be legally mine and we can leave."

"Right, with a monster that likes to eat human skin. Sounds perfect darling."

"I've already told you, I will definitely get the contract right next time."

"I hope so. I really don't want to wake up one night and find myself being spitted and over an open fire."

"I'm sure if you were spitted you would die almost immediately."

"That doesn't really make me feel better."

"I'll control the ogre, the problem is acquiring him."

"So what do we do?"

"If you were willing, there's a very easy way we could get the money we need."

He was not surprised when he saw her glare or felt anger through their bond.

"Don't even suggest that or I am going to kick you again. I wouldn't do it for Elsa when I was single. I certainly won't do it now that I am properly married."

"That's not what I meant. If you would just agree to use your Charm we could raise the funds easily. I'll bet you could get it in a day or two."

She shook her head. "I've already told you I am not going to do that. It would be wrong."

"You said you would do it to help me get the ogre."

"As a one-time thing, I am not going to steal from dozens of men."

"So if we find one who is wealthy enough you'll agree?"

"I am not doing it. It would be wrong."

"That's not how a typical succubus would view it."

"Well it's how I see it."

"This would be so much simpler if you didn't have these ridiculous morals of yours."

"It's how I was brought up. If you have no problem with stealing why don't you do it?"

"I would if I could get away with it, unlike with Roger though we can't simply leave the area afterwards. Given the limits of my spells it wouldn't be safe in a city crawling with armed guardsmen. I also lack mind altering magics, so I would have to resort to force."

As he said this a squad of six guards went past on the other side of the street.

"No," Alice agreed. "That wouldn't be a good idea."

"If only she had been a man."

Alice nodded and gently patted his shoulder. "Yes, but she's not. Too bad you can't make her fall in love with you or something."

Waldo came to sudden halt. He stood there with his eyes staring out into empty space.

"Is something wrong darling?"

Through their bond she could feel him being filled with exhilaration.

"Alice you are brilliant! That's the answer."

"What is?"

"I'll make Carin fall in love with me and just give me the ogre!"

"Uh, darling, while I absolutely love you and think you're the best, you may not be her type."

Laughing he hurried down the street. "That won't matter."

When they arrived at the Inn Waldo ignored Tyrone's greeting and went straight to the back kitchen. Looking about he snatched a small iron cauldron, a measuring cup, an iron pan, a spoon, a bowl, and a wooden pestle.

"Bring me some flowers," he told Alice as he piled everything into his arms. "Roses would be best, but at this point I'll settle for whatever you can find."

"Darling, what are you up to?"

"Isn't it obvious?" He headed toward the door. "I am going to make love potion."

XXX

John Varlos sat back in his chair and listened as Jonas rambled on about what he had seen. The man smelled of alcohol and swayed a bit as he stood there.

"You know Jonas that I do not pay you to get drunk when you are supposed to be working."

He held his hands up. "Weren't like that mister Varlos, I swear. I didn't go drinking 'til after they was back at the Inn. An then I only did it to find out what one of them guards heard. Were just doing my job sir."

"So you just had to get drunk to gather information?"

"It take more than two, three mugs to do me in." Jonas said proudly. "I had to buy this guard some brew to loosen up his tongue. It look downright strange if I not drink right along with him."

"Yes, I see you very diligent in maintaining your hidden identity." Jonas smiled widely as though it were a real compliment. "So this Waldo Rabbit really was trying to purchase an ogre? Not only that but he had his wife try to haggle the price, and didn't seem to have enough coin?"

Jonas bobbed his head up and down. "Not just that now, he was threatening her. He did it real polite now, but Miss Carin went all white when he done it. It sound like he want to get the ogre real bad it does."

"Just not badly enough to actually pay for the creature."

Jonas gave an indifferent shrug. "That what the guard say. His wife ask for a few days, and Miss Carin say that be fine."

"I hope you are not making any of this up or exaggerating. It would be easy enough for me to confirm by asking directly."

"I know better than to be making up things. If anything be a lie it be on the guard, not me." He placed two fingers over his right eye. "May Wotal strike me blind."

Varlos gradually nodded. His agents knew not to bring false reports. He also doubted that Jonas had enough imagination to come up with such a bizarre tale. Varlos opened one of his desk drawers and took out a silver coin. Thinking about it, he took out a second and held them out.

"You've done very well. I want you to get a friend to watch the White Horse when you cannot. I want to be sure to know when Waldo Rabbit leaves, no matter the time day or night."

The man eagerly accepted the two coins. "I do that sir, no worries." Bowing his head Jonas shambled out of the study.

As soon as he was gone Varlos began to drum his fingers upon his desk and consider the information.

A White Mage purchasing a monster, and a Great Monster at that, was contrary to their entire philosophy. They preached absolutes, in their view there was no moral middle ground. Everything was white or black, good or evil, they did not believe in compromise. They moderated their actions only as much as circumstances required, and even then they never bent when it came to their principles.

All monsters were evil. There could be no co-existence. The world belonged to humanity and there was no place in it for any other sentient beings. In the lands they controlled all monsters were exterminated without exception. That one of their order would actually want to purchase an ogre simply did not make sense.

That he was apparently lacking funds was another discrepancy. As a rule, White Mages travelled with a good amount of money. They were expected to not only to pay for their own needs, but to be able to provide charity and assistance when it was called for. It was almost unheard of for one to be short of coin.

And he was staying at an Inn in the poor part of town.

And he was traveling with his wife, a wife who was actually working as a barmaid.

The man was one incongruity after another.

Is he really a White Mage? Varlos wondered.

Normally you would never think anyone would dare to impersonate a white. That was an excellent way to make an enemy of one of the greatest powers in the world. Only a complete fool would do something like that. On the face of it, it seemed most unlikely. Yet if it were so it would explain all of the odd behavior.

How would I go about finding out? What would I do if he really were an imposter? Do I even want to know?

There was a knock on his study door.

"Come."

The door opened and his loyal servant stepped inside. "Pardon sir, but I just got a messenger from the south gate."

Varlos had eyes at each of the city gates, and standing orders that a messenger be sent to him as soon as anyone of importance entered the city. That was how he had originally found out about Master Rabbit.

"Who has arrived Martin?"

Martin told him.

"Well now, isn't that interesting?" He rose to his feet. "Get my cloak and my best clothes ready. I need to go."

XXX

Melissa Cornwall was headed towards the baron's palace. Like everywhere else the people kept their distance as soon as they spotted her white robes. She made a point to smile at them and try to let them know they had nothing to fear from her.

Only the guilty, like the man she was hunting, had any reason to fear.

She hoped that she would find some trace of where this so called Rabbit had run to.

Chapter 40

The Enemy Of My Enemy Is My Friend

Melissa had last been in Middleton about two years ago, and had forgotten what the constant clanging was like. If she stayed here awhile the sound would fade into the background. She wasn't planning on staying that long. Her only priority at the moment was tracking down this Waldo Rabbit before he caused any more harm to the Order's good name.

First things first though, she needed to announce her arrival to the local court and arrange quarters for her stay.

XXX

The baron's palace was not really all that impressive. Alice had travelled all over the northern half of the Shattered Lands and had stayed with kings and dukes and other rulers. The palace was really more of a fortress. It was stuck in the low area between Ardwin Hill and Spring Hill. Just a rectangular block with a tower at each corner and a small inner courtyard. The main building was only two stories, with the outer wall about ten feet higher, and each tower ten feet more. It was all built of granite and was kept in good repair. Good enough for local nobility.

The guards at the gate were noticeably better equipped than the men who patrolled the streets. Melissa was granted immediate entrance and escorted to a formal audience. She noticed that none of them had to rush off to inform the baron of her arrival.

Melissa didn't need the single guard to guide her to the audience chamber, she remembered the lay out quite well. The rooms here were not that spacious, and the furnishings not overly lavish, but they would do. She didn't plan to spend much time in her quarters anyway.

The audience chamber was about the size of a conference room in some of the castles Melissa had visited. The only furniture was a single gilded chair. Baron Gregorie Torrance was already seated, dressed in plate armor and with his blade belted on. He was surrounded by a dozen knights and officials

Melissa noticed one of the faces with interest.

"Welcome Mistress Melissa Cornwall of the Order of Mist," the baron said. "I am most pleased to see you once more."

She strode up to the baron and curtsied for him. "It is a great pleasure to again be in your presence Baron Torrance. May I request lodging within your home? As well as your protection of course."

"Certainly," he replied with a stiff nod. "When you left I was under the impression I would not see you again for some time."

"My duty brought me back sooner than expected, but I likely will not stay long. I am happy for the chance for us to be reacquainted."

"As am I," he murmured as he shifted in his seat. His hand tapped restlessly on the hilt of his sword. "What sort of business has brought you back? Perhaps I can be of assistance."

Melissa bowed her head. "That is most generous of you, but it is a very small matter that I prefer to take care of myself." The absolute last thing she intended to announce was that there was a traitor to the Order going about committing crimes.

"Then I will leave you to settle your affairs." He stood up. "Your old quarters will be made ready for you, and anything else you may require will be provided."

"You have my sincerest thanks baron. I wish upon you the blessings of unity, justice, and peace."

"Yes, now if you will pardon me I have much to do."

He wasted no time in withdrawing, and all but one of his retinue followed on his heels. Melissa soon found herself alone with a well-dressed man in a dark blue cloak.

"It is nice to see you again John Varlos."

"It is also good to meet you again as well Melissa Cornwall." He gave a slight, respectful nod.

"The audience was rather short."

"The baron is a very busy man, the merchant houses and the guilds are always screaming for his attention."

"When I was staying here before he avoided me as much as he could. I think I make him nervous."

"I think you make all of us nervous."

"Should I take that as a compliment?"

"You can if you like."

They both kept a healthy distance as they eyed one another cautiously.

"We last met about, what, a year and a half ago in the capitol? What is King Leo's spymaster doing here so far from Nodol?"

"Spymaster?" He placed a hand to his chest and both eyebrows rose. "Mistress Melissa you exalt me far beyond my rank. I am but a humble merchant."

It was a wonderful performance. "A merchant who just happened to be here to greet me as soon as I arrived. You were the only one without noble blood attending the baron."

"The baron honors me by seeking my advice on minor matters of trade and banking."

Melissa nodded. "As does the king, you were a fixture at the royal court. Always standing in the background listening, ever present yet never noticed."

"Well you certainly noticed me, but I would expect an archmage to have a keen eye."

"I am just a servant to the Order and to The One We Follow."

He frowned. "Is that how you refer to your ruler or to one of your gods?"

"So what are you doing here in Middleton?"

"I am doing what I always do, selling my goods, purchasing materials, and seeking promising business opportunities. A merchant needs to travel constantly."

Melissa nodded. "As do spies." She hesitated just a bit. "Have you any interesting news to share?"

"There is always gossip. Are you concerned with any particular subject?"

"Not really."

"Then how could I guess what you mind find remarkable?"

"I am simply curious if you have heard any rumors that are especially unusual."

"Nothing really comes to mind."

"I see. Well it was just a thought."

There was silence as they both stood there observing the other.

"You don't trust me do you?" Melissa asked.

"Mistress Melissa, I can honestly say that I trust you as much as I trust any White Mage."

"Which is to say not very much at all."

He shrugged. "I am merely a merchant; my opinion does not count for much."

"Your king seems to value it."

"You give me far too much credit."

"I don't think so."

"King Leo has many advisors, and my opinion is not unique."

"I am not your enemy. The Order and the Alliance are not your enemies. Your enemy wears black."

"My enemy, is whoever threatens my country and my king."

She spread her hands. "Avalon is no threat to Lothas. All we want is…"

"Unity, justice, and peace; yes, I have heard that before, many times."

"It is the truth, that is all we want for the world."

"Even if I believed that you would still be a threat."

"How so?"

"Because to achieve those noble ends you would sacrifice my homeland."

She shook her head. "Avalon, and every member of the Alliance, would shed its blood for you."

"That will be a huge comfort as the hordes of zombies overrun us. You are very far away, and Alteroth is on our southern border."

"Yes, poor Lothas, so far from salvation and so near Alteroth."

"I am sure from your point of view that is an inconvenient truth. Being a great power, Avalon can pick and choose its enemies. We do not have that luxury."

"There can be no peace with those who embrace evil. If you put your trust in the Dark Mages instead of us, they will swallow you whole."

"We would be idiots to trust the Dark Mages. At least for now though, they are not a threat, they do not seek to invade our lands. If you had your way you would provoke them into attacking us. That is the last thing the king wants."

"They are evil and must be purged from the land. They are rotten and must be cut out. There is no other way. Soon or late there will be war."

"If those are the only choices then King Leo chooses late."

Melissa shook her head sadly. "Forgive me, but that is cowardly. Wickedness must be opposed, not tamely yielded to."

"That is very easy to say when it is not your people who will be butchered or your lands that will burn."

"King Doran of Dregal has a very different view of things. He understands the wisdom of accepting our protection and our beliefs."

Doran was extremely close to his advisor Ramiel and seemed to be inching his way towards joining the Alliance. That made everyone at the royal court in Nodol very nervous. It was assumed that openly joining the Alliance would provoke an invasion by Alteroth. The ruling families of Lothas, Dregal, and Wylef were all connected by blood. King Leo would be honor bound to come to Doran's aid, which would likely mean the end of Lothas.

"I cannot speak for King Doran, but I know that King Leo does not want to provoke our southern neighbors."

"Then I will pray that he gains the wisdom to understand who his friends are. Know that should he ever truly see the light we will still extend to him our benevolent support." She turned and headed to the door. "If you will excuse me, I have had a long journey and am going to rest."

XXX

As he headed home Varlos was not happy.

Melissa's arrival was a reminder that a day of reckoning was coming.

The sad thing was that in many ways he respected the Order and what they stood for. If he were forced to choose he would choose them over the Dark Mages. The darks were genuine evil; he had no illusions about that. For Varlos, and for his king, the problem with the White Mages was that they were trying to force them to choose. They were zealots, and in their fanaticism were pushing for a confrontation that no one here wanted. That they and their Alliance would fight he did not doubt for a moment. But if Lothas were destroyed regardless of who won, what difference did it make?

When he returned he found a few new reports waiting for him on his desk.

One was from an agent he had in Stratford. It related a very interesting tale about a Dark Mage and a winged monster. The monster had been a beautiful barmaid named Alice.

Chapter 41

What A Guy Will Do Just To Get An Ogre

In one of the blank pages of his spellbook Waldo had written the following:

Recipe for Love Potion

Two servings of ground rose petals.
Three servings of ground mandrake.
Two pinches of sugar.
One pinch of cinnamon.
Two pinches of rosemary.
Two servings of ground lotus blossoms.
Another ingredient.

Mix together with one cup of water and bring to boil.

Add one succubus tear while reciting the following spell:

'Est lothanos carcao, est navarro carcao, aris monk nula.'

Will produce one dose of love potion that will enrapture any heart for a single night.

That was what Waldo *thought* the recipe was. He had learned it along with many others back when he had been an apprentice. The recipes for all the various potions had been written down in his spellbook, the one that was at the bottom of a river now. He had to go by memory and intuition.

Right beneath the first notation was a second one.

Recipe for Love Potion, Rabbit Variant

Two servings of ground dandelions.

Two servings of ground mandrake.
One spoonful of honey.
One pinch of cinnamon.
Two pinches of rosemary.
Two servings of ground lotus blossoms.
One serving of ground devil's grass.

Mix together with one cup of water and bring to boil.

Add two succubus tears while reciting the following spell:

'Est lothanos carcao, est navarro carcao, aris monk nula.'

Will produce something, I pray the Dark Powers, that will act like love potion for at least an hour or two.

Magical incantations and potions were a bit like cooking recipes. If you had the necessary abilities and followed the correct process you could expect to get the same result every time. The same was true of potions and wards.

But, as with cooking, you could make adjustments. Change a syllable here; alter an inflection there, even use a different word and you would get... something. The effect might be close to what you wanted, it could be worse or better, it could be nothing, and occasionally it could be something else entirely.

Walter had once drawn up a summoning circle meaning to call a samalander. He made a mistake with one of the runes and somehow wound up with a talking gerbil who said his name was Ernst.

Mages could create their own spells and potions through experimentation. The spellbooks of former masters were treasures worth killing for, largely because they often contained unique incantations found nowhere else. For the truly great ones (like his mother) it was almost expected.

Circumstances had forced Waldo to come up with an alternate recipe.

Alice hadn't known of any places that sold roses and so had brought him some dandelions she had found growing in an alleyway. Mandrake and lotus blossoms had been among the ingredients he had stolen from Roger, but he'd only had enough mandrake to make two doses. Sugar was an expensive luxury and very hard to find, he had substituted the honey that the Innkeeper had brought just this morning. Cinnamon and rosemary he had, having acquired both while traveling through the forest.

There was a seventh ingredient, Waldo was almost sure of it, but for the life of him he couldn't recall what it was. Devil's grass had been another of the things stolen from Roger. It contained strong magical properties and was used to strengthen the effects of other components. Since he didn't know what was missing it seemed like a good choice as a substitute. Waldo also decided that since the potion was so far from the original formula he would use two tears rather than one. Hopefully using more of the key ingredient would help make up for the other shortcomings.

Back in the castle he'd been quite skilled at brewing potions. He was meticulous and patient and could always see the logical order in things. Unlike with his spell casting, no one had ever questioned his competence when it came to potions or wards. Of course, he always had the correct recipes in front of him. Waldo had never tried to improvise before. Given some of his wretched failures casting he had enjoyed just getting the correct result.

"Well I guess I'll experiment now. At least this shouldn't accidentally poison her." He paused to consider it. "Probably."

With his pestle he slowly, deliberately ground up the dandelions, mandrake, lotus blossoms, and devil's grass in the bowl. Each was emptied into the small cauldron. He filled a spoon with the thick honey, and then watched as it slowly fell. A pinch of cinnamon and two of rosemary. In went a mug of well water.

"Pyro."

There was no fireplace in the room, so Waldo placed an iron pan on the floor and created a magical fire within it. He then placed the cauldron on top of the flames. With a wooden ladle he stirred the mixture together as the water heated up. Just as it began to simmer he took out the glass vial that held Alice's tears. Ever so carefully, he let one drop fall, and then a second.

"Est lothanos carcao, est navarro carcao, aris monk nula."

Waldo felt the familiar warmth of drawing forth mana. He focused on the contents inside the cauldron and let the power flow out and into them. As the arcane power was infused into the stock it boiled over. Most of it was reduced to steam and was gone. What remained was as thick and gooey as syrup, and there was about enough to fill a shot glass.

He had made love potion before, and knew that when it was complete it was a very light, almost translucent, pink.

What he had was golden yellow.

Waldo took a clean cloth and strained it to remove the impurities. He gradually poured it into a glass vial, careful not to spill a drop. Then he pushed in a cork stopper.

He held it in his hand and stared at it. In the afternoon light it shined like liquid gold.

"Well... I made something."

XXX

It was well after sunset when Alice went to the room they shared. It was early evening and the common room was filled with customers eating, drinking, and laughing. The cook was complaining about her missing utensils and had been after her to

443

get them back. Alice was also curious to see how things were going. So despite being busy she hurried upstairs.

She gave a knock. "Darling? Can I come in?"

There was no reply.

Alice cautiously opened the door and stuck her head in. "Darling?"

He was sitting cross legged on the floor. The cook's things were scattered in front of him. He was holding one of the glass containers they had stolen from Roger. He was just sitting there staring at it.

Alice stepped into the room and shut the door. "Darling?"

He finally seemed to hear and turned in her direction. Through their bond she could feel surprise, and underneath that, a sense of worry.

"Alice? Are you done with your work? I hadn't realized it was that late."

"It's not; I just came up to see if I could return all those things to the kitchen."

Waldo nodded. "Go ahead, I am done with them."

She took a couple steps closer and peered at what he was holding. "Is that it? Is that the love potion?"

"I have no idea."

"What is that supposed to mean? Is it love potion or isn't it?"

"I don't have the recipe with me, or even all of the proper ingredients. I had to improvise and use substitutes. What I made is something close, but not exactly what I was aiming for."

She put a hand on his shoulder. "Sometimes I had to make chicken stew with rabbit or squirrel; it tasted different, but was good in its own way. As long as it works that is all that matters."

"Assuming it works."

"It's going to, isn't it?"

"I honestly don't know. I used most of the correct ingredients, including your tears which are the most important component. I'm also sure I used the correct spell when enchanting the potion, but the fact is this is not proper love potion."

"What is it then?"

"I don't know."

"You made it, how can you not know what it is?"

"Simple, because no one has ever made this exact potion before. It's impossible to know beforehand exactly what its effects will be. I *think* it will act like love potion, with the effects being slightly weaker or slightly stronger than with the base formula. However it could have a completely different effect or no effect. There's even a very slight chance it could be poisonous for human consumption."

"It could be poison?"

"It's very unlikely. None of the base ingredients are toxic, but it's possible to mix different herbs, that are all safe individually, into something lethal."

Alice could imagine the merchant woman gagging and clawing at her throat before falling over dead. She then imagined a whole host of guards dragging Waldo away to the nearest dungeon.

"In that case shouldn't we test it first? Maybe we could give it to a horse or something."

"You can't necessarily tell if a horse is in love from simple observation. In any case, I don't have enough mandrake to make a second dose."

"Darling, maybe we should just forget the whole idea."

"I'll consider it, if you can give me an alternate."

Alice clamped her mouth shut.

She had no trouble figuring out ways to raise enough money in just a day or two. The problem was they all involved letting strangers use her body or else using her Charm. During her years working for Elsa she had seen up close how people used each other.

Alice never wanted to be that sort of person. She never wanted to use others just to get what she wanted. While she loved her husband and was ready to do most anything for him, Alice would not deliberately hurt innocent folk.

"From your silence I take it you don't have a different solution?"

"No I don't," she admitted. "Just what do you intend?"

"The gates to the hill and the city all shut at sunset. I will want us to leave immediately, as soon as I have ownership. So I will invite her here early tomorrow to discuss the matter over some wine."

Alice did not like the sound of that at all. Even if it was just a ruse, it had a romantic note to it. She did not want him having wine with any other woman. "We don't serve wine, only ale."

"I'll buy a bottle and keep it behind the bar. You need to serve us and make absolutely sure the cup you give her is the one with the potion in it."

"Right," though she didn't like it, she would do her part. "If she doesn't fall over dead, what then?"

"Well, if this were normal love potion, she would fall in love with the first person she sees after drinking."

"What if she saw another woman?"

"Then she would fall in love with her."

Alice's eyes widened, even with her background the idea was shocking. "That must cause a lot of embarrassment."

"Not really, at least not where I am from."

Alice decided not to go down this road. "All right, say she drinks the wine, looks at you, and falls in love. Then what?"

"Well it depends on how strong the reaction is. Even with the regular potion the effect can vary from one person to another. If her response is weak, she may still not give me the ogre, but there is a chance she would be willing to lower the price to something we can afford."

That was another thing she didn't like hearing. "By that I guess you mean any amount we can actually pay? Even if it's everything we have?"

"That's right."

He really has no respect for money. "Fine."

"If the effect is about what I hope for, she will be happy to do almost anything. I'll ask her to give me the ogre along with whatever coin she happens to have with her."

447

"Wait! You're going to rob her too?"

"Of course."

"Isn't it bad enough you're basically stealing her ogre from her? Do you have to take her purse too?"

"I'm not taking everything she has, and we've already met so she's not a stranger. That makes it all right doesn't it?"

"No it doesn't. Be satisfied with the ogre. Don't you dare ask for her purse too."

Waldo looked defiant, but didn't argue.

"There's also the possibility that the potion may have a stronger effect than normal. In that case Carin may insist on some act of devotion on my part before she agrees to any favors."

"So what, she'll want you to give her flowers or tell her that you love her?"

"Well she might settle for that, more likely she'll demand I physically pleasure her."

Alice stared at him. *He could not possibly mean what I think he means.* "What exactly are you saying?"

"She may insist that I fuck her."

Her jaw dropped and she could feel her heart stop. "Wh… what?"

"She may want me to fuck her," Waldo said slowly and clearly. "You know, have sex with her, mount her, have my way with her, drive in the stake, make her fountain gush, put my sausage in her…"

"I know what it means!"

"Then why were you asking?"

Alice shut her eyes and fought hard against the urge to reach out and strangle him. "You cannot be serious. Didn't you tell me you were a virgin? You even said that when you kissed me that was your first kiss."

"What does my virginity have to do with this? I know the basics of the process, and if I need help I am sure she will assist me."

Alice just stood there.

"Why are you upset?" Waldo asked.

"You're joking, you're about to give your virginity away to some ugly old grandmother, just to get your hands on a monster, and you need to ask why I'm upset?"

"Well... yes, so why are you?"

"I do not believe this! So you're actually going to whore yourself to get an ogre?"

"Did you not see how magnificent he is? I'd call it a small price to pay."

Alice pressed both hands into fists and ground her teeth together before she could speak again.

"Look darling, as your wife, it is not all right with me that you have sex with someone else. But it is especially not all right for your very first time to be with anyone but me."

"Alice, I am not saying I want to have sex with Carin, I mean you did see her right? I am saying that depending on how the potion works I may have to."

"So it would just be a huge sacrifice on your part?"

"Exactly."

She stood there for a moment. "Turn around and face the wall."

"What?"

Alice reached down and hauled him up to his feet. Grabbing his shoulders she faced him towards the wall and away from her. "Just stand there and don't you dare move or look over here until I tell you to."

"You're not going to suddenly attack me are you?"

"Only if you turn around before I say."

Standing just a few feet behind him she took a couple deep breaths. *Do I really want to do this?* These were not the circumstances she had pictured for this moment. She had always imagined her husband carrying her to the bed, speaking tender words of love and devotion. Having him casually tell her he might screw a total stranger just to get his hands on an ugly beast, had somehow never entered her imaginings of her wedding night.

Nothing about him is normal or what I expected, but I really love him.

She slid off her skirt and let it fall to the floor. Next she unbuttoned her blouse and then removed her small clothes. Finally she stepped out of her shoes so that she was well and truly naked.

Her knees pressed together and she instinctively wanted to cover herself up. She had to force her hands to stay by her side. It was so embarrassing.

"You can turn around now." Alice said nervously.

When he did so his eyes widened and his jaw dropped. "What...
what are you doing?"

The way he was staring made her hands twitch and she had to
make a deliberate effort to keep them where they were. "I swear,
if you make fun of me or mention your mother I will kill you."

"Why are you naked?"

"Oh, in Cannassa's name! You need to ask?" Her eyes darted to
the floor. "I love you and I don't want another woman to be your
first. I want to have our wedding night."

"You mean right now?"

"Yes! Now!"

"I thought you wanted to wait."

"I did, right up until you said you might be with someone else. I
don't like the idea of you being unfaithful to me, but given the
situation I suppose I can forgive it, once. But I absolutely refuse
to let the first woman you ever make love to, to be anyone but
me."

He didn't say anything. His feet were the only part of him she
could see. He didn't move or make a sound. As the moment
dragged on she began to fidget.

"Damn it! Am I ugly to you? Are my breasts too small? Does it
sicken you that I am not human? Would you really rather have
Carin or the ogre you kept ogling? Do you have any idea how
many men would kill to be where you are right now? I've had
brawls started just over who I should give myself to. Your wife is
naked and willing and you just stand there! What do I have to do
to make you look at me like you want me? Tell me!"

There was another momentary silence.

"I am sorry."

Her face snapped up. "What?"

His tranquil eyes stared back into hers. "I've hurt you haven't I? I can feel rage and pain and despair through our connection. I've never meant to harm you, yet I have."

Through their bond Alice could feel his concern for her. There was no anger there, no mocking, all she could sense was worry.

"I know you don't do it on purpose," Alice said. "But it would be nice if you could act normal once in a while."

"Honestly Alice, I have no idea what normal is. I have my own idea of normal, and the more time I spend in this world the clearer it becomes that my ideas are a world apart from everyone else's."

He took a step towards her.

"I will tell you something though; if I say things that wound you it is not my intention. You are more precious to me than anything. You are my treasure."

Waldo took a second step that brought him standing right in front of her.

"When we first met you saved my life when any other familiar would have let me drown. You took care of me and fed me. You helped me with Roger even when it went against your beliefs. You faced an archlich and were ready to die for me. You have stayed by my side and been there for me even though you were always free to leave, even though it would have been easier and safer for you to go."

He took both of her hands into his own. His tender words and the way he was looking at her made Alice fee as if she were going to melt. This was the gentle, kind side of him that she loved best.

"I am not well versed with apologies, but I am sorry for hurting you. I think you are wonderful, and I truly thank you for all that you have done for me."

He let go of one of her hands and carefully placed it on the back of her head. He got up on his toes as he pressed her face towards his.

He kissed her with his soft, warm lips. Through their connection she understood his feelings.

He loved her.

He never said the words, but that was all right. In his own way he had shown her what she meant to him. He was strange and full of weird notions, but she understood that in his own way he really did love her.

That was all she'd wanted.

XXX

Somehow or other they wound up on the bed and his clothes ended on the floor.

He might have been a virgin, but she quickly discovered he had a pretty good notion of what to do. His hands fondled and squeezed and he licked and kissed her all over her body. His touch was light and certain. His affection was patient and thorough and brought her mounting pleasure.

When the key moment came he hesitated.

"Are you sure?" He whispered.

The concern in his voice made her happy. As much as he wanted it, he didn't want to hurt her.

"Yes darling, I am."

He paused, and then drove the stake in. She gasped at the pain, but it was not as bad as she expected. It very quickly faded into the background as pleasure began to fill her. She knew from stories that the first time wasn't supposed to be this enjoyable for a woman. Alice momentarily wondered if it was because she was a succubus.

She quickly stopped worrying about it and simply enjoyed all the things Waldo was doing to her.

XXX

"Ooooooooooooohhhhhhhh!!!"

All the men down in the common room were staring up at the stairwell. It turned out Alice was a moaner and they could all clearly hear her erotic cries. A few of the men laughed and made some naughty jokes. Many more were weeping tears of pure jealousy.

The Innkeeper lifted a mug. "To the luckiest bastard on the face of the Earth."

"Yeeeeeeeessssssssss!!!" Came another shout from upstairs in seeming agreement.

All the men lifted their mugs in salute.

Chapter 42

Women Make No Sense At All

Waldo was lying in bed with Alice resting on top of him. His heart was just beginning to slow down. Sex was quite a bit more strenuous than he'd expected. It was also more enjoyable.

With one finger Alice began to lazily draw little circles on his chest.

"There is no way you were a virgin."

He noticed her voice was back to normal. It was too bad; he'd rather liked the sounds she'd been making before. "I assure you that I was."

"Not possible." Alice planted a slight kiss on the side of his neck.

They had shared a bed for a week now, but somehow he had never realized just how amazingly soft she was. The delightful feel of her moist skin sliding against his, had it always felt so luxuriant? How had he not noticed before? Just having her close to him like this was pleasant.

When they performed the physical act of love... it had felt better than he had ever imagined it could. It was so much better than doing it alone. He could understand now why Walter had spent so much time with the sex slaves.

"I suppose I should take that as a compliment. Why do you not believe it?"

"I've heard stories about what men are like when they do it the first time. All the girls say they're like bulls; rough, hard, and quick. They're eager to see what it's like and in too big a rush to even think about the girl they're with. It's never any good for them; it's almost like a chore."

Waldo couldn't help but smile. "I take it I was different?"

Alice giggled. "Darling, if you were any more different I swear I would have lost my mind. You were wonderful." She placed another tender kiss on his neck. "There is no way this was your first time."

"It was."

"Oh really?" She propped herself up on one elbow so that he could see her face clearly. Her amethyst eyes had a playful twinkle. "How were you so good then? Natural talent?"

"No," he said matter of factly. "It just comes from observing the sex slaves when they performed."

"You... you actually watched people do that? Even at the Inn that was always done behind closed doors."

"Really? So you never had people perform for the enjoyment and entertainment of others?"

"Entertainment?" Alice sounded scandalized. "You had people do *that* just to put on a show?"

"Certainly, we would also have plays performed, singers, dancers, jesters, jugglers, and sometimes we would make slaves fight each other to the death. My mother wouldn't allow any of us to leave the castle grounds until she was certain of our strength. Since we were confined she thought we should at least be properly diverted."

Alice's mouth opened, and then closed.

"By the way, do you like being tied up or spanked? Some of the slaves seemed to really enjoy that."

Alice shook her head. "You would think by now I would know better than to ask you certain questions."

Waldo raised a curious eyebrow. "I was being truthful."

"I know, that's what worries me." She paused a moment. "Do you want children?"

"Why are you asking me that?"

"It's a normal thing for a married couple to discuss. So do you?"

"Well of course, I am heir to one of the Seven Great Families of Alteroth. Fathering children is one of my duties."

"That's not what I asked you. Do you want to have children?"

"You mean just to have them?"

"Yes."

"I have never really thought about it."

"Well you're married now and you're going to be having sex with me, a lot, you should begin to think about it."

"We can't have children until I return to Alteroth."

She frowned and he could sense her disappointment through their bond. "When will that be?"

"Not until I complete my quest."

"You mentioned before that you need to beat a knight and find a treasure. What sort of treasure is it? Is it hard to find?"

"Are you sure that is a question you want to ask?"

She nodded.

Waldo thought about just how much to reveal.

"Be honest with me." Alice told him.

"Didn't you just say there were certain things you didn't want to know?"

"Yeah, some subjects I'd sooner avoid. But this is something I need to know. Darling, what are you trying to accomplish? Why are you so determined to get these other monsters? Can you explain it to me so that it makes sense?"

"What if you don't like the answers?"

"I won't leave you whatever you tell me. I love you, and I am staying by your side no matter what."

Waldo slid his fingers along her smooth back. Alice let out a slight gasp and he could feel her tremble slightly. The techniques and moves he had learned from the sex slaves, but he had paid attention to her responses. He liked knowing where to touch her.

"Love is a horrible weakness."

Her eyebrows rose. "No it's not. Why would you say that?"

Waldo let his finger trace a spot on her lower back. He could feel her legs twitch in response. *My feelings are a weakness I cannot afford.* Waldo thought. *I am a fool.*

"My mother is the head of the Corpselover family and I am her seventh child. I tried as hard as I could to be worthy of my position, but no matter how I struggled I was weak. Everyone but my mother and my sister Gwendolyn saw me as a failure."

"How could anyone think that? You can do magic! You're amazing!"

458

"Thank you Alice. From your point of view or that of most of the people of this land I am sure that is true. However, where I am from my abilities were seen as a disappointment. In Alteroth we respect bloodlines, but not in the same way they do here and in other countries. In barbaric lands people assume that your blood is everything. There are weak kings, mad kings, and incompetent kings that are allowed to rule simply because they were born from a queen's womb. That would not be permitted in my homeland. Blood matters only because powerful abilities can be passed down through the generations, it is a matter of breeding, just like with horses or cattle. But the right blood is not enough; no weakling would be allowed to hold power just because of their birth."

"You don't respect royal blood? Really? Isn't it proof of the gods' favor?"

"I don't know about your gods, but the Dark Powers don't care. Blood and family ties do matter, but a person is not respected because of just that. In Alteroth power is what matters above everything else. Your reputation and your position have to be earned. You have to prove your own strength and ability; no one is given power because of their ancestors. You yourself have to be strong."

"That's very different from how we do it here. Knights may fight to get a better reputation and spoils, but they are still knights no matter what they do."

"Barbaric and uncivilized," Waldo told her. "There are no kings or nobles in Alteroth. The Seven Families conquered the land we rule. We remain in control because we remain strong. You are not allowed to hide behind your birth. Only the strong have the right to rule."

Alice nodded silently.

"One of the ways to prove yourself is to go on a First Quest. Each child born into a head family is required to journey out into the world all alone. They are expected to prove themselves by returning with treasure and stories of people they have slaughtered."

"That's horrible!"

"It's necessary," he told her firmly. "It's the only way to really test just how strong you are. I was the seventh child born into the ruling family of Corpselover. I was seen as an incompetent, but since no one ever expected me to lead the family I was tolerated. But one by one, all my older brothers and sisters were killed, and by default I became the heir. The other families did not want someone like me to become head of Corpselover, but my mother was adamant. I am sure they would have killed me if they could, but I was too well protected. So they did the next best thing."

"What was that?"

"They forced me to go on my First Quest and set impossible conditions. Before I can return home I not only have to acquire three monsters and defeat a knight in combat, I have to get a dragon's egg."

"So that's why you are so determined to get the ogre and this next monster?"

"Well, in a sense, getting three monsters is actually the easy part. I could have just bought three goblins and made contracts with them and that would have satisfied the first condition. I need to get three Great Monsters in order to defeat a knight and, most importantly, acquire a dragon's egg."

"How are you going to do that? All the stories I've heard tell that dragons are the most terrible of all monsters. They can burn down cities and slaughter whole armies."

"For once the stories you've heard are true, if anything they underestimate what a dragon can do. Not only can they fly, breathe fire, chew up steel plate, and tear down stone walls; their scales are harder than the strongest iron and they are impervious to most magics. If all that were not enough, their lairs are always well hidden and near impossible to find."

"How will you get an egg then?"

He chortled a bitter laugh. "I have no idea. The men who assigned me this quest consider it impossible. As far as they are concerned I may as well be dead. They assume I will either die or simply give up."

"But you won't, will you?" She asked softly.

He shook his head slightly. "I mean to go home. I want to see my mother again and make her proud of me. No matter what it costs I mean to complete my quest and return in glory." Waldo focused his eyes as he looked at her. "That is why I will do anything to get this ogre. Why I will then go and acquire another Great Monster. Why I am willing to risk my grandfather ripping out my heart. Why I will lie, cheat, steal, and yes, whore myself if it means that someday I can go home again. This may be a fool's quest, and I may be as much of a fool as people think, but I have determined to follow it until the end." He took a breath. "There, now you know why I am doing everything I am doing."

He expected her to tell him he was an idiot, to demand he give up this path and try to find a safe place instead.

So Waldo was very surprised when she smiled and kissed him passionately.

"I am happy darling, I will do everything that I can to make your dream come true."

She gave him another fervent kiss.

He started to slide his arms around her, but she sprung out of bed and quickly began putting her clothes back on.

Waldo sat up and looked at her. "What are you doing?"

"Getting dressed of course, I am still in the middle of my shift. Tyrone will probably be angry with me, but I am sure I can get him to forgive. If we're leaving tomorrow I want to get as many tips tonight as I can."

She gathered up the cauldron and other items he had taken from the kitchen.

"So you're not angry with me or going to call me a fool?"

"For what? Wanting to go home and make your mother proud of you? I think it's wonderful and I am really happy to know the truth." She hurried to his side and gave him one more swift kiss before going to the door with both arms full. "Don't look so upset, I promise to wake you up as soon as I finish my shift."

With that she was out the door and gone.

Waldo sat there in the bed and slowly shook his head. *Women make no sense at all.*

XXX

From downstairs there was a sudden loud cheer and applause.

Chapter 43

A Simple Plan

Everything was packed.

He had purchased a new map and travel rations.

The runes up in their room had been inverted and could not be seen. That was just in case they were forced to stay here for some reason.

Waldo was ready to leave as soon as he had the ogre. He wanted to go before night fall; every mile would improve the odds of avoiding his grandfather. Waldo was eager to be as far away as possible.

He was down in the common room and it was late morning when Alice returned from her errands. She carried a bottle of wine with a fancy seal. Alice did not look happy.

"Well? How did it go?"

Alice set the bottle down in front of him. "It cost me an entire silver dalter, for one bottle of wine! I could have bought two kegs of ale for that much."

"I am sure if you had used your Charm you could have gotten a much better price."

He missed her scowl as he carefully inspected the wax seal on the bottle.

"An Illsyrian Red," he nodded. "Perfect."

"Why did I even have to buy this? Wouldn't the potion have worked in ale?"

"It should work in any drink. The point is she needs to swallow some of it. Illsyrian wines are the best in the world; they're the only sort we ever drank in the castle. I can't take the chance she would refuse to drink the common swill that is served here."

"You've drunk the ale here."

"I know, that's why I had you get the wine."

Waldo again missed the look Alice sent him.

"Did you deliver the message that I wanted to meet with her here at noon?"

"Yes, I went to Baden Hill and told the soldiers there. One of them went to tell her."

"Wait, you didn't go and tell her yourself?"

"I don't know where she lives darling. Anyway, I am sure she will get the invitation."

"True, but I would still have liked it to be confirmed."

"Do you want me to go and track her down and tell her in person?"

"It will be noon before long; I can't have you on your way back when she arrives." From one of the many pockets in his robes he produced the vial with the love potion and placed it in her hand. "You know what you need to do?"

Alice slid the vial into a skirt pocket. "As soon as she sits down with you I bring two goblets of wine over. One goblet will have the potion in it and I will place it in front of her."

"Make very sure the one with the love potion is the one you give her. It will be embarrassing, to say nothing of inconvenient, if you give it to me instead."

"No need to worry darling, I'll keep them straight." Alice put her hands together and fidgeted slightly. "Are you really going to sleep with that old woman?"

"Yes, but only if I have to. I've told you, I don't know how the potion will work or even if it will. If it doesn't have the right effect I will have to come up with another plan."

"I really don't like the idea of you having sex with her."

"Neither do I. Do you dislike it enough to use your Charm to rob strangers?"

"No."

"Then if it comes to that you will just have to accept it." Thinking of Carin's features Waldo made a face. "I'm sure I will suffer much worse than you will. In any case, as soon as she agrees be ready to leave. We will go straight to Baden Hill then to the west gate. The sooner we are gone from this city the better."

A couple men entered and took one of the open tables. The Inn was not usually that busy during the day and the common room was close to empty.

"All right darling, I am going to start my shift."

Alice took the bottle and placed it carefully behind the bar. She then went over to the newly arrived customers.

Waldo didn't hear what she asked them but he heard the response.

"Yeeeeeeeeeeeeesssss!!"

For some reason he felt a sudden burst of embarrassment come through the bond. He couldn't guess why.

XXX

"Have the midday meal brought out." Carin said.

"Have you forgotten?" One of her servants reminded. "That White Mage asked you to have lunch with him."

Carin frowned. "No I haven't forgotten, I just have no intention of accepting such a presumptuous request. Even for a White Mage it's just rude. He wants me to go to some dirty place in the middle of the poor quarter of town, and with no more than a couple hours' notice. Am I a servant to come running at his call?"

She was painfully aware of her social status as a merchant. Even poor nobles talked down to her and made unreasonable demands. But they were at least respectful when they needed something.

"He should be inviting me to the baron's palace, or at the very least to one of the finer establishments. I should be given a day's notice, expecting me to just show up at the snap of his fingers is nothing but an affront."

"Then are you going to just ignore his request?" Her assistant asked nervously. "Won't he take that as an insult?"

Carin wanted to deny it, she really did, but offending a White Mage was dangerous.

"I never said I was going to ignore him, but I am not going to just run at his call either. I will go when I have time. Now bring me my lunch. I need to see Viol about a wool shipment."

XXX

"You're sure it was a White Mage with a woman with red hair walking with him?"

"Course I'm sure, they'd be hard to miss." The soldier told her.

"What was he doing?" Melissa asked.

"Weren't doing much of anything, just saw them go walking by. Not like I talked to him or anything." He shifted his weight from one foot to another.

"I don't suppose by any chance you would know where he was staying?"

"Don't your sort stay with the baron?"

"Normally, but my associate appears to be a bit reluctant to accept the baron's generous accommodations."

"Is he a friend of yours?"

"I can truthfully say I have never met him, but I am most eager to make his acquaintance." She bowed her head in a sign of appreciation. "I thank you for your help, and wish you the blessings of Unity, Justice, and Peace."

"Happy to help." He stepped back from her and walked away as quickly as he could without breaking into a run.

Melissa Cornwall continued down the street at a deliberate and casual pace. She forced herself to smile and maintain a pleasant air.

Inside she seethed!

That man was the twelfth person to report seeing Waldo Rabbit and his so called wife. None of them had known their names, but it was obvious who they were. When she had begun asking around this morning she honestly hadn't expected to find his trail. Melissa had expected him to keep a low profile, or to be fleeing to the nearest border. The last thing she had anticipated was for him to flaunt himself in the middle of a city.

"Arrogant," she muttered beneath her breath. To believe he could commit crimes in the Order's robes and not suffer for it. How could anyone be that foolish?

That so many folk had seen him also meant John Varlos had lied to her. There was no way he would be ignorant of something that appeared to be common knowledge in this city. She would never be able to call him on it. He would claim to be just a merchant and to have been too busy with his trade to have heard. It was another sign that he was no friend to her or the Order.

He might need to be removed, she thought.

That was a problem that could wait though. Her immediate concern was to track down where this deserter was hiding. While many had seen him out and about, no one appeared to know where he resided. She had already visited all the Inns near the palace. Every one of them claimed ignorance. Melissa was slowly expanding her search in hopes of finding anyone who knew where he was staying. She was sure that if he heard a true White Mage was in the city he would try to flee. That could not be allowed; she had to track him down before he could escape.

XXX

Five hours had passed since noon and Waldo was ready to admit defeat, at least for today. Outside the shadows would be growing long. Sunset would be in about an hour and a half. He'd spent the entire time sitting in a corner table expecting the merchant's arrival at any time. Waldo had not eaten or moved from his seat. He had been determined to be ready the instant she arrived. Now he was finally ready to admit she was not coming. Even if she did show up they might not have enough time to run to Baden Hill, purchase the ogre, and make it out the West Gate before the sun set. Being so near Middleton as the night began would be an invitation for his grandfather to attack them. It had been such a simple plan. Waldo hadn't expected anything to go wrong.

Did she not receive Alice's message or did she just ignore it?
Waldo wondered.

The common room was about four fifths empty. It would not fill up until the sun went down and the work day ended. Alice came over to his table. "You haven't eaten anything all day darling. Do you want a bowl of cabbage stew and some ale?"

"Yes, why not. I will eat and go back up to my room. I suppose we will just have to try and do this again tomorrow."

Alice was slowly ringing her hands. "I'm sorry. I should have gone myself to make sure she knew you wanted to see her. I promise to find out where she lives and go see her in person. I will drag her here if I need to."

Waldo could pick up the guilt she was feeling though their bond.

"It's just fine. After all the time we have spent here one more day won't make a difference. You've been wonderful Alice, without you I wouldn't even be here."

He saw her cheeks tinge and felt a surge of happiness from her.

"I am sure we will be able to leave tomorrow."

He nodded.

"I'll get you that stew."

He watched her hurry off to the kitchen.

It was one more failure in a long string of them. He had set out determined to prove himself a great Dark Mage. Waldo had wanted to prove the Council wrong and earn his mother's respect. Instead he had almost been drowned by a pack of commoners, had a disobedient familiar, was dressed in white, had just barely escaped having his heart eaten, had wasted an entire week searching for his second monster, and had now

469

wasted an entire day waiting on an old merchant woman. And if all that were not enough he had fallen in love with his familiar.

"What a pathetic master I am."

Yet I am supposed to get a third monster, defeat a knight, and somehow acquire a dragon's egg. How do I do all that when I can't even get Alice to obey me or force a merchant to sell me her ogre?

Sitting there at the table he felt defeated. Everything he had tried to do since starting on this quest had either ended in disaster or been far harder than he'd ever expected. Maybe... maybe they had all been right. Maybe he really was just an incompetent. Maybe he was as weak as they all said. What sort of fool messes up the binding spell after studying it for weeks? Would any competent mage get himself thrown off a bridge by a bunch of peasants? If he had any real strength at all would he be sitting here, alone and hungry, after wasting hours waiting on a mere merchant?

Waldo tried to imagine any of his brothers or sisters being in a similar situation.

It would never have happened. Every one of them had possessed real power. They would have slaughtered that crowd of commoners at the bridge. They wouldn't have screwed up the contract. None of them would have condescended to actually negotiate with a lowly merchant. Carin would have been compelled to hand over what they wanted or died.

Each of them had been a true Dark Mage.

So what am I?

For a moment, he imagined just giving up on this insane quest. Even if he muddled through somehow, finally got the ogre, acquired the third Great Monster, and used them to defeat a knight. What were the odds of someone like him obtaining a dragon's egg? He was more likely to suddenly sprout wings and hooves.

Waldo could just give up and go into exile. That was what everyone expected him to do. He could go with Alice to some country very far away and start a new life. Magic was rare and much prized nearly everywhere. Even an inept mage like him would be able to make a good living. He could buy some property, have a nice house with servants, and settle down to a pleasant life with Alice.

It was very easy to imagine. A life of luxury with a beautiful succubus. Surely that was something most men dreamed of. He could have it if he wanted. All it really required was for him to give up on this hopeless quest.

To accept never going home again.

To accept being the disgrace and failure people had always considered him.

To accept knowing he brought his mother shame.

His fingernails dug into the wooden table as he imagined the disappointment in his mother's eyes. "I would rather die."

I'll continue this for as long as I am alive, no matter how hard it is. Even if it is impossible, the very least I owe her is to die trying. I would sooner die as Waldo Corpselover, than to truly become Waldo Rabbit.

XXX

Alice came out of the kitchen with a big bowl of cabbage stew and a large chunk of brown bread. She ducked behind the bar just long enough to draw a tankard of ale.

"Here you go darling," she set everything down in front of him. "I know you're hungry so I had the cook load you up."

The stew did look thicker than usual. "I will go back upstairs as soon as I eat."

Waldo picked up his wooden spoon and was about to dig in, when the door to the Inn opened. A grandmother in a simple, but well-tailored, burgundy and white dress entered. Waldo's hand stopped half way to his mouth.

"Now? She comes now?"

Alice glanced at him. "But isn't this good darling?"

"It is about an hour and a half until the gates shut."

"That's enough time isn't it?"

"Yes, if the potion works the way it's supposed to, and if she agrees right away. We have just enough time."

The few other patrons paid Carin no special mind. As soon as she spotted Waldo she began walking stiffly to his table.

Even a normal love potion did not last for more than a night, and very often the victim would realize what had been done to her. He had no idea if his pseudo mix would even work or how well. Waldo wanted to be far away when it wore off. If she drank it and it was slow acting, or she insisted on delaying things, he could find himself trapped in the city until the gates opened again come sunrise. That would be bad.

On the other hand, if he chose not to give it to her now this meeting would surely end in failure. Would she agree to meet him here again? What if she refused to see him, or insisted they meet somewhere else? How much longer might he be trapped in this city? Long enough for his grandfather to lose patience and come try to find him?

Either choice had its risks.

472

"Go and bring her a cup of that special wine."

"Yes dear." Alice hurried to the bar, sending Carin a bow deep enough for the Crown Prince.

Carin rewarded this with a slight nod. She then came to a halt five feet from Waldo's table. She stood there ram rod straight with her arms rigid against her sides. "I apologize for disturbing your dinner."

"Well you wouldn't have if you had come when I asked."

Her eyes narrowed, and she seemed to arch her back like an angry cat.

"Your request came as a surprise, and I had other obligations. I do so hope you can forgive me for not dropping everything and rushing to meet you as you wanted."

"I suppose I can."

The edges of Carin's lips drew back and her arms trembled ever so slightly.

Waldo motioned to the empty chair across from him. "Please take a seat and we can begin."

She remained where she was. "A gentleman would rise and pull the chair out for a woman he has asked to meet with him."

How arrogant, Waldo thought. It was amazing that someone so far beneath him would be so presumptuous. In a truly civilized country she would have given a far more sincere apology, and been properly respectful. He was painfully aware though that time was pressing. If a few empty courtesies would hurry things along he would grin and endure them. *This is what I get for being weak and needing to bargain with people.*

473

"Of course," Waldo rose smoothly to his feet. He pulled the chair well out from the table.

Carin remained standing for a moment. She glanced at the chair and back at him.

"Was there something else?" Waldo asked, trying to keep his impatience from showing.

"Why did you ask me to meet you here, in this place?"

"This is where I am staying, it was convenient for me."

"Do you always just do what is easiest?"

"Yes, doesn't everyone?"

Carin shook her head slightly. "You aren't much for subtlety are you?"

"It is not one of my strong points. My mother always said I needed to be more deceptive."

Carin pursed her lips and looked uncertain. At last she finally sat down.

As soon as she was seated Waldo hurried back around to his own chair. "I hope we can come to an agreement quickly. I am eager to leave Middleton and would like to be on my way tonight."

"Tonight? You are in quite a rush. Normally it takes a few days or weeks to arrange things."

"I hope to move things along a little faster than that."

"Trying to hurry me like this is very poor form." Carin told him. "Some might call it rude."

"I don't care if it's rude so long as I get what I want."

"Yes," Carin said. "I have heard it said that White Mages will do most anything to get what they want. Though usually they do manage to remain polite." Carin put both hands on the table and leaned forward. "All right, we'll just dispense with all the formalities and niceties. If you want to depart so badly I won't stand in your way. We can go to Baden Hill and you can take possession of your ogre. The price is still twelve ducats."

"I was hoping we could negotiate the price down a bit."

Carin's head shook. "Twelve is already a bargain and much less than I would normally ever agree to."

Alice came over with a tray with a single goblet. She deftly placed it before Carin. "With my husband's compliments." Alice bowed her head and retreated back to the bar.

"What's this?"

"It's an Illsyrian Red," Waldo told her with a hint of pride. "It wasn't easy to find, but please accept it as a small sign of my appreciation for your coming here to meet me."

Now we see.

With one hand Carin slid the goblet away. "I hate red wine, I only ever drink gold."

Waldo felt his stomach do a slow turn. "Won't you at least have a sip? It's Illsyrian, the finest wine in all the Shattered Lands."

"That's a matter of opinion. Personally I prefer Companian Golds. Illsyrian wines are too strong and sweet for my taste."

"Could you just give it a try? Since I went to the trouble of acquiring it just for you. Just one swallow, as a courtesy."

"If this were a normal meeting I would drink and praise it, even as it set fire to my throat and burned in my belly. Since you have made it clear though that you are in a hurry to be done with it I will not bother to pretend."

The Dark Powers mock me.

He wondered if anyone would care if he suddenly got up and tried to force it down her throat. It had been such a simple plan.

Waldo looked hard across the table at this plain, blunt, merchant woman. What would she do if he simply threatened her? Commoners were always ignorant of just how magic worked, and the folk in this barbarous land were even more ill-informed than the low people back in Alteroth. Waldo knew he didn't exactly have a threatening demeanor, but he was a mage. If he demanded she give him the ogre or else be cursed how would she react? Would she be terrified or would she be insulted and call his bluff? Openly threatening someone was a bit risky, but he was considering it.

"Well then," Carin said. "Will you pay me my twelve ducats so we can be done?"

Waldo was not sure how to answer. As he opened his mouth he sensed something.

A powerful aura.

A being with great magical ability was approaching.

Waldo turned his face to the door.

"Is something wrong?" Carin looked in the same direction to see nothing out of the ordinary.

"I am afraid you will need to give me a moment." Waldo spoke without turning his gaze back to her. "Could you please go wait by the bar?"

476

Carin frowned. "What are you talking about?"

From behind the bar Alice glanced at Waldo and then at the door. She could sense his sudden alarm through their bond, but could not guess the cause of it.

Just then the door to the Inn opened. In stepped a woman in white robes. Clutched in her right hand was a wand.

"I am afraid I have to deal with someone else first." Sliding his hand into one of the many pockets of his robe he took hold of his own wand.

Chapter 44

Bet You Didn't See That Coming

Everyone in the common room stopped to look at the new arrival. No one did anything more than that though. They all went back to enjoying their meals. Apparently, having had a white wizard staying for over a week had accustomed them to the presence of a magic user.

Carin was not quite so familiar.

She quickly pushed back from the table and got up to her feet. "It seems this was a bad time. I certainly do not want to come between two White Mages who want to talk. I will go."

"Please just wait by the bar." Waldo asked. He did not spare her a glance.

"I have many things still to do and do not have time to waste."

"Oh I wouldn't worry about that, I doubt this will take very long."

Carin paused. "I will give you five minutes. Any longer than that and I will have to go."

Waldo nodded without turning in her direction. "That should be enough."

Carin hurried over to the bar, clearly eager to not get involved in whatever business two White Mages might have.

XXX

"Is she a friend of yours?" Tyrone asked.

Alice was standing rigid behind the bar. She had felt a sudden sharp spike of fear coming through the bond. Alice had wondered what Carin could possibly have said to him to cause that. When the door to the Inn had opened it was suddenly obvious what the cause was.

"No," Alice replied. "Definitely not a friend."

XXX

The woman had spotted him immediately of course. It was rather hard to be inconspicuous wearing snow white robes. She began to deliberately walk across the room to him, steps slow and certain. Her attention was directed entirely on him, she did not bother to so much as glance at the bar or any other part of the common room. Her wand was still not pointed at him. The fact the commoners were all so calm with a mage holding a wand was proof of just how ignorant they were about magic.

Waldo took his own wand out and held it beneath the table. He was tempted to send a gout of fire at her while she was still across the room. He held off because it was almost certain she had protective wards cast. If he could not take her in the first strike he had little hope in a protracted battle. She was unlikely to be as strong as his grandfather, but it was well known that only capable mages were sent out from Avalon. Waldo knew he was nowhere near skilled enough in combat magic to defeat a properly trained White Mage. There was also the inconvenient fact that if he openly attacked her he and Alice would have to immediately flee the city.

The only chance to salvage the situation was to try and talk his way through.

He didn't like his odds very much.

As she drew closer Waldo noted she was very pretty, though clearly older than him by some years. With high cheek bones, a fair complexion, and hair the color of gold.

Her eyes are like mine.

She came to a halt just five feet from his table, her wand still held to the side. Waldo was surprised by her temerity. At this range protective wards would not be enough to blunt a lethal spell.

"You are Waldo Rabbit."

His eyebrows rose, and despite the situation he couldn't keep a pleased smile from his lips. "You've heard of me? I had no idea my reputation had already spread."

"Don't sound so proud. What I know about you is shameful. I recently spoke to Master Roger of Bittford."

"Oh, well that would explain it."

The woman frowned. "You seem to be taking this rather lightly."

"Why wouldn't I? Roger is nothing but a backwoods hedgewizard. He is an independent. Why would he matter to a couple of White Mages like us?"

Waldo felt a little relieved. Upon her arrival with wand in hand, he had assumed she knew he was a fake. If instead she was here about the incident with Roger, Waldo was sure they could work something out.

He quickly changed his mind about that when she at last pointed her wand directly at his face.

"You think you can bring shame to the Order and not pay the penalty?"

Waldo tilted his chair back, his tone casual, "The penalty would be?"

"Death," she said voice as hard and unforgiving as iron. "I intend to execute you, but first you will give me the property that was stolen."

"You plan to kill me for robbing some half trained spell caster from the boonies?"

Her grip on her wand tightened. "Even as a deserter could you truly have fallen so far as to forget our sacred cause? Everything that we do is to protect and serve the Order and The One We Follow. How dare you disgrace them? That you should abandon our hallowed cause and yet still wear the robes... have you no shame?"

"No actually, none at all." He saw her eyes widen at his unexpected answer. "You do realize I have a wand pointed at you beneath the table?"

She gave a curt nod. "I have protective wards."

"So do I, but at this range they won't matter."

"Perhaps, what is most important is that you be brought to justice and not allowed to do any further harm to the Order."

Waldo studied her for a long moment.

"You mean it," he said in plain disbelief. "You are actually willing to die over this."

"Of course, we are always ready to die for the sake of the cause."

Fanatic, Waldo thought. There were things he was willing to die for too, but a theft from some third rate wizard was not one of them.

"I do not know why or for how long you have you have been a traitor, but I would hope you still have some sense of honor. I would prefer not to cause any further rumor or scandal.

481

Surrender yourself, return what you have stolen, and I will grant you a quick, clean death. It is a chance for you to restore a little of your honor before you die."

"Sorry, I have about as much honor as I do shame. And tempting as your offer is I will have to decline it."

"Is that why you deserted?"

She believes I'm a White Mage, but one who abandoned the cause. "You say you don't want to bring any embarrassment to the Order. I think even the mundanes will begin to notice if you keep standing there with your wand pointed at me." With his free hand he motioned to the seat across from him. "I would be honored if you would join me, Mistress…?

"I am the Archmage Melissa Cornwall," she paused. "I don't suppose you would tell me your name? Your real name I mean."

"Waldo Rabbit is real enough." He again waved at the chair. "Please."

Moving cautiously she sat down. Both of them held their wands beneath the table where others in the room could not see them.

"I don't suppose you'd care for a drink?" The goblet was still sitting there.

"I don't drink with criminals."

"Of course not," he sighed.

"I want you to surrender yourself and leave with me quietly."

"Well I hope you can forgive me, but I don't intend to let you kill me out of politeness."

"You cannot hope to escape me. Surrender peacefully and return the stolen items and I promise you a quick clean death."

"Your aura is immense, I can sense just how strong you are, but our wands are practically touching. If I cast you will not survive."

"Nor will you."

"Which leaves us in a very troublesome predicament."

"Not really," she shook her head ever so slightly. "I was very lucky to track you down as quickly as I did. Some soldiers I ran into just happened to know that you and your wife were staying here. I was determined to deal with you before you could get away. Your wife I will deal with later for her part in the crime."

She hasn't noticed Alice yet. "Why don't we try and negotiate? Maybe I could give you something in exchange for my life? That way we could both walk out of here alive. I mean is Roger really worth dying for?"

"Roger is not what is important. What truly matters is that you have committed a crime while pretending to still be a White Mage. That cannot be forgiven. Abandoning the Order is also punishable by death. I will not let you escape justice."

"You know you are the second woman who hasn't wanted to bargain with me today. I suppose I am not very charming."

"Tell me something Master Waldo. Why did you run away?"

He snorted a laugh. "Maybe I just wasn't enough of a fanatic."

"Fanatic? That is what our enemies call us. Are you saying you lacked faith in our sacred cause? Was your will weak?"

"I don't lack faith or will," he told her firmly. "But what I believe in is myself and my family. I like to think I have too much common sense to go around spouting about, 'Unity, Justice, and Peace.' Those are meaningless concepts. Why would anyone with any intelligence waste their life following them?" He stopped and gave her a slight grin. "No offense."

"I would expect more deference for our beliefs."

"I don't care about imaginary causes." He raised his hand. "Waitress, you can clear the table." He leaned forward slightly. "All that matters in this world is power, once you have it you can do whatever you want with it. Living your life for the sake of some ridiculous ideal is simply a waste."

Her body locked. Her next words were spoken, as someone passing judgment. "If you were not obviously from Avalon I would think you an imposter. You sound like a Dark Mage."

"Thank you."

Her lips thinned. "Tell me, who is The One We Follow? Speak his name to me."

Is that what they call their strongest god? "Why would you ask me that?"

"It's a name that only those in the Order would know, now speak it."

"And if I don't?"

"Then despite your eyes you are something even worse than a deserter or thief, you are an imposter. If that is the case I will ring out the truth before I end you. I will learn your name and why you did this. You will suffer and regret ever putting on those robes."

"You really need a drink." He nodded to the waitress standing behind her. "The lady would like some wine."

"Yes."

Not bothering to turn her face Melissa spoke. "No, I don't want…"

Alice snatched the goblet off the table, and in one smooth motion tossed its contents into Melissa's face.

Startled Melissa choked and spat as she jumped to her feet knocking over the chair.

Waldo jumped up as well and took a couple steps back, all while keeping his wand at the ready.

Alice stood there, fists cocked ready to fight.

Everyone else was suddenly looking at them wondering what was happening.

Melissa wiped the wine from her face, looking furiously at Waldo and then at the waitress. "How dare you! Do you know…" Melissa stopped as she finally paid attention to the barmaid. "You're Alice the wife!" She aimed her wand at Alice's head.

He rushed to get between Melissa and Alice. "Don't do anything rash!" Waldo warned.

Melissa switched back to Waldo's head. She looked absolutely murderous. "Is this some sort of game to you? You're...mocking me! Us! Our...no, My Order! Do you enjoy insulting White Mages? I will make you beg for death! I will… will…" Her eyes blinked, and there was a slight tremble to her arm.

Waldo took a deep breath. "Feeling all right?"

Her mouth opened, panting, she wanted to say something, but there was conflict. Her mouth twisted and her arm shook, for a second Waldo thought her about to attack him. Then, slowly, she appeared to relax.

485

Melissa lowered her wand. "Yes, yes I feel… wonderful. Do you know you have the most beautiful eyes?"

"I am very glad you think so." Waldo replied as he did the same. "If it's not too much trouble would you mind handing me your wand? Oh and I'll take your purse too while I'm at it."

"Whatever you want," Melissa cooed.

Only when Waldo had her wand did he completely relax. Apparently not only had the recipe he'd come up with worked, it was rather potent. That or Melissa was naturally susceptible. Inspecting Melissa's wand he was not surprised to find it was made of soulwood. Three words of power were carved into it.

Unity. Justice. Peace.

"Is there anything else I can do for you my sweetheart?" She wrapped herself around his right arm and began to snuggle.

Startled Waldo instinctively tried to pull free. He didn't want to be this close to someone who would kill him if not for the effects of a temporary and untried potion.

Alice's mouth opened at the shameless display.

Melissa took his hand and tried to lead him towards the stairs. "Do you have a room? I'm not too good at these things, but I'll do my best."

Really potent recipe. I will have to make more whenever I get Alice to cry again.

"I am sorry, but I can't right now. There is something else you could do for me though."

"Anything."

"Could you get your spellbook as well as any spell components and meet me at Baden Hill? I will be there shortly so you need to really run to meet me before I depart."

"I am happy to my love!" She planted a quick kiss on his cheek before bolting from the Inn.

Alice watched her go before turning a sharp eye Waldo's way.

"She isn't coming with us is she?"

"No, definitely not."

"Good!"

It was then that Waldo noticed everyone in the room staring.

"Old lover," Waldo told them. "She wasn't happy that I'm taken now."

Heads bobbed up and down.

Alice put a hand to her face and muttered.

Opening Melissa's purse he emptied its contents on the table. A number of copper and silver coins spilled out, as well as nineteen gold guilders.

XXX

"Twelve gold coins, your asking price. I trust there's no issue with them being guilders instead of ducats?"

Carin took the money from him. She inspected them to make sure they were not shaved or damaged. Putting one to her mouth she bit down, when her teeth sank into the soft metal she nodded and made all twelve disappear. "They'll do. You still want to get the ogre right now?"

"Yes, absolutely," he turned to Alice. "Get our things from upstairs, we are leaving now."

"Right darling."

Tyrone and the customers wept when Alice told them they were going. Still, after a few quick goodbyes they were all rushing to get to Baden Hill. Carin did not much like being hurried along, but was willing to put up with it for the sake of business. When they got to the hill Carin told her guards to find the ogre and bring him out. As they waited Waldo kept looking at the setting ball of fire.

At last he was brought out, clinking at every step. A dozen guards were waiting along with Carin, Waldo, and Alice. Most of the guards had their weapons in hand.

The eight foot tall ogre looked about. "Gronk no do it. No know what it is but Gronk no do."

"Remove his chains," Carin ordered.

The guards all looked at one another, none of them eager.

"You heard her," the sergeant snapped. "Get on with it."

A couple men finally stepped forward and unlocked the manacles on the ogre's wrists, ankles, and about his waist.

"I have sold you ogre." Carin told him nodding to Waldo. "He is your new owner, you belong to him now."

The ogre rubbed his wrists. "Gronk happy to belong to little man."

"From now on you will refer to me as master."

The ogre gave a tusked grin. "Yes master."

Waldo turned to send Alice a triumphant look. "See? That's how you were supposed to be!"

She just sighed and shook her head.

"If there is nothing else Master Waldo I take it our business is concluded." Carin was clearly eager to see the last of him.

"Yes, we're done." Waldo agreed. "Gronk, carry our packs, we are going to the west gate right now and leaving."

The ogre easily took both packs in one hand. "Yes master."

Waldo was smiling from ear to ear.

Alice fought the urge to smack him.

Melissa arrived shortly afterwards. She had in her hand a spellbook as well as a sack containing various components. She handed them over to him without complaint.

"Thank you Mistress Melissa. You can go now."

"What? Without you?"

"I am sorry, but I am leaving the city."

"I'll come with you then. I can teach you about the philosophy of the Order. I am sure once you understand the truth you will want to give your life over to the cause."

"I really, really doubt that."

"But you need to be saved." Melissa told him. "If you go on the way you do you'll only die a horrible death."

"I will take my chances, please go now."

489

She crossed her hands over her heart. "I will go because you ask me to, but there is something you should know. I realize you gave me a love potion."

"You do?"

She nodded. "It's obvious, there is no other explanation for these feelings. But even though I understand what I am feeling is false, I can't help loving you. However we both know this is temporary. I am sure once it wears off I will be absolutely furious. I will definitely hunt you down and give you a slow, torturous death." She said all that with a look of adoration.

"Good to know." Waldo told her and wasted no more time. He wanted to get as far away as possible from her.

"Stay safe my love!" Melissa called out with a wave.

They made it to the west gate with time to spare. The guards stared at him and his companions but made no issue of their departure. As they went Waldo took out Melissa's wand and snapped it in two before tossing it away like trash.

XXX

They didn't stop until the ball of fire was gone and they were more than a mile from the gate.

"It actually worked." Waldo said. "I actually got my second Great Monster and I have more coin now than when we arrived."

"We have more coin," Alice said pointedly. "We also have a crazy woman chasing us now along with your grandfather."

"I am sure we'll manage." Having somehow succeeded despite everything he was brimming with confidence. *Maybe this quest isn't impossible after all.* "Gronk."

"Yes master?"

"I am going to make you my familiar, bend down."

Gronk blinked, but did as he was told.

"Darling, are you sure you know what you are doing?"

"No need to worry, I will definitely get it right this time."
Placing a hand on Gronk's cheek he began the binding ritual.
*"Until the moment of my death, or the moment of your release, I
bind you to me. Your life is one with mine. You shall obey me and
do me no harm. You shall answer my summons. You shall never
be parted from me or be hidden from my sight. This is our
contract."*

He put his lips to Gronk's.

The spell activated and Waldo's magic surged through the ogre.
Gronk let out a startled gasp and shook. He stumbled back and
stared wide eyed.

Waldo could sense him in the back of his mind, the ogre was
now his second familiar. "Now you truly belong to me Gronk.
You will be my most obedient servant and I will be your master."

"Oooh, okay master, make me your bitch." The eight foot tall
ogre put his hands together and let out a girlish giggle.

"Huh?"

Then without warning Gronk grabbed Waldo about the shoulders
and planted a **real** kiss.

Waldo gagged and his arms flailed about as he felt ogre tongue
being rammed down his throat.

Alice was speechless with the horror of it.

"What the hell are you doing to my husband?!!" She grabbed Waldo and yanked him free.

Waldo stumbled and landed on his butt. He was spitting and gagging, trying to get the taste of ogre out of his mouth.

"Why did you do that?" Alice yelled.

"What?" Gronk spoke in a high pitched, lilting voice. "He said he wanted that kind of relationship, and I'm okay with being the submissive."

Still sitting on the ground Waldo stared up in mounting dismay. "I may have gotten the contract wrong again."

"YOU THINK?!!!" Alice screamed.

Waldo shut his eyes. *I really hope my third familiar is just a regular blood thirsty vampire.*

THE END